"The Man c

and

"The Land of Terror"

THE CLASSIC DEBUT ADVENTURES OF

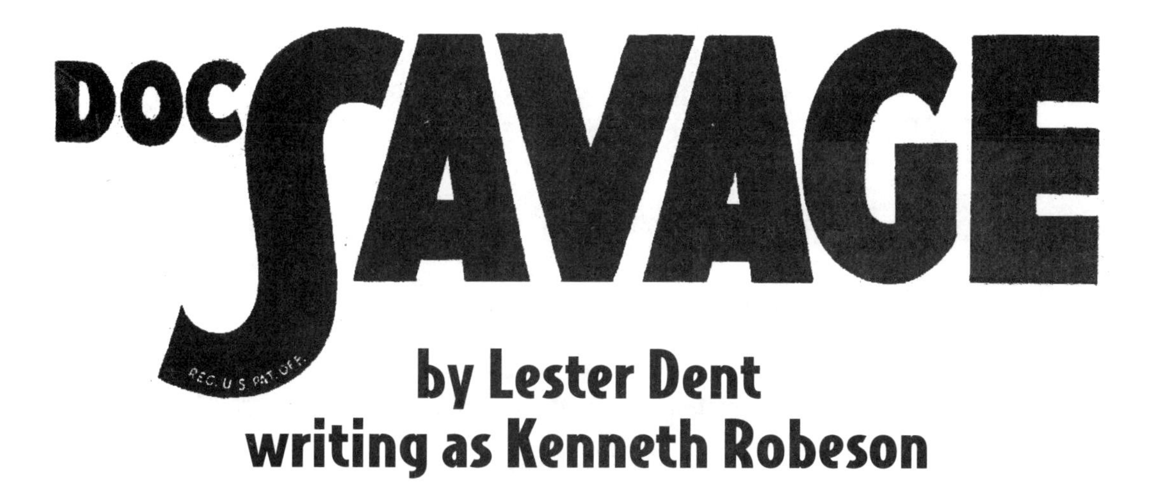

by Lester Dent
writing as Kenneth Robeson

with new historical essays
by Will Murray

Published by Sanctum Productions for
NOSTALGIA VENTURES, INC.
P.O. Box 231183; Encinitas, CA 92023-1183

Lester Dent teletype photo courtesy of Shirley Dungan.

This Nostalgia Ventures edition is an unabridged republication of the text and illustrations of two stories from *Doc Savage Magazine,* as originally published by Street & Smith Publications, Inc., N.Y.: *The Man of Bronze* from the March 1933 issue, and *The Land of Terror* from the April 1933 issue. This is a work of its time. Consequently, the text is reprinted intact in its original historical form, including occasional out-of-date ethnic and cultural stereotyping. Typographical errors have been tacitly corrected in this edition.

Walter M. Baumhofer cover classic edition:
ISBN: 1-932806-89-X 13 digit: 978-1-932806-89-2

James Bama cover variant edition:
ISBN: 1-932806-90-3 13 digit 978-1-932806-90-8

First printing: February 2008

Series editor: Anthony Tollin
P.O. Box 761474
San Antonio, TX 78245-1474
sanctumotr@earthlink.net

Consulting editor: Will Murray

Copy editor: Joseph Wrzos

Cover restoration: Michael Piper

The editors gratefully acknowledge the contributions of Bob Chapman of Graphitti Designs, James Bama, Tom Stephens, John Workman, Brian M. Kane and Scott Cranford in the preparation of this volume, and William T. Stolz of the Western Historical Manuscript Collection of the University of Missouri at Columbia for research assistance with the Lester Dent Collection.

Nostalgia Ventures, Inc.
P.O. Box 231183; Encinitas, CA 92023-1183

Visit Doc Savage at www.shadowsanctum.com & www.nostalgiatown.com.

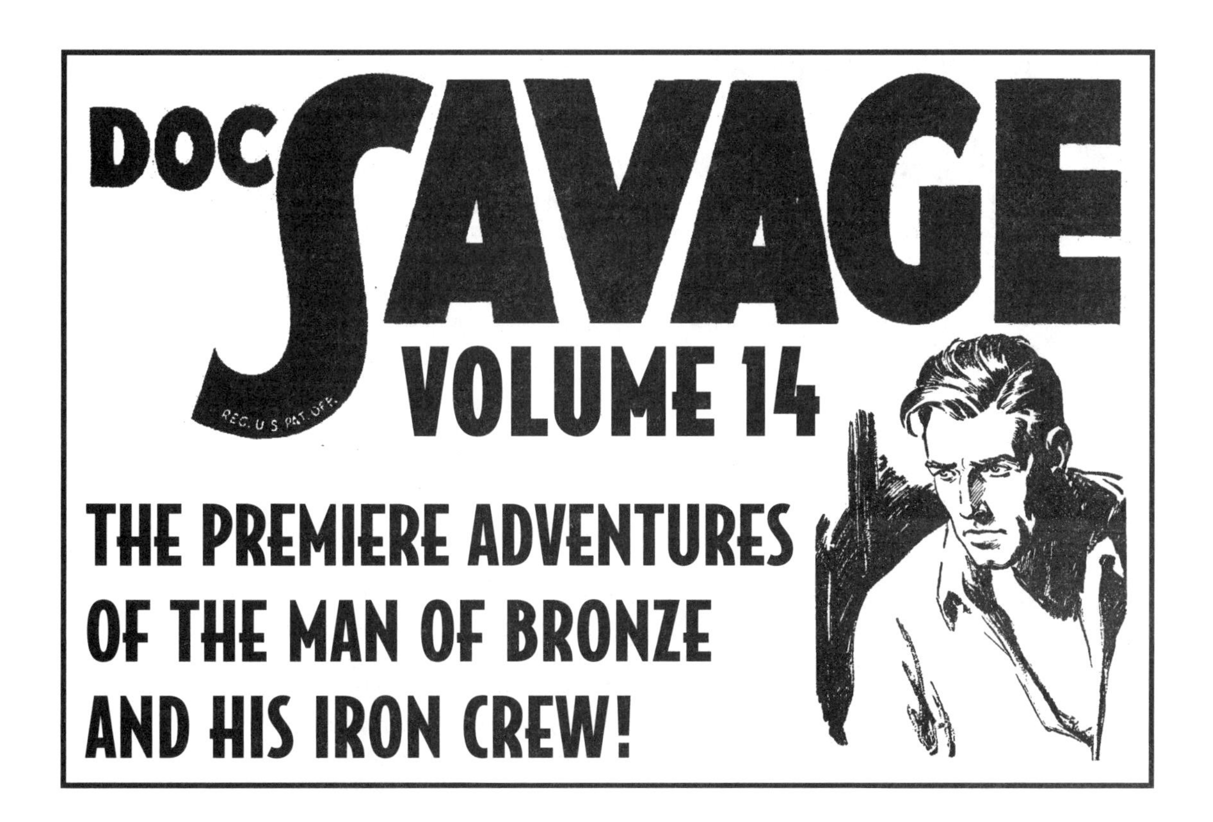

Thrilling Tales and Features

Front cover art by Walter Baumhofer (classic edition) and James Bama (variant edition)

Back cover art by Walter Baumhofer and Emery Clarke

Interior illustrations by Paul Orban

FOREWORD by Lester Dent

The character of Doc Savage was "born" on December 10, 1932, in a story conference in the old Street & Smith building in the Chelsea section of New York—a huge old brick building the color, appropriately enough, of coagulated blood. Appropriate, I always thought, because the building had been built by blood spilled on the pages of many a dime novel including Dick Merriwell and Nick Carter. Anyway, midwifery at the birth was done by John Nanovic and H. W. Ralston. They were Street & Smith editors.

The first issue of *Doc Savage* hit the newstands on February 17, 1933, and two weeks later President Roosevelt called the "Bank Holiday" which closed every bank in the nation. We were at the hard bottom of the Depression that day. No magazine ever chose a more inauspicious spot of time for birth. Magazines and publishers were going bust right and left.

Doc Savage was the first one-character magazine of its type. Within six months, there were nineteen imitators of which I knew. The stands were flooded with one-character magazines. The success of Doc was fabulous for its period. It ran the race during the worst of the Depression of the thirties.

I am quite sure that after the fourth issue, *Doc* had topped in circulation per issue the pulp magazine field. Circulation figures are jealously guarded, but it was a conceded fact that Doc led the pulp magazine field, not only the one-character books which came in a swarm in imitation, but quickly topped such long-established pulp favorites as *Argosy, Adventure* and *Blue Book.*

None of the imitators was able to approach *Doc* in circulation. All eventually fell away, although some lasted a dozen years.

I do not have exact circulation figures. The publisher refused to reveal them to me consistently, this being a bitter point in contract negotiations, and a common practice of publishers. However, years later, when a figure was revealed to me in a moaning session preliminary to trying a contract cut, the figure was two hundred thousand monthly. This, during the Depression, was fabulous.

Foreign editions of the magazine in English went into Canada, England, Australia. Foreign translations were published.

For example, an Argentine publisher, Editorial Molino Argentina, Buenos Aires, has published one hundred and eighty-one of the series, in Spanish.

In 1940 the character was issued in comic magazine form.

Earlier in the Thirties, the character was on radio, sponsored by a patent medicine outfit in Kansas City, and staged by what was then the Don Lee outfit on the Pacific coast. There were other radio shows using the character with which I am unfamiliar, because I was out of the country at the time.

Editor John Nanovic instigated a Doc Savage Club operated in conjunction with the magazine and it attained a quite impressive membership. Again, I don't know the exact figures, being out of the country. (I had bought a schooner and was living on it in the Caribbean at the time; later we were in Europe.) The club awarded medals for bravery in a number of cases where impressive publicity was involved. I know that once in Paris I thought it would be nice to drop each fan letter writer a note from abroad and asked for a batch of the fan mail, got nearly three thousand letters dumped on me to answer. That cured my interest in the Doc fan mail, which is a hell of a horrible thing to say, but practical.

I believe that more books written by one author have been published about Doc Savage than by any other writer in history. I think the figure is one hundred eighty-one or eighty-two, written by myself. Very few ghosted Docs appeared.

I say "books" meaning book-length novels, although some did appear in hardback in the early thirties.

The last U.S. edition appeared in 1949. At this time Street & Smith turned exclusively to slick magazine publication, having cannily founded such magazines as *Mademoiselle* with the profits from *Doc Savage* and other pulps.

At one time I was treasure hunting in the Caribbean and got a little behind with Doc novels and, rushing back to New York, managed to turn out nine 60,000 word books in eight weeks. I believe this is a record of some sort. Although as a matter of fact at one period I had a 200,000-word monthly average of published material for two years. Of course the obvious happened: a nervous breakdown.

The Doc Savage novels are laid in every part of the world against many backgrounds.

Doc was a "gadget" man. We tried to keep him as scientific as possible without becoming pseudo-scientific; in others words, anything Doc did was possible on at least a laboratory scale.

"Firsts" which appeared in *Doc Savage* long before they were actually presented to the public included: wire recorders; automatic telephone-answering gadgets; sea-trace used by the navy; shark-repellent; sonic detectors; proximity fuses, and many others which I do not recall at the moment.

Doc was, frankly, a superman. Physically as well as morally. He had the clue-following ability of Sherlock Holmes, the muscular tree-swinging ability of Tarzan, the scientific sleuthing of Craig Kennedy and the morals of Jesus Christ. He was an ideal, surrounded by five assistants who were human enough to temper his severity. I think such a character, a character made up of ideals, cannot fail if presented with force and sincerity. If the sincerity is there, cleverness and skill are not even necessary.

Lester Dent

La Plata, Missouri
March 1, 1953

The MAN of BRONZE

. . A COMPLETE BOOK-LENGTH NOVEL . .

of the exploits of Doc Savage and his five companions; a thrilling saga of a scrappy outfit hunting a treasure and being hunted in turn

By KENNETH ROBESON

Chapter I
THE SINISTER ONE

THERE was death afoot in the darkness.

It crept furtively along a steel girder. Hundreds of feet below yawned glass-and-brick-walled cracks—New York streets. Down there, late workers scurried homeward. Most of them carried umbrellas, and did not glance upward.

Even had they looked, they probably would have noticed nothing. The night was black as a cave bat. Rain threshed down monotonously. The clammy sky was like an oppressive shroud wrapped around the tops of the tall buildings.

One skyscraper was under construction. It had been completed to the eightieth floor. Some offices were in use.

Above the eightieth floor, an ornamental observation tower jutted up a full hundred and fifty feet more. The metal work of this was in place, but no masonry had been laid. Girders lifted a gigantic steel skeleton. The naked beams were a sinister forest.

It was in this forest that Death prowled.

Death was a man.

He seemed to have the adroitness of a cat at finding his way in the dark. Upward, he crept. The girders were slick with rain, treacherous. The man's progress was gruesome in its vile purpose.

From time to time, he spat strange, clucking words. A gibberish of hate!

A master of languages would have been baffled trying to name the tongue the man spoke. A profound student might have identified the dialect. The knowledge would be hard to believe, for the words were of a lost race, the language of a civilization long vanished!

"He must die!" the man chanted hoarsely in his strange lingo. "It is decreed by the Son of the Feathered Serpent! Tonight! Tonight death shall strike!"

Each time he raved his paean of hate, the man hugged an object he carried closer to his chest.

This object was a box, black, leather-covered. It was about four inches deep and four feet long.

"This shall bring death to him!" the man clucked, caressing the black case.

The rain beat him. Steel-fanged space gaped below. One slip would be his death. He climbed upward yard after yard.

Most of the chimneys which New Yorkers call office buildings had been emptied of their daily toilers. There were only occasional pale eyes of light gleaming from their sides.

The labyrinth of girders baffled the skulker a moment. He poked a flashlight beam inquisitively. The glow lasted a bare instant, but it disclosed a remarkable thing about the man's hands.

The fingertips were a brilliant red! They might have been dipped an inch of their length in a scarlet dye.

The red-fingered man scuttled onto a workmen's platform. The planks were thick. The platform was near the outside of the wilderness of steel.

The man lowered his black case. His inner pocket disgorged compact, powerful binoculars.

ON the lowermost floor of a skyscraper many blocks distant, the crimson-fingered man focused his glasses. He started counting stories upward.

The building was one of the tallest in New York. A gleaming spike of steel and brick, it rammed upward nearly a hundred stories.

At the eighty-sixth floor, the sinister man ceased to count. His glasses moved right and left until they found a lighted window. This was at the west corner of the building.

Only slightly blurred by the rain, the powerful binoculars disclosed what was in the room.

The broad, polished top of a massive and exquisitely inlaid table stood directly before the window.

Beyond it was the bronze figure!

This looked like the head and shoulders of a man, sculptured in hard bronze. It was a startling sight, that bronze bust. The lines of the features, the unusually high forehead, the mobile and muscular, but not too-full mouth, the lean cheeks, denoted a power of character seldom seen.

The bronze of the hair was a little darker than the bronze of the features. The hair was straight, and lay down tightly as a metal skullcap. A genius at sculpture might have made it.

Most marvelous of all were the eyes. They glittered like pools of flake gold when little lights from the table lamp played on them. Even from that distance they seemed to exert a hypnotic influence through the powerful binocular lenses, a quality that would cause the most rash individual to hesitate.

The man with the scarlet-tipped fingers shuddered.

"Death!" he croaked, as if seeking to overcome the unnerving quality of those strange, golden eyes. "The Son of the Feathered Serpent has commanded. It shall be death!"

He opened the black box. Faint metallic clickings sounded as he fitted together parts of the thing it held. After that, he ran his fingers lovingly over the object.

"The tool of the Son of the Feathered Serpent!" he chortled. "It shall deliver death!"

Once more, he pressed the binoculars to his eyes and focused them on the amazing bronze statue.

The bronze masterpiece opened its mouth, yawned—for it was no statue, but a living man!

THE bronze man showed wide, very strong-looking teeth, in yawning. Seated there by the immense desk, he did not seem to be a large man. An onlooker would have doubted his six feet height—and would have been astounded to learn he weighed every ounce of two hundred pounds.

The big bronze man was so well put together that the impression was not of size, but of power. The bulk of his great body was forgotten in the smooth symmetry of a build incredibly powerful.

This man was Clark Savage, Jr.

Doc Savage! The man whose name was becoming a byword in the odd corners of the world!

Apparently no sound had entered the room. But the big bronze man left his chair. He went to the door. The hand he opened the door with was long-fingered, supple. Yet its enormous tendons were like cables under a thin film of bronze lacquer.

Doc Savage's keenness of hearing was vindicated. Five men were getting out of the elevator cage, which had come up silently.

WHAT IS THE LEGACY?

What is the doubtful heritage which is left to Doc Savage to secure? And will it bring him the woe that is foretold, or the success which is hoped for?

Take a scrapper like Doc, and a prize such as the message offers—and you've got the makings of a real he-man's story in this yarn.

Go through with Doc and his pals to the end. You'll like it.

These men came toward Doc. There was wild delight in their manner. But for some sober reason, they did not shout boisterous greetings. It was as though Doc bore a great grief, and they sympathized deeply with him, but didn't know what to say.

The first of the five men was a giant who towered four inches over six feet. He weighed fully two fifty. His face was severe, his mouth thin and grim, and compressed tightly, as though he had just finished uttering a disapproving, *"tsk tsk!"* sound. His features had a most puritanical look.

This was "Renny," or Colonel John Renwick. His arms were enormous, his fists bony monstrosities. His favorite act was to slam his great fists through the solid panel of a heavy door. He was known throughout the world for his engineering accomplishments, also.

Behind Renny came William Harper Littlejohn, very tall, very gaunt. Johnny wore glasses with a peculiarly thick lens over the left eye. He looked like a half-starved, studious scientist. He was probably one of the greatest living experts on geology and archaeology.

Next was Major Thomas J. Roberts, dubbed "Long Tom." Long Tom was the physical weakling of the crowd, thin, not very tall, and with a none-too-healthy-appearing skin. He was a wizard with electricity.

"Ham" trailed Long Tom. "Brigadier General Theodore Marley Brooks," Ham was designated on formal occasions. Slender, waspy, quick-moving, Ham looked what he was—a quick thinker and possibly the most astute lawyer Harvard ever turned out. He carried a plain black cane—never went anywhere without it. This was, among other things, a sword cane.

Last came the most remarkable character of all. Only a few inches over five feet tall, he weighed better than two hundred and sixty pounds. He had the build of a gorilla, arms six inches longer than his legs, a chest thicker than it was wide. His eyes were so surrounded by gristle as to resemble pleasant little stars twinkling in pits. He grinned with a mouth so very big it looked like an accident.

"Monk!" No other name could fit him!

He was Lieutenant Colonel Andrew Blodgett Mayfair, but he heard the full name so seldom he had about forgotten what it sounded like.

THE men entered the sumptuously furnished reception room of the office suite. After the first greeting, they were silent, uncomfortable. They didn't know what to say.

For Doc Savage's father had died from a weird cause since they last saw Doc.

The elder Savage had been known throughout the world for his dominant bearing and his good work. Early in life, he had amassed a tremendous fortune—for one purpose.

That purpose was to go here and there, from one end of the world to the other, looking for excitement and adventure, striving to help those who needed help, punishing those who deserved it.

To that creed he had devoted his life.

His fortune had dwindled to practically nothing. But as it shrank, his influence had increased. It was unbelievably wide, a heritage befitting the man.

Greater even, though, was the heritage he had given his son. Not in wealth, but in training to take up his career of adventure and righting of wrongs where it left off.

Clark Savage, Jr., had been reared from the cradle to become the supreme adventurer.

Hardly had Doc learned to walk, when his father started him taking the routine of exercises to which he still adhered. Two hours each day, Doc exercised intensively all his muscles, senses, and his brain.

As a result of these exercises, Doc possessed a strength superhuman. There was no magic about it, though. Doc had simply built up muscle intensively all his life.

Doc's mental training had started with medicine and surgery. It had branched out to include all arts and sciences. Just as Doc could easily overpower the gorillalike Monk in spite of his great strength, so did Doc know more about chemistry. And that applied to Renny, the engineer; Long Tom, the electrical wizard; Johnny, the geologist and archaeologist; and Ham, the lawyer.

Doc had been well trained for his work.

Grief lay heavily upon Doc's five friends. The elder Savage had been close to their hearts.

"Your father's death—was three weeks ago," Renny said at last.

Doc nodded slowly. "So I learned from the newspapers—when I got back today."

Renny groped for words, said finally: "We tried to get you in every way. But you were gone—as if you had been off the face of the earth."

Doc looked at the window. There was grief in his gold eyes.

Chapter II
A MESSAGE FROM THE DEAD

FALLING rain strewed the outer side of the windowpane with water. Far below, very pallid in the soaking murk, were streetlights. Over on the Hudson River, a steamer was tooting a foghorn. The frightened, mooing horn was hardly audible inside the room.

Some blocks away, the skyscraper under construction loomed a darksome pile, crowned with a spidery labyrinth of steel girders. Only the vaguest outlines of it were discernible.

Impossible, of course, to glimpse the strange,

crimson-fingered servant of death in that wilderness of metal!

Doc Savage said slowly: "I was far away when my father died."

He did not explain where he had been, did not mention his "Fortress of Solitude," his rendezvous built on a rocky island deep in the Arctic regions. He had been there.

It was to this spot that Doc retired periodically to brush up on the newest developments in science, psychology, medicine, engineering. This was the secret of his universal knowledge, for his periods of concentration there were long and intense.

The Fortress of Solitude had been his father's recommendation. And no one on earth knew the location of the retreat. Once there, nothing could interrupt Doc's studies and experiments.

Without taking his golden eyes from the wet window, Doc asked: "Was there anything strange about my father's death?"

"We're not certain," Renny muttered, and set his thin lips in an expression of ominousness.

"I, for one, am certain!" snapped Littlejohn. He settled more firmly on his nose the glasses which had the extremely thick left lens.

"What do you mean, Johnny?" Doc Savage asked.

"I am positive your father was murdered!" Johnny's gauntness, his studious scientist look, gave him a profoundly serious expression.

Doc Savage swung slowly from the window. His bronze face had not changed expression. But under his brown business coat, tensing muscles had made his arms inches farther around.

"Why do you say that, Johnny?"

Johnny hesitated. His right eye narrowed, the left remaining wide and a little blank behind the thick spectacle lens. He shrugged.

"Only a hunch," he admitted, then added, almost shouting: "I'm right about it! I know I am!"

That was Johnny's way. He had absolute faith in what he called his hunches. And nearly always he was right. On occasions when he was wrong, though, he was very wrong indeed.

"Exactly what did the doctors say caused death?" Doc asked. Doc's voice was low, pleasant, but a voice capable of great volume and changing tone.

Renny answered that. Renny's voice was like thunder gobbling out of a cave. "The doctors didn't know. It was a new one on them. Your father broke out with queer circular red patches on his neck. And he lasted only a couple of days."

"I ran all kinds of chemical tests, trying to find if it was poison or germs or what it was caused the red spots," Monk interposed, slowly opening and closing his huge, red-furred fists. "I never found out a thing!"

Monk's looks were deceiving. His low forehead apparently didn't contain room for a spoonful of brains. Actually, Monk was in a way of being the most widely known chemist in America. He was a Houdini of the test tubes.

"We have no facts upon which to base suspicion!" clipped Ham, the waspish Harvard lawyer whose quick thinking had earned him a brigadier generalship in the World War. "But we're suspicious anyway."

Doc Savage moved abruptly across the room to a steel safe. The safe was huge, reaching above his shoulders. He swung it open.

It was instantly evident explosive had torn the lock out of the safe door.

A long, surprised gasp swished around the room.

"I found it broken into when I came back," Doc explained. "Maybe that has a connection with my father's death. Maybe not."

DOC'S movements were rhythmic as he swung over and perched on a corner of the big, inlaid table before the window. His eyes roved slowly over the beautifully furnished office. There was another office adjoining, larger, which contained a library of technical books that was priceless because of its completeness.

Adjoining that was the vast laboratory room, replete with apparatus for chemical and electrical experiments.

This was about all the worldly goods the elder Savage had left behind.

"What's eating you, Doc?" asked the giant Renny. "We all got the word from you to show up here tonight. Why?"

Doc Savage's strange golden eyes roved over the assembled men; from Renny, whose knowledge of engineering in all its branches was profound, to Long Tom, who was an electrical wizard, to Johnny, whose fund of information on the structure of the earth and ancient races which had inhabited it was extremely vast, to Ham, the clever Harvard lawyer and quick thinker, and finally to Monk, who, in spite of his resemblance to a gorilla, was a great chemist.

In these five men, Doc knew he had five of the greatest brains ever to assemble in one group. Each was surpassed in his field by only one human being—Doc Savage himself.

"I think you can guess why you are here," Doc said.

Monk rubbed his hairy hands together. Of the six men present, Monk's skin alone bore scars. The skin of the others held no marks of their adventurous past, thanks to Doc's uncanny skill in causing wounds to heal without leaving scars.

But not Monk. His tough, rusty iron hide was so marked with gray scars that it looked as if a flock of chickens with gray-chalk feet had paraded on him. This was because Monk refused to let Doc treat him. Monk gloried in his tough looks.

"Our big job is about to start, huh?" said Monk, vast satisfaction in his mild voice.

Doc nodded. "The work to which we shall devote the rest of our lives."

At that statement, great satisfaction appeared upon the face of every man present. They showed eagerness for what was to come.

Doc dangled a leg from the corner of the table. Unwittingly—for he knew nothing of the red-fingered killer lurking in the distant skyscraper that was under construction—Doc had placed his back out of line with the window. In fact, since the men had entered, he had not once been aligned with the window.

"We first got together back in the War," he told the five slowly. "We all liked the big scrap. It got into our blood. When we came back, the humdrum life of an ordinary man was not suited to our natures. So we sought something else."

Doc held their absolute attention, as if he had them hypnotized. Undeniably this golden-eyed man was the leader of the group, as well as leader of anything he undertook. His very being denoted a calm knowledge of all things, and an ability to handle himself under any conditions.

"Moved by mutual admiration for my father," Doc continued, "we decided to take up his work of good wherever he was forced to leave off. We at once began training ourselves for that purpose. It is the cause for which I had been reared from the cradle, but you fellows, because of a love of excitement and adventure, wish to join me."

Doc Savage paused. He looked over his companions. One by one, in the soft light of the well-furnished office, one of the few remaining evidences of the wealth that once belonged to his father.

"Tonight," he went on soberly, "we begin carrying out the ideals of my father—to go here and there, from one end of the world to the other, looking for excitement and adventure, striving to help those who need help, and punishing those who deserve it."

THERE was a somber silence after that immense pronouncement.

It was Monk, matter-of-fact person that he was, who shattered the quiet.

"What flubdubs me is who broke into that safe, and why?" he grumbled. "Doc, could it have any connection with your father's death?"

"It could, of course," Doc explained. "The contents of the safe had been rifled. I do not know whether my father had anything of importance in it. But I suspect there was."

Doc drew a folded paper from inside his coat. The lower half of the paper had been burned away, it was evident from the charred edges. Doc continued speaking.

"Finding this in a corner of the safe leads me to that belief. The explosion which opened the safe obviously destroyed the lower part of the paper. And the robber probably overlooked the rest. Here, read it!"

He passed it to the five men. The paper was covered with the fine, almost engraving-perfect writing of Doc's father. They all recognized the penmanship instantly. They read:

> DEAR CLARK: I have many things to tell you. In your whole lifetime, there never was an occasion when I desired you here so much as I do now. I need you, son, because many things have happened which indicate to me that my last journey is at hand. You will find that I have nothing much to leave you in the way of tangible wealth.
>
> I have, however, the satisfaction of knowing that in you I shall live.
>
> I have developed you from boyhood into the sort of man you have become, and I have spared no time or expense to make you just what I think you should be.
>
> Everything I have done for you has been with the purpose that you should find yourself capable of carrying on the work which I so hopefully started, and which, in these last few years, has been almost impossible to carry on.
>
> If I do not see you again before this letter is in your hands, I want to assure you that I appreciate the fact that you have lacked nothing in the way of filial devotion. That you have been absent so much of the time has been a secret source of gratification to me, for your absence has, I know, made you self-reliant and able. It was all that I hoped for you.
>
> Now, as to the heritage which I am about to leave you:
>
> What I am passing along to you may be a doubtful heritage. It may be a heritage of woe. It may even be a heritage of destruction to you if you attempt to capitalize on it. On the other hand, it may enable you to do many things for those who are not so fortunate as you yourself, and will, in that way, be a boon for you in carrying on your work of doing good to all.
>
> Here is the general information concerning it:
>
> Some twenty years ago, in company with Hubert Robertson, I went on an expedition to Hidalgo, in Central America, to investigate the report of a prehistoric—

There the missive ended. Flames had consumed the rest.

"The thing to do is get hold of Hubert Robertson!" clipped the quick-thinking Ham. Waspish, rapid-moving, he swung over to the telephone, scooped it up. "I know Hubert Robertson's phone number. He is connected with the Museum of Natural History."

"You won't get him!" Doc said dryly.

"Why not?"

Doc got off the table and stood beside the giant Renny. It was only then that one realized what a big man Doc was. Alongside Renny, Doc was like dynamite alongside gunpowder.

"Hubert Robertson is dead," Doc explained. "He died from the same thing that killed my father—a weird malady that started with a breaking out of red spots. And he died at about the same time as my father."

RENNY'S thin mouth pinched even tighter at that. Gloom seemed to settle on his long face. He looked like a man disgusted enough with the evils of the world to cry.

Strangely enough, that somber look denoted that Renny was beginning to take interest. The tougher the going got, the better Renny functioned and—the more puritanical he looked.

"That flooeys our chances of finding out more about this heritage your father left you!" he rumbled.

"Not entirely," Doc corrected. "Wait here a moment!"

He stepped through another door, crossed the room banked with the volumes of his father's great technical library. Through a second door, and he was in the laboratory.

Cases laden with chemicals stood thick as forest trees on the floor. There were electrical coils, vacuum tubes, ray apparatus, microscopes, retorts, electric furnaces, everything that could go into such a laboratory.

From a cabinet Doc lifted a metal box closely resembling an old-fashioned magic lantern. The lens, instead of being ordinary optical glass, was a very dark purple, almost black. There was a cord for plugging into an electric-light socket.

Doc carried this into the room where his five men waited, placed it on a stand, aiming the lens at the window. He plugged the cord into an electric outlet.

Before putting the thing in operation, he lifted the metal lid and beckoned to Long Tom, the electrical wizard.

"Know what this is?"

"Of course." Long Tom pulled absently at an ear that was too big, too thin and too pale. "That is a lamp for making ultraviolet rays, or what is commonly called black light. The rays are invisible to the human eye, since they are shorter than ordinary light, but many substances when placed in the black light will glow, or fluoresce after the fashion of luminous paint on a watch dial. Examples of such substances are ordinary vaseline, quinine—"

"That's plenty," interposed Doc. "Will you look at the window I've pointed this at. See anything unusual about it?"

Johnny, the gaunt archaeologist and geologist, advanced to the window, removing his glasses as he went. He held the thick-lensed left glass before his right eye, inspecting the window.

In reality, the left side of Johnny's glasses was an extremely powerful magnifying lens. His work often required a magnifier, so he wore one over his left eye, which was virtually useless because of an injury received in the World War.

"I can find nothing!" Johnny declared. "There's nothing unusual about the window!"

"I hope you're wrong," Doc said, sobriety in his wondrously modulated voice. "But you could not see the writing on that window, should there be any. The substance my father perfected for leaving secret messages was absolutely invisible. But it glows under ultraviolet light."

"You mean—" hairy Monk rumbled.

"That my father and I often left each other notes written on that window," Doc explained. "Watch!"

Doc crossed the room, a big, dynamic man, light on his feet as a kitten for all his size, and turned out the lights. He came back to the black-light box. His hand, supple despite its enormous tendons, clicked the switch that shot current into the apparatus.

Instantly, written words sprang out on the darkened windowpane. Glowing with a dazzling, electric blue, the effect of their sudden appearance was uncanny.

A split second later came a terrific report! A bullet knocked the glass into hundreds of fragments, wiping out the sparkling blue message before they could read it. The bullet passed entirely through the steel-plate inner door of the safe! It embedded in the safe back.

THE room reeked silence. One second, two! Nobody had moved.

And then a new sound was heard. It was a low, mellow, trilling sound, like the song of some strange bird of the jungle, or the sound of the wind filtering through a jungled forest. It was melodious, though it had no tune; and it was inspiring, though it was not awesome.

The amazing sound had the peculiar quality of seeming to come from everywhere within the room rather than from a definite spot, as though permeated with an eerie essence of ventriloquism.

A purposeful calm settled over Doc Savage's five men as they heard that sound. Their breathing became less rapid, their brains more alert.

For this weird sound was part of Doc—a small, unconscious thing which he did in moments of utter concentration. To his friends it was both the cry of battle and the song of triumph. It would come upon his lips when a plan of action was being arranged, precursing a master stroke which made all things certain.

It would come again in the midst of some struggle,

when the odds were all against his men, when everything seemed lost. And with the sound, new strength would come to all, and the tide would always turn.

And again, it might come when some beleaguered member of the group, alone and attacked, had almost given up all hope of survival. Then that sound would filter through, some way, and the victim knew that help was at hand.

The whistling sound was a sign of Doc, and of safety, of victory.

"Who got it?" asked Johnny, and he could be heard settling his glasses more firmly on his bony nose.

"No one," said Doc. "Let us crawl, brothers, crawl. That was no ordinary rifle bullet, from the sound of it!"

At that instant, a second bullet crashed into the room. It came, not through the window, but through some inches of brick and mortar which comprised the wall! Plaster sprayed across the thick carpet.

Chapter III
THE ENEMY

DOC SAVAGE was the last of the six to enter the adjoining room. But he was inside the room in less than ten seconds. They moved with amazing speed, these men.

Doc flashed across the big library. The speed with which he traversed the darkness, never disturbing an article of furniture, showed the marvelous development of his senses. No jungle cat could have done better.

Expensive binoculars reposed in a desk drawer, a highpower hunting rifle in a corner cabinet. In splits of seconds, Doc had these, and was at the window.

He watched, waited.

No more shots followed the first two.

Four minutes, five, Doc bored into the night with the binoculars. He peered into every office window within range, and there were hundreds. He scrutinized the spidery framework of the observation tower atop the skyscraper under construction. Darkness packed the labyrinth of girders, and he could discern no trace of the bushwhacker.

"He's gone!" Doc concluded aloud.

No sound of movement followed his words. Then the window shade ran down loudly in the room where they had been shot at. The five men stiffened, then relaxed at Doc's low call. Doc had moved soundlessly to the shade and drawn it.

Doc was beside the safe, the lights turned on, when they entered.

The window glass had been clouted completely out of the sash. It lay in glistening chunks and spears on the luxuriant carpet.

The glowing message which had been on it seemed destroyed forever.

"Somebody was laying for me outside," Doc said, no worry at all in his well-developed voice. "They evidently couldn't get just the aim they wanted at me through the window. When we turned out the light to look at the writing on the window, they thought we were leaving the building. So they took a couple of shots for wild luck."

"Next time, Doc, suppose we have bulletproof glass in these windows!" Renny suggested, the humor in his voice belying his dour look.

"Sure," said Doc. "Next time! We're on the eighty-sixth floor, and it's quite common to be shot at here!"

Ham interposed a sarcastic snort. He bounced over, waspish, quick-moving, and nearly managed to thrust his slender arm through the hole the bullet had tunneled in the brick wall.

"Even if you put in bulletproof windows, you'd have to be blame careful to set in front of them!" he clipped dryly.

Doc was studying the hole in the safe door, noting particularly the angle at which the powerful bullet had entered. He opened the safe. The big bullet, almost intact, was embedded in the safe rear wall.

Renny ran a great arm into the safe, grasped the bullet with his fingers. His giant arm muscles corded as he tried to pull it out. The fist that could drive bodily through inch-thick planking with perfect ease was defied by the embedded metal slug.

"Whew!" snorted Renny. "That's a job for a drill and cold chisels."

Saying nothing, merely as if he wanted to see if the bullet was stuck as tightly as Renny said, Doc reached into the safe.

Great muscles popping up along his arm suddenly split his coat sleeve wide open. He glanced at the ruined sleeve ruefully, and brought his arm out of the safe. The bullet lay loosely in his palm.

RENNY could not have looked more astounded had a spike-tailed devil hopped out of the safe. The expression on his puritanical face was ludicrous.

Doc weighed the bullet in his palm. The lids were drawn over his golden eyes. He seemed to be giving his marvelous brain every chance to work—and he was. He was guessing the weight of that bullet within a few grains, almost as accurately as a chemist's scale could weigh it.

"Seven hundred and fifty grains," he decided. "That makes it a .577 caliber Nitro-Express rifle. Probably the gun that fired that shot was a double-barreled rifle."

"How d'you figure that?" asked Ham. Possibly the most astute of Doc's five friends, Doc's reasoning nevertheless got away from even Ham.

"There were only two shots," Doc clarified. "Also, cartridges of this tremendous size are usually fired from double-barreled elephant rifles."

"Let's do somethin' about this!" boomed Monk. "The bushwhacker may get away while we're jawin'!"

"He's probably fled already, since I could locate no trace of him with the binoculars," Doc replied. "But we'll do something about it, right enough!"

With exactly four terse sentences, one each directed at Renny, Long Tom, Johnny, and Monk, Doc gave all the orders he needed to. He did not explain in detail what they were to do. That wasn't necessary. He merely gave them the idea of what he wanted, and they set to work and got it in short order. They were clever, these men of Doc's.

Renny, the engineer, picked a slide rule from the drawer of a desk, a pair of dividers, some paper, a length of string. He probed the angle at which the bullet had passed through the inner safe door, calculated expertly the slight amount the window had probably deflected it. In less than a minute, he had his string aligned from the safe to a spot midway in the window, and was sighting down it.

"Snap out of it, Long Tom!" he called impatiently.

"Just keep your shirt on!" Long Tom complained. He was doing his own share as rapidly as the engineer.

Long Tom had made a swift swing into the library and laboratory, collecting odds and ends of electrical material. With a couple of powerful lightbulbs he unscrewed from sockets, some tin, a pocket mirror he borrowed from—of all people—Monk, Long Tom rigged an apparatus to project a thin, extremely powerful beam of light. He added a flashlight lens, and borrowed the magnifying half of Johnny's glasses before he got just the effect he desired.

Long Tom sighted his light beam down Renny's string, thus locating precisely in the gloomy mass of skyscrapers, the spot from whence the shots had come.

In the meantime, Johnny, with fingers and eye made expert by years of assembling bits of pottery from ancient ruins, and the bones of prehistoric monsters, was fitting the shattered windowpane together. A task that would have taken a layman hours, Johnny accomplished in minutes.

Johnny turned the black-light apparatus on the glass. The message in glowing blue sprang out. Intact!

Monk came waddling in from the laboratory. In the big furry hands that swung below his knees, he carried several bottles, tightly corked. They held a fluid of villainous color.

Monk, from the wealth of chemical formulas within his head, had compounded a gas with which to fight their opponents, should they succeed in cornering whoever had fired that shot. It was a gas that would instantly paralyze anyone who inhaled it, but the effects were only temporary, and not harmful.

THEY all gathered around the table on which Johnny had assembled the fragments of glass. All but Renny, who was still calculating his angles. And as Doc flashed the light upon the glass, they read the message written there:

Important papers back of the red brick—

Before the message could mean anything to their minds, Renny shouted his discovery.

"It's from the observation tower, on that unfinished skyscraper," he cried. "That's where the shot came from—and the sharpshooter must still be somewhere up there!"

"Let's go, brothers!" Doc ordered, and the men surged out into the massive, shining corridor of the building, straight to the battery of elevators.

If they noticed that Doc tarried behind several seconds, none of them remarked the fact. Doc was always doing little things like that—little things that often turned out to have amazing consequences later.

The men piled into the opened elevator with a suddenness that startled the dozing operator. He wouldn't be able to sleep on the job the rest of the night!

With a whine like a lost pup, the cage sank.

Grimly silent, Doc and his five friends were a remarkable collection of men. They so impressed the elevator operator that he would have shot the lift past the first floor into the basement, had Doc not dropped a bronze, long-fingered hand on the control.

Doc led out through the lobby at a trot. A taxi was cocked in at the curb, driver dreaming over the wheel. Four of the six men piled into the machine. Doc and Renny rode the running board.

"Do a Barney Oldfield!" Doc directed the cab driver.

The hack jumped away from the curb as if stung.

Rain sheeted against Doc's strong, bronzed face, and his straight, close-lying bronze hair. An unusual fact was at once evident. Doc's bronze skin and bronze hair had the strange quality of seeming impervious to water. They didn't get appreciably wet; he shed water like the proverbial duck's back.

The streets were virtually deserted in this shopping region. Over toward the theater district, perhaps, there would be a crowd.

Brakes giving one long squawk, the taxi skidded sidewise to the curb and stopped. Doc and Renny were instantly running for the entrance of the new skyscraper. The four passengers came out of the cab door as if blown out. Ham still carried his plain black cane.

"My pay!" howled the taxi driver.

"Wait for us!" Doc flung back at him.

In the recently finished building lobby, Doc yelled for the watchman. He got no answer. He was puzzled. There should be one around.

They entered an elevator, sent it upward to the topmost floor. Still no watchman! They sprang up a staircase to where all construction but steel work ceased. There they found the watchman.

The man, a big Irishman with cheeks so plump and red they looked like the halves of Christmas apples, was bound and gagged. He was indeed grateful when Doc turned him loose—but quite astounded. For Doc, not bothering with the knots, simply freed the Irishman by snapping the stout ropes with his fingers as easily as he would cords.

"Begorra, man!" muttered the Irishman. "'Tis not human yez can be, with a strength like that!"

"Who tied you up?" Doc asked compellingly. "What did he look like?"

"Faith, I dunno!" declared the son of Erin. "'Twas not a single look or a smell I got of him, except for one thing. The fingers of the man were red on the ends. Like he had dipped 'em in blood!"

ON up into the wilderness of steel girders, the six men climbed. They left the Irishman behind, rubbing spots where the ropes had hurt him, and mumbling to himself about a man who broke ropes with his fingers, and another man who had red fingertips.

"This is about the right height!" said the gaunt Johnny, bounding at Doc's heels. "He was shooting from about here."

Johnny was hardly breathing rapidly. A tall, poorly looking man, Johnny nevertheless exceeded all the others, excepting Doc, in endurance. He had been known to go for three days and three nights steadily with only a slice of bread and a canteen of water.

Doc veered right. He had taken a flashlight from an inside pocket.

It was not like other flashlights, that one of Doc's. It employed no battery. A tiny, powerful generator, built into the handle and driven by a stout spring and clockwork, supplied the current. One twist of the flash handle would wind the spring and furnish light current for some minutes. A special receptacle held spare bulbs. There was not much chance of Doc's light playing out.

The flash spiked a white rod of luminance ahead. It picked up a workman's platform of heavy planks.

"The shot came from there!" Doc vouchsafed.

A steel girder, a few inches wide, slippery with moisture, offered a shortcut to the platform. Doc ran along it, surefooted as a bronze spider on a web thread. His five men, knowing they would be flirting with death among the steel beams hundreds of feet below, decided to go around, and did it very carefully, too.

Doc had picked two empty cartridges off the platform, and was scrutinizing them when his five friends put relieved feet on the planks.

"A cannon!" Monk gulped, after one look at the great size of the cartridges.

"Not quite," Doc replied. "They are cartridges for the elephant rifle I told you about. And it was a double-barreled rifle the sniper used."

"What makes you so sure, Doc?" asked big, sober-faced Renny.

Doc pointed at the plank surface of the platform. Barely visible were two tiny marks, side by side. Now that Doc had called their attention to the marks, the others knew they had been made by the muzzle of a double-barreled elephant rifle rested for a moment on the boards.

"He was a short man," Doc added. "Shorter, even, than Long Tom, here. And much wider."

"Huh?" This was beyond even quick-thinking Ham.

Seemingly unaware of their great height, and the certain death the slightest misstep would bring, Doc swung around the group and back the easy route they had come. He pointed to a girder which, because of the roof effect of another girder above, was dry on one side. But there was a damp smear on the dry steel.

"The sniper rubbed it with his shoulder in passing," Doc explained. "That shows how tall he is. It also shows he has wide shoulders, because only a wide-shouldered man would rub the girder. Now—"

Doc fell suddenly silent. As rigid as if he were the hard bronze he so resembled, he poised against the girder. His glittering golden eyes seemed to grow luminous in the darkness.

"What is it, Doc?" asked Renny.

"Someone just struck a match—up there in the room where we were shot at!" He interrupted himself with an explosive sound. "There! He's lighted another!"

Doc instantly whipped the binoculars—he had brought them along from the office—from his pocket. He aimed them at the window.

He got but a fragmentary glimpse. The match was about burned out. Only the tips of the prowler's fingers were clearly lighted.

"His fingers—the ends are red!" Doc voiced what he had seen.

Chapter IV
THE RED DEATH PROMISE

AN interval of a dozen seconds, Doc waited.

"Let's go!" he breathed then. "You fellows make for that room, quick!"

The five men spun, began descending from the platform as swiftly as they dared. But it would take them minutes in the darkness, and the jumble of girders, to reach the spot where the elevators could carry them on.

"Where's Doc?" Monk rumbled when they were down a couple of stories.

Doc was not with them, they now noted.

"He stayed behind!" snapped waspish Ham. Then, as Monk accidentally nudged him in the dangerous murk: "Listen, Monk, do you want me to kick you off here?"

Doc, however, had not exactly remained behind. He had, with the uncanny nimbleness of a forest-dwelling monkey, flashed across a precarious path of girders, until he reached the supply elevators, erected by the workmen on the outside of the building for fetching up materials.

The cages were hundreds of feet below, on the ground, and there was no one to operate the controls. But Doc knew that.

On the lip of the elevator shaft, balanced by the grip of his powerful knees, he shucked off his coat. He made it into a bundle in his hands.

The stout wire cables which lifted the elevator cab were barely discernible. A full eight feet out over space they hung. But with a gentle leap, Doc launched out and seized them. Using his coat to protect his palms from the friction heat sure to be generated, he let himself slide down the cables.

Air swished past his ears, plucked at his trouser legs and shirtsleeves. The coat smoked, began to leave a trail of sparks. Halfway down, Doc braked to a stop by tightening his powerful hands, and changed to a fresh spot in the coat.

So it was that Doc had reached the street even while thin, waspish Ham was threatening to kick the gigantic Monk off the girder if Monk shoved him again.

It was imperative to get to the office before the departure of the prowler who had lighted the match. Doc plunged into the taxi he had left standing in front, rapped an order.

Doc's voice had a magical quality of compelling sudden obedience to an order. With a squawl of clashing gears and a whine of spinning tires, the taxi doubled around in the street. It covered the several blocks in a fraction of a minute.

A bronze streak, Doc was out of the cab and in the skyscraper lobby. He confronted the elevator operator.

"What sort of a looking man did you take up to eighty-six a few minutes ago?"

"There ain't a soul come in this building since you left!" said the elevator operator positively.

DOC'S brain fought the problem an instant. He had naturally supposed the sniper had invaded the room above. It seemed not.

"Get this!" he clipped at the operator. "You wait here and be ready to sic my five men on anybody who comes out of this building. My men will be here in a minute. I'm taking your cage up!"

In the cage with the last word, Doc sent it sighing upward a couple of city blocks. He stopped it one floor below the eighty-sixth, quitted it there, crept furtively up the stairs and to the suite of offices which had been his father's, but which was now Doc's own.

The suite door gaped ajar. Inside was sepia blackness that might hold anything.

Doc popped the corridor lights off as a matter of safety. He feared no encounter in the dark. He had trained his ears by a system of scientific sound exercises which was a part of the two hours of intensive physical and mental drill Doc gave himself daily. So powerful and sensitive had his hearing become that he could detect sounds absolutely inaudible to other people. And ears were all important in a scrimmage in the dark.

But a quick round of the three rooms, a moment of listening in each, convinced Doc the quarry had fled.

His men arrived in the corridor with a great deal of racket. Doc lighted the offices, and watched them come in. Monk was absent.

"Monk remained downstairs on guard," Renny explained.

Doc nodded, his golden eyes flickering at the table. On that table, where none had been before, was propped a blood-red envelope!

Crossing over quickly, Doc picked up a book, opened it and used it like pincers to pick up the strange scarlet missive. He carried it into the laboratory, and dunked it in a bath of concentrated disinfectant fluid, stuff calculated to destroy every possible germ.

"I've heard of murderers leaving their victims an envelope full of the germs of some rare disease," he told the others dryly. "And remember, it was a strange malady that seized my father."

Carefully, he picked the crimson envelope apart until he had disclosed the missive it held. Words were lettered on scarlet paper with an odious black ink. They read:

> SAVAGE: Turn back from your quest, lest the red death strike once again.

There was no signature.

A silent group, they went back to the room where they had found the vermilion missive.

IT was Long Tom who gave voice to a new discovery. He leveled a rather pale hand at the box which held the ultraviolet light apparatus.

"That isn't sitting where we left it!" he declared.

Doc nodded. He had already noticed that, but he did not say so. He made it a policy never to disillusion one of his men who thought he had been first to notice something or get an idea, although Doc himself might have discovered it far earlier. It was this modesty of Doc's which helped endear him to everybody he was associated with.

"The prowler who came in and left the red note used the black-light apparatus," he told Long Tom. "It's a safe guess that he inspected the window Johnny put together."

"Then he read the invisible writing on the glass!" Renny rumbled.

"Very likely."

"Could he make heads or tails of it?"

"I hope he could," Doc said dryly.

They all betrayed surprise at that, but Doc, turning away, indicated he wasn't ready to amplify on his strange statement. Doc borrowed the magnifying glass Johnny wore in his left spectacle lens, and inspected the door for fingerprints.

"We'll get whoever it was!" Ham decided. The waspish lawyer made a wry smile. "One look at Monk's ugly phiz and nobody would try to get out of here."

But at that instant the elevator doors rolled back, out in the corridor.

Monk waddled from the lift like a huge anthropoid.

"What d'you want?" he asked them.

They stared at him, puzzled.

Monk's big mouth crooked a gigantic scowl. "Didn't one of you phone downstairs for me to come right up?"

Doc shook his bronze head slowly. "No."

Monk let out a bellow that would have shamed the beast he resembled. He stamped up and down. He waved his huge, corded arms that were inches longer than his legs.

"Somebody run a whizzer on me!" he howled. "Whoever it was, I'll wring his neck! I'll pull off his ears! I'll—"

"You'll be in a cage at the zoo if you don't learn the manners of a man!" waspish Ham said bitingly.

Monk promptly stopped his apelike prancing and bellowing. He looked steadily at Ham, starting with Ham's distinguished shock of prematurely gray hair, and running his little eyes slowly down Ham's well-cared-for face, perfect business suit, and small shoes.

Suddenly Monk began to laugh. His mirth was a loud, hearty roar.

At the gusty laughter, Ham stiffened. His face became very red with embarrassment.

For all Monk had to do to get Ham's goat was laugh at him. It had all started back in the war, when Ham was Brigadier General Theodore Marley Brooks. The brigadier general had been the moving spirit in a little scheme to teach Monk certain French words which had a meaning entirely different than Monk thought. As a result, Monk had spent a session in the guardhouse for some things he had innocently called a French general.

A few days after that, though, Brigadier General Theodore Marley Brooks was suddenly haled up before a court-martial, accused of stealing hams. And convicted! Somebody had expertly planted plenty of evidence.

Ham got his name right there. And to this day he had not been able to prove it was the homely Monk who framed him. That rankled Ham's lawyer soul.

Unnoticed, Doc Savage had reached over and turned on the ultraviolet light apparatus. He focused it on the pieced-together window, then called to the others: "Take a look!"

The message on the glass had been changed!

THERE now glowed with an eerie blue luminance exactly eight more words than had been in the original message. The communication now read:

Important papers back of the red brick house at corner of Mountainair and Farmwell Streets.

"Hey!" exploded the giant Renny. "How—"

With a lifted hand, a nod at the door, Doc silenced Renny and sent them all piling into the corridor.

As the elevator rushed them downward, Doc explained: "Somebody decoyed you upstairs so they could get away, Monk."

"Don't I know it!" Monk mumbled. "But what I can't savvy is who added words to that message?"

"That was my doing," Doc admitted. "I had a hunch the sniper might have seen us working with the ultraviolet light apparatus, and be smart enough to see what it was. I hoped he'd try to read the message. So I changed it to lead him into a trap."

Monk popped the knuckles in hands that were near as big as gallon pails. "Trap is right! Wait'll I get my lunch shovels on that guy!"

Their taxi was still waiting outside. The driver began a wailing: "Say—when am I gonna get paid? You gotta pay for the time I been waitin'—"

Doc handed the man a bill that not only silenced him, but nearly made his eyes jump out.

North on Fifth Avenue, the taxi raced. Water whipped the windshield and washed the windows. Doc and Renny, riding outside once more, were pelted with the moisture drops. Renny bent his face away from the stinging drops, but Doc seemed no more affected than had he really been of bronze. His hair and skin showed not the least wetness.

"This red brick house at the corner of Mountainair and Farmwell Streets is deserted," Doc called once. "That's why I gave that address in the addition to the note."

Inside the cab, Monk rumbled about what he would do to whoever had tricked him.

A motorcycle cop fell in behind them, opened his siren, and came up rapidly. But when he caught sight of Doc, like a striking figure of bronze on the side of the taxi, the officer waved his hand respectfully. Doc didn't even know the man. The officer must have been one who knew and revered the elder Savage.

The cab reeled into a less frequented street, slanting around corners. Rows of unlighted houses made the thoroughfare like a black, ominous tunnel.

"Here we are!" Doc told their driver at last.

GHOSTLY described the neighborhood. The streets were narrow, the sidewalks narrower; the cement of both was cracked and rutted and gone entirely in places. Chugholes filled with water reached half to their knees.

"You each have one of Monk's gas bombs?" Doc asked, just to be sure.

They had.

Doc breathed terse orders of campaign. "Monk in front, Long Tom and Johnny on the right, Renny on the left. I'll take the back. Ham, you stay off to one side as a sort of reserve if some quick thinking and moving has to be done."

Doc gave them half a minute to place themselves. Not long, but all the time they needed. He went forward himself.

The red brick house on the corner had two ramshackle stories. It had been deserted a long time. Two of the three porch posts canted crazily. Shingles still clung to the roof only in scabs. The windows were planked up solid. And the brick looked rotten and soft.

The street lamp at the corner cast light so pale as to be near nonexistent.

Doc encountered brush, eased into it with a peculiar twisting, worming movement of his powerful, supple frame. He had seen great jungle cats slide through dense leafage in that strangely noiseless fashion, and had copied it himself. He made absolutely no sound.

And in a moment, he had raised his quarry.

The man was at the rear of the house, going over the backyard a foot at a time, lighting matches in succession.

He was short, but perfectly formed, with a smooth yellow skin, and a seeming plumpness that probably meant great muscular development. His nose was curving, slightly hooked, his lips full, his chin not particularly large. A man of a strange race.

The ends of his fingers were dyed a brilliant scarlet.

Doc did not reveal himself at once, but watched curiously.

The stocky, golden-skinned man seemed very puzzled, as indeed he had reason to be, for what he sought was not there. He muttered disgustedly in some strange clucking language.

Doc, when he heard the words, held back even longer. He was astounded. He had never expected to hear a man speaking that language as though it were his native tongue. For it was the lingo of a lost civilization!

The stocky man showed signs of giving up his search. He lit one more match, putting his box away as though he didn't intend to ignite more. Then he stiffened.

Into the soaking night had permeated a low, mellow, trilling sound like the song of some exotic bird. It seemed to emanate from underfoot, overhead, to the sides, everywhere—and nowhere. The stocky man was bewildered. The sound was startling, but not awesome.

Doc was telling his men to beware. There might be more of the enemy about than this one fellow.

The stocky man half turned, searching the darkness. He took a step toward a big, double-barreled elephant rifle that leaned against a pile of scrap wood near him. It was of huge caliber, that rifle, fitted with telescopic sights. The man's hand started to close over the gun—

And Doc had him! Doc's leap was more expert even than the lunge of a jungle prowler, for the victim gave not even a single bleat before he was pinned, helpless in arms that banded him like steel, and a hand that cut off his wind as though his throat had been poured full of lead.

SWIFTLY, the others came up. They had found no one else about.

"I'd be glad to hold him for you!" Monk suggested hopefully to Doc. His furry fingers opened and shut.

Doc shook his head and released the prisoner. The man instantly started to run. But Doc's hand, floating out with incredible speed, stopped the man with a snap that made his teeth pop together like clapped hands.

"Why did you shoot at us?" Doc demanded in English.

The stocky man spewed clucking gutturals, highly excited.

Doc looked swiftly aside, at Johnny.

The gaunt archaeologist, who knew a great deal about ancient races, was scratching his head with thick fingers. He took off the glasses with the magnifying lens on the left side, then nervously put them back on again.

"It's incredible!" he muttered. "The language that fellow speaks—I think it is ancient Mayan. The lingo of the tribe that built the great pyramids at Chichen Itza, then vanished. I probably know as much about that language as anybody on earth. Wait a minute, and I'll think of a few words."

But Doc was not waiting. To the squat man, he spoke in ancient Mayan! Slowly, halting, having difficulty with the syllables, it was true, but he spoke understandably.

And the squat man, more excited than ever, spouted more gutturals.

Doc asked a question.

The man made a stubborn answer.

"He won't talk," Doc complained. "All he will say is a lot of stuff about having to kill me to save his people from something he calls the Red Death!"

Chapter V
THE FLY THAT JUMPED

ASTOUNDED silence gripped the group.

"You mean!" Johnny muttered, blinking through his glasses, "You mean this fellow really speaks the tongue of ancient Maya?"

Doc nodded. "He sure does."

"It's fantastic!" Johnny grumbled. "Those people vanished hundreds of years ago. At least, all those that comprised the highest civilization did. A few ignorant peons were probably left. Even those survive to this day. But as for the higher class Mayan"—he made a gesture of something disappearing—*"pouf!* Nobody knows for sure what became of them."

"They were a wonderful people," Doc said thoughtfully. "They had a civilization that probably surpassed ancient Egypt."

"Ask him why he paints his fingers red," Monk requested, unfazed by talk of lost civilizations.

Doc put the query in the tongue-flapping Mayan tongue.

The stocky man gave a surly answer.

"He says he's one of the warrior sect," Doc translated. "Only members of the warrior sect sport red fingertips."

"Well, I'll be daggone!" Monk snorted.

"He won't talk anymore," Doc advised. Then he added grimly: "We'll take him down to the office, and see if he won't change his mind!"

Searching the prisoner, Doc dug up a remarkable knife. It had a blade of obsidian, a darksome, glasslike volcanic rock, and the edge rivaled a razor in cutting qualities. The handle was simply a leather thong wrapped around and around the upper end of the obsidian shaft.

This knife Doc appropriated. He picked up the prisoner's double-barreled elephant rifle. The marvelous weapon was manufactured by the Webley & Scott firm, of England.

Monk eagerly took charge of the captive, booting him ungently out to the street and to their taxi.

Swishing downtown through the rain, Doc, speaking through the taxi window, tried again to persuade the stocky prisoner to talk.

The fellow disclosed only one fact—and Doc had already guessed that.

"He says he's really a Mayan!" Doc translated for the others.

"Tell him I'll pull his ears off an' feed 'em to him if he don't come clean!" Monk suggested.

Doc, anxious himself to note the effect of torture threats on the Mayan, repeated Monk's remarks.

The Mayan shrugged, clucked in his native tongue.

"He says," Doc explained, "that the trees in his country are full of those like you, only smaller. He means monkeys."

Ham let out a howl of laughter at that, and Monk subsided.

RAIN was threshing down less vigorously when they pulled up before the gleaming office building that spiked up nearly a hundred stories. Entering, they rode the elevator to the eighty-sixth floor.

The Mayan again refused to talk.

"If we just had some truth serum!" suggested Long Tom, running pale fingers through his blond, Nordic hair.

Renny held up a monster fist. "This is all the truth serum we need! I'll show you how it works!"

Big, with sloping mountains of gristle for shoulders, and long kegs of bone and tendon for arms, Renny slid over to the library door. His fist came up.

Wham! Completely through the stout panel Renny's fist pistoned. It seemed more than bone and tendon could stand. But when Renny drew his knuckles out of the wreckage and blew off the splinters, they were unmarked.

Renny, having demonstrated what he could do, came back and towered threateningly over their captive.

"Talk to him in that gobble he calls a language, Doc! Tell him he's in for the same thing that door got if he don't tell us whether your father was murdered, and if he was, who did it. And we want to know why he tried to shoot us."

The prisoner only sat in stoical silence. He was scared—but determined to suffer any violence rather than talk.

"Wait, Renny," Doc suggested. "Let's try something more subtle."

"For instance?" Renny inquired.

"Hypnotism," said Doc. "If this man is of a savage race, his mind is probably susceptible to hypnotic influence. It's no secret that many savages hypnotize themselves to such an extent that they think they see their pagan gods come and talk to them."

Positioned directly before the stocky Mayan, Doc began to exert the power of his amazing golden eyes. They seemed to turn into shifting, gleaming piles of the flaked yellow metal, holding the prisoner's gaze inexorably, exerting a compelling, authoritative influence.

For a minute the squat Mayan was quiet, except for his bulging eyes. He swayed a little in his chair. Then, with a piercing yell in his native tongue, the prisoner lunged backward out of his chair.

The Mayan's plunge carried him toward Renny. But the big-fisted giant had been watching Doc so intently he must have been a little hypnotized himself. He was slow breaking the spell. Reaching for the Mayan, he missed.

Straight to the window, the squat Mayan sped. A wild jump, and he shot headfirst through it—to his death!

AWED silence was in the room for a while.

"He realized he was going to be made to talk," Ham clipped, whipping his waspish frame over to the window to look callously down. "So he killed himself."

"Wonder what can be behind all this!" Long Tom puzzled, absently inspecting his unhealthy looking features as reflected by the polished tabletop.

"Let's see if the message my father left written on the window won't help," Doc suggested.

They followed Doc to the library in a group. "Important papers back of the red brick," read the message in invisible ink which could only be detected by ultraviolet light. They were all curious to know where the papers were, anxious to see that they were intact. Above all, they wanted to know the nature of these "important papers."

Doc had the box which manufactured ultraviolet rays, under his arm. On into the laboratory, he led the cavalcade.

Everyone noticed instantly that the laboratory floor was of brick, with a rubber matting scattered here and there.

Monk looked like he understood, then his jaw fell. "Huh!"

The floor bricks were *all* red!

Doc plugged the ultraviolet apparatus into a light socket. He switched off the laboratory lights. Deliberately, he played the black-light rays across the brick floor. The darkness was intense.

And suddenly one brick was shining with an unholy red luminance. The brick was the lid of a secret little cavity in the floor, and the elder Savage had treated it with some substance that had the property of glowing red under the black-light beams.

From the secret cavity, Doc lifted a packet of papers wrapped securely in an oilskin cloth that looked like a fragment of slicker. Ham clicked on the lights. They gathered around, eagerly waiting.

Doc opened the papers. They were very official looking, replete with gaudy seals. And they were printed in Spanish.

One at a time, as he finished glancing over them, Doc passed the papers to Ham. The astute lawyer studied them with great interest. At last Doc was completely through the papers. He looked at Ham.

"These papers are a concession from the government of Hidalgo," Ham declared. "They give to you several hundred square miles of land in Hidalgo, providing you pay the government of Hidalgo one hundred thousand dollars yearly and one fifth of everything you remove from this land. And the concession holds for a period of ninety-nine years."

Doc nodded. "Notice something else, Ham! Those papers are made out to me. *Me*, mind you! Yet they were executed twenty years ago. I was only a kid then."

"You know what I think?" Ham demanded.

"Same thing I do, I'll bet!" Doc replied. "These papers are the title to the legacy my father left me. The legacy is something he discovered twenty years ago."

"But what *is* the legacy?" Monk wanted to know.

Doc shrugged. "I haven't the slightest idea, brothers. But you can bet it's something well worthwhile. My father was never mixed up in piker deals. I have heard him treat a million dollar transaction as casually as though he were buying a cigar."

Pausing, Doc looked steadily at each of his men in turn. The flaky gold of his eyes shimmered strange lights. He seemed to read the thoughts of each.

"I'm going after this heritage my father left," he said at length. "I don't need to ask—you fellows are with me!"

"And how!" grinned Renny. And the others echoed his sentiment.

PLANTING the papers securely in a chamois money belt about his powerful waist, Doc walked back into the library, thence into the other room.

"Did the Mayan race hang out in Hidalgo?" Renny asked abruptly, eyeing his enormous fist.

Johnny, fiddling with his glasses that had the magnifying lens, took it upon himself to answer.

"The Mayans were scattered over a large part of Central America," he said. "But the Itzans, the clan whose dialect our late prisoner spoke, were situated in Yucatan during the height of their civilization. However, the republic of Hidalgo is not far away, being situated among the rugged mountains farther inland."

"I'm betting this Mayan and Doc's heritage are tied up somewhere," declared Long Tom, the electrical wizard.

Doc stood facing the window. With his back to the light, his strong bronze face was not sharply outlined except when he turned slightly to the right or left to speak. Then the light play seemed to accentuate its remarkable qualities of character.

"The thing for us to do now is corner the man who was giving the Mayan orders," he said slowly.

"Huh—you think there's more of your enemies?" Renny demanded.

"The Mayan showed no signs of understanding the English language," Doc elaborated. "Whoever left the warning in this room wrote it in English, and was educated enough to understand the ultra-violet apparatus. That man was in the building when the shot was fired, because the elevator operator said no one came in between the time we left and got back. Yes, brothers, I don't think we're out of the woods yet."

Abruptly, Doc went over to the double-barreled elephant rifle which had been in possession of the Mayan. He inspected the manufacturer's number. He grasped the telephone.

"Get me the firearms manufacturing firm of Webley & Scott, Birmingham, England," he told the phone operator. "Yes, of course—England! Where the Prince of Wales lives."

To his friends, Doc explained: "Perhaps the firm that made the rifle will know to whom they sold it."

"Somebody will cuss over in England when he's called out of bed by long-distance phone from America," Renny chuckled.

"You forget the five hours' time difference," clipped waspish Ham. "It is now early morning in England! They'll just be getting up."

Doc was facing the window again, apparently lost in thought. Actually, while standing there a moment before, he had felt vaguely that something was out of place about the window.

Then he got it! The mortar at one end of the granite slab which formed the windowsill was fresher than on the other side. The strip of mortar was no wider than a pencil mark, yet Doc noticed it. He leaned out the window.

A fine wire, escaping from the room through the mortared crack, ran downward! It entered a window below.

Doc flashed back into the room. His supple, sensitive, but steel-strong hands explored. He brought to light a tiny microphone of the type radio announcers call lapel mikes.

"Somebody has been listening!" His powerful voice throbbed through the room. "In the room below! Let's look into that!"

NO puff of wind could have gone out of the room and down the stairs more speedily than Doc made it. The distance was sixty feet, and Doc had covered it all before his men were out of the upstairs room. And they had moved as quickly as they could.

Whipping over where the wall could shelter him from ordinary bullets, Doc tried the doorknob. Locked! He exerted what for him was a mild pressure. Wood splintered, brass mechanism of the lock gritted and tore—and the door hopped ajar.

A pistol crashed in the room. The bullet came close enough to Doc's bronzed features that he felt the cold stir of air. A second lead missile followed. The powder noise was a great bawl of sound. Both bullets chopped plaster off the elaborately decorated corridor wall.

Within the room, a door slammed.

Doc instantly slid inside. Sure enough, his quarry had retreated to a connecting office.

All this had taken flash parts of a second—Doc's men were only now clamoring at the door.

"Keep back!" Doc directed. He liked to fight his own battles. And there seemed to be only one man opposing him.

Doc crossed the office, treading new-looking cheap carpet. He circled a second-hand oak desk with edges blackened where cigarette stubs had been placed carelessly. He tried the connecting door.

It was also locked—but gave like wet cardboard before his powerful shove. Alert, almost certain a bullet would meet him, he doubled down close to the floor. He knew he could bob into view and back before the man inside could pull trigger.

But the place was empty!

Once, twice, three times, Doc counted his own heartbeats. Then he saw the explanation.

A stout silken cord, with hardwood rods about the size of fountain pens tied every foot or so for handholds, draped out of the open window. The end of the cord was tied to a stout radiator leg. And a tense jerking showed a man was going down it.

With a single leap, Doc was at the window. He looked down.

Of the man descending the cord, little could be told. In the streaming darkness he was no more than a black lump.

Doc drew back, whipped out his flashlight. When he played it down the cord, the man was gone!

The fellow had ducked into a window.

The flash went into Doc's pocket. Doc himself clambered over the windowsill. Grasping the silken cord, he descended. Thanks to the coördination of his great muscles, Doc negotiated the cord just about as fast as a man could run.

He passed the first window. It was closed, the office beyond darkened and deserted-looking.

Doc went on down. He had not seen what window the quarry had disappeared into. The second window was also closed. And the third! Doc knew then that he had passed the right window. The man could not have gone this far down the cord.

It was typical of Doc that he did not give even a glance to what was below—a sheer fall of hundreds of feet. So far downward did the brick-and-glass wall extend that it seemed to narrow with distance until it was only a yard or so across. And the street was wedge-shaped at the bottom, as though cut with a great, sharp knife.

Doc had climbed a yard upward when the silk cord gave a violent jerk. He looked up.

A window had opened. A man had shoved a chair through it, and was pushing on the cord so as to swing Doc out away from the building. The murk of the night hid the man's face. But it was obvious he was Doc's quarry.

Like a rock on the end of the silken rope, Doc was swung out several feet from the building. He would have to chance to grab a windowsill.

The man above flashed a hand for the cord. A long knife glistened in the hand.

Chapter VI
WORKING PLANS

AT no time had Doc Savage ever put his ability to think like chain lightning to better use than he did now. In the fractional split of time that it took his golden eyes to register the deadly menace of that knife, he formulated a plan of action.

He simply let go completely of the silken cord!

This, in spite of the sheer fall of more than eighty stories directly below him—with not a possible chance of saving himself by clutching a projecting piece of masonry. This building was of the modernistic architecture which does not go in for trick balconies and carved ledges.

But Doc knew what he was doing. And it was a thing that called for iron nerve and stupendous strength and quickness of movement.

The silken cord, going abruptly slack before the chair the man above pushed against it, nearly caused the would-be murderer to pitch headlong out of the window. The fellow dropped both the chair and his knife and by a wild grab, saved himself from the fall he had meant for Doc.

Doc, with a maneuver little short of marvelous, caught the end of the silken cord as it snaked past. A drop of a few feet, which his remarkable arm muscles easily cushioned, and he was swinging close to a windowsill, none the worse for his narrow escape.

Doc stepped easily to the window ledge.

Not a moment too soon! The man above had recovered and, desperate, had employed a small penknife to cut the silken line. It slithered down past Doc, writhing and twisting into fantastic shapes as it dropped those eighty stories to the street.

The window on the ledge of which Doc found himself was locked. Using an elbow, he popped the pane inward, and sprang into the office. He lunged across the room.

The door literally jumped out of its casing, lock and all, when he took hold of it. He halted in the corridor, stumped.

His attuned ear could detect the windy noise of an elevator dropping downward. He knew it was his quarry in flight!

A couple of floors above, Renny was yelling, his voice more than ever like thunder deep in a cave. "Doc! What's become of you?"

Doc paid no attention. He ran across the corridor to the elevator doors. So quickly that he seemed to spring directly to it, he found the cage shaft that was in operation. His fist came back, jumped forward so swiftly as to defy the eye.

The sound as Doc's knuckles hit the sheet-steel elevator door was like the boom of a hard-swung sledge. An onlooker would have sworn the blow would shatter every bone in his fist. But Doc had learned how to tighten the muscles and tendons in his hands until they were like cushioned steel, capable of withstanding the most violent shock.

As a matter of fact, it was part of Doc's daily two-hour routine of exercises to subject all parts of his great body to terrific blows in order that he might be able always to steel himself against them.

The sheet-metal elevator door caved in like a kicked tin can. In a moment Doc had thrown the safety switch which the door, closing, ordinarily operated. Such safety switches are a part of all elevator doors, so the cage cannot move up or down and leave a door open for some child or careless person to fall through into the shaft. They controlled the motor current.

Many floors below, the elevator car halted, motor circuit broken.

Doc thrust his head in and looked down the shaft. He was disappointed. The elevator car was nearly at the street level.

Five minutes elapsed before the lackadaisical elevator operator got a cage up and ferried Doc and his friends down to the street.

By that time, their quarry was hopelessly gone.

The indifferent elevator chauffeur could not even give them a description of the would-be killer who had fled the building.

THERE was considerable uproar around to the side of the skyscraper, when a sleepy pedestrian got the shock of his life by falling over the body of the Mayan who had jumped from the window.

Doc Savage told a straightforward story to the police, explaining exactly how the Mayan had come to his death. And such was the power of Doc, and the esteem in which his departed father was held, that the New York police commissioner gave instant orders that Doc be not molested, and, moreover, that his connection with the suicide be not revealed to the newspapers.

Doc was thus left free to depart for the Central American republic of Hidalgo to investigate the mysterious legacy his father had left him.

Back up in the eighty-sixth-floor lair, Doc made plans and gave orders looking to their execution.

To waspish, quick-thinking Ham, he gave certain of the papers which had been under the brick in the laboratory.

"Your career as a lawyer has given you a wide acquaintance in Washington, Ham," Doc told him. "You're intimate with all the high government officials. So you take care of the legal angle of our trip to Hidalgo."

Ham picked back a cuff to look at an expensive platinum wristwatch. "A passenger plane leaves New York for Washington in four hours. I'll be on it." He twirled his black, innocent-looking sword cane.

"Too long to wait," Doc told him. "Take my autogyro. Fly it down yourself. We'll join you at about nine this morning."

Ham nodded. He was an expert airplane pilot. So were Renny, Long Tom, Johnny, and Monk. Doc Savage had taught them, managing to imbue them with some of his own genius at the controls.

"Where is your autogyro?" Ham inquired.

"At North Beach airport, out on Long Island," Doc retorted.

Ham whipped out, in a hurry to get his share done.

"Renny," Doc directed, "whatever instruments you need, take them. Dig up maps. You're our navigator. We are going to fly down, of course."

"Righto, Doc," said Renny, his utterly somber, puritanical look showing just how pleased he was.

For this thing promised action. Excitement and adventure aplenty! And how these remarkable men were enamored of that!

"Long Tom," said Doc Savage, "yours is the electrical end. You know what we might need."

"Sure!" Long Tom's pale face was flaming red with excitement.

Long Tom wasn't as unhealthy as he looked. None of the others could remember his suffering a day of illness. Unless the periodic rages, the wild tantrums of temper into which he flew, could be called illness. Long Tom sometimes went months without a flare-up, but when he did explode, he certainly made up for lost time.

His unhealthy look probably came from the gloomy laboratory in which he conducted his endless electrical experiments. The enormous gold tooth he sported directly in front helped, too.

Long Tom, like Ham, had earned his nickname in France. In a certain French village there had been ensconced in the town park an old-fashioned cannon of the type used centuries ago by rovers of the Spanish Main. In the heat of an enemy attack, Major Thomas J. Roberts had loaded this ancient relic with a sackful of kitchen cutlery and broken wine bottles, and wrought genuine havoc. And from that day, he was Long Tom Roberts.

"Chemicals," Doc told Monk.

"Oke.," grinned Monk. He sidled out. It was remarkable that a man so homely could be one of the world's leading chemists. But it was true. Monk had a great chemical laboratory of his own in a penthouse atop an office building far downtown, only a short distance from Wall Street. He was headed there now.

Only Johnny, the geologist and archaeologist, remained with Doc.

"Johnny, your work is possibly the most important." Doc's golden eyes were thoughtful as he looked out the window. "Dig into your library for dope on Hidalgo. Also on the ancient Mayan race."

"You think the Mayan angle is important, Doc?"

"I sure do, Johnny."

The telephone bell jangled.

"That's my long-distance call to England," Doc guessed. "They took their time getting it through!"

Lifting the phone, he spoke, got an answer, then rapidly gave the model of the double-barreled elephant rifle, and the number of the weapon.

"Who was it sold to?" he asked.

In a few minutes, he got his answer.

Doc rung off. His bronze face was inscrutable; golden gleamings were in his eyes.

"The English factory says they sold that gun to the government of Hidalgo," Doc said thoughtfully. "It was a part of a large lot of weapons sold to Hidalgo some months ago."

Johnny adjusted his glasses which had the magnifying lens.

"We've got to be careful, Doc," he said. "If this enemy of ours persists in making trouble, he may try to tamper with our plane."

"I have a scheme that will prevent danger from that angle," Doc assured him.

Johnny blinked, then started to ask what the scheme was. But he was too slow. Doc had already quitted the office.

With a grin, Johnny went about his own part of the preparations. He felt supreme confidence in Doc Savage.

Whatever villainous moves the enemy made against them, Doc was capable of checkmating. Already, Doc was undoubtedly putting into operation some plan which would guarantee them safety in their flight southward.

The plan to protect their plane would be one worthy of Doc's vast ingenuity.

Chapter VII
DANGER TRAIL

THE rain had stopped.

A bilious dawn, full of fog, shot through with a chill wind, was crawling along the north shore of Long Island. The big hangars at North Beach airport, just within the boundary line of New York City, were like pale-gray, round-backed boxes in the mist. Electric lights made a futile effort to dispel the sodden gloom.

A giant trimotored, all-metal plane stood on the tarmac of the flying field near by. On the fuselage, just back of the bow engine, was emblazoned in firm black letters:

Clark Savage, Jr.

One of Doc's crates!

Airport attendants, in uniforms made very untidy by mud, grease, and dampness, were busy transferring boxes from a truck to the interior of the big plane. These boxes were of light, but stout, construction, and on each was imprinted, after the manner of exploration expeditions, the words:

CLARK SAVAGE, JR., HIDALGO EXPEDITION.

"What's a Hidalgo?" a thick-necked mechanic wanted to know.

"Dunno—a country, I reckon," a companion greaseball told him.

The conversation was unimportant, except in that it showed what a little-known country Hidalgo was. Yet the Central American republic was of no inconsiderable size.

The last box was finally in the plane. An airport worker closed the plane door. Because of the murky dawn and moisture on the windows, it was impossible to see into the pilot's compartment of the great trimotor plane.

A mechanic climbed atop the tin pants over the big wheels, and standing there, cranked the inertia starter of first one motor, then the other. All three big radial engines thundered into life. More than a thousand throbbing horsepower.

The big plane trembled to the tune of the hammering exhaust stacks. It was not an especially new ship, being about five years old.

Perhaps one or two attendants about the tarmac heard the sound of another plane which had arrived overhead. Looking up, maybe they saw a huge gray bat of a shape go slicing through the mist. But that was all, and the noise of its great, muffled exhaust was hardly audible above the bawl of the stacks of the old-fashioned trimotor.

The trimotor was moving now. The tail was up, preliminary to taking off. Faster and faster it raced across the tarmac. It slowly took the air.

Without banking to either side, climbing gently, the big all-metal plane flew possibly a mile.

An astounding thing happened then.

The trimotor ship seemed to turn instantaneously into a gigantic sheet of white-hot flame. This resolved into a monster ball of villainous smoke. Then ripped fragments of the plane and its contents rained downward upon the roofs of Jackson Heights, a conservative residential suburb of New York City.

So terrific was the explosion that windows were broken in the houses underneath, and shingles even torn off roofs.

No piece more than a few yards in area remained of the great plane. Indeed, the authorities could never have identified it, had not the airport men known it had just taken off from there.

No human life could have survived aboard the trimotor aircraft.

DOC SAVAGE merely blinked his golden eyes once after the blinding flash which marked the blast that annihilated the trimotor ship.

"That was what I was afraid of!" he said dryly.

The rush of air thrown by the explosion caused his plane to reel. Doc stirred the controls expertly to right it.

For Doc and his men had not been in the ill-fated trimotor plane. They were in the other craft which had flown over the airport a moment before the trimotor took off. Indeed, Doc himself had maneuvered the takeoff of the trimotor, using remote radio control to direct it.

Doc's radio remote control apparatus was exactly the same type used by the army and navy in extensive experiments, employing changing frequencies and sensitive relays for its operation.

Doc did not know how their mysterious enemy had managed to blow up the trimotor. But thanks to his foresight, Doc's men had escaped the devilish blast. Doc had used the trimotor plane for a decoy. It was one of his old ships, almost ready to be discarded, anyway.

"They must have managed to slip high explosive into one of our boxes," Doc concluded aloud. "It is too bad we lost the equipment in the destroyed plane. But we can get along without it."

"What dizzies me," Renny muttered, "is how they fixed their bomb to explode in the air, and not on the ground."

Doc banked his plane, set a course directly for the city of Washington, using not only the gyroscopic compass with which the craft was fitted, but calculating wind drift expertly.

"How they made the bomb explode in the air can be simply explained," he told Renny at last. "They probably put an altimeter or barometer in the bomb. The altimeter would register a change in height. All they had to do was fix an electrical contact to be closed at a given height, and—*bang!"*

"Bang, is right!" Monk put in, grinning.

Their plane flashed past the upraised arm of the Statue of Liberty, and sang its song of speed southward over the Jersey marshes.

Unlike the trimotor which had been destroyed, this plane was of the latest design. It was a trimotor craft also, but the great engines were in eggs built directly into the wings. It was what pilots call a low-wing job, with the wings attached well down on the fuselage, instead of at the top. The landing gear was retractible—folded up into the wings so as not to offer a trace of wind resistance.

It was the ultra in an airman's steed, this supercraft. And two hundred miles an hour was only its cruising speed.

No small point was the fact that the cabin was soundproof, enabling Doc and his friends to converse in ordinary tones.

The really essential portion of their equipment was loaded into the rear of the speed-ship cabin. Packed compactly in light metal containers, an alloy metal that was lighter even than wood, each carton was fitted with straps for carrying.

In a surprisingly short time they picked up the clustered buildings of Philadelphia. Doc whipped the plane past a little east of the city hall, the center of the downtown business district.

Onward they swept, to zoom down on an airport at the outskirts of Washington.

THE landing Doc made was feather-light, a sample of his wizardry with the controls. He tailed the plane about with sharp blurps of the nose motor, and taxied for the little airport administration office.

In vain did he look about for his autogyro. Ham should have left the windmill plane here, had he already arrived. But the whirligig ship was not in evidence.

An attendant, a spick-and-span dude in a white uniform, ran out to meet them.

"Didn't Ham show up here?" Monk demanded of the man.

"Who?"

"Brigadier General Theodore Marley Brooks!" Monk explained.

The airport attendant registered shock, then great embarrassment at the words. He opened his mouth to speak, but instead, excitement made him merely stutter.

"What has happened?" Doc asked in a gentle but powerful tone that compelled an instant answer.

"The airport manager is holding a man over in the field office who says his name is Brigadier General Theodore Marley Brooks," the attendant explained.

"Holding him—why?"

"The manager is also a deputy sheriff. We got a call that this fellow had stolen an autogyro from a man named Clark Savage. So we arrested him."

Doc nodded absently. He was clever, this unknown enemy of theirs. He had decoyed Ham by a neat ruse.

"Where is the autogyro?" Doc asked.

"Why, this Clark Savage who telephoned the plane had been stolen asked us to send a man with it to bring him here and confront the thief!"

Monk let out a loud snort. "You dumb dude! You're talkin' to Clark Savage!"

The attendant stuttered again. "I don't understand—"

"Someone foxed you," Doc said without noticeable malice. "The pilot who flew that plane to get the fake Clark Savage may be in danger. Do you know where he went?"

"The manager knows."

They hurried over to the administration building. They found a Ham who was burning up. Ham could ordinarily talk himself out of almost any situation, given a little time. But he hadn't made an impression on the blond, bullet-headed airport manager.

Doc handed Ham a phone. "Get the nearest army flying field, Ham. See if you can raise me a pursuit ship fitted with machine guns. It's against regulations, but—"

"Hang regulations!" Ham snapped, and seized the instrument.

From the blond airport manager Doc learned where the autogyro had gone to meet the man who had put over the trick. The spot was in New Jersey.

Doc located it on the map. It was in the mountainous, or, rather, hilly, western portion of Jersey.

Ham cracked the telephone receiver onto its hook. "They're warming up a pursuit job for you, Doc."

It required less than ten minutes for Doc to ferry over to the army drome, plug his powerful frame into a cockpit, saw the throttle back, and take off. He had a regulation warplane now.

FLYING northward, Doc had a fair idea of the purpose of their enemy in decoying the autogyro. The place was within motor distance of New York, so the villainous unknown one would probably be on hand. He would destroy the autogyro, thus hampering Doc and his friends as much as possible.

"Whoever it is, they're willing to do anything to keep us from getting to that legacy of mine in Hidalgo!" Doc concluded.

Over the Delaware River, Doc dived and tested

his machine guns by shooting at the shadow of his plane on the water.

Knobby green hills sprang up underneath. Doc used a pair of binoculars to scrutinize the terrain.

Farmhouses were scattering, ramshackle. Very few of the roads were paved.

Doc discovered his autogyro at last.

The windmill plane sat in a clearing. Near by ran a paved road.

In the clearing with the plane was a green coupé and two men. One of the men was holding a gun upon the other.

The gun wielder, Doc perceived when he came nearer, was masked. The man discovered Doc's army pursuit plane, diving with motor cans a-thunder. The fellow took flight.

Deserting the other man, who must be the autogyro pilot, the masked fellow raced to the windmill plane. The gun in his fist spat a bullet into the fuel tank of the plane. Gasoline ran out in two pale strings. The masked man struck a match and tossed it into the fuel. Instantly the autogyro was bundled in hot flame.

One thing Doc noted about the masked man—the fellow's fingers were a deep scarlet hue for an inch of their length!

The man was also squat and wide. He ran with shortlegged, pegging steps for the green coupé, dived into it. The green car ran out of the field like a frightened bug.

Doc's cowl machine guns released a spray of lead that forked up dust behind the coupé. The car skewered onto the road and turned north.

Again Doc's Browning guns tore off their ripping cackle of death. After the army fashion, every fifth bullet in the ammo cans was a phosphorous-filled tracer. These burst with hot red blots directly behind the green coupé.

Slowly, inexorably, the gray cobwebs of tracer smoke climbed into the rear of the automobile.

With a wild swing, the green car suddenly left the pavement. It vaulted a ditch, miraculously remaining upright, and skewered to a stop amid tall brush that practically hid it.

Doc distinctly saw the passenger quit the car and take to the concealment of the timber.

A couple of times Doc dived and let the Browning guns spew their twelve hundred shots a minute into the timber. He did it more to give the masked man one last scare than from any hope of bagging the fellow. The timber offered perfect concealment.

Not a little disgusted, Doc landed and launched a hunt afoot for the masked man. But it was too late.

The airport attendant who had flown the autogyro here could give no worthwhile description of the masked man when Doc consulted him. The fellow had merely sprung out of the green car with a gun.

Doc telephoned the authorities and had a net spread for the masked man before he took off again for Washington. But he was pretty certain the fellow would evade the Jersey officers. The man was smart, as well as very dangerous.

Doc took the chagrined airport attendant with him in the army pursuit plane back to Washington.

HAM and the others were waiting when Doc arrived, after restoring the pursuit plane to the army field.

"Have any trouble getting our papers up?" Doc asked.

Ham tightened his mobile orator's mouth. "I did have a little trouble, Doc. It was strange, too. The Hidalgo consul seemed very reluctant to O. K. our papers. At first he wasn't going to do it. In fact, I had to have our own secretary of state make some things very clear to Mr. Consul before he gave us the official high sign."

"What's your guess, Ham?" Doc asked. "Was the official directly interested in keeping us out of Hidalgo, or had someone paid him money to make it tough for us?"

"He was paid!" Ham smiled tightly. "He gave himself away when I accused him of accepting money to refuse his O. K. on our papers. But I was not able to learn who had put the cash on the line."

"Somebody!" Renny rumbled, his puritanical face very long. "Somebody is taking a lot of trouble to keep us out of Hidalgo! Now, I wonder why?"

"I have a hunch!" Ham declared. "Doc's mysterious heritage must be of fabulous value. Men are not killed and diplomatic agents bribed without good reasons. That concession of several hundred square miles of mountainous territory in Hidalgo is the explanation, of course. Someone is trying to keep us away from it!"

"Does anybody know what they raise down in that neck of the woods?" Monk inquired.

Long Tom hazarded a couple of guesses, "Bananas, chicle for making chewing gum—"

"No plantations in the region Doc seems to own," Johnny, the geologist, put in sharply. "I soaked up all I could find on the precise region. And you'd be surprised how little it was!"

"You mean there was not much information available about it?" Ham prompted.

"You said it! To be exact—the whole region is unexplored!"

"Unexplored!"

"Oh, the district is filled with mountains on most maps," Johnny explained. "But on the really accurate charts the truth comes out. There's a considerable stretch of country no white men have penetrated. And Doc's strange heritage is located slap-dab in the middle of it!"

"So we gotta play Columbus!" Monk snorted.

"You'll think Columbus's trip across the briny was a pipe when you see this Hidalgo country!" Johnny informed him. "That region is unexplored for only one reason—white men can't get into it!"

Doc had been standing by during the exchange of words. But now his calm, powerful voice commanded quick attention.

"Is there any reason we can't be on our way?" he asked dryly.

They took off at once in the monster, low-wing speed plane. But before their departure, Doc telephoned long distance to Miami, Florida, where he got in touch with an airplane supplies concern. He ordered pontoons for his plane, after determining the company kept them in stock.

THE approximately nine-hundred-mile flight to Miami they made in something more than five hours, thanks to the tremendous cruising speed of Doc's superplane.

Working swiftly, with lifting cranes and tools and mechanics supplied by the plane parts concern, they installed the pontoons before darkness flung its pall over the lower end of Florida.

Doc taxied the low-wing speed ship out over Biscayne Bay a short distance, making sure the pontoons were seaworthy. Back at the seaplane base he took on fuel and oil from a seagoing filling station built on a barge.

To Cuba was not quite another three hundred miles. They were circling over Havana before the night was many hours old. Another landing for fuel, and off again.

Doc flew. He was tireless. Renny, huge and elephantine, but without equal when it came to angles and maps and navigation, checked their course periodically. Between times he slept.

Long Tom, Johnny, Monk, and Ham were sleeping as soundly among the boxed supplies as they would have in sumptuous hotel beds. A faint grin was on every slumbering face. This was the sort of thing they considered real living. Action! Adventure!

Across the Caribbean to Belize, their destination on the Central American mainland, was somewhat over five hundred miles. It was an all-water hop.

To avoid a headwind for a while, Doc flew quite near the sea, low enough that at times he sighted barracudas and sharks. There was an island or two, flat, white beaches bared to the lambent glory of a tropical moon that was like a huge disk of rich platinum.

So stunningly beautiful was the southern sea that he awoke the others to observe the play of phosphorescent fire and the manner in which the waves creamed in the moonlight, or were blown into faintly jeweled spindrift.

They thundered across Ambergris Cay at a thousand feet, and in no time at all were swinging wide over the flat, narrow streets of Belize.

Chapter VIII
PERSISTENT FOES

THE sun was up, blazing with a wild revelry. Away inland, the jungle was lost in a horizon infinitely blue.

Doc slanted the big plane down and patted the pontoons against the small waves. Spray fanned up and roared against the idling propellers. He taxied in toward the mud beach.

Renny stretched, yawned. The yawn gave his extremely puritanical face a ludicrous aspect.

"I believe that in the old pirate days they actually built a foundation for part of this town out of rum bottles," Renny offered. "Ain't that right, Johnny?"

"I believe so," Johnny corroborated from his wealth of historical lore.

Plink!

The sound was exactly like a boy shooting at a tin can with a small air rifle.

Plink! It came again.

Then—*bur-r-r-rip!* One long roar!

"Well, for—" Monk swallowed the rest and sat down heavily as Doc slammed the engine throttles wide open.

Engines thundering, props scooping up water and turning it into a great funnel of mist behind the tail, the plane lunged ahead—straight for the mud beach.

"What happened?" demanded Ham.

"Machine gun putting bullets through our floats!" Doc said in a low voice. "Watch the shore! See if you can get a glimpse of whoever it was!"

"For the love of mud!" muttered Monk. "Ain't we never gonna get that red-fingered guy out of our hair?"

"No doubt he radioed ahead to someone he knows here!" Doc offered.

Distinctly audible over the bawl of the motors came two more metallic *plinks,* then a series. The unseen marksman was doing his best to perforate the pontoons and sink the craft.

All five of Doc's men were staring through the cabin windows, seeking trace of the one who was shooting.

Abruptly bullets began to whiz through the plane fuselage itself. Renny clapped a hand to his monster left arm. But the wound was no more than a shallow scrape. Another blob of lead wrought minor havoc in the box that held Long Tom's electrical equipment.

It was Doc who saw the sniper ahead of all the others, thanks to an eye of matchless keenness.

"Over behind that fallen palm!" he said.

Then the rest perceived. The sharpshooter's weapon projected over the bole of a fallen royal palm that was like a pillar of dull silver.

Rifles leaped magically into the hands of Doc's five men. A whistling salvo of lead pelted the palm log, preventing the sniper from releasing further shots.

The plane dug its pontoons into the mud beach at this point. It was not a moment too soon, either. They were filling rapidly with water, for some of the bullets, striking slantwise, had opened sizeable rips.

SWIFTLY, grim with purpose, three men bounded out of the plane. They were Doc, Renny, and Monk. The other three, Johnny, Long Tom, and Ham, all excellent marksmen, continued to put a barrage of rifle lead against the palm log.

The log lay on a finger of land which reached out toward a very small cay, or island. Between cay and the land finger stretched about fifty yards of water.

The sniper tried to reach the mainland, only to shriek and drop flat as a bullet from the plane creased him. Meantime Doc, Renny, and Monk had floundered to solid ground and doubled down in the scrawny tropical growth. The smell of the beach was strong in their nostrils—seawater, wet logs, soft-shell crabs, fish, kelp, and decaying vegetation making a conglomerate odor.

To the right of the friends lay Belize, with scraggly, narrow streets and romantic houses with protruding balconies, brightly painted doorways, and every window as becrossed with iron bars as if it were a jail.

The sniper knew they were coming upon him. He tried again to escape. But he had not reckoned with the kind of shooting that was coming from the plane. He couldn't make it to the mainland.

Desperately, the fellow worked out toward the end of the land finger. Stunted mangroves offered puny shelter there. The man shrieked again as he was creased.

In his circle of acquaintances, it must have been customary to shoot prisoners—give no quarter—because he didn't offer to surrender. Evidently he was out of ammunition.

Wild with terror, he leaped up and plunged into the water. He was going to try to swim to the little island.

"Sharks!" grunted Renny. "These waters are full of the things!"

But Doc Savage was already a dozen yards ahead, leaping out on the land finger.

The sniper was a squat, dark-skinned fellow—but his features did not resemble those of the Mayan who had committed suicide in New York. He was a low specimen of the Central American half-breed.

He was not a good swimmer, either. He splashed a great deal. Suddenly he let out a piercing squawl of terror. He had seen a dark, sinister triangle of fin sizzling through the water toward him. He tried to turn and come back. But so frightened was he that he hardly moved for all his slamming of the water with his arms.

The shark was a gigantic man-eater. It came straight for its prospective meal, not even circling to investigate. The mouth of the monster thing was open, revealing the horrible array of teeth.

The unfortunate sniper let out a weak, ghastly bleat.

It seemed too late for anything to help the fellow. Renny, in discussing the affair later, maintained Doc purposely waited until the last minute so that terror would teach the sniper a lesson—show the man the fate of an evildoer. If true, Doc's lesson was mightily effective.

With a tremendous spring, Doc shot outward and cleaved headfirst into the water.

THE dive was perfectly executed. And Doc, curving his powerful bronze body at the instant of impact with the water, seemed to hardly sink beneath the surface.

It looked like an impossible thing to do, but Doc was beside the unfortunate man even as the big shark shot in with a last burst of speed. Doc put himself between the shark's teeth and the sniper!

But the bronzed, powerful body was not there when the needled teeth slashed. Doc was alongside the shark. His left arm flipped with electric speed around the head of the thing, securing what a wrestler would call a stranglehold.

Doc's legs kicked powerfully. For a fractional moment he was able to lift the shark's head out of the water. In that interval his free right fist traveled a terrific arc—and found the one spot where his vast knowledge told him it was possible to stun the man-eater.

The shark became slack as a kayoed boxer.

Doc shoved the sniper ashore. The breed's swarthy face was a study. He looked like someone had jerked the cover off hell and let him see what awaited men of his ilk.

Now that the shark was atop the water, where rifle bullets could reach it, Renny and Monk put the finishing touch to the ugly monster.

"Why did you fire upon us?" Doc asked the breed, couching the words in Spanish. Doc spoke Spanish fluently, as he did many other tongues.

Almost eagerly, so grateful was he for what Doc

had done, the breed made answer:

"I was hired to do it, señor. Hired by a man in Blanco Grande, the capital of Hidalgo. This man rushed me here during the night in a blue airplane."

"What was your employer's name?" Doc questioned.

"That I do not know, señor."

"Don't lie!"

"I am not lying to you, señor! Not after what you did for me a while ago. Truly, I do not know this man." The breed squirmed uneasily. "I have been a low *mozo*, hiring out for evil work to whoever pays me, and asking no questions. I shall desert that manner of living. I can take you to the spot where the blue airplane is hidden."

"Do that!" Doc directed.

They started off, reached the outskirts of town. Doc prepared to hail a *fotingo*, or dilapidated flivver taxi. Then he lifted his golden eyes to the heavens.

An airplane was droning in the hot copper sky. It came into view, a brilliant blue, single-motor monoplane.

"That is the plane of the man who hired me to shoot at you!" gasped the breed prisoner.

The gaudy blue craft whipped overhead, engine stacks bawling, and sped directly for the mud beach.

Without a word, Doc spun and ran with tremendous speed for the beach where Johnny, Long Tom, and Ham waited with his own plane.

HALF-NAKED children gaped at the blur of bronze Doc made in passing them. And women muffled in *rebozos*, a combination shawl and scarf, scampered out and yanked them clear of the thundering charge of Renny and Monk and the prisoner, coming in Doc's wake.

On the beach a machine gun suddenly cackled. Doc knew by the particularly rapid rate of its fire that it was one he had brought along. His friends had set it up, were firing at the blue monoplane.

The blue plane dipped back of the tufted top of a royal palm, going down in a whistling dive. Then came a loud explosion. A bomb!

Up above the palm fronds the blue plane climbed. It was behaving erratically now. The pilot or some part of his azure ship was hit.

Straight inland it flew. And it did not come back.

Doc, reaching the beach, saw the bomb had been so badly aimed as to miss his plane fully fifty yards. His three men were sitting on the wing with the machine gun, grinning widely.

"We sure knocked the feathers off that bluebird!" Long Tom chuckled.

"He won't be back!" Ham decided, after squinting at the distant blue dot that was the receding aircraft. "Who was it?"

"Obviously one of the gang trying to prevent us reaching that land of mine in Hidalgo," Doc replied. "The member of the gang in New York radioed to Blanco Grande, the capital of Hidalgo that we were coming by plane. Right here is the logical place for us to refuel after a flight across the Caribbean. So they set a trap here. They hired this breed to machine-gun us, and when that didn't work, the pilot tried to bomb us."

At that moment Renny and Monk came up. They were both so big the breed looked like a little brown boy between them.

"What do we do with his nibs?" Monk asked, shaking the breed.

Doc replied without hesitation: "Free him."

The swarthy breed nearly broke down with gratitude. Tears stood in his eyes. He blubbered profuse thanks. And before he would depart, he came close to Doc and murmured an earnest question. The others could not hear the breed's words.

"What did he ask you?" Monk inquired after the breed had departed, with a strange new confidence in his walk.

"Believe it or not," Doc smiled, "he wanted to know how one went about entering a monastery. I think there is one chap who will walk the straight and narrow in the future."

"We better catch a shark and take him along if a close look at one reforms our enemies like that!" Monk laughed.

With ropes from a local warehouse, and long, thin palms which Doc hired willing natives to cut, the plane was snaked to dry land. The news was bad. The floats were badly torn. Renny, a genius with tools, made repairs, using a compact welding torch and spare sheet metal.

When he had the work underway, Doc sought a secluded spot for his exercises. He never missed the two-hour routine each day, although he might have been on the go for many hours previously.

His muscular exercises were similar to ordinary setting-up movements, but infinitely harder, more violent. He took them without apparatus. For instance, he would make certain muscles attempt to lift his arm, while the other muscles strove to hold it down. That way he furthered not only muscular tissue, but control over individual muscles as well. Every part of his great, bronzed body he exercised in this manner.

From the case which held his equipment, Doc took a pad and pencil and wrote a number of several figures. Eyes closed, he extracted the square and cube root of this number in his head, carrying the figures to many decimal places. He multiplied and divided and subtracted the number with various figures. Next he did the same thing with a number of an even dozen figures. This disciplined him in concentration.

Out of the case came an apparatus which made sound waves of all tones, some of a wavelength so short or so long as to be inaudible to the normal ear. For several minutes Doc strained to detect these waves inaudible to ordinary people. Years of this had enabled him to hear many of these customarily unheard sounds.

His eyes shut, Doc rapidly identified by the sense of smell several score of different odors, all very vague, each contained in a small vial racked in the case.

The full two hours Doc worked at these and other intensive exercises.

When he returned to the plane, the floats were repaired and emptied of water.

THEY took off for Blanco Grande, capital of Hidalgo.

It was jungle country they flew over, luxuriant, unhealthily rank trees in near solid masses. Lianas and grotesque aerial roots tied these into a solid carpet.

Confident of his motors, Doc flew low enough that they could see tiny parakeets and pairs of yellow-headed parrots feeding off *chichem* berries that grew in abundance.

Some hours later they were over the border of Hidalgo. It was a typical country of the southern republics. Wedged in between two mighty mountains, traversed in its own right by a half dozen smaller but even more rugged ranges, it was a perfect spot for those whose minds run to revolutions and banditry.

In such localities governments are unstable not so much because of their own lack of equilibrium, but more because of the opportunities offered others to gather in revolt.

Half of the little valleys of Hidalgo were lost even to the bandits and revolutionists who were most familiar with the terrain. The interior was inhabited by fierce tribes, remnants of once powerful nations, each still a power in its own right, and often engaging in conflict with its neighbors. Woe betide the defenseless white man who found himself wandering about in the wilder part of Hidalgo.

The warlike tribes, the utter inaccessibility of some of the rocky fastnesses, probably explained the large unexplored area Renny had noted on the best maps of Hidalgo.

The capital city itself was a concoction of little, crooked streets, balconied-and-barred houses, ramshackle mud huts, and myriads of colored tile roofs, with the inevitable park for parading in the center of town.

In this case the park was also occupied by the presidential palace and administration buildings. They were imposing structures which showed past governments had been free with the taxpayers' money.

There was a small, shallow lake to the north of town.

On this Doc Savage landed his plane.

Chapter IX
DOC'S WHISTLE

DOC gave some necessary instructions at once. The work fell to Ham, whose understanding of law made him eminently capable.

"Ham, you pay the local secretary of state a visit and check up our rights in this land grant of mine," Doc directed.

"Maybe somebody had better go along to see he don't steal some hams, or something," Monk couldn't resist putting in.

Ham bristled instantly.

"Why should I want a ham when I associate with a crowd of them all the time?" he demanded.

"Monk, you'd better accompany Ham as bodyguard," Doc suggested. "You two love each other so!"

As a matter of fact, despite the mutual ribbing they were always handing each other, Monk and Ham made a good team of quick thinking and brawn, and they got along perfectly, regardless of the fact that to hear them talk, one would think violence was always impending.

Ham shaved and changed to a natty suit of white flannels before departing. He was sartorial perfection in his white shoes, panama, and innocent-looking black sword cane.

Monk, more to aggravate Ham than anything else, didn't even wash his homely face. He cocked a battered hat over one eye, and with pants seemingly on the point of dropping off his tapering hips, he swaggered behind Ham.

It was later afternoon when they were ushered into the presence of Don Rubio Gorro, Secretary of State of Hidalgo.

Don Rubio was rather short, well knit. His face was entirely too handsome for a man's. His complexion was olive, his lips thin, his nose straight and a bit too sharp. His eyes were dark and limpid as a señorita's.

Don Rubio had ears exactly like those artists put on pictures of the devil. They were very pointed.

Extreme politeness characterized the welcome Don Rubio gave Ham, after the Latin fashion. Monk remained in the background. He didn't think Don Rubio was so hot, taking snap judgment.

And Don Rubio lived up to Monk's impression as soon as Ham made his business known.

"But my dear Señor Brooks," said Don Rubio smugly, "our official records contain nothing concerning any concession giving anyone named

Clark Savage, Jr., even an acre of Hidalgo land, much less some hundreds of square miles. I am very sorry, but that is the fact."

Ham executed a twirl with his cane. "Was the present government in power twenty years ago?"

"No. This government came into being two years ago."

"The gang before you probably made the concession grant."

Don Rubio flushed slightly at the subtle inference he was one of a gang.

"In that case!" he said snappishly, "we have nothing to do with it. You're just out of luck."

"You mean we have no rights to this land?"

"You most certainly have not!"

HAM'S cane suddenly leveled at a spot directly between Don Rubio Gorro's devil-like ears. "You've got another guess coming, my friend!"

Don Rubio began: "There is nothing that—"

"Oh, yes, there is!" Ham poked his cane for emphasis. "When this government came into power, it was recognized by the United States only on condition that the new regime respect property rights of American citizens in Hidalgo! That right?"

"Well—"

"You bet it's right! And do you know what will happen if you don't live up to that agreement? The U. S. government will sever relations and class you as a plain crowd of bandits. You couldn't obtain credit to buy arms and machinery and other things you need to keep your political opponents in check. Your export trade would be hurt. You would— But you know all that would happen as well as I do. In six months your government would be out, and a new one in.

"That's what it would mean if you refuse to respect American property. And if this land concession isn't American property, I'm a string on Nero's fiddle."

Don Rubio's swarthy face was flushed a smudgy purple, even to his pointed ears. His hands trembled with rage—and worry. He knew all Ham was telling him was true. Uncle Sam was not somebody to be fooled with. He seized desperately at a straw.

"We cannot recognize your right because there is no record in our archives!" he said wildly.

Ham slapped Doc's papers on the desk. "These are record enough. Somebody has destroyed the others. I'll tell you something else—there are some people who will go to any length to keep us away from this land. They've made attacks on us—no doubt they destroyed the papers."

As he made that statement, Ham watched Don Rubio intently. He felt there was something behind Don Rubio's attitude, had felt that from the first. Ham believed Don Rubio was either one of the gang trying to keep Doc from his heritage, or had been hired by the gang. And Don Rubio's agitation tended to corroborate Ham's suspicion.

"It's going to be just too bad for whoever is causing the trouble!" Ham stated. "We'll get them in the end."

Various emotions played on Don Rubio's too-handsome, swarthy face. He was scared, worried. But gradually a desperate determination came uppermost. He clipped his lips together, shot out his jaw, and offered his final word.

"There is nothing more to be said! You have no claim to that land. That's final!"

Ham twiddled his cane and smiled ominously. "It will take me just about one hour to get a radio message to Washington," he promised grimly. "Then, my friend, you'll see more diplomatic lightning strike around you than you ever saw before!"

Don Rubio bowed, tight-lipped.

LEAVING the government building, Ham and Monk ascertained the location of the radio station and set a course for it. Darkness had arrived while they were talking to Don Rubio. The city, quiet during the heat of the afternoon when they had entered, was awakening. Carriages occupied by staid Castilians, the blue blood of these southern republics, clattered over the rough streets. Here and there was an American car.

"You talked kinda tough to that Don Rubio gink, didn't you?" Monk suggested. "I thought you was always supposed to be polite to these Spaniards. Maybe if you'd handled him with gloves on, you'd have got somewhere."

"Hur-r-rump!" said Ham in his best courtroom manner. "I know how to handle men! That fellow Don Rubio has no principles. I give politeness where politeness is due. And it is never due a crook!"

"You said a mouthful!" rumbled Monk, for once forgetting himself and agreeing with Ham.

They soon found the anglings and meanderings of Blanco Grande streets most bewildering. They had been told the radio station and message office was but a few hundred yards' walk. But when they had covered that distance, there was no sign of any radio station.

"Fooey—we're lost!" Monk grunted, and looked about for someone to accost regarding directions.

There was only one man in the street, a shabby side thoroughfare in what, as they only now perceived, was a none-too-savory-looking part of Blanco Grande. The sole pedestrian was ahead of them, loitering along as though he had no place to go, and plenty of time to reach there.

He was a broad-backed fellow with a short body and a block of a head. He wore dungarees, a bright-green calico shirt, and no shoes. His head, ludicrously enough, was topped with a rusty black derby.

He had his hands in his pockets.

Ham and Monk overhauled the loafer.

"Can you direct us to the radio station?" Ham asked in Spanish.

"Si, señor!" replied the loafer. "Better yet, for a half a peso I will guide you there myself."

Ham, baffled by the crookedness of the Blanco Grande streets, thought it cheap at the price. He hired the native on the spot.

Not once did the stocky, ill-clad fellow take his hands out of his pockets. But Ham and Monk thought nothing of that, passing it up as laziness on their guide's part.

If anything, the streets which they now traversed became more offensive to the eye and nostril. Stale fruit odors came from the darkened mud houses, mingling with the far from weak smell of unwashed humanity.

"Strange district for a radio station," Monk muttered, beginning at last to get suspicious.

"Only a little distance now, señor!" murmured their guide.

Monk, studying the man's plumpness, his curving nose, his prominent lips, was struck by something vaguely familiar. It was as though he had known the guide, or one of his relatives. Monk cudgeled his brains, trying to place the fellow.

And then the whole thing became unpleasantly clear!

Their guide halted suddenly. He pulled his hands from his pockets. The fingertips were stained red for an inch of their length!

The fellow released a loud shout. Instantly from every doorway and darkened cranny for yards around, shadowy forms sprang.

They had been trapped!

MONK emitted a great howl. Monk's fights were always noisy, unless there was reason for them being quiet. Like a gladiator of old, Monk fought best when the racket was loudest.

Knives glittered in the dark. Sandals, made of tapir hide and held on with coarse henequin rope, slammed the cobbles.

Monk lunged and got the man who had been their guide by the nape and the seat of his dungaree pants. As though he were a straw, Monk whirled the man up and back, let him fly. The victim screamed in a strange tongue. A clot of the attackers went down like ten-pins before his hurtling body.

The scream, the ex-guide's red fingertips, told Monk something. The man was a Mayan! The same race as the fellow who had committed suicide in New York! That was why he seemed familiar.

Like the gigantic anthropoid he resembled, Monk went into action. His first fist blow jammed a ratty, dark-skinned man's jaw back under his ear. The fellow dropped, convulsively throwing his knife high in the air.

Ham, dancing like a fencer, tapped a swarthy skull with his sword cane. The cane looked very light, but the tubelike case over the long, keen blade of steel was heavy. The blade itself was by no means light.

As the first assailant went over backward, Ham unsheathed his sword cane. He expertly skewered a fellow who tried to stab him.

But where one besieger went down, a half dozen took his place. The street was full of snarling, vicious devils. None of these had red fingertips, or even resembled Mayans.

The one who was a Mayan, their late guide, had regained his feet, dazed, spouting commands in Spanish.

Men were clinging like leeches to Monk. One sailed fully ten feet straight up when Monk threw him off. But suddenly, weighted by hopeless odds, Monk was borne down.

Ham, with his sword in another unlucky one, was overcome an instant later.

A resounding blow delivered on the head of each one rendered Monk and Ham senseless.

MONK'S awakening was one long blaze of pain. He rolled his eyes. He was in a mud-walled, mud-floored room. There was not a single window, and the one door was low and narrow. Monk tried to sit up and found himself tied hand and foot—not with rope, but with heavy wire.

Ham sprawled nearby on his back. Ham was also wired.

The red-fingered Mayan was bending over Ham. He had just appropriated Ham's papers—Doc's sole documentary proof to his ownership of the tract of land in interior Hidalgo.

"This is what I wanted, Senor!" He hissed a number of words in Mayan, which neither Ham nor Monk understood. It didn't sound complimentary, whatever it was.

The Mayan whipped a knife from inside his bright-green shirt.

"You die now!" he gritted. But even as his knife started up, he seemed to get a more satisfactory thought. From within the capacious green shirt he drew an evil-looking little statuette. The features carved on this faintly resembled those of a human being, a tremendously long nose being most notable. It was artfully sculptured out of a dark obsidian rock.

The Mayan mumbled words, and there had suddenly come into his voice a religious fervor. Monk caught the name "Kukulcan" a time or two, and recognized it as the name of an ancient Mayan deity. The fellow was going to offer them as a sacrifice to his hideous little idol!

Monk heaved against the wires, but only bruised his huge muscles and started crimson running from torn skin. Numberless turns of the wire held him.

The Mayan concluded his paean to the idol. A wild light inflamed his nigrescent eyes. He was slavering like an idiot.

Faint light scintillated from the knife as it uplifted once more.

Monk shut his eyes. He opened them instantly—it was all he could do to stem a yell of utter joy.

For into that unsavory room had penetrated a low, mellow sound that trilled up and down the scale like the song of some rare bird. It seemed to filter everywhere. The sound was strengthening, inspiring.

The sound of Doc!

The Mayan was puzzled. He looked about, saw nothing. The idol-worshipping fervor seized him again. The knife poised.

The blade rushed down.

But no more than a foot did it travel. Out of the narrow black doorway flashed a gigantic figure of bronze. A Nemesis of power and speed, Doc Savage descended upon the devilish but luckless Mayan.

Doc's hand seemed hardly to touch the Mayan's knife arm before the bone snapped loudly and the knife gyrated away.

The Mayan twisted. With surprising alacrity, his other hand darted inside his green shirt and came out with a shiny pistol. He aimed at Ham, not Doc. Ham was handiest.

There was only one thing Doc could do to save Ham. He did it—chopped a blow with the edge of his hand that snapped the Mayan's neck instantly. The fellow died before he could pull trigger.

It took only a moment for Doc to free Ham and Monk of the wires.

A swarthy native—one of the Mayan's hirelings—popped through the door with a long-bladed knife that resembled nothing so much as an ordinary corn knife. In fact, it *was* a corn knife, with "Made in U.S.A." on the handle. But the native would have called it a *machete.*

His precipitous arrival was just his hard luck. A leap, a blow so swift the native probably never saw it, and the fellow was flying head over heels back the way he came.

Doc guided Ham and Monk outside. They turned left. Doc seized Ham and gave him a toss that lifted him to a low roof. Monk managed the jump unassisted, and Doc followed. They leaped to another roof, another.

On that one lay the silken folds of a parachute.

"That's how I got here," Doc explained. "News of that fight you had spread fast. I heard it and took off in the plane. Two thousand feet up I touched off a parachute flare. That lighted the whole town. I was lucky enough to see the gang haul you into that joint. So I simply jumped down to help you."

"Sure!" Monk grinned. "There wasn't nothin' to it, was there, Doc?"

Chapter X
TROUBLE TRAIL

DOC, Ham, and Monk strolled through the moonlight to the spot on the lake shore where they had pitched camp. A crowd of curious natives were there inspecting the plane, talking among themselves. Aircraft were still a novelty in this out-of-the-way spot.

Doc, a bronze giant nearly twice as tall as some of the swarthy fellows, mingled among them and asked questions in the mixture of Spanish and Indian lingo they spoke. He wanted to know about the blue plane which had attacked him at Belize.

The blue plane had been seen a few times by the natives. But they did not know from whence it came or where it went.

Doc noticed that some of the swarthy little men were very superstitious about the blue plane. These would give him little information. In each case the features of such men showed they were of Mayan ancestry.

Doc recalled then that blue was the sacred color of the ancient Mayans. It only added to this mysterious thing confronting him.

Renny and the others had erected a silken tent. But they had also dug inside the tent a deep hole, sort of a dugout in which to sleep. From the outside, the excavation would escape detection. They were taking no chance on a sudden machine-gun burst in the night.

Monk and Ham, completely recovered from their narrow brush with death, decided to sleep in the plane cabin, alternating on keeping guard.

Doc himself set off alone through the night. Thanks to the marvelous faculties he had developed by years of intensive drill, he had little fear of his enemies attacking him successfully.

He went to the presidential palace. To the servant who admitted him, Doc gave simply his name and a request to see the President of Hidalgo.

In a surprisingly brief interval, the flunky was back. Carlos Avispa, President of Hidalgo, would see Doc at once.

Doc was ushered into a great, sumptuously fitted room. The chamber was in twilight, and a small motion-picture projector was throwing shifting images onto a white screen. However, the film being run off was one concerning military tactics instead of a mushy love drama.

Carlos Avispa came forward with a warmly outstretched hand. He was a powerful man, a few inches shorter than Doc. His upstanding shock of white hair lent him a distinguished aspect. His face was lined with care, but intelligent and pleasant. He was near fifty.

"It is a great honor indeed to meet the son of the great Señor Clark Savage," he said with genuine heartiness.

That surprised Doc. He was not aware his father had known Carlos Avispa. But Doc's father had many friends of whom Doc was not aware.

"You knew my father?" Doc inquired.

Carlos Avispa bowed. There was genuine esteem in his voice as he replied: "Your father saved my life with his wonderful medical skill. That was twenty years ago, when I was but an unimportant revolutionist hiding out in the mountains. You, I believe, are also a great doctor and surgeon?"

Here *was* a break, Doc reflected. He nodded that he was a doctor and surgeon. For that was the thing he knew more about than all others.

In the course of a few minutes Doc had told his story and mentioned that Don Rubio Gorro, the Secretary of State, had refused to honor his grant to the territory in interior Hidalgo.

"I shall remedy that at once, Señor Savage!" declared President Carlos Avispa. "Anything I have, any power I control, is yours."

AFTER he had thanked the elderly, likable man properly, Doc inquired whether President Avispa had any idea what made the tract of land so valuable that many men were anxious to do murder to prevent him reaching it.

"I cannot imagine" was the reply. "I do not know what your father found there. He was bound for the interior of Hidalgo when he came upon me ill in camp twenty years ago. He saved my life. And I never saw him again. As for the region, it is very near impregnable, and the natives are so troublesome I have given up trying to send soldiers to explore."

President Carlos Avispa reflected deeply, then went on.

"It worries me, this action of my secretary of state, Don Rubio Gorro," he said. "Some sneak has destroyed the records of this heritage your father left you. They should be in our archives. But I cannot understand why Don Rubio should act as he did. Your papers were enough, even though ours had vanished. He shall be punished for his impertinence."

Doc was silent. The moving-picture machine was still running off the reel of military maneuvers—the type of picture shown at war colleges.

With a smile, President Avispa indicated the cinema machine. "I must keep myself advised of the latest fighting methods. It is indeed regrettable. But it seems we can never have peace here in the south. There is always a revolution brewing.

"Just recently I have heard strong rumors that an attempt is to be made to assassinate me and seize power. Many of my people of Mayan ancestry are involved. But I do not know the ringleaders. I understand they await only money to buy arms before making the attempt."

There came into the elderly chief executive's eyes a fiery, warlike glint. "If I could but find from what source their money is expected to come, I would soon put a quietus on them. And, best of all, it would be done without bloodshed!"

Doc conversed for a considerable time, mostly about his great father. Politely declining an invitation to spend the night at the presidential palace, he departed at a late hour.

Striding through Blanco Grande's sleepy streets, Doc was thoughtful. Could it be that the money for the revolution against President Carlos Avispa was tied up directly with his heritage? The fact that Mayans were involved in both pointed that way. Maybe his enemies were trying to rob him of his legacy, and use it to finance a revolution to overthrow President Avispa!

The enemies had tried hard enough from the first to prevent him even finding out about the legacy. Strange—the whole thing!

Then Doc stopped suddenly.

Before him on the dimly moonlit cobbles lay a knife. It had an obsidian stone blade, a hilt of wound leather—exactly such a knife as the Mayan in New York had carried.

SOME fifteen minutes later, there was a curious meeting in a top-floor room of Blanco Grande's one hotel modern enough to be fitted with running water and a radio in every room. The hotel happened to be the pride of all Hidalgo. Three stories high!

But the gentry meeting in the top-floor room were easily the scourge of Hidalgo. They were the ringleaders of the latest crop of revolutionists. These men were motivated by no high ideals of freedom. If so, they wouldn't have been here, because no kinder or more upright official ever administered a nation than elderly President Carlos Avispa.

Greed was behind every act of these men. They wanted to overthrow President Avispa's honest, low-cost government, so they could loot the public treasury, tax the citizens to bankruptcy for a year or two, then skip to Paris and the fleshpots of Europe for a life of luxury on the proceeds.

Eleven outlaws from the hills were congregated on one side of the room. Shaggy, vicious fellows, everyone of them was a murderer many times over.

Before them was a curtain. Behind the curtain was a door into an adjoining room. This door opened, and the assembled bandits could hear a man enter. They grew tense, wary. But when the man spoke, they relaxed.

For the man was their boss! The brains behind the revolution! *He* was going to fill their pockets from the Hidalgo treasury.

"I am late!" said the ringleader whom none of them could see—and, indeed, whom none of them even knew! "I lost my sacred knife, and had to go back and hunt it."

"Did you find it?" interrupted one of the bandits.

The speaker ... sprang forward, taking the curtain with him ...

"That thing is important. You need it to impress those Mayans. They think only members of their warrior sect can have one and live. If an ordinary man gets one, they think he will die. So you need it to make them think you're the son of that god of theirs they call the Feathered Serpent."

"I found it," said the man behind the curtain. "Now, let's get down to business. This Savage person has proved to be more of a menace than we ever dreamed."

The speaker paused, and when he continued, there was a distinct twinge of fear in his voice. "Savage visited President Avispa tonight, and Avispa O. K.'d everything. The old fool! We shall soon be shut of him! But we must stop Savage! We must wipe him out, and those five fighting devils with him!"

"Agreed," muttered a hairy cutthroat. "They must not reach the Valley of the Vanished!"

"Why not let them go ahead into the Valley of the Vanished?" growled another bandit. "That would be the end of them. They'd never get out!"

Greater became the fear in the voice of the revolution mastermind. "You idiot! You do not know Savage! The man is uncanny. I went to New York, but I failed to stop him. And I had with me two members of that fanatical sect of warriors among the inhabitants of the Valley of the Vanished. Those men are accomplished fighters. Their own people are in terror of them. But Savage escaped!"

UNEASY was the silence that impregnated the room.

"What if the members of this warrior sect should find you are not one of them?" asked an outlaw. "You've led them to believe you are the flesh-and-blood son of one of their old deities. They worship you. But suppose they get wise that you are a faker?"

"They won't!" snapped the man behind the curtain. "They won't, because I control the Red Death!"

"The Red Death!" gulped one man.

Another breathed: "The Red Death—what is it?"

Loud, ugly laughter came from the man back of the curtain. "A drunken genius of a scientist sold the secret of causing the Red Death, and curing it. He sold it to me! And then I killed him so no one would ever get it—or, rather, the cure for it."

A nervous shifting passed over the assembled bandits.

"If we could just solve the mystery of that gold that comes out of the Valley of the Vanished," one mumbled. "If we could find where they get it, we could forget this revolution."

"We can't!" declared the man back of the curtain. "I've tried and tried. Morning Breeze, the chief of the warrior sect of which I have made myself head, does not know where it comes from. Only old King Chaac, ruler of the Valley of the Vanished, knows. And you couldn't torture it out of him."

"I'd like to take my men in there with machine guns!" a bandit chieftain muttered angrily.

"You tried that once, didn't you?" snapped the curtain speaker. "And you were nearly wiped out for your pains. The Valley of the Vanished is impregnable. The best we can do is get enough gold as offerings to finance this revolt."

"How do you get the gold?" asked a robber, evidently not as well posted as the others.

Again the man laughed back of the curtain. "I simply turn the Red Death loose on the tribe. Then they make a big offering of gold which reaches my hands. Then I give them the cure for the Red Death." He snorted mirthfully. "The ignorant dupes think their deity sends the Red Death, and the gold offering appeases his wrath."

"Well, you had better turn the Red Death loose soon," suggested a man. "We need an offering bad. If we don't get it, we can't pay for those guns we must have to put over the revolt."

"I will, very shortly. I have been sending my blue plane over the Valley of the Vanished. That's a new idea of mine. It impresses the inhabitants of the Valley a lot. Blue is their sacred color. And they think the plane is a big winged god flying around."

There was a lot of evil laughter in appreciation of their leader's cleverness.

"That Red Death is great stuff!" grated the man behind the curtain. "It put old man Savage out—"

The speaker suddenly emitted a frenzied scream and sprang forward, taking the curtain with him. He plunged head over heels across the floor.

The stunned bandits saw, towering in the door back of the curtain, a great bronze, frightsome figure of a man.

"Doc Savage!" one squawked.

DOC SAVAGE it was, right enough. Doc, when he had seen that knife in the street, had a moment later heard footsteps approaching. He had followed the man who had picked up the knife to this hotel room.

Doc had heard the whole vile plot!

And for probably the first time in his career, Doc had failed to get his man. Rage at the leader of the revolutionists, the murderer of his father, had momentarily blinded Doc. A tiny gasp had escaped from his great chest—and the man had heard.

A bandit drew a pistol. Another doused the lights. Guns roared deafeningly. Blows smacked. Terrific blows that tore flesh and bone! Blows such as only Doc Savage could deliver!

The window burst with a glassy rattle as somebody leaped through, heedless of the fact that it was three floors to the earth. A second man took the same leap.

The fight within the room was over in a matter of thundering seconds.

Doc Savage turned on the lights. Ten bandits in various stages of stupor and unconsciousness and even death, were strewed on the floor. Three of them would never murder again. And the Blanco Grande police, already clamoring in the corridor outside, would make short shrift of the rest.

To the window, Doc swept. Poising a moment easily, he took the three-story drop as lightly as if he were leaping off a table.

Under the window, he found another cutthroat. The man had broken his neck in the plunge.

There was no trace of the leader. The man had survived the jump and escaped.

Doc stood there, rage tingling all through his powerful bronze frame. The murderer of his father! And he didn't even know who the man was!

For Doc, in following the fellow to the hotel, had not once been able to glimpse the master villain's face. Up there in the room, the curtain had enveloped the fiend until the lights went out.

Doc slowly quitted the vicinity of the hotel with its holocaust of death. In that hostelry room, he had left something that would become a legend in Hidalgo. A dozen men whipped in a matter of seconds!

For days, the Blanco Grande police puzzled over what manner of superman had overpowered these worst of Hidalgo's bandits in a hand-to-hand fray.

Every cutthroat had a reward on his unkempt head. The reward went unclaimed. Finally, by decree of President Avispa, it was turned over to charity.

Doc Savage, with hardly a thought about what he had done, went to his camp and turned in.

Chapter XI
VALLEY OF THE VANISHED

BY the time the sun had crawled off one of Hidalgo's spike-like mountaintops, Doc and his men were ready for departure.

Doc had taken his usual two-hour exercise long before dawn, while the others still slept.

After that, Doc had awakened his men, and they had all seized brushes and quick-drying blue paint, and gone over their entire plane. The ship was now blue, the sacred color of the Mayans!

"If the inhabitants of this mysterious Valley of the Vanished think we're riding in a holy chariot," Doc had commented, "they may let us hang around long enough to make friends."

Ham, waspish and debonair, carrying his inevitable sword cane—for he had several of them—offered jocosely: "And if they believe in evolution, we can arouse their interest by passing Monk off as the missing link."

"Oh, yeah?" Monk grinned. "Someday you're gonna find yourself in a pile that will pass for hamburger steak, and you won't know anymore about who done it than you do about who framed that ham-stealing charge on you."

Red-necked, Ham twiddled his cane and had nothing more to say.

Gasoline for twenty hours' flying reposed in the tanks of the big trimotor speed plane.

Doc, in the control bucket, turned the radial motors over with the electro-inertia starting mechanism. He let the cylinders warm so there would be no such unpleasantness as a cold motor stopping at a critical moment in the take-off.

Out across the lake, Doc ruddered the plane. He rocked the Deperdussin-type control wheel. The floats went on step—skimming the lake surface. Then they were off. Doc banked about and headed directly for the most rugged interior region of Hidalgo.

It was Doc's own idea, borne out by Johnny's intensive study of the country's topography, to use pontoons instead of landing wheels on the plane. Due to the wildly rank jungle and the unbelievably craggy nature of the region, chances were one in a thousand of finding a clearing large enough for a setdown.

On the other hand, Hidalgo was in a sphere of great rainfall, of tropical downpours. The streams were small rivers, and here and there in a mountain chasm lay a tiny lake. Hence the floats on the plane.

While Doc lifted the plane to ten thousand feet to find a favorable air current, and thus cut gasoline consumption, his five friends used binoculars through the cabin windows.

They hoped to find trace of their enemy, the blue monoplane. But not a glimpse of its hangar did they catch in the nodular, verdurous carpet of jungle. It must be concealed, they reasoned, somewhere very near the capital city of Blanco Grande. But they didn't sight it.

Below was an occasional patch of *milpa*, or native corn, growing in jungle clearings. Through the glasses, they could see natives carrying burdens in *macapals*, or netting bags suspended by a strap about the forehead. These became scarcer. Where had once been *milpa* patches was only a thick growth of *uamil* bushes ten to twenty feet high. They were leaving civilization behind. Hours passed.

Great *barrancas*, or gorges, began to split the terrain. The earth seemed to tumble and writhe and pile atop itself in inconceivable derangement. Mountains lurched up, gigantic, made black and ominous by the jungle growth. From above, the fliers could look down into canyons so deep their floors were nothing but gloomy space.

"There's not a level place down there big enough to stick a stamp on!" Renny declared in an awed voice.

Johnny laughed. "I told Monk that Columbus tackling the Atlantic Ocean had a pipe compared to this."

Monk snorted. "You're crazy. Us settin' in comfortable seats in this plane, and you call it somethin' hard! I don't see nothin' dangerous about it."

"You wouldn't!" Ham said dryly. "If we should be forced down, *you* could take to the trees. The rest of us would have to walk. And a half mile a day is good walking in that country under us!"

Renny, up in the pilot's well with Doc, called: "Heads up, you eggs! We're getting close!"

RENNY had checked their course figures again and again. He had calculated angles and inscribed lines on the map. And they were nearing their destination, the tract of land that was Doc's legacy! It lay directly ahead.

And ahead was a mountain range more nodular and sheer than any they had sighted yet. Its foothill peaks were like stone needles. To the rampant sides of the mountains clung stringy patches of jungle, wherever there was a roothold.

The great speed plane bucked like a plains cayuse as it encountered the tremendous air currents set up by the precipitous wastes of stone below. This in spite of Doc's masterful hand at the controls. An ordinary pilot would have succumbed to such treacherous currents, or prudently turned back.

It was as though they were flying the tumultuous heart of a vast cyclone.

Monk, hanging tightly to a wicker seat, which was in turn strapped with metal to the plane fuselage, had become somewhat green under his ruddy brick complexion. Plainly, he had changed his ideas about the ease of their exploration method. Not that he was scared. But he was about as seasick as man ever became.

"These devilish air currents explain why this region has not been mapped by plane," Doc offered.

Four or five minutes later, he leveled an arm. "Look! That canyon should lead to the center of this tract of land we're hunting!"

The eyes, all of them, followed Doc's pointing arm.

A narrow-walled gash that seemed to sink a limitless depth into the mountain met their gaze. This cut was of bare stone, too steep and too flintlike in hardness to support even a trace of green growth.

The plane careened closer.

So deep was the gash of canyon that twilight swathed the lower recesses. Renny, keen of eye and using binoculars, advised: "There is quite a stream of water running in the bottom of the canyon."

Fearlessly, Doc nosed the plane down. Another pilot would have banked away in terror from those malicious air currents. Doc, however, knew just how much his plane could stand. Although the craft might be tossed about a great deal, they were all as yet quite safe—as long as Doc's hand was on the controls.

Into the monster slash of a chasm, the plane rumbled its way. The motor thunder was tossed back in waves from the frowning walls. Suddenly air, cooled by the small river rushing through the cut and thus contracting and forming a down current, seemed to suck the plane into the depths. Wheeling, twisting, the speed ship plummeted among murky shadows.

Monk was now a striking example of the contention that sudden danger will cure seasickness—for he was entirely normal again.

Doc had the throttles against the wide-open pins. The three radial motors moaned and labored, and the exhaust pipes lipped blue flame.

The progress of the craft along the chasm was a procession of leaps and drops and side-whippings, as though they were riding an amusement park jack rabbit, or roller coaster.

"It'll be a long old day before another gang of white explorers penetrate into this place!" Renny prophesied.

Doc's arm suddenly leveled like a bronze bar.

"The Valley of the Vanished!" he cried.

QUITE suddenly, it had appeared before them—the Valley of the Vanished!

A widening in the strange, devilish chasm formed it. The valley had roughly the shape of an egg. The floor was sloping, of such a steepness that to land a wheel-equipped plane on it would be an impossibility.

There was only one spot of comparative levelness, and that was no greater than an acre or two in area.

It was on this level spot that the eyes of Doc and his five men instantly focused. They stared, unbelieving.

"Good Heaven!" gasped Johnny, the archaeologist.

From the little flat towered a pyramid! It adhered in a general way to the architecture of the Egyptian type of pyramids, but there were differences.

For one thing, the sides, instead of drawing inward in a series of steplike shelves, were smooth as glass from top to bottom. Only in the front was there a flight of steps. Not more than twenty feet wide was this flight, and the steps were less high and deep than those in an American home. The stairway was like a ribbon up the glittering, sleek side of the pyramid.

The top of the structure was flat, and on this stood a sort of temple, a flat stone roof supported by square, wondrously carved pillars. Except for the pillars, this was open at the sides, permitting glimpses of fantastically wrought idols of stone.

Strangest of all, perhaps, was the color of the pyramid. Of a grayish-brown stone, yet it glowed all over with a strange yellow, metallic aurora of tiny lights caught and cast back.

"Priceless!" murmured Johnny, the archaeologist.

"You said it!" grunted Renny, the engineer.

"From a historical standpoint, I mean!" corrected Johnny.

"I meant from a pocketbook standpoint!" Renny snorted. "If I ever saw quartz absolutely full of wire gold, I see it now. I'll bet the stone that pyramid is made of would mill fifty thousand dollars to the ton in free gold!"

"Forget the gold!" snapped Johnny. "Don't you realize you're looking at a rare sample of ancient Mayan architecture? Something any archaeologist would give both hands and a leg to inspect!"

As the plane dived closer, another thing about the pyramid became noticeable. This was a sizeable volume of water which poured steadily down the pyramid side, coursing in a deep trough inlaid near the steps.

This water came out of the pyramid top by some artesian effect. Continuing away from the structure, it fed a long, narrow lake. This body of water in turn emptied into the stream that ran down the chasm up which Doc and his friends had flown.

Upon the sides of the egg-shaped valley, not far from the pyramid, stood rows of impressive stone houses. These were lavishly carved, strange of architecture. It was as though the fliers had slipped back into an age before history.

There were people—many of them. They were garbed weirdly.

Doc dropped the plane pontoons on the narrow lake surface.

IT was an awed group of men who peered from the plane as it grounded floats on the clean white sand of the tiny beach.

The natives of this Valley of the Vanished were running down the steep sides to meet them. It was difficult to tell whether their reception was going to be warlike or not.

"Maybe we'd better unlimber a machine gun?" Renny suggested. "I don't like the looks of that gang getting together in front!"

"No!" Doc shook his head. "After all, we haven't any moral right here. And I'll get out rather than massacre some of them!"

"But this land is all yours."

"In the eyes of civilized law, probably so," Doc agreed. "But there's another way of looking at it. It's a lousy trick for a government to take some poor savage's land away from him and give it to a white man to exploit. Our own American Indians got that kind of a deal, you know. Not that these people look so savage, though."

"They've got a pretty high type of civilization, if you ask me!" Renny declared. "That's the cleanest little city I ever saw!"

The men fell to watching the on-coming natives.

"They're every one a pure Mayan!" Johnny declared. "No outside races have intermarried with these people!"

The approaching Mayans were going through a strange maneuver. The bulk of the populace was holding back to let a group of men, all of whom were garbed alike, come ahead.

These men were slightly larger in stature, more brutelike, of a thickness of shoulder and chest advertising powerful muscles. They wore a short mantle over the shoulders, a network of leather which had projecting ends rather like modern epaulets. They wore broad girdles of a dark blue, the ends of these forming aprons to the front and rear. Each man wore leggings not unlike football shin guards, and sandals which had extremely high backs.

They carried spears and short clubs of wood into which vicious-looking, razor-edged flakes of stone were fitted in the manner of sawteeth. In addition, each had a knife with an obsidian blade, and a hilt of wound leather.

Every one of these men also had his fingertips dyed scarlet for an inch of their length! None of the other tribesmen seemed to have the red fingers.

Suddenly the man who led this group halted. Turning, he lifted his hands above his head and harangued his followers in a voice of vast emotion and volume. This man was more stocky than the others. Indeed, he had Monk's anthropoid build without Monk's gigantic size. His face was dark and evil.

Doc listened with interest to the Mayan dialect as shouted by the speaker.

"That fellow is Morning Breeze, and the gang he is talking to are the sect of warriors, his followers!" Doc translated for his men, giving his own accurate deductions rather than the gist of Morning Breeze's speech.

"He looks more like an alley wind at midnight to me!" Monk muttered. "What's he ribbin' 'em up to do, Doc?"

Angry little lights danced in Doc Savage's golden eyes. "He is telling them the blue plane is a holy bird."

"That's what we wanted them to think!" said Renny. "So it's all right if—"

"It's not as right as you think," Doc interposed. "Morning Breeze is telling his warriors we are a human offering the holy blue bird has brought to be sacrificed."

"You mean—"

"They're going to kill us—if Morning Breeze has his way!"

Chapter XII
THE LEGACY

MONK instantly whirled for the plane, rumbling: "I'm gonna meet 'em with a machine gun in each hand!"

But Doc's low voice stopped him.

"Wait," Doc suggested. "Morning Breeze's warriors haven't worked up their nerve yet. I have a scheme to try."

Doc stepped forward, advancing alone to meet the belligerent fighting sect of this lost clan of the ancient Mayans. There were fully a hundred red-fingered men in the conclave, every one armed to the teeth.

Seized with the insane fervor which comes upon addicts of exotic religions, they would be vicious customers in a fight. But Doc stepped up to them as calmly as he would go before a chamber of commerce luncheon gathering in the States.

Morning Breeze stopped shouting at his followers to watch Doc. The chief warrior's features were even less likeable at close range. They were tattooed in colored designs, making them quite repulsive. His little black eyes glittered like a pig's.

Doc dropped his right hand into his coat pocket. Here reposed the obsidian knife he had taken from the Mayan who had killed himself in New York. Doc knew, from what he had heard in the Blanco Grande hotel room, that great significance attached to these knives.

With dignity, Doc elevated both bronze hands high above his head. In doing so, he carefully kept the sacred obsidian knife hidden from the Mayans. He had palmed it like a magician.

"Greetings, my children!" he said in the best Mayan he could manage.

Then, with a quick flirt of his wrist, he brought the knife into view. With such expert sleight-of-hand did he accomplish this that it looked to the Mayans like the obsidian blade had materialized in thin air.

The effect was noticeable. Red-fingered hands moved uncertainly. Feet shod in high-backed sandals shifted about. A low murmur arose.

While the time was opportune, Doc's powerful voice vibrated over the group.

"Myself and my friends come to speak with King Chaac, your ruler!" he said.

Morning Breeze didn't like this at all. A variety of emotions played on his unlovely face.

Watching the warrior chief, Doc catalogued the man's character accurately. Morning Breeze was hungry for power and glory. He wanted to be supreme among his people. And for that reason, he was an enemy of King Chaac, the ruler. The darkening of Morning Breeze's countenance at mention of King Chaac apprised Doc of this last state of affairs.

"Tell me your business here!" commanded Morning Breeze in substance, seeking to give his coarse voice a ring of overbearing authority.

Doc, knowing that if he gave Morning Breeze an inch of rope, the fellow would take the whole lasso, made his tone more commanding.

"My business is not with underlings, but with King Chaac himself!" he thundered.

This also had its effect. Both on Morning Breeze, who turned purple with humiliation and rage, and on the other warriors, who were plainly impressed. Doc could see they were of a mind to postpone the sacrificing and take the white strangers to King Chaac.

Putting a volume of dignity and command in his voice which few other men could have managed, Doc directed: "Do not delay longer!"

Doc's sleight of hand with the knife, his knowledge of their language, his dominant bearing, all worked triumphantly to his advantage.

The phalanx of red-fingered men melted away in the middle, forming an encircling group to escort Doc and his men to King Chaac.

"That is what I call runnin' a whizzer!" Monk grinned admiringly.

"Here's something to remember!" Doc told him. "Anything that smacks of magic impresses these red-fingered fighters. That's the principal thing that saved us a lot of trouble."

They left the plane on the narrow sand beach, depending on superstitious fear to keep the Mayan populace away. The yellow-skinned folk would hardly be irreligious enough to finger the holy blue bird.

JUDGING from their physical appearance, the other Mayans were an entirely sociable people. They were not hard on the eyes, either, especially some of the young women. Their clothing showed expert weaving and dyeing, and in some of it, fine wire gold had been interwoven with luxuriant effect.

Their skins were a beautiful golden color; absolutely without blemish.

"I don't believe I ever saw better complexions in a race of people," Ham declared.

The young women and some of the younger men wore high headdresses of gorgeous tropical flowers. Some had trains that fell in graceful manner about their shoulders.

Monk remarked on the uniform beauty of the Mayans, with the exception of the red-fingered warriors.

"Looks like they pick out the ugly ducklings and make fighters of them!" he chuckled.

And they later found this very thing was true. To become a warrior, a Mayan had to attain a certain degree of ugliness, both physically and of mind. The Mayans had no prison system. When one of their number committed a minor crime, he was sentenced, not to exile or prison, but to become a fighting man—a protector of the tribe.

These red-fingered warriors fought off invaders, and kept the Valley of the Vanished for the Mayans alone. Thus, many of them were slain in battle, and hence actually punished.

They were the most ignorant and superstitious in the Valley of the Vanished, these crimson-fingered fighting men.

The cavalcade trod the streets of the little Mayan city.

Johnny, with the excitement of a born archaeologist making new discoveries of stupendous interest, could hardly be kept in line.

"These buildings!" he gasped. "They are erected exactly as in the great ruined city of Chichen Itza and elsewhere. See, they never use the arch in construction of roofs or doorways!"

One peculiarity about the buildings struck the others, who, with the exception of Doc, did not know a great deal about the Mayan type of architecture. The structures were replete with carvings of animals, grotesque human figures and birds. Not a square inch but was sculptured in some likeness. The Mayans seemed to abhor leaving even a tiny bit of unadorned space.

They came finally to a stone house larger than the rest. It was lifted slightly above the others upon a foundation of masonry.

They were ushered inside, into the presence of King Chaac.

KING CHAAC was a distinct shock. But a pleasant one.

He was a tall, solid man, only a little stooped with age. His hair was a snowy white, and his features were nearly as perfect as Doc's own! Dressed in an evening suit, Chaac would have been a distinct credit to any banquet table in New York. He wore a *maxtli*, or broad girdle, of red, with the ends forming an apron in front and back.

He was stationed in the middle of a large room.

Beside him stood a young woman. She was by a long stretch the most attractive of the Mayan girls they had seen. The perfection of her features revealed instantly that she was King Chaac's daughter. She was nearly as tall as her father. The exquisite fineness of her beauty was like the work of some masterly craftsman in gold.

"A pippin!" gasped Monk.

"Not bad," admitted Renny, his long, tight-lipped face losing a bit of its puritanical look.

Doc, in a low voice only the pair discussing the girl could hear, said sharply: "Dry up, you gorillas! Can't you see she understands English?"

Monk and Renny looked sharply at the girl—and both instantly became red as well-cooked beets.

For it was evident the ravishing young Mayan lady had heard their remarks and understood them. Her features were flushed, and she was distinctly embarrassed.

Doc, in his halting Mayan, began to greet King Chaac.

"You may speak your own language," interposed King Chaac.

He spoke English that was fair enough!

For once, Doc was taken with surprise. It was a long twenty seconds before he thought of something to say. Then he waved an arm slowly to take in all his surroundings.

"I don't quite understand all this," he murmured. "Here you are, obviously descendants of an ancient civilization. You are in a valley practically impregnable to outsiders. The rest of the world does not even dream you are here. You live exactly as your ancestors did, hundreds of years ago. Yet you greet me in excellent English!"

King Chaac bowed easily. "I can dispel your curiosity, Mr. Clark Savage, Jr."

Had Doc been less of a man than he was, that would have knocked him over.

He was known here!

"Your esteemed father taught me the English tongue," smiled King Chaac. "I recognize you as his son. You resemble him."

Doc nodded slowly. He should have guessed that. And it was very good to know his great father had been here. For wherever Savage, Sr., had gone, he had made friends among all people who were worthy of friendship.

The next few words exchanged had to do with introductions. The ravishing young Mayan lady's name was Monja. She was, as they had surmised, a princess; King Chaac's daughter.

The squat, surly chief of the red-fingered warriors, Morning Breeze, was ordered outside by King Chaac. His going was slinky, reluctant. And he paused in the door for a final, avid look at Princess Monja.

That glance told Doc something else. Morning Breeze had a crush on Monja. And judging from Monja's uplifted nose, she didn't think much of the chief of fighting men.

"I don't blame her, either," Monk whispered to Ham, making very sure his voice was so low nobody else heard. "Imagine having to stare at that phiz of his across the breakfast table every morning!"

Ham looked at Monk—and released a loud laugh. Monk's face was fully as homely as Morning Breeze's, although in a more likable way.

DOC SAVAGE put the query that was uppermost in his mind. "How does it happen your people are here—like this—as they lived hundreds of years ago?"

King Chaac smiled benignly. "Because we are satisfied with our way of living. We lead an ideal existence here. True, we must fight to keep invaders away. But the warlike tribes surrounding this mountain do most of that for us. They are our friends. It is only every year or two that our red-fingered warriors must drive off some especially persistent invader. Thanks to the impregnable nature of this valley, that is not difficult."

"How long have you been here—when did you settle here, I mean?" Doc asked.

"Hundreds of years ago—at the time of the Spanish conquest of Mexico," explained the old Mayan. "My ancestors who settled the valley were a clan of the highest class Mayans, the royalty. They fled from the Spanish soldiers to this valley. We have been here since, satisfied, as I said, to exist without the rest of the world."

Doc, reflecting on the turmoil and bloodshed and greed that had racked the rest of the world in the interim, could not but agree that the course these people had taken had its merits. They might be without a few conveniences of modern homes, but they probably didn't miss them.

Elderly King Chaac spoke up unexpectedly: "I know why you are here, Mr. Savage."

"Eh?"

"Your father sent you. It was agreed that upon the passage of twenty years, you were to come to me. And I was to be the judge of whether or not to give you access to the gold which is of no value to we of the Valley of the Vanished."

Lights of understanding flickered in Doc's golden eyes. So this had been the text of the remainder of that letter, the burned first portion of which he had found in his father's robbed safe!

It was all plain now. His father had discovered this lost valley with its strange inhabitants and its fabulous hoard of gold. He had decided to leave it as a legacy to his son. He had secured possession of the land enclosing the Valley of the Vanished. And he had made some arrangement with King Chaac. The thing to do was to find out what kind of arrangements!

Doc put the inquiry: "What sort of an agreement did my father have with you?"

"He did not tell you?" the old Mayan asked in surprise.

Doc lowered his head. Slowly, he explained his father had died suddenly. The elderly Mayan maintained a reverent silence for a time after he heard the sad news. Then he outlined the business aspects of the gold deal.

"You will necessarily give a certain portion to the government of Hidalgo," he said.

Doc nodded. "The agreement is one fifth to the government of Hidalgo. That is eminently fair. The President of Hidalgo, Carlos Avispa, is a fine old gentleman."

"A third of all gold removed is to be placed in a trust fund in the name of my people," explained King Chaac. "You are to establish that fund and see that suitable honest administrators are appointed. The other two thirds you are to have, not to build up a personal fortune, but to spend as you see fit in furthering the work in which your father was engaged—in righting wrongs, relieving the oppressed, in benefiting mankind in every way possible."

"A third to your people doesn't seem like a very big percentage," Doc suggested.

King Chaac smiled. "You will be surprised at the sum it will come to. And we may never need it. This Valley of the Vanished, you understand, remains just as it is—unknown to the world. And the source of this gold will also be unknown to the world."

JOHNNY, twiddling his glasses which had the magnifying lens on the left side, had been an interested listener to all this. Now he broke in with a puzzled query.

"I noticed the nature of the rock about here," he said. "And, although the pyramid is made of high-grade gold ore, there is no sign of quantities of the rock nearby. If you're figuring on giving us the pyramid, will your people stand for it?"

"The pyramid remains untouched!" There was a sharpness in King Chaac's voice. "That is our shrine! It shall stand always!"

"Then where is the gold?"

King Chaac turned to Doc. "You will be shown to it within thirty days—or sooner, if I decide it is time. But until then, you will know no more."

"Why this condition?" Doc inquired.

There seemed the slightest of twinkles in the old

Mayan's eyes as he retorted: "That I do not care to disclose."

Throughout the entire confab, pretty Princess Monja had been standing to one side. And almost the whole time, she had been watching Doc, a strange, veiled expression in her eyes.

"I wish she'd look at me like that!" Monk confided to Ham.

King Chaac's declaration of the thirty-day moratorium on all information concluded the interview. He gave orders to his followers that Doc and his men should be treated with the best.

Doc and his men spent the remainder of the day making friends with the Mayans. They did little tricks of magic that highly entertained the simple people. Long Tom with an electrical shocking apparatus he rigged up, and Monk with some chemical displays, were the favorites.

Morning Breeze and his warriors, however, kept severely aloof. They were often seen chatting in surly groups.

"They're gonna give us trouble," Renny declared, playfully cracking soft rocks with his ironlike fists to awe and amuse a young Mayan.

Doc agreed. "They're more ignorant than the others. And this devil who is behind the Hidalgo revolution is a nabob in the sect of fighting men. He's going to send the Red Death on the tribe before long."

"Can't we stop it? That infernal Red Death, I mean?"

"We can try," Doc said seriously. "But I'm doubtful that we can do much until it strikes. We don't even know how they spread it, much less what the cure is."

"Maybe if we got them the gold in the form of a bribe so they wouldn't inflict this Red Death—"

"That would mean the success of the Hidalgo revolt, and hundreds of people killed, Renny!"

"That's right," Renny muttered soberly.

For sleeping quarters, they were allotted a many-room house not a great distance from the gleaming golden pyramid.

They turned in early. The night gave promise of not being as chilly as they had expected it to be up here in the mountains.

Chapter XIII
DEATH STALKS

THE following day was devoted to nothing more glorious than killing time. Exhibiting little tricks soon palled. So Doc and Renny set out to explore the Valley of the Vanished.

They found it as much a prison as a fortress. The narrowest of paths chiseled into the sheer gorge side was the only route out, afoot. And by air, nothing except a seaplane could land. No dirigible could withstand those terrific air currents.

The sides of the valley were in cultivation, growing vegetables and many *milpa* patches. There was cotton, and domesticated, long-haired goats, for clothing. Jungle growth was rank everywhere else.

"They're pretty well fixed," Doc remarked. "Not fancy. But you couldn't want more."

Strolling back to the little city beside the golden pyramid, Doc and Renny encountered the attractive Princess Monja. Obviously, she had maneuvered this meeting. She was, it could plainly be seen, greatly taken with the handsome Doc.

This embarrassed Doc no little. He had long ago made up his mind that women were to play no part in his career. Anyway, his was not a nature to easily lend itself to domestication. So he answered Princess Monja's eager patter in monosyllables, and carefully avoided being led into discussions about how pretty American girls were in comparison to, well—Monja, for instance.

It was not an easy course to take. Monja was one of the most ravishing young women Doc had ever encountered.

Back at the city, they could not help but notice a subtle change in the attitude of many of the Mayans. Even those who were not of the red-fingered sect now looked at Doc and his friends with unfriendly eyes.

The red-fingered warriors were mingling with the populace, doing a lot of talking.

Doc chanced to overhear one of these conversations. It told him what was happening. The red-fingered men were poisoning the minds of the other Mayans against the whites. Doc and his men, the warriors claimed, were pale-skinned devils that had ridden here like worms in the innards of the great blue bird that landed on the water. And so, as worms, they should be destroyed.

It was clever work on the part of the red-fingered ones. Doc went away thoughtful.

That night, Doc and his five friends turned in early again, largely because the Mayans seemed to go to roost with the chickens. Whether it was the hardness of the stone benches that served these golden-skinned folk for beds, or because of nervous excitement over their position here in the Valley of the Vanished, they didn't sleep well.

LONG TOM, occupying a large room with Johnny and Ham, stuck it out on his stone slab exactly one hour. Then insomnia got the best of him. He yanked on his trousers and took a stroll in the moonlight that penetrated faintly to the floor of the great chasm of which the valley was a part.

For no particular reason, Long Tom's footsteps took him toward the pyramid. The thing fascinated him. So rich was the ore of which it was built that it was literally a mound of gold. What a fabulous value it must have!

Long Tom hoped looking at such wealth would make him sleepy.

It didn't. It cost him dearly.

For while he was having his first eye-filling look at the golden pyramid with the stream of water running steadily out of its top, a man sprang onto his back. A vile hand clapped over Long Tom's mouth.

Long Tom might look none too healthy, but under his sallow hide were some very ropy, powerful muscles. He couldn't have stood the gaff with Doc's bunch without them. He could probably whip ninety-nine out of every hundred men you meet on the street, and not shown fatigue in doing it.

He angled both fists around, drove them behind him. He hit nobody. He bit the unclean fingers that held his mouth. The fingers jerked away. Long Tom started a yell. A hand, thoroughly protected by cloth this time, stoppered his jaws.

Other attackers rushed in. They were bounding dervishes in the moon glow. The red-fingered warriors!

Long Tom kicked mightily backward. He peeled a shin. He and his assailants toppled among round rocks and soft dirt.

One of Long Tom's clawlike hands found a rock. He popped it against a skull—knew by the feel of the blow that one of the red-fingered fiends was through with this world.

Sheer weight of numbers mashed Long Tom out before he could do more damage. He was securely bound at wrist and ankle with stout cotton cords, then drawn into a helpless knot as his wrists and ankles were tied in a single wad.

A red-fingered Mayan who had kept well away from the fight now came up. Long Tom recognized Morning Breeze, chief of the fighting men.

Morning Breeze clucked a command in the Mayan tongue, which Long Tom did not understand.

Lifting Long Tom, they bore him around to the rear of the pyramid. They shoved through a high growth of brush, coming then to a circular flooring of stone blocks. In the center of this gaped a sinister, black, round aperture.

Long Tom was left in doubt as to what this was for only a moment.

Morning Breeze picked up a pebble, smirked evilly at Long Tom, then tossed the rock into the round opening.

One second dragged, another! The pebble must have fallen two hundred feet! There was a loud clatter as it struck a rock bottom. Then out of the ghastly hole came a bedlam of hissings and grisly, slithering noises!

The hole was a sacrificial well! Long Tom recalled reading how the ancient Mayans had tossed human offerings into such wells. And the hissings and slitherings were snakes! Poisonous, beyond a doubt. There must be hundreds of them in the well bottom!

Morning Breeze callously gave a command.

Long Tom suffered unutterable tortures as he was lifted and tossed bodily into the awful black opening.

Morning Breeze listened. A moment later came a horrible thump from the well bottom. The poisonous serpents hissed and slithered.

Morning Breeze and his evil followers turned away, highly pleased.

UNKNOWN to Long Tom when he left the sleeping quarters, Ham had not been sleeping soundly. One eye drowsily open, Ham had watched Long Tom pull on his trousers and go out.

Ham drowsed a while after that. But Long Tom's departure had done something to what little desire he had for sleep, so it was not long before Ham also got up and pulled on his trousers. Thanks to the balmy night, no more clothing was needed.

Ham took his sword cane along, although for no particular reason. He just liked the feel of it in his hands.

Outside, he saw no sign of Long Tom. But a little use of his keen brain told Ham where the electrical wizard would be likely to stroll; the most fascinating spot in the Valley of the Vanished, if one disregarded the really entrancing Mayan girls. The golden pyramid, of course! Long Tom, like the rest of Doc's men, would not be wooing a Mayan damsel at this hour. They were not interested in women, these supreme adventurers.

Ham ambled toward the pyramid, breathing in deeply of the lambent night air. He heard no sound, certainly nothing to alarm him. He clipped the gaudy flower off a tropical vine with a jaunty swing of his cane.

A split second later, Ham was buried under an avalanche of red-fingered men!

No gallant of old ever bared his steel quicker than Ham unsheathed his sword cane. He got it out in time to skewer two of the devils who piled atop him!

Outnumbered hopelessly, Ham was bound and gagged.

They carried Ham to the sacrificial well, and without a word, threw him in.

Morning Breeze, poised on the well rim, listened until he heard the loud smash come up from the pit floor two hundred feet below. The snakes, disturbed, made enraged noises.

Morning Breeze nodded and clucked to himself. Two of them gone! He gave another command.

The three red-fingered warriors who had been killed by Long Tom and Ham were hauled up. One after the other, the dead forms were pitched into the sacrificial well. Three loud thumps and snake sounds arose.

Very elated indeed, Morning Breeze led his followers to get further victims.

MONK had been sleeping soundly, but the stone bed was hard, and Monk had got a nightmare. In the nightmare, he was fighting a million clawing, crimson-tipped fingers while a beautiful Mayan princess looked on. Monk whipped all the red fingers in his dream, but as he started toward the entrancing princess to claim his reward, a man who looked suspiciously like Doc came up and took her away. That woke Monk up.

He sat erect, then stood on his feet to stretch. Looking about, he made a discovery that surprised him. Both Doc and Renny should have been slumbering in this same room.

But their stone couches were unoccupied!

Monk thought a bit, concluded they were out talking somewhere, and decided to join them. He started to put on his trousers, then changed his mind. He had noted a *maxtli*, one of the broad girdles the Mayan gentlemen wore. Evidently it had belonged to whoever gave up the house for their comfort, since it hung on the wall.

Monk whipped the *maxtli* twice about his middle in lieu of pants, and sauntered out. He had an idea he'd go swimming if nothing better turned up.

Unable to locate either Doc or Renny, Monk made for the lakeshore. He was not worried about his two friends. That anything could happen to them without an alarm being raised was hardly likely.

The lake was an appealing blue. Away from the shore a few yards, were large rocks. Monk wended his good-natured way through these.

Suddenly he got a tremendous start by encountering pretty Princess Monja face to face. She was evidently out strolling in the moonlight. Alone, too.

Monk felt a great deal of confusion. He made a move to go back hastily the way he had been coming.

But Princess Monja smiled sweetly at Monk's pleasantly ugly face, and requested: "Do not leave so quickly, please! I wish to ask you a question."

Monk hesitated. He asked bluntly, "What's the question?"

Princess Monja blushed prettily. For a moment it looked like she was going to be too bashful to put the query. Then, out it came.

It was: "What is there about myself that your leader finds undesirable?"

"Huh?" Monk stuttered, at a loss for an answer. "Oh, Doc likes you all right. He likes everybody."

"I do not believe so," said the entrancing Mayan. "He remains aloof."

"Well," floundered Monk, "I guess that's just Doc's way."

"There is a girl—he is—?"

"In love with anybody?" Monk snorted. "Heck no! There ain't a girl livin' who could make Doc's heart—"

Monk abruptly swallowed the rest. But it was too late. He had said the wrong thing.

Princess Monja spun on her heel and vanished among the large rocks. The trace of a sob lingered behind her.

MONK stood there in the moonlight a while. Then he went back to his sleeping quarters. Doc and Renny were still missing.

Just to ascertain that things were all right, Monk stepped into the adjoining room where Johnny, Long Tom, and Ham were supposed to be slumbering.

All three were gone!

Monk's huge fingers curled and uncurled. He knew something was wrong now! All five of his friends would not be out taking the night air at once!

A giant, animal-like figure, Monk sprang outside. His keen ears strained. They detected faint noises. To the right! He made for them, his leaps enormous, bounding.

Quite a number of men seemed to be receding furtively through the night. Monk put on a burst of speed to overhaul them.

The golden pyramid came in view.

On the left of it, Monk discerned the men he was following. Fully a dozen of them! They carried a limp, bound form in their midst.

Monk had a technique for running in the dark. His unnaturally long arms played an important part. He simply doubled over and traveled by great bounds, balancing himself with his long arms when he stumbled. He could make unbelievable speed.

He raced his best now. He tried repeatedly to see who it was the men—they were red-fingered warriors—were carrying.

Johnny! They had Johnny!

Monk did not know Long Tom and Ham had already gone into the sacrificial well, or he would have been even more horrified than he was.

The red-fingered men had seen him now. They quickened their own pace, shedding caution. They ran out on the stone pavement around the sacrificial well.

Still fifty feet from them, Monk saw them lift Johnny's bound and gagged frame and toss him into the fiendish pit!

Monk heard the loud, heavy thump come up from the well bottom!

That turned Monk into such a fighting devil as he seldom became. His great hands scooped up two rocks. He hurled them with the velocity of cannon balls.

Both rocks downed their men.

So sudden was the attack, so fearsome a figure did Monk present that the red-fingered group turned to a man and fled wildly into the brush. Monk overhauled one before they got away. He heaved the loathsome creature up like a feather and dashed him against a tree. The lifeless body bounced back almost to his feet, so terrific was the impact.

Into the undergrowth Monk dived. He searched like a terrier after rats. But the warriors knew the vegetation. They evaded him.

It was high tribute to the fright Monk inspired that they did not even dare throw a knife or a spear at him, but crept away like sneaking coyotes into the night.

Slowly, with his heart the heaviest it had ever been, Monk went back to the sacrificial well. He had heard that thump come up from the bottom—he knew the well must be at least two hundred feet deep.

Poor Johnny! To meet a fate like that! One of the most brilliant living geologists and archaeologists snuffed out at the dawn of his career. It was awful.

Nearing the well, Monk could hear the gruesome hissing and swishing of serpent bodies deep in the black Gehenna of a pit. He recognized the noises for what they were. Johnny didn't stand a chance of being alive! Salty tears came to Monk's eyes.

With an effort, he brought himself to look over the rim of the sacrificial well.

Out of the pit came Ham's sarcastic drawl.

"I ask you, brothers, did you ever see an uglier face than that?"

Chapter XIV
DOC PULLS A RESURRECTION

SO astounded was Monk that he came within a hair of toppling headfirst into the sacrificial well. He hastily got away from the brink.

A sibilant "Sh-h-h!" came out of the hole, warning silence.

Johnny then appeared, shoved from behind. Johnny was a little scuffed and pale, but otherwise none the worse for his grisly encounter. He kept low, behind the screen of bushes that surrounded the sacrificial well.

Long Tom was helped out next. Then Ham. They, too, were unharmed. And finally Renny.

At last, Doc himself appeared.

"You wait here," Doc whispered. "I'm going to the plane to get some materials."

He vanished like a bronze ghost in the moonlight.

"What happened to you birds?" Monk demanded.

"The red-fingered rascals got us, one at a time, bound and gagged us, and threw us in the well," Long Tom explained.

"Aw-w-w! I mean, what saved you?"

"Doc."

"How?"

"It beat anything you ever saw," Long Tom murmured admiringly. "Doc and Renny were out prowling, and saw the warriors grab me. Doc ran to the plane and got a stout silk rope, or, rather, two of them." Long Tom pointed. "There they are!"

Monk looked, and perceived what he had not before noted in the moonlight. The two ropes, thin but extremely strong, were tied to a couple of the stout shrubs surrounding the paved circle. The ends of the ropes dangled in the well. The Mayans, too, had missed seeing them.

"Doc and Renny slid down into the well before the warriors got here," Long Tom continued. "Renny held a big rock in his arms. He tied the rope end around his waist to support him."

Long Tom laughed softly—but not very heartily. "When the red-fingered men tossed me in, Renny dropped the rock to make it sound like I had hit bottom. And—"

"And Doc simply swung out and caught them, one at a time, as they came down," Renny chimed in. "Then they clung to the sides of the well. That was not much of a job, because the sides are very rough, some blocks sticking out enough for a man to sit on in comfort."

"You looked like you were crying when you stuck your mug into the pit," Johnny chided Monk. "Did you really hate to see me go that much?"

"Aw-w, fooey on you!" Monk grinned.

Doc came back, appearing with the silent unexpectedness of an apparition.

"Why didn't you and Renny pitch in and clean up on the warriors when you saw them grab Long Tom?" Monk asked.

"Because I reasoned he'd be thrown into the sacrificial well alive," Doc replied. "That is the customary manner of sacrificing offerings. And I wanted the red-fingered devils to think Long Tom, Johnny, and Ham are dead. I've got an idea to pull."

"What?"

"The warriors are our immediate trouble here," Doc explained. "If we can convince them we are really supernatural beings, we'll have half the battle won. Then we can concentrate on trapping this man who is behind the Hidalgo revolution scheme."

"Sure," Monk agreed. "But how to convince them is the catch." He rubbed his big knuckles. "I'm in favor of glomming onto Morning Breeze and the rest of them, and have an old-fashioned lynching party. That'd fix it."

"And have the rest of the Mayans on top of us," Doc pointed out. "No. I'm going to convince those superstitious fighters I am an extra sort of a guy. I'll run such a whizzer on them that they won't dare to listen to Morning Breeze telling them we're ordinary men!"

Doc paused dramatically, then revealed his plan. "I'm going to bring Long Tom, Johnny, and Ham to life for the warrior sect's benefit!"

Monk digested that. "How?"

"Watch us," Doc suggested, "and you'll catch on."

WORKING rapidly, Doc pried up paving stones in a line to the thickest part of the surrounding jungle. In the soft earth beneath, he dug a narrow trench.

He had brought with him from the plane a coil of stout piano wire. No greater in diameter than a match, it had a strength sufficient to support several men. This he laid in the trench, afterward replacing the paving stones, careful no evidence remained of their having been disturbed.

The end of the piano wire he ran into the sacrificial well, and straight across and out the other side. To a dead-man-stick anchor some yards beyond he secured the end, uprooting other paving blocks and replacing them so the whole work would go unnoticed.

Directly below the well mouth he rigged a sort of saddle on the wire.

"Catch on?" he asked.

Monk did. "Sure. I hide out there in the brush and give the wire a big pull when you pass the word. Long Tom, Johnny, and Ham take turns sitting in that saddle arrangement. When I pull the wire tight, they will be tossed out of the well. Just like an arrow is thrown from a bow."

"Or a rock from a kid's bean shooter," Doc agreed. "One more little detail."

Inside the well, close to the anchored end, Doc cut the wire. He tied the end in a loop. The other end he secured to that in such a manner that, by yanking on an ordinary twine string which Doc attached, the last man thrown out by the ingenious catapult could separate the wire.

"And you pull in the end, saddle and all," Doc pointed out to Monk. "That gets rid of the evidence, in case anybody is suspicious enough to look into the well."

Johnny, Long Tom, and Ham climbed down into the well, to spend the rest of the night roosting on the jutting ends of the huge rocks which formed the masonry wall.

"Don't get drowsy and fall off!" Monk chided.

"Not much danger!" Long Tom shuddered. "Just you don't let the end of that wire slip out of your hands while I'm in the saddle!"

Monk leered delightedly at his old roasting mate, Ham. "Now, there *is* an idea!" he chuckled with mock threat. "I've got the ugliest face in the world, have I?"

To which Ham grinned: "You're a raving beauty until I get out of that saddle, Monk!"

A FAIR degree of daylight came long before the sun actually could be seen from the floor of the Valley of the Vanished, due to the tremendous depth of the chasm.

With the first flush of luminance, Doc was in conference with old King Chaac, benign sovereign of the lost clan of Maya.

The elderly ruler was very enraged when he heard Morning Breeze and his red-fingered men had consigned three of Doc's friends to the sacrificial well during the night.

Doc had neglected to mention that his three men were still quite alive.

"The time has come for a firm hand!" the Mayan chief said in his surprisingly good English. "In the past the people have put the warrior sect in its place when their depredations became unbearable.

"Morning Breeze has been working for a long time, slowly undermining my authority. Not satisfied with being chief of the fighting men, which is not such an honorable post, he desires to rule. It is also no secret that he wishes my daughter in marriage! I shall call together men and seize Morning Breeze and those next him in authority. They shall follow your men into the sacrificial well!"

Likable old King Chaac, Doc reflected, had waited a little too long before putting a firm hand upon Morning Breeze.

"Your people are under the spell of Morning Breeze's eloquence," Doc pointed out. "To lay hands on him would cause an uprising."

The Mayan winced a little at the blunt statement that his power had ebbed. Reluctantly he agreed.

"I have let Morning Breeze go too far, hoping to avert violence," he admitted. Then he looked wryly at Doc. "I should have been more alert. Our warriors have never been considered members of an honorable profession. It is not like your country, where soldiers are fine men. We Mayans are by nature a peaceable folk. To us war is a low thing."

He shrugged. "Those of our men who are inclined to violence naturally turn to the warrior sect. Many lazy men join the fighting group because the warriors do no labor. Too, petty criminals are sentenced to join the red-fingered ones. The fighting guild are a class apart. No upstanding Mayan would think of taking one of them into his home."

"But they seem to have more influence than that now," Doc smiled.

"They do," King Chaac admitted. "The red-fingered men fight off invaders from the Valley of the Vanished. Otherwise their sect would have been abolished hundreds of years ago."

Doc now broached the subject of his visit. "I have a plan which will dwarf the influence of the red-fingered sect."

Renewed energy flowed into the elderly Mayan sovereign at Doc's statement. He looked at this bronze Apollo of a man before him, and seemed to gather confidence.

"What is your plan?"

"I am going to bring my three friends who were thrown in the sacrificial well back to life," Doc disclosed.

This brought varied expressions to the staid Mayan's face. Uppermost was skepticism.

"Your father spent some months in this Valley of the Vanished," he told Doc. "He taught me many things—the fallacy of belief in evil spirits and heathen deities. And along with the rest he taught me that what you have just promised to do is impossible. If your men were hurled into the sacrificial well, they are dead until Judgment Day."

A faint smile warped Doc's strong bronze lips; appreciation glowed in his flaky golden eyes. The Mayan sovereign was as free of superstitious, heathen beliefs as any American. Probably more so than many.

So Doc explained how he had caught his friends as they were thrown into the fiendish sacrificial pit. A bystander would have marveled at how insignificant Doc made his feat sound.

Elderly King Chaac fell in heartily with the resurrection scheme.

EVERY community of human beings has certain individuals who are more addicted to talking than others. These gossips no sooner get a morsel of news than they start imparting it to everyone they meet.

King Chaac, using his deep understanding of his Mayan subjects, selected about fifty of these walking newspapers to witness the reanimation of Johnny, Long Tom, and Ham. There was not room for the whole tribe, which would have been the best audience. They would have overflowed the stone paving about the sacrificial well and surely discovered Monk hidden in the luxuriant tropical growth. And the whole resurrection depended on Monk's tremendous strength to jerk the wire, the tightening of which would fling Johnny, Long Tom, and Ham out of the well mouth.

Doc, since his knowledge of the Mayan language was not sufficient to make a public speech, left the oratory to King Chaac. The elderly Mayan was an eloquent speaker, his mellow voice making the clattering gutturals of the language pleasantly liquid.

King Chaac told of the fate of Doc's three friends during the night. He gave the impression, of course, they had perished among the sharp rocks and poisonous serpents in the depths of the sacrificial well.

Finally he announced Doc's act.

Truly impressive was the figure Doc Savage presented as he made dignified progress to the gaping, evil mouth of the sacrificial well. His face was serious; not the slightest humor flickered in his golden eyes.

The situation had little comedy. If his trick failed, there would be serious consequences indeed. The crimson-fingered warriors would brand him a faker, set upon him. The other Mayans wouldn't object.

He glanced at the warriors. The entire clique of fighting men stood to one side, varying expressions on their unlovely faces—from frank unbelief to fear. They were all curious. And Morning Breeze glared surly hate.

Doc brought his bronze arms out rigidly before him. His fists were closed tightly, dramatically. In his left hand was a quantity of ordinary flash powder, such as photographers use. In his right was a cigarette lighter.

After what he considered the proper amount of incantations and mysterious rigmarole, Doc stooped at the well mouth. So none could see, he poured out a little pile of the flash powder. He touched a lighter spark to it.

There was a flash, a great bloom of white smoke. And when the smoke blew away a loud howl of surprise went up from the red-fingered men.

For Long Tom stood upon the well lip!

The trick had worked perfectly.

Doc followed exactly the same procedure and got Ham out of the sacrificial pit.

Immediately Morning Breeze tried to dash up and look into the well. But Doc, with an ominous thunder in his voice, informed Morning Breeze that powerful invisible spirits, great enemies of his, were congregated about the sacrificial well mouth. And Morning Breeze retreated, scared in spite of himself.

Johnny was resurrected next. As Johnny came out of the pit, he jerked the trip string which separated the wire. And Monk, concealed in the brush, drew wire and saddle out of the well.

When Doc turned after the last reanimation and saw the effect on the red-fingered men, it was difficult not to show his satisfaction. For every warrior was on his knees, arms upstretched. Only Morning Breeze alone stood. And, after a compelling, hypnotic look from Doc's golden eyes, even Morning Breeze slouched reluctantly to his knees along with the rest.

It was a perfect victory. The lay tribesmen present were as impressed as the red-fingered men. The news would spread as though broadcast by radio. And to Doc would come the type of superstitious power, but an infinitely greater amount, that Morning Breeze had held.

Hearts were light as Doc and his five friends and King Chaac and entrancing Princess Monja turned away.

BUT their jubilation was short-lived.

With a piercing howl, Morning Breeze was on his feet. He urged his satellites erect, even kicking some of the less willing.

Shouting again in dramatic fashion, Morning Breeze pointed at the lakeshore.

All eyes followed his arm.

Doc's low-wing speed plane had floated into view around a rocky headland. It was being pushed by a number of red-fingered warriors who had not attended the session at the sacrificial well.

The plane was no longer blue!

It was daubed with a bilious, motley assortment of grays and pallid yellows. And prominent upon the fuselage sides were large red spots.

"The Red Death!" The words rose in a low moan from the Mayans!

Morning Breeze was quick to seize his advantage.

"Our gods are angered!" he shrieked. "They have sent the Red Death upon the blue bird which brought these white-skinned devils!"

Renny knotted and unknotted his gigantic, steel-hard fists.

"The whelp is clever! He repainted our plane last night."

Doc spoke in a voice so low it carried only to his five friends. "Morning Breeze did not have the intelligence to think that up, if I am any judge. Somebody is prompting him. And that somebody can only be the murderer of my father, the fiend who is planning the Hidalgo revolution."

"But how could that devil get in touch with Morning Breeze so soon?"

"You forget the blue monoplane," Doc pointed out. "The craft could have dropped him by parachute in the Valley of the Vanished."

They ceased speaking to listen to Morning Breeze harangue his uncertain followers.

"The gods are wroth that we permit these white heretics in our midst!" was the gist of his exhorting. "We must wipe them out!"

He was rapidly undoing the good work Doc had accomplished.

King Chaac addressed Doc in a voice that was strained but full of violent resolve. "I have never executed one of my subjects during my entire reign, but I am going to execute one now—Morning Breeze!"

But before things could progress further, there came a new and startling interruption.

Chapter XV
THE BLUE BIRD BATTLE

MORNING BREEZE it was who called attention to the new development. And it was evident from the way he did it that the whole thing was planned. More of the scheme to discredit Doc which had started with the painting of Doc's plane!

Straight above his head Morning Breeze pointed.

"Behold!" he shouted. "The genuine holy blue bird has returned! The same holy blue bird of which we obtained glimpses before these impostors arrived!"

Everyone stared upward.

Perhaps five thousand feet above, a blue plane was circling slowly. Doc's keen eyes ascertained instantly that it was the monoplane which had attacked his expedition in Belize. The plane the instigator of the Hidalgo revolt was using to impress the superstitious Mayans!

Loud gasps came from the assembled people. The scarlet-fingered warriors recovered their punctured dignity and cast ominous glances at Doc and his friends. It was plain the tide was turning against the adventurers.

High overhead, the blue plane continued to spiral. Its presence had a ghostly quality, for no sound of its motor reached their ears. Doc, with all his keenness of hearing, could detect but the faintest drone of the motor. But he knew the explanation. The terrific winds that comprised the air currents over the chasm were sweeping the sound waves aside.

"I am worried!" benign King Chaac confided in shaky tones. "My people and the warriors are being whipped into a religious frenzy by Morning Breeze. I fear they will attack you."

Doc nodded. He could see that very thing impending. There was certain to be violence unless he did something to prevent it.

"The blue bird you see above is supreme!" Morning Breeze was shrieking. "It is all-powerful. It is the chosen of your gods! It has no white-skinned worms inside it! Therefore, destroy these white worms in your midst!"

Doc reached a decision.

"Stand by your guns!" he directed his men. "If you have to, shoot a few red-fingered men. But try holding them off a while. Renny, you come with me!"

Doc's friends whipped out automatic pistols, which they had kept under their clothing. These automatics were fed by sixty-cartridge magazines, curled in the shape of compact rams' horns below the grips. The guns were what is known as continuously automatic in operation—they fired steadily as long as the trigger was held back. Both guns and magazines were of Doc's invention, infinitely more compact than ordinary submachine guns.

At the display of firearms, excited cries arose from the populace. Ample proof, this, that they understood what guns were.

Doc and Renny sprinted for their plane.

AMID a great splashing, Doc and Renny waded out to the low-wing craft and hoisted themselves into the cabin. Doc planted his powerful frame in the pilot's bucket.

"Now if the engines haven't been tampered with!" Renny grated, anxiety on his long, puritanical face.

Doc stepped on the electro-inertia starter buttons. The port motor popped black smoke out of the stacks, then started turning over. Nose engine, starboard—both functioned.

Vastly relieved, Renny lunged back in the cabin. His monster, flinty hands tore the top from a metal case as another man would open a cigarette pack. Out of the case came the latest model of Browning machine gun, airplane type. An ammo box gave way to his iron fingers. The cartridges were already in long snakes of metal link belt.

The low-wing speed plane was going down the narrow lake now. Renny threaded a belt into the Browning. The gun was fitted with a riflelike stock.

At the lake end, Doc jacked the ship about with sharp bloops of the engines. The craft gathered speed, a run of the whole lake length ahead of it. On step, it went. Then into the air.

With a touch little short of wizardry, Doc banked the speedy plane before it shattered itself against the sheer stone sides of the chasm. In tight, corkscrew turns, climbing, using all the power of the motors, Doc mounted out of the great cut.

Overhead the blue monoplane still lurked.

The treacherous air currents seized Doc's plane, worried it like a Kansas whirlwind would a piece of paper. Once, despite his expertness, Doc found himself doing a complete wingover. He recovered, continued to climb out of the Valley of the Vanished.

The air currents, after an interminable battle, became less violent. Doc pointed the great ship's nose up more steeply.

Suddenly the blue monoplane came hoicking down the sky lanes to the attack. Grayish wisps like spectral ropes suddenly streaked past Doc's ship. Tracer bullets! The monoplane was evidently fitted with a machine gun synchronized to shoot through the propeller blades!

Doc had not expected that—the blue plane had not possessed such armament when it attacked him in Belize. But he was not greatly perturbed. At his back was Renny, whose equal with a machine gun would be hard to find. Renny knew just how to lean into the firing weapon so as to withstand the recoil and still maintain an accurate aim.

Renny's Browning abruptly released a long, ripping burst.

The blue monoplane rolled wildly to get clear of the slugs that searched horribly for its vitals.

"Good work!" Doc complimented Renny.

Then it was Doc's turn to sideslip—skid his ship out of the procession of slugs that were eating vicious holes in the left wing end. The pilot of the blue plane was no tyro.

WARILY the ships jockeyed. Doc's plane was infinitely the larger, but that was certainly no advantage. And its control surfaces were not designed for combat flying. The two crafts were nearly evenly matched, with Doc having the great edge in speed on a straightaway. But this was no straightaway.

Lead from the other ship chewed at the fuselage, well to the rear.

"Now, Renny!" Doc breathed—and stood his ship on one wing tip.

Renny's Browning hammered and forked one long tongue of red from the barrel.

The burst punctured the pilot of the blue plane! The ship careened over, motor full on. It bored in a howling, unguided dive for the craggy mountaintop.

Its antics were even wilder as the air currents gripped it. Far to one side it skittered, then back. A gigantic suction drew it down into the Valley of the Vanished.

Striking in the deeper part of the lake, it raised a great geyser of foam.

By the time Doc had battled the rigorous air down to the lake surface, not a trace of the blue monoplane was to be seen.

Doc taxied over to the beach below the pyramid. He sprang ashore and ran up the sloping floor of the valley. Directly for Morning Breeze Doc raced. Now was the time for slam-bang stuff!

Long Tom, Johnny, Ham, and Monk had not been harmed as yet. But they were ringed around with agitated Mayans. The Mayans seemed to want to attack the white men as Morning Breeze advised, but at the same time were afraid of Doc's wrath. For the resurrection had given them the idea Doc was a superior being. He had killed the blue bird, too.

Morning Breeze saw Doc bearing down on him. Terror seized the squat, ugly-faced culprit. He shouted for his fellow warriors to protect him. Four of these advanced. Two had short spears. Two had the terrible clubs with razor-sharp flakes of obsidian embedded in the heads. Emboldened by Morning Breeze's shrieked orders, they rushed Doc. And fully fifteen more warriors, all armed, joined the attack.

What followed went into Mayan history. They carved the story of it on their temple atop the golden pyramid.

Fully fifteen warriors, all armed, joined the attack ...

Doc's bronzed body seemed to make a single move—forward. His great, powerful arms did things with a blurred, unbelievable speed.

The two spearsmen reeled away without making a thrust. One had a face knocked almost flat by Doc's fist; the other's right arm was broken and nearly jerked from his body.

The two club wielders found themselves suddenly pushed forcibly together by two hands which apparently possessed the power of a hundred ordinary hands. Their heads banged; they saw stars—and nothing else.

Doc grasped each of these unconscious warriors by the woven leather mantles they wore secured about their necks. He slung them, blue girdles flopping, into the midst of the other attackers. A full half dozen of these went down, mightily bruised and bewildered. The others milled, all tangled up with each other.

Suddenly Doc was among them! Not satisfied with overpowering the four, he pitched into the whole crew. Terrific blows came from his flashing fists. Red-fingered men began to drop in the milling, fighting mob. Piercing yells of pain arose.

As one, the mob of warriors fled! They couldn't fight this bronze being who moved too quickly for them to land a single blow.

Morning Breeze, tremendously chagrined, spun to flee with his satellites. One leap, two, he took. Then Doc, with a great spring, had him by the neck.

Doc took Morning Breeze's sacred knife, his only weapon, away from him.

"Have you someplace we can lock him up so he won't give more trouble?" Doc asked King Chaac. Doc was not even breathing heavily.

The Mayan sovereign was both amazed and highly elated. "I have!" he declared.

To one side, entrancing Princess Monja of the Mayans had been an admiring observer. Her dark eyes, as she watched Doc, radiated a great deal of feeling.

MORNING BREEZE was cast into a dark, windowless stone dungeon of a room, the only access to which was through a hole in the ceiling. Over this was fitted a stone lid of a door which required the combined strength of four squat Mayans to lift.

King Chaac was all for expelling the troublesome chief warrior from the Valley of the Vanished. He saw the undesirability of this, though, when Doc pointed out that Morning Breeze would only disclose to the world the existence of the golden pyramid.

"Give him a chance to cool off there in the cell," Doc suggested. "A chance to think over the error of his way has done wonders for many a criminal."

The Mayan sovereign concluded to follow that course.

Such was the simple temperament of these golden-skinned Mayans that Doc and his friends now found themselves generally accepted in defiance to the red-fingered men's solemn warnings. The influence of the latter was deflated to such a degree that the other Mayans refused to even listen to their sinister propaganda—for the warriors quickly tried to talk themselves into power again.

"We're sitting pretty!" Monk declared, rubbing his big, furry hands together.

"Knock on wood, you lunk!" Ham muttered somberly.

Monk grinned and tried to knock on Ham's head. "I wonder why his nibs, the king, is making us wait a month before he concludes arrangements about this gold?"

"I have no idea," Ham admitted. "But you recall he mentioned it might not be thirty days."

Monk stretched and yawned tremendously.

"Well, this ain't a bad place to spend a month's vacation," he decided. "It'll probably be quiet around here now."

Chapter XVI
CURSE OF THE GODS

THAT night, in the Valley of the Vanished, darkness lay everywhere with the black intensity of drawing ink. Impenetrable clouds massed above the great chasm caused this. The air was a bit sultry. Even a novice forecaster could have told one of the tropical downpours common to Hidalgo was on its way.

Doc and his friends took the precaution of posting a guard and keeping a light burning. They alternated on guard, but nothing eventful came to their notice.

At the stone hut where Morning Breeze was incarcerated, two Mayan citizens kept alert vigil. From time to time the surly Morning Breeze called them uncomplimentary names and promised them the wrath of the gods if they didn't release him at once. But the watchmen had been promised the wrath of Doc Savage if they let Morning Breeze escape, and they feared that the greater. To them, also, the night gave nothing portentous.

In one spot in the Valley of the Vanished, however, a devil's cauldron of evil simmered and stewed.

This was near the lower end of the egg-shaped valley, where the stream cut through the great chasm. In a tiny pock of a hole among the boulders had congregated most of the red-fingered warriors. There they lighted a fire and offered a chant to the fire god, one of their principal deities. There were also prayers to Quetzalcoatl, the Sky God; and to Kukulcan, the Feathered Serpent.

They seemed to be waiting for something, these villainous ones, and killing the ensuing time with chants calculated to redeem their sadly depreciated standing. They launched into a ritual devoted to the Earth Monster, another pagan deity.

This was interrupted by a low rustling of the leafage that edged the recess where the red-fingered men had gathered. An amazing figure clambered down and joined them.

A man it was, but he wore a remarkable masquerade. The body of the garment consisted of an enormous snakeskin, the hide of a giant boa constrictor. The head of the reptile had been carefully skinned out, and probably enlarged by some stretching process until it formed a fantastic hood and mask for the one who wore it.

The man's arms and legs, projecting from the masquerade garment, were painted a gaudy blue, the Mayan holy color. Starting on the forehead and down the middle of the back, and nearly to the dragging end of the snake tail, were feathers. They resembled the trains on the feather headdress of an American Indian.

The newcomer was obviously made up in some weird likeness of the Mayan god, Kukulcan, the Feathered Serpent.

The gathering of red-fingered warriors were greatly impressed. To a man they sank upon their knees and kowtowed to the hideous apparition in snakeskin and feathers. They undoubtedly knew there was a man inside the rigmarole, but they were overawed anyway, such superstitious souls did they possess.

HALTINGLY, with the greatest of difficulty, the snake man began to speak Mayan. A large proportion of his words were so poorly uttered as to convey no meaning to his listeners. At such times the blank expression of the warriors warned him to go back and repeat. The snake man was plainly an outsider.

But the red-fingered men were completely under his sway.

"I am the son of Kukulcan, blood of his blood, flesh of his flesh," the serpent one told his awed audience. "Did you seize such of the white invaders as you could and throw them into the sacrificial well? Did you change the color of the white devils' blue plane, painting marks of the Red Death upon it? This I commanded. Did you do it?"

"We did," muttered a warrior.

The brain back of the snake mask sensed something wrong. The hideous head jerked, surveying the assembled Mayans. "Where is your commander, Morning Breeze?"

"He is imprisoned." The information came reluctantly.

A great rage shook the masked figure. "Then Savage and his men are still in the good graces of your people?" he grated.

Slowly the serpent one extracted the story of what had happened from the humiliated gathering. The information seemed to stun him. He sat in morose silence, thinking.

A warrior, bolder than the rest, inquired: "What, O master, became of the two of our number we sent with you into the outer world to slay this Savage and his father?"

That disclosed who the snake man was. The murderer of Doc Savage's father! The master of the Red Death! The brains behind the Hidalgo revolution movement!

Words of answer were slow coming from the evil mask. The fiendish brain was racing. It would not do to let these red-fingered men know their two fellows had succumbed to the power of that supreme adventurer, Doc Savage. It might wipe out some of their faith in the impostor who was pretending to be the son of the sacred Feathered Serpent.

He needed all his power now, did the snake man. His plane and pilot destroyed by Doc Savage! This *was* a blow! He had intended to use that machine-gun-equipped plane in his revolution against President Carlos Avispa's government of Hidalgo.

And Savage and his friends were soundly entrenched in the Valley of the Vanished. Soon all chance to secure the vast sum needed to finance the revolution would be gone.

"Has Savage gained access to the gold?" asked the snake man.

"No," replied a well-posted Mayan. "He does not know but what the pyramid contains all the yellow metal in the Valley of the Vanished. King Chaac has not told him the truth yet."

None of the red-fingered ones heard the words next breathed into the serpent mask. They were: "Thank Heaven for that!"

The collected warriors began to stir uneasily. This Son of the Feathered Serpent had been full of egoism and orders on other occasions. Now he was silent. And he had not explained what had happened to their two comrades. One Mayan repeated the question about their two fellows.

"They are alive and well!" lied the snake man. "Listen! Hear me well, my children, for here are my words of wisdom."

The warriors came under the spell again.

"The Red Death shall strike very soon!" rumbled the voice back of the serpent mask.

GENUINE terror now seized upon the Mayans. They shuddered and drew together as if for protection. Not a one voiced a word.

"The Red Death strikes soon!" repeated the snake man. "It is the way of Kukulcan, the Feathered Serpent, my father, to show you he will not have these white men in your midst. You have sinned grievously in letting them stay. You were warned to destroy them. I, the voice of my father, the Feathered Serpent, warned you."

A warrior began: "We tried—"

"No excuses!" commanded the voice from the mask. "By doing two things only can you avert the Red Death, or stop its progress after it has descended upon you. First, you must destroy Savage and his men. Second, you must deliver to me, Son of the Feathered Serpent, as much gold as ten men can carry. I will see the gold gets to the Feathered Serpent."

The Mayans muttered, squirmed, shuddered.

"Destroy Savage—and bring me all the gold ten men can carry!" repeated the one they feared. "Only that will cause the Feathered Serpent to take back his Red Death. I have spoken. Go."

With steps driven to haste by their terror of this feathered snake of a thing, the red-fingered men took their departure. They would sit in their huts and talk about it the rest of the night. And the more they talked, the more likely they would be to do as they had been commanded. For it is a strange fact that a crowd of men are less brave in the face of threat than a single individual. They add to each other's fear.

The snake man did not linger after they had gone. He quitted the rendezvous, walking furtively, wincing as his bare feet were mauled by the sharp rocks.

Reaching a low bush, he drew from under it two ordinary gallon fruit jars. One of these was filled with a red, viscous fluid. The other contained a much thinner, paler fluid.

On one jar was written:

Germ culture which causes Red Death.

On the other was inscribed:

Cure for Red Death.

These the man in the serpent masquerade carried most carefully as he made his way in stealth toward the gilded pyramid.

WITHOUT being observed or arousing any slumbering Mayans, the snake man reached the pyramid. As he came near the monster pile of fabulously rich gold ore, he could not control his breathing, so strong was his lust for the yellow metal. The noisy purling of the stream of water down the pyramid side eliminated any chance of his being heard, though.

Up the steps the man felt his way in the intense darkness. The water raced by at his side. He reached the flattened top of the structure. There he felt about in the sepia murk until he found what he sought—a small, tanklike pool.

It was this pool that fed the racing brook down the pyramid side. Just how the pool was kept continuously supplied with water, in spite of its position high atop the pyramid, the man did not know or care.

He furtively lit a match.

The contents of the jar labeled *Germ culture which causes Red Death*, he emptied into the pool.

From experience, the fiend in the serpent mask knew the deadly germs would be fed down the pyramid water stream for about two days. And the entire clan of Mayans obtained their drinking water from that stream!

Two days and every person in the valley would be a victim of the gruesome Red Death. Only one thing could save them—treatment with the stuff in the other jar. Previously—for he had obtained many offerings of gold from this valley—the man in the snake mask had administered the cure exactly as he had the disease, by dumping it into the Mayan water supply.

It was because he saw the end of the golden offerings once Doc Savage appeared on the scene that the man had sought to keep Doc from reaching the Valley of the Vanished.

Carrying the empty jar, and the full jar of the cure, the man retreated down the pyramid. He made his way in silence to the remote end of the valley, where he had his hiding place. It was here he had concealed himself after his plane pilot had dropped him by parachute into the valley the previous night. No one had noticed the falling chute.

En route, the man paused to smash the empty jar.

The clatter of the breaking glass instilled an ugly thought in his brain. He toyed with it.

"I will never learn the source of this gold from old Chaac," he growled. "And no one else knows the secret. So why should I trouble with curing them after they get sick?"

He made angry noises with his teeth. "If all in the valley were dead, I could take my time hunting the gold. And there is a fortune in that pyramid for the taking."

A mean grin crooked the lips back of the snake-head mask. "They will make many gold offerings before they find out I am not going to cure them!"

He had reached a decision that showed how evil and cruel he was. He had no regard at all for human life.

He crashed the bottle of Red Death cure against a rock, destroying it.

He intended to let the Mayans perish!

Chapter XVII
THE BATTLE OF MERCY

DOC SAVAGE, up ahead of the sun, spent the usual time at the exercises which kept his amazing bronze body the wonderful mental and physical thing it was. From force of habit he liked to go through his ritual while alone. Bystanders were always asking questions as to what this and that was intended to do, pestering him.

Morning Breeze was still a prisoner. Doc paid the cell hut a visit to be sure. The guards on duty eyed Doc's bronze form in open wonder, marveling at its perfection. Doc had not as yet donned his shirt.

Doc's bared arms looked like those of an Atlas. The muscles, in repose, were not knotty. They were more like bundled piano wires on which a thin bronze skin had been painted. And across his chest and back great, supple cables of tendon lay layer upon layer. It was a rare sight, that body of Doc's. The Mayans' eyes popped.

Some of the morning Doc spent in conversation with King Chaac. Considering the elderly sovereign had never heard of a modern university, he had some remarkably accurate knowledge about the universe.

Pretty Princess Monja, Doc discovered also, would pass in any society as a well-educated young woman. All she lacked was a course in the history of the rest of the world. It was amazing.

"We lead a life of leisure here in the Valley of the Vanished," King Chaac explained. "We have much time to think, to reason things out."

A little later King Chaac made an unexpected—and pleasant—revelation.

"You may have wondered why I said I would delay thirty days or possibly less before I disclosed to you the location of the gold supply?" he asked.

Doc admitted he had.

"It was my agreement with your father," smiled King Chaac. "I was to satisfy myself you were a man of sufficient character to put this fabulous wealth to the use to which it should be put."

"That was not a bad idea," Doc agreed.

"I am satisfied," said King Chaac in a pleased tone. "Tomorrow I show you the gold. But first, tomorrow morning you must be adopted into our Mayan clan. You and your men. That is necessary. For centuries the word has come down that none but a Mayan should ever remove the gold. Your adoption into the tribe will fulfill that command."

Doc expressed the proper appreciation. The conversation came around to how the gold was to be transported to civilization.

"We can hardly take it in the plane, due to the terrific air currents," Doc pointed out.

The elderly Mayan sovereign smiled. "We have donkeys here in the Valley of the Vanished. I will simply have a number of them loaded with gold and dispatched to your banker at Blanco Grande."

Doc was surprised at the simplicity of the scheme. "But the warlike natives in the surrounding mountains—they will never let a pack train through."

"In that you are mistaken," chuckled King Chaac. "The natives are of Mayan ancestry. They know we are here; they know why. And for centuries it has been their fighting which has kept this valley lost to white men. Oh, yes, they will let the pack train through. And no white man will ever know from whence it came. And they will let others through as the years pass."

"Is there that much gold?" Doc inquired.

But King Chaac only smiled secretively and gave no other answer.

THE Red Death struck in the middle of that afternoon.

A cluster of excited Mayans about a stone house drew Monk's curious attention. Monk looked inside.

A Mayan was sprawled on a stone bench. His yellow skin was mottled, feverish, and he was calling for water.

On his neck were vile red patches.

"The Red Death!" Monk muttered in a horror-filled voice. He ran for Doc, and found him politely listening to attractive Princess Monja. The young lady had finally cornered Doc alone.

Doc raced to the plane, got his instrument case.

Entering the Mayan's stone dwelling, Doc became at once the thing for which he was eminently fitted above all others—a great doctor and surgeon. From the highest credited medical universities and the greatest hospitals in America, from the best that Europe had to offer, Doc garnered his fabulous fund of knowledge of medicine and surgery. He had studied with the master surgeons in the costliest clinics in the world. And he had conducted unnumbered experiments of his own when he had advanced beyond the greatest master's ability to teach.

With his instruments, his supersensitive ear, his featherlight touch; Doc examined the Mayan.

"What ails him?" Monk wanted to know.

"It escapes me as yet," Doc was forced to admit. "Obviously it is the same thing that seized my father. That means it was administered to this man in some fashion by that devil who is behind all our troubles. Whoever he is, the fiend must be in the valley now. Probably the blue airplane brought him and dropped him by parachute at night."

In that Doc's reasoning could not have been more accurate had he witnessed the arrival of the enemy.

At this juncture Long Tom ran up.

"The Red Death!" he puffed. "They're collapsing with it all over the city!"

Doc administered an opiate to the first Mayan to be stricken to ease his pain, then visited a second sufferer. He questioned each closely on where he had been, what he had eaten. Four more Mayans he asked the same thing.

Deduction then told him how the Red Death was being spread!

"The water supply!" he guessed with exactness.

He showed Long Tom, Johnny, Ham, and Renny how to administer the opiates that lessened suffering.

"Monk, your knowledge of chemistry is going to be in need," he declared. "Come on."

Securing test tubes for obtaining samples of the water, Doc and Monk hurried toward the gleaming yellow pyramid.

Although the epidemic of Red Death had been underway less than an hour, the cult of red-fingered warriors had been making full use of the panic it engendered. They were falling over themselves to spread word that the disease was a punishment inflicted upon the Mayans for permitting Doc and his friends to remain in the Valley of the Vanished.

Ominous mutterings were arising. Blue-girdled men everywhere harangued madly, seeking to fan the flames of hatred.

"And just when things were sailing smooth for us!" Monk muttered.

DOC and Monk reached the golden pyramid and started up. Instantly a loud roar of anger lifted from a crowd of Mayans who had followed them. The crowd was composed of about half red-fingered fighting men.

They made threatening gestures, indicating Doc and Monk should not ascend the pyramid. It was an altar, inviolate to their gods, they screamed. Only Mayans could ascend without bringing bad luck.

It was the red-fingered men who howled the loudest.

"We're going to have a fight on our hands if we go up," Monk whispered.

It was Doc who solved the delicate situation. He did it simply. He beckoned to attractive Princess Monja, gave her the test tubes, and told her to dip water from whatever sort of a tank or pool was on top of the pyramid.

The confidence the young woman showed Doc did its bit to allay the anger of the Mayans.

Back at the stone house assigned himself and his friends, Doc set to work.

He had brought a compact quantity of apparatus. And Monk had his tiny, wonderfully efficient chemical laboratory. Doc combined the two, went to work analyzing the water.

He had trouble with the Mayans before he had hardly started. Two of the homeliest of the ugly, red-fingered gentry came dancing and screaming into the place. They had rubbed some evil-smelling lotion on themselves, and the odor angered Doc, who depended a great deal on his sense of smell in his analyzing.

Doc kicked both warriors bodily outdoors. For a moment it looked like the house was going into a state of siege. Hundreds of Mayans shrieked and waved arms and weapons outside. It was astounding the number of spears and terrible clubs they had unearthed.

But memory of what had happened to the gang of warriors who had attacked Doc the day before made them hesitate.

"Monk," Doc questioned, "did you bring that gas you made up in my laboratory in New York? The stuff that paralyzes without harming, I mean."

"I sure did," Monk assured him. "I'll go get it."

Doc heaved the heavy stone door shut and continued his analyzing.

Rocks began to bounce against the stone walls and the flat stone roof. A couple whizzed in the square window.

The yelling had risen to a bedlam.

Suddenly the note of the howling changed from rage to fear. It diminished greatly in volume. Doc looked out the window.

Monk had broken a bottle of his gas where the wind carried it over the besieging Mayans. Fully half of the malefactors were stiff and helpless on the earth. They would be thus for possibly two hours; then the effects would wear off.

This eased the tension for a time, enabling Doc to continue his work undisturbed.

Test after test he ran on the water. He had very early isolated a tiny quantity of red, viscous fluid which he had determined was some sort of germ culture. The question was to find out what kind of germs.

There was not much time. His father had succumbed less than three days after being stricken. Probably that was about the time required for the ghastly disease to prove fatal.

An hour dragged past. Another. Doc worked tirelessly, with every ounce of his enormous concentration.

The humor of the Mayans rapidly became worse. Johnny, Ham, and Renny were driven to the stone house where Doc worked. They were joined by elderly King Chaac and entrancing Princess Monja. Of all the Mayans, the faith of these two in Doc remained utterly unshaken.

However, there were other Mayans who remained aloof from the turmoil—people who would probably side with Doc when the showdown came.

Doc worked without hardly lifting his head all that afternoon. He labored the night straight through, his experiments lighted by electric bulbs Long Tom fixed up.

ANOTHER dawn had come before Doc straightened from the stone bench where he had placed his apparatus.

"Long Tom!" he called.

Long Tom sprang to Doc's side and listened to Doc explain what was wanted.

It was an intricate apparatus Long Tom was to rig, a mechanism to create one of the newest and most marvelous healing rays known to medical science. Long Tom, electrical wizard that he was, knew pretty much how it should be made. Doc supplied such details as Long Tom was not familiar with.

Then Doc quitted the stone building.

His friends flocked to the doors and windows, armed with machine guns, Monk with his gas bombs. They were certain Doc would be attacked by the Mayans, who had kept vigil outside all night.

But they witnessed something little short of a miracle. Doc walked through the crowd untouched! Not a warrior dared lay a hand upon him, such a hypnotic quality did his golden eyes contain. No doubt his reputation of a superman in a fight helped.

Fifty or so Mayans trailed Doc. Afraid to attack him, they nevertheless followed him. But not for far.

Doc reached the jungle-carpeted lower end of the little valley. With a bound he lifted high from the earth and seized a limb. A monkey-like flip put him atop it. He ran along it, balancing perfectly, and sprang to another bough.

Then he was gone, silent as a bronze owl flitting along the jungle lanes.

The Mayans milled a while, then returned to their city.

They were met by a group of red-fingered fellows who upbraided them fiendishly for permitting Doc to walk through their hands. The white man, they screamed, must be slaughtered.

Somebody had freed squat, tattooed, ugly Morning Breeze from his dungeon. He was rapidly whipping the Mayans into a frenzy. He herded them toward the stone house where Doc's friends were barricaded. Exerting all his powers of persuasion, Morning Breeze got them to attack.

Monk promptly expended all his gas on the assailants. They fled, such of them as could, repulsed. But they reunited at a short distance, a great mob, and listened to the red-fingered men talk.

Now and then a Mayan would stumble off to his stone home, seized with the horrible Red Death. Perhaps a fourth of the tribe were already prostrate from the malady.

HALF the morning had gone when Doc returned. He came via the roofs of the closely spaced houses, crossing the narrow streets with gigantic leaps only he could manage. He was inside the stone house with his besieged friends before the Mayans even awakened to his nearness.

The natives sent up a rumble of anger, but did not advance.

Doc had brought, tied with roots in a great bundle, many types of jungle herbs.

With these he set to work. He boiled some, cooked others, treated some with acids. Slowly he refined the product.

Noon came. The fourth of stricken Mayans had risen to a third. And with the increased rate of collapse, the temper of the besiegers was getting shorter. The red-fingered warriors had them believing that the death of the white men would solve their problem, vanquish the malady.

"I think I've got it!" Doc said at last. "The cure!"

"I'm out of gas," Monk muttered. "How are we going to get out of here to treat them?"

For answer, Doc pocketed vials of the thin pale fluid he had concocted. "Wait here," he directed.

He shoved the stone door ajar suddenly, stepped outside. The Mayans saw him, rumbled. A couple of spears sped through the air. But long before the obsidian spear tips shattered against the stone house, Doc had vaulted to the roof and was gone.

Furtively he prowled through the strange city. He found a Mayan who had been stricken and forcibly administered some of the pale medicine. At another home he repeated the operation on an entire family.

When molested by armed Mayans, he simply evaded them. His bronzed form would flash around a corner—and all trace would be gone when the Mayans reached the spot. Once, about mid-afternoon, he did show resistance to three red-fingered men who happened upon him treating a household of five Mayans. When Doc left the vicinity, all three warriors were still unconscious from the blows he had delivered.

Thus, as furtively as though he were a criminal instead of the angel of mercy he was in reality, he was forced to skulk and give by main strength the treatment he had devised.

By nightfall, however, his persistence began to tell. Word spread that the bronze god of a white man was *curing the Red Death!*

Doc's concoction, thanks to his unique medical skill, was proving effective.

By nine o'clock Long Tom could venture forth without danger and treat unfortunates with his health-ray apparatus. This had remarkable properties for healing tissue burned out by the ravages of the Red Death.

"Doc says the Red Death is a rare tropical fever," Long Tom explained to the greatly interested Princess Monja. "Originally it must have been the malady of some jungle bird. Probably similar to an epidemic known as 'parrot fever' which swept the United States a year or two ago."

"Mr. Savage is a remarkable man!" the young Mayan woman murmured.

Long Tom nodded soberly. "There is not a thing he can't do, I reckon."

Chapter XVIII
FRIENDSHIP

A WEEK passed. During that time, Doc Savage's position among the Mayans not only returned to what it had been before the epidemic of the Red Death, but it far surpassed that.

As man after man of the yellow-skinned people recovered, a complete change of feeling came about. Doc was the hero of every stone home. They followed him about in droves, admiring his tremendous physique, imitating his little manners.

They even spied upon him taking his inevitable exercise in the mornings. By the end of the week, half the Mayans in the city were also taking exercises.

Renny, who never took any exercise except to knock things to pieces with his great fists, thought it very funny.

"Exercise never hurt anybody, unless they overdid it," Doc told him.

The red-fingered warriors were a chagrined lot. In fact, Morning Breeze lost a large part of his following. His erstwhile satellites scrubbed the red stain off their fingers, threw their blue *maxtlis,* or girdles, away, and forsook the fighting sect, with King Chaac's consent.

Less than fifty of the most villainous remained in Morning Breeze's fold. These were careful not to make themselves noticed too much, because there was some talk among the upright Mayan citizens of seeing if there wasn't enough warriors to fill the sacrificial well.

Things seemed to have come to an ideal pass.

Except, possibly, in the case of pretty Princess Monja. She was plainly infatuated with Doc, but making no headway. She was, of course, well bred enough not to show her feelings too openly. But all of Doc's friends could see how it was.

Doc removed all firearms to their stone headquarters house. He locked the weapons in a room. Long Tom installed a simple electrical burglar alarm. Monk made up more of his paralyzing gas. He stored this with the arms. In the face of the peace, such preparations seemed unnecessary, though.

Everyone noted Doc was inexplicably missing from the city at times. These absences lasted several hours. Then Doc would reappear. He offered no explanation. Actually, he had been ranging the jungle sections of the Valley of the Vanished. He was seeking his father's murderer. He traveled, apelike, among the trees, or silent as a bronze shadow on the ground.

Near the lower end of the valley he found what his keen senses told him was the camp of his quarry. But it was a cold trail. The camp had been deserted some time. Doc tracked the killer a considerable distance. The scent ended at the trail out of the valley.

THERE came the day when elderly King Chaac decided things were normal enough to adopt Doc and his men into the tribe. There was to be a great ceremony.

After, they would be shown the gold source.

The ceremony got underway at the pyramid.

Since Doc and his friends were to become honorary Mayans, it was needful that they don Mayan costume for the festivities. King Chaac furnished the attire.

The garb consisted of short mantles of stout fiber interwoven with wire gold, brilliant girdles, and high-backed sandals. Each had a headdress to denote some animal. These towered high, and interwoven trains of flowers fell down their backs.

Ham took one look at Monk in this paraphernalia and burst into laughter. "If I just had a grind organ to go with you!" he chuckled.

Because pistols did not harmonize with this garb, they left them behind. No danger seemed to threaten, anyway.

The entire populace assembled at the pyramid for the ceremony. The Mayan men wore the same costume as Doc and his friends. In addition, some wore a cotton padlike armor, stuffed with sand. These resembled baseball chest protectors. Those attired in the armor also carried ceremonial spears and clubs.

Doc noted one thing a little off color.

Morning Breeze and his red-fingered followers were nowhere about!

Doc gave some thought to that. But there seemed no serious harm Morning Breeze could do. His fifty men were hopelessly outnumbered in case they started trouble.

The rituals got under way.

Doc and his men first had their faces daubed with sacred blue. Mystic designs in other colors were painted on their arms.

They were next offered various viands to which ceremonial significance was attached. They each drank honey—honey by the strange bees of Central America which store it in liquid in the hive, not in combs. Next was *atole*, a drink made from maize, and kept in most elaborate and beautiful jars.

Atop the pyramid, native incense was now burning in an immense *quiche*, or ceremonial burner. The fumes, sweeping down the great golden pyramid in the calm, bracing air, were quite pleasant.

Seated in orderly rows about the pyramid base, the entire Mayan populace kept up a low chanting. The sound was rhythmic, certain musical words repeated over and over. There were a few musical instruments, well handled.

The affair moved rapidly toward the climax. This would be when Doc and his friends were led up the long flight of steps bearing offerings of incense for the great burner and little stone images of the god Kukulcan to place at the feet of the larger statue.

It was necessary, King Chaac had explained, to mount the steps only on their knees. To do otherwise would not be according to Hoyle.

The Mayan women were taking an equal part in the ritual with the men. Most of these were very attractive in their shoulder mantles and knee-length girdles.

The time came when Doc and his friends started up the long line of steps. It was tricky business balancing on their knees. Around them, the Mayan chanting pulsed and throbbed with an exciting, exotic quality.

Yard after yard the adventurers ascended.

Suddenly Morning Breeze appeared. Shrieking, he sprang through the hundreds of Mayans ringed about the pyramid base.

THAT halted everything.

It was an unheard-of thing. The ritual was sacred. For one to interrupt was highest sacrilege.

Hundreds of angry Mayan eyes bore upon the chief of the red-fingered fighting guild.

Morning Breeze commanded attention with uplifted arms.

"O children!" he shrilled. "You cannot do this thing! The gods forbid! They do not want these white men!"

At this juncture some Mayan muttered loudly that the Mayans didn't want Morning Breeze, either.

Ignoring the hostility, the warrior leader continued: "Fearsome will be the fate to fall upon you if you make these outsiders Mayans. It is forbidden!"

Doc Savage made no move. He saw in this dramatic interruption a last wild bid by Morning Breeze. The fellow was desperate. His hotly blazing eyes, the shaking in his arms, showed that.

Anyhow, Doc wanted to see just how deeply the golden-skinned Mayans loved him. He had confidence in them. They wouldn't listen to Morning Breeze lampoon the white men for long.

And they didn't!

Dignified King Chaac called a sharp command. Mayans—the fellows who wore the quilted armor and carried the weapons—surged for Morning Breeze.

The warrior chief took flight. Like a jackrabbit in spite of his short legs, the ugly fellow bounded away. At the crowd skirts he halted.

He screamed: "You fools! For this you must come to Morning Breeze with your noses in the dirt and beg his mercy! Otherwise you die! All of you!"

With that proclamation he spun and fled. Four or five well-cast javelins lent wings to his big, ungainly feet.

The dissenter disappeared in the jungle.

Doc was very thoughtful. He had learned to judge by men's voices when they were bluffing. Morning Breeze sounded like a man who had an ace in the hole.

What could it be? Doc pondered. He became more uneasy. The fiend who had murdered the elder Savage was still at large. That man was clever, capable of anything. Doc wished his men had their guns.

The ceremonials resumed where they had left off. For four or five minutes the chanting continued. Bodies swayed rhythmically. The savage cadence had a quality to arouse, incite strange feelings.

Again Doc and his friends advanced up the pyramid stairs, keeping balanced on their knees. The bundles of incense, and the stone images they carried were getting burdensome.

All eyes were on Doc's magnificent frame. Truly, thought the yellow-skinned people, here was a worthy addition to the clan of Maya.

Doc and his five men were almost at the top. King Chaac was before them, showing where the incense should be placed.

The final words of ritual were about to be spoken by the sovereign of the Valley of the Vanished.

Then the holocaust broke.

SUDDEN staccato reports rattled. Shots! They were so closely spaced as to be almost one loud roar. Their noise beat against the great yellow pyramid in terrible waves.

"Machine guns!" Renny barked.

Piercing screams, moans of agony, arose from the assembled Mayans. Several had dropped from the murderous leaden hail!

There had apparently been four rapid-fire guns. They were situated on the four sides of the pyramid. So well screened were the weapons that no trace of them or the operators could be seen.

Doc shoved his friends, as well as King Chaac and the Princess Monja, down in the shelter of the large images on the pyramid top.

Not a moment too soon! Lead stormed the spot where they had been. Rock chips showered off the images. One big, long-nosed likeness even toppled over. Flattened bullets fell about them.

Doc picked up one of those lead blobs, studied it. His brain, replete with ballistics lore, instantly catalogued the bullet.

"This is not the caliber of our guns!" he declared. "That means they haven't seized our weapons. So someone has brought in machine guns from the outside!"

The adventurers looked at each other. They knew the answer to the question. The murderer of Doc's father had brought in the guns!

The hail of lead ceased.

To the right, on a low knoll backed by brush, Morning Breeze made his appearance.

"You behold the fulfilling of my prophecy!" he shouted. "Destroy these white men! Crawl to me and beg for your lives! Acknowledge me as your ruler! Otherwise you shall all die!"

Even from that distance they could see Morning Breeze's wild look.

"He's insane," Monk muttered. "Plumb dingy!"

A flight of spears gave Morning Breeze's answer. With wild yells of anger, a group of the Mayan citizens attired in quilted armor charged the warrior chief. A machine gun forced them back, slaying several.

Then elderly King Chaac raised a great shout. He called some command at his people. So rapidly did he speak that Doc's knowledge of Mayan was not sufficient to follow him.

The Mayan people began to run up the pyramid steps. They came with orderly speed, in a column the full twenty feet wide.

Doc stared at them, not realizing what they were intent on. The first of the yellow-skinned people passed him.

Doc now observed King Chaac had exerted pressure on the large Kukulcan idol beside the water tank that was always flowing. The idol had levered back. Revealed was a large cavity! Well-worn stone steps stretched downward into darkness!

Into this opening the column of Mayans dived. Like well-trained soldiers they sped up the side of the pyramid. But they seemed as surprised as the white men at sight of the opening.

Doc glanced askance at the elderly Mayan sovereign.

"Of all my people, only I knew of this hidden door," explained King Chaac.

The machine guns of the red-fingered warriors were silent. The orderly retreat up the pyramid side must have them puzzled. And no doubt they thought they had wrought enough havoc with their weapons to bring the Mayans to terms.

Doc watched the gun emplacements closely—his sharp eye had located each one. He saw the red-fingered devils show themselves.

He saw one other man—a fellow masquerading in a repulsive snakeskin costume. Colored feathers were arrayed down the back of the hideous serpent outfit.

This revolting figure seemed to be directing the whole thing. He even gave Morning Breeze orders. Doc, catching the man's voice faintly, knew by the accent he was no Mayan.

Suddenly the machine guns went into operation again.

But they had waited too long. Practically all the Mayans were inside the pyramid. Even as the hail of metal started anew, the last of the golden-skinned people ducked into the wide, secret door.

King Chaac and Princess Monja now descended. Doc and his five friends followed.

The Mayan ruler showed them slits in the masonry. Through these, it was possible to observe whether anyone was coming up the steps.

Even as they looked, some of the red-fingered warriors ran to the foot of the pyramid and started up the stairs.

"If we just had our guns!" Renny groaned, his puritanical face genuinely forlorn. But Doc and his men had left their weapons in their stone house.

"Watch!" commanded King Chaac. He called a low order to some of his men far down the darkened passage into the depths of the pyramid.

Great, round rocks were passed up and chucked outside. The dornicks bounded down the steps. The warriors were battered back. They picked themselves up and fled.

"They cannot get to us here," said King Chaac.

DOC SAVAGE listened to the shouting voice of the man in the snake masquerade. The tones reached them faintly.

Doc identified the coarse voice! The snake man was the slayer of the elder Savage, and the prime mover in the planned Hidalgo revolution. It was the voice Doc had heard in that hotel room in the Hidalgo capital city, Blanco Grande.

Doc knew now why he had found no trace of the killer during the past week. The man had been away from the Valley of the Vanished, getting the machine guns.

"How about food supplies?" Doc asked.

Reluctantly, King Chaac admitted: "There is no food."

"Then we're penned up," Doc pointed out. "There is plenty of water, I presume?"

"Plenty. The stream that supplies the pool atop the pyramid—we have access to it."

"That helps," Doc admitted. "Your people may be able to hold out a few days. My men and myself, accustomed to hardship, might beat that. But we've got to do something."

Suddenly Doc bounded upward to the lip of the opening in the pyramid top. He glanced quickly about. He decided to take a chance. It was a chance so slim only a man of Doc's unique powers could wrench success from it.

"No one shall try to follow me!" he warned.

Then, with a swift spring, he was out of the passage that dived down into the innards of the golden pyramid.

So unexpected was Doc's appearance that a moment elapsed before the clumsy red-fingered machine gunners could turn a stream of lead on the pyramid top and the tiny temple there. By the time metal did storm, Doc had bounded off the top.

He did not select the stairs. He had a better means of descent. The steep, glass-smooth side of the pyramid! The gold-bearing ore of which the great structure was made was hard. The ages it had stood there had not weathered away enough of the soft gold to roughen the original sleekness much.

Leaning well back, Doc coasted downward on his heels. His leap had given him great momentum.

Twenty feet, and he spun over and over expertly. Thus, he flashed to one side several yards. It was well he did. Machine-gun bullets clouted into the course he had been following, and screamed off into space.

Rich gold ore, broken loose, clattered down the pyramid. But Doc left it far behind. Mere sliding speed was not enough. He jumped outward, did it again, until he traveled faster than a falling object.

He hit the foot of the pyramid at a speed that would have shattered the body of an ordinary man. Tremendous muscles of sprung steel cushioned Doc's landing. He never as much as lost his balance. Like a whippet, he was away.

Into a low depression, he sank. Hungry lead slugs rattled like hail—but always a yard or two behind Doc. The speed of his movements was too tremendous for inexperienced marksmen. Even an expert shot at moving objects would have had trouble getting a bead on that bronze, corded form.

The depression let Doc into low bushes. And from that moment he was lost to the murderers with the machine guns.

To the red-fingered warriors, it was incredible! They clucked among themselves, and looked about wildly for the flashing thing of bronze that was Doc. They did not find it.

Their leader, the repulsive figure masqueraded in snakeskin and feathers, was more perturbed than the others. He cowered among them. He kept very close to a machine gun, as though he expected that great, bronzed Nemesis of his kind to spring upon him from thin air.

Great was the snake man's terror of Doc Savage.

Chapter XIX
THE BRONZE MASTER

DOC SAVAGE sped for the stone city. It lay only a few rods away. He haunted low tropical vegetation to the first stone-paved street. Among the houses he glided.

So quiet was his going that wild tropical birds perched on the projecting stone roofs of the houses were unfrightened by his passage; no more scared than had he been the bronze reflection of some cloud overhead.

Doc was making for the building which had been his headquarters. In it, he had left his machine guns, rifles, pistols, and the remarkable gas that was Monk's invention.

He wanted those weapons. With them, the fifty or so warriors could be defeated in short order. Armed equally, the men of Morning Breeze could not stand against Doc and his five veteran fighters. So Doc had taken tremendous chances to get guns.

The headquarters house appeared ahead. Low, replete with stone carving, it was no more elaborate than the other Mayan homes. It seemed deserted.

The door, which could be closed solidly with a pivoted stone slab, but which was ordinarily only curtained, gaped invitingly. Doc paused and listened.

Back toward the pyramid, a machine gun snarled out a dozen shots. He heard nothing else.

Doc pushed back the curtain and slid into the stone house.

No enemies were there.

Doc went across the room, seeming to glide on ice, so effortlessly did he move. He tried the door of the room in which they had placed their arms.

He perceived suddenly that Long Tom's electric burglar alarm had been expertly put out of commission.

No Mayan knew enough to do that!

"The man in the snakeskin!" Doc decided. "He did it!"

The room door gave before a shove by a great bronze arm. Doc had expected what he saw when he looked in.

The weapons were gone!

A faint sound came from the street.

Doc spun. Across the room he flashed—not to the door, but to the window. His keen senses told him a trap was closing upon him.

Before he reached the window, an object flashed into it, thrown from the outside. The object—a bottle—broke on the stone wall. It was filled with a vile-looking fluid. This sprayed over most of the room.

Doc surmised what the stuff was. Monk's gas!

His bronze features set with determination, Doc continued for the window. But a gun muzzle snaked in. It spat flame. Doc ducked clear of the screaming lead. Gas was everywhere in the room.

There was no escape that way. He whirled on the door. But the muzzles of two automatic pistols met him. They were the guns he had invented. He knew just how fast they could deal death.

Then, slowly, Doc Savage collapsed.

He made a great bronze figure on the stone floor.

"THE gas got him!" snarled the man in the snake masquerade, appearing from a haven of safety behind several red-fingered fighters.

Then, realizing he had spoken in a language the Mayans could not understand, the man translated: "The all-powerful breath of the Son of the Feathered Serpent has vanquished the chief of our enemies."

"Indeed, your magic breath is powerful!" muttered the warriors in great awe.

"Retreat from the doorway and windows until the wind has time to sweep my magic breath away," commanded the snake man.

A gentle breeze had sprung up, slightly stronger in the streets of the Mayan city than elsewhere. In ten minutes, the serpent man decided all the gas had been swept out of the stone house.

"Go in!" he directed. "Seize the bronze devil and drag him to the street!"

His orders were complied with. It was, however, with the greatest fear that the red-fingered ones laid hands upon the magnificent bronze form of Doc Savage. Even though the great figure was still and limp, they feared it.

In the street, they dropped the bronze giant hastily.

"Cowards!" sneered the snake man. He was quite brave now. "Can you not see he has succumbed to my magic? He is helpless! Never again will he defy the son of Kukulcan, the Feathered Serpent!"

The red-fingered Mayans did not look as relieved as they might. All too well, they remembered an occasion when Doc had brought three of his white companions out of the sacrificial well, very much alive, when they should have been dead. Doc might do the same for himself, they reasoned.

"Fetch tapir-hide thongs!" commanded the snake man. "Bind him. Not with a few turns, but with many! Tie him until he is a great bundle of tapir thongs!"

The warriors hurried to obey. They returned, bearing long strings of the tough hide.

"Fear him not!" said the serpent man. "My magic breath has stricken him, so that he will lie helpless for two hours."

The fellow had profited by talking to the victim of Monk's gas. He had learned about how long its effects lasted.

"I shall go now to send my magic breath into the interior of the pyramid!" snarled the snake man. "Six of you remain here and bind the bronze devil. Bind him well! Death shall strike all six of you if he escapes! He is to be sacrificed to the Feathered Serpent."

With that warning, the fellow departed, the long, feather-studded snake tail scraping behind him. He was even more sinister than the reptilian monster after which he was disguised.

He moved from view.

The six evil Mayans seized their festoons of tapir-hide thongs and leaned over to lay violent hands on Doc. They got the shock of their lives.

STEEL talons seemed to trap the throats of two. Another pair bounced away, driven by pistoning bronze legs.

At no time had Doc Savage been unconscious.

Monk's remarkable gas depended for its action upon inhalation. Unless some of it penetrated to the lungs, the stuff was quite ineffective.

Because of his conscientious exercises, Doc had lungs of tremendous capacity. An ordinary man can, by straining himself, usually hold his breath about a minute. Several minutes is not uncommon for pearl divers in the South Seas. And Doc Savage, thanks to years of practice, could hold his breath fully twice as long as the most expert pearl diver.

He had held his breath all the while the snake man was waiting for the gas fumes to blow from the stone house.

By this ruse, which only he could manage, Doc had escaped being shot on the spot.

Doc shook the two Mayans whose throats he held. He brought their heads together, knocking their senses out. The other two were tangled in the tapir-hide strands, trying to reach their obsidian knives.

Using the two men in his hands as human clubs, Doc beat the others down. The two his powerful legs had knocked away had collapsed where they fell.

A single piercing squawl of agony, one warrior managed to emit. Then all six were sprawled unconscious in the stone-paved street.

Doc straightened. Into the stone house he leaped. He would only have a moment. That yell of the red-fingered man would spread an alarm.

The metal case which contained Monk's chemicals was not behind the stone bench where Monk had kept it.

Doc was disappointed. He had hoped to get enough chemicals to rig up gas masks effective against Monk's remarkable vapor. But the snake man had evidently appropriated the chemicals.

Out of the building, Doc ran. A machine gun blasted at him from down the narrow street. But it was poorly aimed. The slugs went wide.

Before the serpent-skin-clad man—it was he who had fired—could correct his aim, Doc's metallic form had vanished like smoke. It seemed to float to a building top.

To another roof, Doc leaped, thence onward. Dropping down into a street, he ran several hundred feet.

There, he purposefully let the red-fingered crew glimpse him. He disappeared with lightning speed before they could fire. Howling like a wolf pack, they rushed the spot.

Dozens of them quitted the siege of the pyramid to aid in the chase.

That was what Doc had maneuvered for. It was imperative that he get back into the pyramid and devise something to defend the Mayans against the gas now in the possession of the fiendish warrior sect.

Unseen by any, Doc raced for the pyramid. So silently did he come, and so swiftly, that he was gliding up the steps before they saw him. And then it was too late.

A machine gun cackled angrily. Lead ricocheted off the steps, or splattered like raindrops.

But Doc was already up the stairs and inside the pyramid.

EVEN Renny and the others were a little startled at the suddenness of his appearance. They were awed, too. It was near unbelievable that even Doc could go and come as he had, with four alert machine guns emplaced about the pyramid.

"They have secured Monk's gas," Doc explained. "They'll try to toss bottles of it into the secret doorway exposed by moving the idol."

"Then we'll move the idol back!" Monk grunted.

Straightway, exerting his enormous strength, Monk shifted the massive stone image of Kukulcan back.

A light sprang up below. One of the Mayans had lighted a torch. This was composed of a bowl filled with animal oils and equipped with a wick, not unlike an ordinary lamp. Evidently it had been placed in this weird place for just such an emergency.

"Chink the cracks with mud," Doc directed. "They'll break the glass bottles of the liquid that makes the gas, hoping it will seep inside."

"But what about our peepholes!" Renny objected. "We can't see them if they start up the stairs!"

For answer, Doc reached over and took off Johnny's glasses which had the powerful magnifying lens on the left side.

"Use the right glass—the one that does not magnify," he suggested. "Pack mud around it, and where could you find a better porthole. It will keep the gas out."

"Daggone!" Monk grinned. "I don't believe anything will ever stump Doc!"

The Mayans were stirring about below. Hundreds of them had gone into the pyramid, Doc reflected. There must be something in the nature of an underground room, or perhaps passages below.

"If they throw the gas bottles," Doc told Renny, "they won't rush the steps until they know the fumes have blown away. So when you see them coming, you'll know it is safe to open the secret door and roll rocks down the stairs. You can tell the Mayans to pass up rocks, using sign talk."

"Where you goin'?" Renny wanted to know.

"To explore. I am very curious about this place!"

Chapter XX
GOLDEN VAULTS

DOC SAVAGE took Johnny and Monk with him as he wended into the depths of the golden pyramid.

He was surprised at the amount of wear the steps underfoot showed. In spots, they were pitted to half their depth. It must have taken thousands of human feet to do that.

The sovereign of the Mayans, King Chaac, had said only he knew of the existence of this place. That meant it had not been used extensively for generations—possibly not for hundreds of years. For information about a place such as this would be handed down from father to son for ages.

At a spot which Doc's expert sense of distance told him was several feet below the surface of the surrounding ground, they entered a large room.

Doc noted a cleverly constructed stone pipe which bore the water that fed the pool on top of the pyramid. This crossed the room and vanished into another, larger chamber beyond.

This latter was a gigantic hallway, narrow and low of roof, but of unfathomable length. In fact, it was more of a tremendous tunnel. It stretched some hundreds of yards, then was lost in a turn upward.

Down the middle of it ran the finely constructed stone conduit carrying water.

In this subterranean corridor, King Chaac and pretty Princess Monja waited with their subjects.

The entrancing young Mayan princess had retained her nerve remarkably well during the attack. Her golden skin was a trifle pale, but there was no nervousness in her manner.

King Chaac was maintaining a mien befitting a ruler.

Doc drew the aged Mayan sovereign aside.

"Would you care to guide Johnny and Monk and myself into the depths of this cavern?"

The Mayan hesitated. "I would, gladly! But my people—they might think I had deserted them in their need."

That was good reasoning, Doc admitted. He had about decided to go on alone with Monk and Johnny when King Chaac spoke again.

"My daughter, Princess Monja, knows as much of these underground passages as I do. She can guide you."

That was agreeable to Doc. It seemed very welcome to Princess Monja, too.

They set off at once.

"This has the appearance of having been built and used centuries ago," Doc offered.

Princess Monja nodded. "It was. When the Mayan race was in its glory, rulers of all this great region, they built this tunnel and the pyramid outside. A hundred thousand men were kept working steadily through the span of many lifetimes, according to the history handed down to my father and myself."

Johnny murmured wonderingly. Johnny had been taking notes on bits of little-known Mayan lore, intending to write a book if he ever got time. He probably never would.

Princess Monja continued. "This has been a guarded secret for centuries. It has been handed down through the rulers of the Mayans in the Valley of the Vanished. Only the rulers! Until a few minutes ago, when the attack came, only my father and myself knew of it."

"But why all the secrecy?" Johnny inquired.

"Because word of its existence might reach the outer world."

"Huh?" Johnny was puzzled.

Princess Monja smiled slyly. "Wait. I will show you why knowledge that this existed would inflame the outside world."

They had reached the upswing in the tunnel, having covered many hundred yards. Doc knew they were far under the walls of the chasm that hid the Valley of the Vanished.

Suddenly Princess Monja halted. She pointed and spoke in a voice low and husky.

"There is the reason! There is the gold you are to have, Mr. Savage. The gold you are to expend in doing good throughout the world!"

Johnny and Monk were staring. Their eyes protruded. They were stunned until they could not even voice astonishment.

DOC SAVAGE himself, in spite of his marvelous self-control, felt his head swim.

It was unbelievable!

Before them, the corridor had widened. It became a vast room. Solid rock made walls, floor, roof.

The rock showed veinings of gold! It was the same kind of rock of which the pyramid was made!

But it was not this that stunned them.

It was the row after row of deep niches cut into the walls. Literally hundreds of thousands of the cupboardlike recesses!

In each were stacked golden vessels, plaques, goblets, amulets. Everything the ancient Mayans had made of the precious yellow metal could be seen.

"This is the storeroom," said Princess Monja in a low voice. "Legend has it forty thousand artisans were continuously employed making the articles, which were then stored here."

Doc, Monk, and Johnny hardly heard her. Sight of this fabulous wealth had knocked them blind, deaf, and dumb to everything else.

For the niches held only a fraction of the hoard here! It lay on the floor in heaps. Great stacks of the raw, rich gold! And the treasure cavern stretched far beyond the limits to which their wick-in-a-bowl lamp projected light.

Doc shut his eyes tightly. His bronze lips worked. He was experiencing one of the great moments of his life.

Here was wealth beyond dream. The ransom of kings! But no king could ever pay a ransom such as this! It was enough to buy and sell realms. It was fabulous.

Doc's brain raced. This was the legacy his father had left him. He was to use it in the cause to which his life was dedicated—to go here and there, from one end of the world to the other, looking for excitement and adventure; striving to help those who need help; punishing those who deserve it.

To what better use could it be put?

Pretty Princess Monja, in whose life here in the Valley of the Vanished, gold meant not a thing, spoke.

"The metal was taken from deeper within the mountain. Much yet remains. Much more, indeed, than you see stacked here."

Gradually, the three adventurers snapped the trance which had seized them. They moved forward.

Ahead of them ran the stone pipe which fed water to the pyramid pool.

Monk started to count his steps the length of the treasure vault. He got to three hundred and lost track, his faculties upset by looking at so much gold. The piles seemed to get higher.

Their route narrowed abruptly. The tunnel floor slanted upward steeply. A couple of hundred feet, they nearly crawled. Then they came to a tiny lake, where the stone pipe ended. This was in a small room.

The walls of this room had been but partially hewn by human hands. Water had excavated a great deal. The stream ran on the floor.

Ahead stretched the cavern. It seemed to go on infinitely.

Doc now realized the cavern was partially the work of the underground stream. It probably extended for miles. Originally, the Mayans had found gold in the stream mouth. They had ventured into the cavern, knowing it must have washed out of there.

And they had found this fabulous lode.

PRINCESS MONJA put a query. "Do you wish to go on?"

"Of course," Doc replied. "We are seeking an outlet. Some manner in which the Mayans can escape starvation or surrender."

They continued into the depths. The air was quite cool. There was a wide path, hewn by human hands.

Sizeable stalagmites, like icicles of stone growing upward from the path's middle, showed convincingly that ages had passed since feet had last trod here.

Often, great rocks near blocked the trail. They had fallen from the ceiling. And everywhere, gold inlaid the stone in an ore of fantastic richness.

Doc and his friends had lost interest in the ore. After the vast riches in the storage cavern, nothing could excite them much.

Upward wound the underground stream.

Two hours, they toiled ahead. By then, they had gotten beyond the area of gold ore. There was no path now. No gold glistened in the stone.

The way grew more tortuous. The character of the rock walls changed. Johnny stopped often to examine the formations. Monk ranged off into every cranny they came to, hoping to find an exit.

"There is one, somewhere!" Doc declared. "Not far off, either."

"How can you tell?" Princess Monja wanted to know.

Doc indicated the flame of their torch. It was blowing about in a manner that showed a distinct breeze.

Johnny dropped behind as far as he could, and still kept them in sight. In darkness as he was, he knew he would be more liable to discover an opening into the outer sunlight.

For the same reason, Monk went ahead. The hairy anthropoid of a fellow had more confidence in his ability to get over unknown ground.

Doc was himself an interested observer of the formations of rock through which they were now passing. A villainous, yellowish-gray deposit attracted him. He scratched it with a thumbnail, and burned a little in the torch flame. It was a sulphur deposit.

"Sulphur," he repeated aloud. But no solution to their troubles presented.

They came soon to a rather large side cavern. The formation was mostly limestone here.

While they waited, Johnny ventured up the side cavern to explore for an opening. Five minutes passed. Ten.

Johnny returned, shaking his head.

"No luck!" He shrugged.

He was juggling a white, crystalline bit of substance in a hand.

Doc looked at this. "Let me inspect that, Johnny!"

Johnny passed it over. Doc touched the end to his tongue. It had a saline taste.

"Saltpeter," he said. "Not pure, but pure enough."

"I don't understand," Johnny murmured.

Doc recited a formula: "Saltpeter, charcoal, and sulphur! I noticed the sulphur back a short distance. We can burn wood and get the charcoal. What does that add up to?"

Johnny got it. "Gunpowder!"

Even as he exclaimed the word, they received fresh cause for elation.

Monk had gone ahead a hundred yards, exploring. His howl of delight came to them.

"I see a hole—"

MONK'S hole proved to be a rip in solid rock of considerable size. Sunlight blazed through.

Doc, Princess Monja, Johnny, and Monk clambered up to it. They found crude steps, proof the ancient Mayans had known of this exit. They sidled cautiously outside, squinting in the sun glare.

They stood on a shelf. Above, to each side, and below, stretched a sheer wall of rock. It looked almost vertical.

But a close inspection showed a procession of steps leading downward. Only from close range could these be discovered. They offered a way to safety, precarious though it might be.

Doc addressed his companions:

"Monk, you go back inside and start work on that sulphur deposit. Get it out as rapidly as you can. Select the purest stuff." He told Monk where he had noticed the sulphur.

"Johnny, you harvest a supply of the saltpeter. Was there much of it?"

"Quite a little," Johnny admitted.

"Dig it out. I think it is pure enough for our purpose. Maybe we can refine it a little."

Doc turned to pretty Princess Monja. He hesitated, then said: "Monja, you've been a brick."

"What's that?" she asked. Evidently her supply of English slang was limited.

"A wonderful girl," Doc grinned. "Now, will you do something else? It'll save time."

She smiled. "I will do anything you say."

The unmistakable adoration in her voice escaped Doc's notice.

He directed: "Return to the Mayans gathered under the pyramid. Select the most powerful and active among the men, and send them here, along with Long Tom, Renny, and Ham."

"I understand," she nodded.

"One thing more—send along a number of those gold vases. Select those with thick walls, very heavy. Say about fifty of them. Tell Renny, Long Tom, and Ham I want to make bombs out of them. They will know which ones will serve best."

"Bombs of gold!" Monk gulped.

"The only thing handy," Doc pointed out. "And when the men reach you fellows, load them up with the saltpeter and sulphur."

Before departing, Johnny asked a question. "Know where we are?"

Doc smiled and pointed. There was another wall of rock opposite them a few hundred yards. A thousand feet or so below poured a rushing stream.

"We're in the chasm. The Valley of the Vanished is somewhere upstream. And it can't be very far."

"The entrance to the valley is through the chasm, isn't it?" Monk queried.

"It is. Unless you count the new entrance we've just found."

Johnny, impatient, said: "Come on, Princess. Come on, Monk. Let's get going!"

WHEN the three had left him, Doc made his way along the precarious steps to more level footing. He found a patch of jungle. Gathering the proper woods, he selected a spot for making his charcoal where the smoke would not be noticed.

The charcoal oven he built of stone and mortar. Two rocks flinty enough to spark a fire could not be located. So, with a leather string from his mantle, and a curved stick, he made a fire bow. This twirled a stick until friction started a tiny glow. In a moment he had a fire.

The charcoal-manufacturing process was well underway when his friends appeared. They had about a hundred of the most manly Mayan men. And from the way they were laden with golden jars, they might have thought they would not have another chance at the fabulous wealth.

The making of the charcoal was tedious. Work on the saltpeter and sulphur called for a great deal of Doc's vast ingenuity and knowledge.

All that afternoon and through the night, they prepared and mixed.

"We won't rush it," Doc explained. "This time we want to settle this red-fingered warrior menace once and for all."

He was ominously silent a bit, then added: "And one in special—the man in the snake suit."

From time to time, runners dispatched back through the long reaches of the cavern of treasure to its termination beneath the Mayan pyramid reported the defenders holding out successfully.

"They have repulsed several attacks," one messenger brought notice. "One of the fire-spitting snakes the red-fingered men are using brought hurt to our ruler, King Chaac, though."

"Is he hurt bad?" Doc demanded.

"In the leg only. He cannot walk about. But otherwise, he is not in bad shape."

"Who has charge of the defense?" Doc wanted to know.

"Princess Monja."

Monk, who had overheard, grinned from ear to ear. "Now there *is* a girl!"

The bombs were rapidly pushed to completion. Obsidian, glasslike rock flakes were placed in the gold jars. A quantity of the powder was poured in to form a core. The gold, being pure and soft, permitted the jars to be pounded together at the top. The pounding was done carefully.

Fuses offered a problem. Doc solved that by selecting lengths of a tough tropical vine which had a soft core. Using long, hardwood twigs, he poked out the core, leaving a hollow tube. One of these he left extending down into the powder of each bomb.

Making use of his vast fund of knowledge, Doc concocted a slow-burning variety of the gunpowder. He filled the improvised fuses with this, after experiments to see what lengths were proper.

With the first silvery glow of dawn, Doc led the attacking party on the march.

Some of the Mayans were familiar with the trail into the Valley of the Vanished. It seemed these men had been outside a time or two to further friendly relations with surrounding natives, who, though not pure Mayans after the passage of these centuries, were of Mayan ancestry. Hence the friendship with the lost clan.

Through the treacherous entrance to the valley, the grim little cavalcade worked. There was no lookout posted at the chasm path—the first time that had happened in centuries, a Mayan muttered.

Since the lookouts were usually red-fingered warriors, Doc understood how the snake man had been able to come and go, unnoticed.

Without revealing themselves to the besieging warriors, they closed in. The Mayans understood how to light the bombs. They carried smoldering pieces of punklike wood.

At Doc's signal, an even dozen bombs rained upon the red-fingered killers.

Chapter XXI
THE GOLDEN DEATH

THUNDEROUS explosion of those twelve bombs was the first warning those of the warrior sect had of the attack.

Doc had apportioned three explosive missiles to each of the four emplaced machine guns. He had instructed his Mayan followers in the art of hurling grenades. Just how well was instantly evident.

All four rapid-fire guns went out of commission at once!

The devilish warriors, rent and torn by the obsidian shrapnel, were tossed high into the air. Many perished instantly, paying in a full measure for their murderous attack on the Mayan citizenry during the ceremonials.

But plenty remained to put up a fierce fight.

And some had the guns which had belonged to Doc and his friends!

With piercing howls, the Mayans fell upon the surviving rascals. They bombed them wherever four or five were together.

Monk had picked up two stout clubs en route. One in either hand, he laid about with terrific results.

Renny needed no more than his great iron fists. Long Tom, Ham, and Johnny stood off and pitched bombs wherever opportunity presented.

Doc, his golden eyes throwing glances seemingly everywhere at once, moved back and forth through the combat. Time after time, red-fingered fiends dropped before his skill and strength without even knowing what manner of blow had downed them.

The great stone likeness of Kukulcan atop the pyramid gave a sudden lurch to one side, uncovering the secret entrance to the mammoth treasure vault of ancient Maya.

Tribesmen poured out. Roaring for vengeance on the red-fingered ones, they flooded down the pyramid stairs. Some fell in their excitement. They bounded up unhurt. Rocks, sticks, anything handy, they seized for the fray.

A spike of steel poked furtively out of a clump of jungle shrubs. It was the snout of a machine gun. It snarled two shots, four—

A bronze hand closed on the warming barrel. A hand with the strength of alloy steel. It jerked. The gunman, a finger unluckily hung in the trigger guard, was hauled out of the tropical foliage.

A warrior! The man probably never saw for sure it was Doc Savage who had seized the weapon. A block of bronze knuckles belted the man's temple. He went to his spirit hunting grounds as suddenly as Mayan man ever did.

Doc was disappointed. He had hoped to get the snake man or Morning Breeze. The machine gun was one of Doc's own weapons. He tossed it to Renny.

Rapidly, Doc glided among the combatants. His attitude was detached, disinterested. He showed fight only when tackled. Then the consequences were invariably disastrous.

Doc was hunting the man masquerading in the serpent skin. He wanted Morning Breeze, too. Both had warranted his wrath.

DOC perceived shortly that the snake man and Morning Breeze were not taking part in the battle.

With this discovery, Doc slid over and was swallowed by the luxuriant tropical leafage. He had an idea the two leaders were skulking somewhere until they saw the outcome of the battle. Around the scene of the engagement, Doc skirted. No one saw him.

Fully half of the red-fingered men had now perished. The Mayan populace, terribly incensed, were giving no quarter. The sect of warriors was being wiped out forever.

Nowhere about the battlefield could Doc find the two he sought.

He began a second search—and found the trail. The tracks of two men! The mark left by the dragging serpent tail identified them with certainty.

Like a hound on a scent, Doc followed the spoor. Most of the time the tracks were lost to the eye of an ordinary observer. The snake man and Morning Breeze had taken the greatest care to conceal them. They went down rocky gullies. They even waded a distance in the lake edge.

It was plain the pair had fled the moment they saw their cause was lost.

They were seeking to fly from the Valley of the Vanished! Their course was set directly for the entrance trail in the chasm.

Doc suddenly abandoned the tracking process. He had been moving swiftly, but it was like the wind he now traveled. He knew whence they were bound. Straight for the chasm exit, he sped.

The snake man and Morning Breeze beat him there!

The villainous pair had been running. They had perspired. They had left the smell of sweat on rocks they touched with their hands. So precarious was the route that they were continually clutching handholds.

Into the chasm, Doc swung. He traversed fifty yards, then stopped to kick off his high-backed Mayan sandals. He needed a delicate touch on this fearsome trail. The way slanted upward.

A few hundred feet below, the little stream threshed and plunged. So tortuous was his channel that the water became a great, snarling rope of white foam.

Doc caught sight of his quarry. The pair were ahead. They looked back—discovered Doc about the same time he saw them.

Over the bawl of the water through the chasm, Morning Breeze's scream of terror penetrated. It was a piping wail of fear.

The snake man still wore his paraphernalia. Probably there had not been time to take it off. He wheeled at Morning Breeze's shriek.

Evidently they thought Doc had a gun.

Morning Breeze, cowardly soul that he was,

sought madly to get past the snake man. There was not room on the trail for that.

Angered, the snake man slugged Morning Breeze with his fist. The Mayan warrior chief fought back. The fellow in the serpent garb struck again.

Morning Breeze was knocked off the trail.

OVER and over spun the squat, vicious Mayan's body. It struck a rock spur. Morning Breeze probably died then. If he did, he was saved the terror of watching the rock-fanged bottom of the abyss reach for him. The foaming river was like slaver on those ravenous stone teeth.

Thus, indirectly, did mere terror of Doc bring death to Morning Breeze.

The snake man continued onward. He had one of Doc's pistol-like machine guns. It could be seen hanging at his belt. But he did not try to use it. No doubt he thought he would let Doc get closer.

The chase resumed. Doc did not go as swiftly now. He was unarmed. Wily, he was biding his time. His great brain sought a plan.

A mile was traversed. Better than two more! The chasm walls became a vague bit less steep. The stone was crisscrossed with tiny weather cracks. Most of these were no wider than pencils.

Doc suddenly quitted the trail. He had another plan.

Upward, he worked. Where seemingly no possible foothold offered, he clung like a fly. His steel fingers, his mobile and powerful feet, materialized solid support where the eye said there was none.

Doc could make the barest projection support his weight, thanks to his highly developed sense of balance.

The speed he made was astounding. Nearly a thousand feet above the snake man, Doc passed the fellow. He went on. His course was now downward, so as to intercept his quarry.

Doc found the sort of a spot he sought. The trail rounded a sharp angle. A thousand feet below, hundreds above, was almost vertical stone. Doc waited around the angle.

Before long, he heard the hard, rattling breath of the snake man. The fellow was nearly exhausted.

The man was looking back as he came around the angle in the trail, wondering if Doc had come closer.

Doc reached out a great, bronzed steel hand. The long, powerful fingers closed over the snake man's gun belt. They jerked downward. Like an aged string, the gun belt snapped before that tremendous strength. Doc tossed gun and belt into the abyss.

Only when he felt the terrific wrench about his middle did the snake man turn his head and discover Doc. He had thought his Nemesis was behind him.

The man had removed his serpent-head mask. His features were disclosed.

THERE was a terrible silence for a moment.

Then, coming from everywhere, and yet nowhere, arose a low trilling sound. Like the song of some exotic bird it was, or the sound of wind filtering through pinnacles of ice. It had an amazing quality of ventriloquism.

Even looking directly at Doc's lips, one would not realize from whence the sound emanated.

It was doubtful if Doc even knew he was making the sound. For it was the small, unconscious thing he did in moments of utter concentration. It could mean many things. Just now it was a sign of victory.

The very calmness of the terrible quality in that whistling sound made the snake man tremble from head to foot. The fellow's mouth worked. But words would not come. He took a backward step.

Doc did not move. But his inexorable golden eyes seemed to project themselves toward his quarry. They were merciless. They chilled. They shriveled. They promised awful things.

Those eyes, far better than words could have, told the snake man what he could expect.

He tried to speak again. He tried to make his nerveless legs carry him in flight. He couldn't.

Finally, by a tremendous effort, he did the one thing that could get him away from those terrifying eyes of Doc's.

The snake man jumped off the trail!

Slowly, his body spun on its way to death. The face was a pale, grotesque mask.

It was the face of Don Rubio Gorro, secretary of state of the republic of Hidalgo.

Chapter XXII
TREASURE TROVE

GREAT was the jubilation when Doc Savage returned to his Mayan friends in the Valley of the Vanished. Doc's five men gave him a tumultuous welcome. King Chaac's wound proved to be minor.

"We cleaned the slate!" Monk grinned. "Not a red-fingered warrior survived."

Elderly King Chaac put in with a firm declaration. "The sect of red-fingered men will never be permitted to revive. Henceforth, we shall punish minor criminals by making them mine the gold. The most manly of our men will do whatever fighting has to be done."

So jovial did the Mayans feel that they insisted the ceremony of inducting Doc and his friends into the clan be picked up at once where it had been interrupted.

The rituals went through without a hitch.

"This makes us members of the lodge," Ham chuckled, eyeing the gaudy Mayan trappings they wore. Fresh clothing had been supplied.

Renny, whom Doc had dispatched to check over their plane, returned.

"The ship is O. K.," he reported. "And thanks to the big supply of gasoline we started out with, there's plenty left to take us to Blanco Grande."

"You are not leaving so soon?" King Chaac inquired sorrowfully.

And entrancing Princess Monja, standing near, looked as disappointed as a pretty young lady could.

Doc did not answer immediately. It was with genuine unwillingness that he had resolved to depart at once. This Valley of the Vanished was an idyllic spot in which to tarry. One could not desire more comforts than it offered.

"I would like to remain—always," he smiled at the Mayan sovereign. "But there is the work to which my life and the lives of my friends are dedicated. We must carry on, regardless of personal desires."

"That is true," King Chaac admitted slowly. "It is the cause to which goes the gold from the treasure trove of ancient Maya. Have you any further instructions about how the wealth should be moved? We will send it by burro train to Blanco Grande, to whoever you designate as your agent—"

"To Carlos Avispa, President of Hidalgo," Doc supplied. "It would be difficult to find a more honorable man than he. I shall designate him my agent."

"Very well," nodded the Mayan.

Doc repeated the other details. "A third of the gold I shall use to establish a gigantic trust fund in America. It shall be for the Mayan people, to be used should they ever have need of it. One fifth goes to the government of Hidalgo. The rest is for my cause."

Preparations for departure now got underway.

Long Tom, the electrical wizard, at Doc's command, rigged a radio receiving set in the palace of the Mayan sovereign. The current for this was supplied by a small generator and waterwheel which Long Tom installed beside the stream flowing from the pyramid top. He made the work very solid. The set should function perfectly for years. He left spare tubes.

With long-lasting ink, Doc made a mark on the radio dial. This designated a certain wavelength.

"Tune in at that spot every seventh day," Doc commanded King Chaac. "Do so at the hour when the sun stands directly above the Valley of the Vanished. You will hear my voice sometimes. But not always, by any means. I shall broadcast to you at that hour—but only when we are in need of more gold. Then you are to send a burro train of the precious metal to me."

"It shall be done," agreed the Mayan ruler.

PRETTY PRINCESS MONJA was a sensible girl. She saw bronze, handsome Doc Savage was not for her. So she made the best of it. Bravely, she hid her disappointment within her bosom.

She even discussed it philosophically with homely Monk.

"I suppose he will find some American girl," she finished, with a catch.

"Now you listen," Monk said seriously. "There won't be any women in Doc's life. If there was, you'd be the one. Doc has come nearer falling for you than for any other girl. And some pippins have tried to snare Doc."

"Is that the truth?" Princess Monja demanded coyly.

"So help my Aunt Hannah if it ain't!" Monk declared.

Then Monk got the shock of his eventful life. Princess Monja suddenly kissed him. Then she fled.

Monk stared after her, grinning from ear to ear, carefully tasting the young Mayan princess's kiss on his lips.

"Gosh! What Doc is passin' up!" he ejaculated.

Two days later, Doc Savage and his five men took their departure. Their sturdy plane battled the air currents up out of the Valley of the Vanished.

Their regret at leaving the idyllic paradise was assuaged by the thought of what was ahead of them. The yearning for adventure and excitement warmed them. Wealth untold was in their hands. It was ample for even their great purpose in life.

Many parts of the world would see the coming of this bronze man and his five friends of iron. Many a human fiend would rue the day he pitted himself against them. Countless rightful causes would receive help from their powerful hands and superbly trained minds.

Indeed, these men were destined hardly to reach New York before new trouble struck them like lightning bolts. They were to meet Kar—with his horrible schemes and a fighting weapon such as civilization never saw!

The giant bronze man and his five friends would confront undreamed of perils as the very depths of hell itself crashed upon their heads.

They would spend terrible days and ghastly nights in a lost land infested by ferocious prehistoric reptilian monsters and flying horrors. A land which they found exactly as it had been countless ages ago! A fearsome, bloodcurdling land where survival of the fiercest was the only law!

And through all that, the work of Savage would go on!

THE END

INTERMISSION by Will Murray

The origins of Doc Savage are not easy to piece together. Lester Dent sometimes claimed to have created the character. Yet his editor John L. Nanovic placed most of the credit on the broad shoulders of Street & Smith's brilliant business manager, Henry William Ralston.

"We grabbed him right out of thin air," Ralston recalled. "We made him a surgeon and scientist, because we wanted him to know chemistry, philosophy, and all that stuff. We also made him immensely wealthy—he'd inherited a huge fortune from his father. He crusaded against crime of all kinds—plots against the United States, against industry, against society at large. He was very strong physically, a giant man of bronze with eyes whose pupils resembled pools of flake gold, always in gentle motion. You might say he was the poor man's Monte Cristo."

Dent put it this way: "I suppose I created the character of Doc Savage, although that is hardly an allowable claim. Doc seems to be an unconscious composite of the physical qualities of Tarzan of the Apes, the detective ability of Sherlock Holmes, the scientific sleuthing mastery of scientific dick Craig Kennedy, and the morals of Jesus Christ."

Norma Dent, Lester's widow, probably had it right when she said, "It came from a combination of minds, not only Les but his editor and others as well."

The truth was that Doc Savage was not so much created as developed, and even after being presented to the Depression reading public early in 1933, the character continued to evolve until he was perfected.

The trigger was *The Shadow*, which pulp magazine powerhouse Street & Smith released in 1931. By the beginning of 1932, it was selling so well plans were made to issue it twice every month. The Shadow was to become the nucleus around which a new generation of pulp heroes would coalesce.

"The Shadow was going so good, it fooled hell out of everybody," writer Walter Gibson explained.

Henry W. Ralston and John L. Nanovic

"Ralston wanted to start another adventure magazine, but for a long time he didn't even have a title."

Ralston reached back into his youth for inspiration. He recalled a former Street & Smith writer of the previous century, a hero of the Spanish-American War who had been an amazing combination of soldier, engineer, attorney and diplomat. Richard Henry Savage, known to intimates as Dick Savage, was transmuted into a superhero for the 20th century, Doc Savage.

"... the beginning of Doc Savage was in the mind of Mr. Ralston," insisted Nanovic, who helped develop the concept. "When he brought this up with me, one lunch, he had all the characters in mind, with names and descriptions. He also had the purpose of Doc Savage strongly in his mind, and passed all this on to me, and then to Lester Dent."

Dent was a bright new star in the pulp-paper firmament. In the field only two years, he was bucking the Depression. Early in '32, Street & Smith approached him to write a Shadow novel to test his ability to do the kind of fiction they wanted. After turning in *The Golden Vulture* that July, Dent went on an extended vacation touring the U. S. Southwest and Mexico. The Depression was deepening. The pulp-magazine industry wallowed in the doldrums. Street & Smith was canceling magazines left and right. Plans for the new hero were put on hold.

Over the summer, Dent panned for gold all over the Far West. He visited Death Valley, California. There, lived a fabulous personage known as the "Mysterious Midas of Death Valley," Walter E. Scott. "Death Valley" Scotty dwelled in a castle built from, it was rumored, the proceeds from a secret gold mine somewhere in the blistering furnace that was Death Valley. The gold mine was guarded by Shoshone Indians who kept Scotty's secret. Dent hoped to interview Scotty, and maybe grab off some loose gold nuggets.

Although Dent returned from his trek with precious little gold, he did harvest a gold mine of ideas for future stories, some of which he would pour into Doc Savage. One of these may have been the image of Doc's flake-gold eyes—inspired by the bottle full of golden flakes panned from Southwestern rivers. Another was the premise of stoic Native Americans guarding the golden hoard of a man of mystery.

"I had dreamed up this idea for Doc Savage," Dent later recounted. "While I wrote and sold other stories—the publishing depression was over enough for me to make a little money—I hounded the Street and Smith people to bring out Doc."

Autumn came. *The Shadow Magazine* started coming out every two weeks. Miraculously, sales held steady. Finally, after the November election that

Doc Savage was inspired by Colonel Richard Henry Savage—engineer, war hero, diplomat, lawyer and author.

catapulted Franklin D. Roosevelt to the Presidency of the beleagured nation, Dent was again called into Street & Smith. Ralston finally felt ready to go ahead with the new adventure magazine.

John Nanovic takes up the tale:

> After one of the discussions with Les, I wrote a condensed version of what Ralston and I thought the first story should be. And Les worked from that.
>
> However, this does not mean that Les Dent did not have a major part in the development and "creation" of Doc Savage. Les put the life and the action into these characters. He made them real, and he made the plots—whether from joint ideas or his own—really zing.

Dent certainly did. Where Ralston had pictured Doc Savage as the supreme adventurer, Lester reimagined him as a virtual superman he dubbed the Man of Bronze. And the character blueprint, "Doc Savage, Supreme Adventurer," was brimming with Lester Dent concepts, including a skyscraper headquarters, an idea he'd been using in another series about a scientific detective named Lynn Lash.

Although Ralston did indeed conceive Doc Savage and his comrades of iron, Dent clearly recast them in the fertile fires of his own imagination. Many of his earlier pulp heroes were identical to big-fisted Renny Renwick, for example, whom Nanovic recalled was added late in the year-long creative process. Any number of apish characters nicknamed "Monk" cavorted through Dent stories, although they were invariably bad guys.

One of the most critical contributions Dent made, and which Nanovic incorporated into "Doc Savage, Supreme Adventurer," is the Mayan backstory that lies behind Doc's origin. Lester had set several of his pre-Doc Savage soldiers of fortune off in search of Mayan gold and treasure. The extinct Central American empire fascinated him.

Nanovic recalled, "That whole Mayan thing was Dent's, I'm sure, because he was the expert on that, and knew all about it."

The roots of Dent's interest in Mayan lore are unknown. In 1946, he touched on it in a letter to a correspondent:

> A long time ago, 1934 to be exact, I did a little exploration of some of the Yucatan Mayan ruins, but not being an archeologist or anthropologist, what stuff I dug up was mostly interesting rather than contributing much to scientific knowledge of the subject. It is a fascinating thing, and some hair-raising thoughts can be connected to the vanishing of the race, the reason for which is still mysterious. Have you ever heard this angle to it—the Mayans, it is believed, began going to wherever they went—vanishing—about the twelfth century; and almost simultaneously, our own cliff-dwellers in the Mesa Verde vanished with equal mystery, although in the latter case the cause has been attributed to a terrific drouth of long duration. The two cultures had many similarities, although the cliff-dwellers might be considered heathen outlanders, for they did not approach the Mayan culture in perfection.
>
> Sometime I plan to go back down there primed with more time to work. In the meantime, I still hack out an occasional yarn with the locale, although not many lately.

Dent had explored the cliff ruins in Arizona's Painted Desert and Mesa Verde, and visited Venezuela in 1933. When he joined the Explorers Club in 1936, his sponsor, pulp writer J. Allan Dunn, listed one of Dent's qualifications thusly: "1935, Caribbean, investigating reports Mayan civilization existent on cays, concluding that such relics were cached by crews of old-time ships." Lester planned to look at Mexico's Mayan ruins in 1938, but it's not recorded whether or not he did. During the summer of 1939, he poked about a different pueblo section of Mesa Verde.

Probably Ralston and Nanovic were unaware of it, but the plot for *The Man of Bronze* went back to an incomplete outline Dent had been working on at the very beginning of his career. Entitled "The Green Gods of Kukulkhan," it told the tale of adventurer Cramer Dorn, who discovers a lost city of golden-skinned Mayans in Old Mexico. They dwell in the Valley of Eternity, and claim to be

Lester Dent, Summer 1932

descendants of the people of "Calantis"—which Dent clearly meant to evoke Atlantis. The essential character conflict is similar—a Mayan priestess pitted against an evil pretender to the throne.

Cramer Dorn was the hero of his third published story, *Buccaneers of the Midnight Sun.* The reason Dent abandoned this planned serial is obscure. But unquestionably, Lester dusted it off in 1932, recreating from its unfinished pages the Valley of the Vanished, Princess Monja and the others. He left out the echoes of Atlantis, but would return to it several times in the Doc Savage adventures to come.

But these were just some of the trappings Dent brought to Ralston's original idea.

"Now, where did Ralston get the idea?" Nanovic once mused. "I think he simply got it from his reading, and his thinking. He was an extremely well-read man. This group of men might have come to mind because of some similar group he read about.

"But he was also a very imaginative man, and it is just possible that this group, etc., came right out of his imagination.

"The fact remains that he initiated it; he kept his finger on it; and he made Doc Savage so good and so important because of his interest in it."

Nanovic didn't possess Ralston's encyclopedic knowledge of prior S&S heroes, so he didn't know that the original Nick Carter, who was trained by his father to become the world's greatest detective, provided the basis of Doc's purpose in life. When Carter's own father is murdered, Nick Carter begins his career in earnest, just as a generation later Doc Savage would as well.

Certainly other S&S pulp heroes contributed to the amalgam that became the Man of Bronze. There was the South Seas Tarzan called Kroom who appeared in Street & Smith's *Top-Notch Magazine* in 1930-31. Various writers wrote his adventures under the house name of "Valentine Wood." No doubt Kroom's prodigious ability to hold his breath underwater was inherited by Doc.

Ten years before Doc, Erle Stanley Gardner penned a series for *Top-Notch* featuring a heroic Human Fly named Speed Dash. To keep himself in top shape, Dash performed daily exercises that began with squeezing raw potatoes into pulp until he could climb brick buildings with iron-fingered ease. This was followed by an elaborate "mental gymnasium" designed to give Speed superhuman memory powers. These were the ancestors of Doc's daily exercise routine, and the bronze man's own skill at climbing tall buildings barehanded.

But Speed Dash was an important Doc Savage precursor in another way. Gardner recalled that an unnamed S&S executive took *Top-Notch* editor Arthur E. Scott aside after the first Speed Dash story was printed:

"Listen," he said, "we're trying to inspire youth. We're trying to get the confidence of parents. Take this guy Speed Dash and make him into a series character. Tell the author you can use more stories, provided he makes it apparent that Speed Dash gets his almost superhuman powers because he lives a pure life. Get it? We inspire the youth of the country! Speed Dash neither smokes, drinks, nor chases. He lives a life of exemplary purity, and because he leads this pure life, he is able to bring his splendid body to such a high pitch of physical fitness that he can climb these buildings. Get it?"

Doubtless that executive was Ralston, who remembered the days when Street & Smith dime novels were forbidden reading for children. Avoiding that same stigma with the pulps was foremost in his mind.

And no doubt it was Ralston or Nanovic's idea to name Doc after one of Hollywood's most successful movie stars, Clark Gable, and order interior artist Paul Orban to depict him as resembling Gable. That was good public relations too.

Clark Gable

For his part, Dent wanted to name Doc himself, but Ralston

1934 house ad for *Doc Savage*

balked. Doc Savage was Street & Smith property and would bear a Street & Smith name.

The Man of Bronze was written at a sprint in December, 1932. Nanovic remembered: "Lester pounced on the idea. He wanted to know when we wanted the story. I told him two weeks. He turned it in ten days later and there was no major change in it."

Dent himself marked the beginning of the Man of Bronze by compiling a dossier of Doc and his aides in a black notebook. The first page reads:

THIS THING STARTED DECEMBER 10, 1932.

Street & Smith issued Dent a check on the 23rd. It was quite a Christmas at the Dent home that year.

There was only one hitch in the birth of Doc Savage: the house name Street & Smith chose to conceal the identity of Lester Dent was "Kenneth Roberts." This did not sit well with the famous historical novelist of the same name. With the next issue, the byline was quietly modified to "Kenneth Robeson"—perhaps as a nod to the black-robed Shadow, since it can truly be said that Doc Savage was the "son" of The Shadow.

In deciding which novel to reprint with *The Man of Bronze,* many were considered, but the final choice was *The Land of Terror,* Doc's second exploit, which Dent turned in a month after the first.

Stylistically, both novels are very different. And therein lies a mystery.

Did Ralston instruct Dent to write *The Man of Bronze* like a turn-of-the-century Nick Carter dime novel? Or emulate a contemporary boys' book in the vein of the popular Hardy Boys? Or as Walter Gibson did in *The Shadow*?

No one living knows. But Dent's first Doc Savage novel is unusually restrained in its telling. Perhaps this is partly due to his having to work from Nanovic's rather dry and reportorial outline. Yet only one issue later the true Lester Dent style emerges in all its cockeyed glory. The difference is arresting.

Mrs. Dent recalled Lester saying early on, "I don't care what old man Ralston says. I'll write it any damn way I choose."

This statement may explain why *The Land of Terror* is the most violent Doc Savage novel Lester Dent ever penned. Here, the bronze man is a vengeful, unstoppable metallic juggernaut, dispensing swift justice in a way that would startle even The Shadow. It was as if Dent suddenly and stubbornly decided to write in his own voice, and on his own terms.

No doubt, reaction to this novel's headlong carnage caused Ralston and Nanovic to rein in Lester over subsequent stories, and demand that Dent temper Doc Savage into a more restrained superhero. In the novels which immediately followed, Nanovic trimmed some of Dent's more violent scenes until a compromise was reached. Out of this evolution emerged various nonlethal tactics such as mercy bullets, anesthetic gas grenades, and others for which Doc Savage is renowned.

Initially, Lester Dent may not have agreed with this approach to pulp fictioneering, but in time he grew to appreciate the wisdom of it. Doc Savage became one of the pulp magazine successes of the Great Depression.

And now you know why Doc Savage turned out the way he did.

Early in Dent's career, he wrote a story called *Time's Domain,* about a tropical area in the Arctic where prehistoric life continued to thrive. Although the story was never published, and the manuscript no longer survives, odds are Dent ransacked it when writing *The Land of Terror.*

Outlined as "The Mountain of Terror," this second Doc Savage exploit, teeming with dinosaurs, had the good fortune to break into print in the early weeks of RKO's initial release of *King Kong.* Or perhaps it was planned that way. Prerelease publicity on *King Kong* had been gearing up for months, and was surely known in the halls of Street & Smith. Think of Thunder Island as Dent's version of Skull Island.

For his second *Doc Savage Magazine* cover, artist Walter M. Baumhofer played up Renny Renwick, whom Dent early on painted as Doc's right-hand man. As the series wore on, that role naturally fell to Monk Mayfair—who may have been based on Clark Gable's *Hell Divers* costar, Wallace Beery, one of Dent's favorite actors.

We're restored *The Man of Bronze* slightly for this 75th anniversary edition. *The Land of Terror* required no restoration. Although it packs enough plot for two Doc novels, amazingly nothing was cut from it.

Here are Doc Savage's formative first exploits, in print together at last! •

Doc Savage, scrapper supreme, with his five companions, braves danger and death in

The LAND of TERROR

A COMPLETE BOOK-LENGTH NOVEL

By KENNETH ROBESON

Chapter I
THE SMOKING DEATH

THERE were no chemists working for the Mammoth Manufacturing Company who could foretell future events. So, as they watched white-haired, distinguished Jerome Coffern don hat and topcoat after the usual Friday conference, none knew they were never to see the famous chemist alive again.

Not one dreamed a gruesome right hand and a right forearm was all of Jerome Coffern's body that would ever be found.

Jerome Coffern was chief chemist for the Mammoth concern. He was also considered one of the most learned industrial scientists in the world.

The Mammoth Manufacturing Company paid Jerome Coffern a larger salary than was received by the president of the corporation. It was Jerome Coffern's great brain which gave the Mammoth concern the jump on all its competitors.

Jerome Coffern plucked back a sleeve to eye a watch on his right wrist. This watch was later to identify the grisly right hand and forearm as Coffern's.

"I wonder how many of you gentlemen have heard of Clark Savage?" he inquired.

Surprise kept the other chemists silent a moment. Then one spoke up.

"I recall that a man by the name of Clark Savage recently did some remarkable work along lines of ultimate organic analysis," he said. "His findings were so advanced in part as to be somewhat bewildering. Some points about chemistry generally accepted as facts were proven wrong by Clark Savage."

Jerome Coffern nodded delightedly, rubbing his rather bony hands.

"That is correct," he declared. "I am proud to point to myself as one of the few chemists to realize Doc Savage's findings- are possibly the most important of our generation."

At this juncture, another chemist gave an appreciable start.

"Doc Savage!" he ejaculated. "Say, isn't that the man who some weeks ago turned over to the surgical profession a new and vastly improved method of performing delicate brain operations?"

"That is the same Doc Savage." Jerome Coffern's none-too-ample chest seemed about to burst with pride.

"Whew!" exploded another man. "It is highly unusual for one man to be among the world's greatest experts in two lines so widely different as chemistry and surgery."

Jerome Coffern chuckled. "You would be more astounded were you to know Doc Savage fully. The man is a mental marvel. He has contributed new discoveries to more than surgery and chemistry. Electricity, archaeology, geology and other lines have received the benefit of his marvelous brain. He has a most amazing method of working."

Pausing, Jerome Coffern gazed steadily at the assembled men. He wanted them to understand he was not exaggerating.

"As I say, Doc Savage has a most amazing method of working," he continued. "At intervals, Savage vanishes. No one knows where he goes. He simply disappears as completely as though he had left the earth. And when he returns, he nearly always has one or more new and incredible scientific discoveries to give to the world.

"It is obvious Doc Savage has a wonderful laboratory at some secret spot where he can work in solitude. Nobody can even guess where it is. But any scientific man would give half a lifetime to inspect that laboratory, so remarkable must it be."

The eminent chemist smiled from ear to ear. "And I will add more. You will, perhaps, find it hard to believe. I have said Doc Savage is a mental marvel. Well, he is also a muscular marvel as well. He has a body as amazing as his brain.

"His strength and agility are incredible. Why, for Doc Savage it is child's play to twist horseshoes, bend silver half-dollars between thumb and forefinger and tear a New York telephone directory in half.

"Were Doc Savage to become a professional athlete, there is no doubt in my mind but that he would be the wonder of all time. But he will not employ his astounding strength to earn money, because he is one of those very rare persons—a genuinely modest man. Publicity and world-wide fame do not interest him at all."

Jerome Coffern halted abruptly, realizing his enthusiasm was getting away with his dignity. He reddened.

"I could not resist the temptation to tell you of this remarkable man," he said proudly. "Doc Savage studied under me many years ago. He quickly learned all I knew. Now his knowledge is vastly beyond mine."

He tugged back his right sleeve to display the watch.

"This timepiece was presented to me by Doc Savage at that time, as a token of gratitude," he smiled. "I am proud to say he is still my friend."

Jerome Coffern gave his topcoat a final straightening tug.

"I am on my way now to have dinner with Doc Savage," he smiled. "He is to meet me in front of the plant immediately. So I shall now bid you gentlemen good afternoon." The eminent chemist quitted the conference room.

It was the last time his colleagues saw him alive.

THE plant of the Mammoth Manufacturing Company was located in New Jersey, only a short distance from the great new George Washington Bridge across the Hudson River into New York City.

The brick buildings of the plant were modern and neat. Spacious grounds surrounded them. Shrubbery grew in profusion and was kept neatly trimmed. The walks were of concrete.

Standing on the high steps in front of the building where the conference of chemists had been held, Jerome Coffern glanced about eagerly. He was anxious to get a glimpse of the man he considered the most remarkable in the world—his friend, Doc Savage.

It was perhaps a hundred yards across a vista of landscaped shrubbery to the main highway.

A car stood on the highway. It was a roadster, very large and powerful and efficient. The color was a reserved gray.

Seated in the car was a figure an onlooker would have sworn was a statue sculptured from solid bronze!

The effect of the metallic figure was amazing. The remarkably high forehead, the muscular and strong mouth, the lean, corded cheeks denoted a rare power of character. The bronze hair was a shade darker than the bronze skin. It lay straight and smooth.

The large size of the roadster kept the bronze man from seeming the giant he was. Too, he was marvelously proportioned. The bulk of his great frame was lost in its perfect symmetry.

Although he was a hundred yards from the bronze man, Jerome Coffern could almost make out the most striking feature of all about Doc Savage.

For the bronze man was Doc Savage. And the most striking thing about him was his eyes. They were like pools of fine flake gold glistening in the sun. Their gaze possessed an almost hypnotic quality, a strange ability to literally give orders with their glance.

Undeniably, here was a leader of men, as well as a leader in all he undertook. He was a man whose very being bespoke a knowledge of all things, and the capacity to dominate all obstacles.

Jerome Coffern waved an arm at the bronze man.

Doc Savage saw him and waved back.

Jerome Coffern hurried forward. He walked with a boyish eagerness. The path he traversed took him through high, dense shrubbery. The bronze figure of Doc Savage was lost to sight.

Suddenly two ratty men lunged from the shrubs.

Before Jerome Coffern could cry an alarm, he was knocked unconscious.

THE blow which reduced the white-haired chemist to senselessness was delivered with a bludgeon of iron pipe about a foot long. The smash probably fractured distinguished Jerome Coffern's skull. He fell heavily to the concrete walk, right arm outflung to one side.

"Put the pipe on top of the body!" hissed one ratty man.

"O. K., Squint!" muttered the other man.

He placed the iron-pipe bludgeon on the chest of prone Jerome Coffern, thrusting one end inside the famous chemist's waistcoat so it would stay there.

The two rodentlike men now retreated a pace. They were excited. A trembling racked their bony, starved hands. Nervous swallowing chased the Adam's apples up and down their stringy necks. The rough, unwashed skin of those necks gave them a turtle aspect.

Squint dived an emaciated claw inside his shirt. The hand clutched convulsively and drew out a strange pistol. This was larger even than a big army automatic. It had two barrels, one the size of a pencil, the other a steel cylinder more than an inch in diameter. The barrels were placed one above the other.

At prone Jerome Coffern's chest, Squint aimed the weapon.

"H-hurry up!" stuttered his companion. The man twitched uneasy glances over the adjacent shrubbery. No one was in sight.

Squint pulled the trigger of the strange pistol. It made a report exactly like a sharp human cough.

An air pistol!

That accounted for the two barrels, one of which, the larger, was in reality the chamber which held the compressed air that fired the gun.

The missile from the air pistol struck the center of Jerome Coffern's chest.

Instantly a puff of grayish vapor arose. It was as though a small cloud of cigarette smoke had escaped from the chemist's body at that point.

No sound of an explosion accompanied the phenomena, however. There was only the dull impact of the air-gun missile striking.

The grayish vapor increased in volume. It had a vile, oily quality. Close to Jerome Coffern's body, it was shot through and through with tiny, weird flashes. These were apparently of an electrical nature.

It was as though a small, foul gray thundercloud were forming about the distinguished chemist's dead body.

About two minutes passed. The repulsive gray fog increased rapidly. It was now like a ball of ash-colored cotton twelve feet thick. From the ground upward about half way, the green and blue and white of the electric sparks played in fantastic fashion.

The whole thing was eerie. It would have baffled a scientific brain.

The balmy spring breeze, whipping along the narrow concrete path, wafted the vile gray cloud to one side.

Both ratty men stared at the source of the cloud.

"It's w-w-workin'!" whined Squint. Stark awe had gripped him. He hardly had the courage to look a second time at the source of the gray vapor.

For Jerome Coffern's body was dissolving!

THE ghastly melting-away effect had started where the mysterious missile from the air pistol had struck.

In all directions from the point of impact, the form of the great chemist was literally turning into the vile grayish vapor. Clothing, skin, flesh and bones—everything was going.

Nor did the dissolution stop with the human body. The concrete walk immediately below was becoming ashen vapor as well. The trowel-smoothed upper surface of the walk was already gone, revealing the coarse gravel below. As by magic, that, too, was wafted away. Rich black earth could be seen.

In the midst of the weird phenomenon glistened a bit of shiny metal. This resembled the crumpled tinfoil wrapper from a candy bar. It alone was not dissolving.

"Let's get outa here, Squint!" whined one of the ratty men. It was obvious from the man's manner that he was getting his first glimpse of the terrible weapon in their possession.

A substance with the power to dissolve all ordinary matter as readily as a red-hot rivet turns a drop of water into steam!

"Aw, whatcha scared of?" sneered "Squint." He pointed a skinny talon at the spot where the iron pipe bludgeon had reposed on Jerome Coffern's chest. "Only thing around here that had our fingerprints on it was that pipe. And it's gone up in smoke."

"I ain't s-scared!" disclaimed the other, trying to snarl bravely. "Only we're two saps to hang around here!"

"Maybe you're right at that," Squint agreed.

With this, the two men fled. The alacrity with which Squint dived into the shrubbery showed he was every bit as anxious as his companion to quit the spot.

Hardly had they gone when the vaporizing of Jerome Coffern's body abruptly ceased. It was apparent that the hideous power of the weird dissolver substance had been exhausted. Only a small quantity could have been contained in the air-pistol cartridge. Yet its effect had been incredible.

Of Jerome Coffern's form, a right hand and forearm remained intact. This right arm had been outflung when the chemist fell after being knocked unconscious. The potency of the dissolver had been exhausted before it reached the hand and forearm. The two ratty men had fled before they noticed this.

On that grisly right wrist was the expensive watch Doc Savage had given Jerome Coffern as a token of gratitude.

The grayish vapor climbed upward in the air like smoke. And like smoke it slowly dispersed.

Chapter II
BRONZE VENGEANCE

DOC SAVAGE, seated in his large and powerful roadster, saw the cloud of grayish vapor lift above the landscaped shrubbery.

Although it was sixty yards distant, his sharp eyes instantly noted an unusual quality about the vapor. It did not resemble smoke, except in a general way.

But at the moment Doc was doing a problem of mathematics in his head, an intricate calculation concerning an advanced electrical research he was making.

The problem would have taxed the ability of a trained accountant supplied with the latest adding machines, but Doc was able, because of the remarkable efficiency of his trained mind, to handle the numerous figures entirely within his head. He habitually performed amazing feats of calculus in this fashion.

Hence it was that Doc did not investigate the cloud of ash-hued fog at once. He finished his mental problem. Then he stood erect in the roadster.

His keen eyes had discerned the play of tiny electric sparks in the lower part of the cloud! That jerked his attention off everything else. Such a thing was astounding.

The rumble of machinery in the nearby manufacturing plant of the Mammoth concern blotted out whatever conversation or sounds which might have arisen in the neighborhood of the weird fog.

Doc hesitated. He expected his old friend, Jerome Coffern, to appear momentarily. There was no sign of the eminent chemist, however.

Doc quitted the roadster. His movements had a flowing smoothness, like great springs uncoiling in oil.

The grounds of the manufacturing plant were surrounded by a stout woven wire fence. This was more than eight feet high and topped off with several rows of needle-sharp barbs. Its purpose was to keep out intruders. A gate nearby was shut, secured by a chain and padlock. No doubt Jerome Coffern had carried a key to this.

Doc Savage approached the fence, running lightly.

Then a startling thing happened.

It was a thing that gave instant insight into Doc Savage's physical powers. It showed the incredible strength and agility of the bronze giant.

For Doc Savage had simply jumped the fence. The height exceeded by more than two feet the world record for the high jump. Yet Doc went over it with far more ease than an average man would take a knee-high obstacle. The very facility with which he did it showed he was capable of a far higher jump than that.

His landing beyond the fence was light as that of a cat. His straight, fine bronze hair was not even disturbed.

He went toward the strange gray cloud. Coming to a row of high shrubs, his bronze form seemed literally to flow through the leaves and branches. Not a leaf fluttered; not a branch shook.

It was a wonderful quality of woodcraft, and Doc did it instinctively, as naturally as a great jungle cat. It came easier to him than shoving through the bushes noisily, this trick he had acquired from the very jungle itself.

Suddenly he stopped.

Before him a pit gaped in the concrete walk. The black, rich earth below the walk was visible.

On this black earth reposed a crumpled bit of metal that resembled wadded tinfoil.

Beside the pit lay a grisly hand and forearm. About the gruesome wrist was an expensive watch.

DOC studied the watch. Strange lights came into his amazing golden eyes.

Of a sudden, a weird sound permeated the surrounding air. It was a trilling, mellow, subdued sound, reminiscent of the song of some strange jungle bird, or the dulcet note of a wind filtering through a leafless forest. Having no tune, it was nevertheless melodious. Not awesome, it still had a quality to excite, to inspire.

This sound was part of Doc—a small, unconscious thing which accompanied his moments of utter concentration. It would come from his lips when a plan of action was being evolved, or in the midst of some struggle, or when some beleaguered friend of Doc's, alone and attacked, had almost given up hope of life. And with the filtering through of that sound would come renewed hope.

The strange trilling had the weird essence of seeming to emanate from everywhere instead of from a particular spot. Even one looking directly at Doc's lips would not realize from whence it arose.

The weird sound was coming now because Doc recognized the watch on that pitiful fragment of an arm.

It was the token he had presented to Jerome Coffern. The eminent scientist had always worn it. He knew this grisly relic was a part of Jerome Coffern's body!

Doc's unique brain moved with flashing speed. Some fantastic substance had dissolved the body of the famous chemist!

The bit of crumpled metal that resembled tinfoil had obviously escaped the ghastly effects of the dissolver material.

Doc picked this up. He saw instantly it was a capsulelike container which had split open, apparently from the shock of striking Jerome Coffern's body.

It was the air-gun missile which had carried the dissolving substance. The metal was of some type so rare that Doc Savage did not recognize it offhand. He dropped it in a pocket to be analyzed later.

Doc's great bronze form pivoted quickly. His golden eyes seemed to give the surrounding shrubbery the briefest of inspections, but not even the misplaced position of a grass blade escaped their notice.

He saw a caterpillar which had been knocked from a leaf so recently it still squirmed to get off its back, on which it had landed. He saw grass which had been stepped on, slowly straightening. The direction in which this grass was bent showed him the course pursued by the feet which had borne it down.

Doc followed the trail. His going was as silent as a breeze-swept puff of bronze smoke. A running man could hardly have moved as swiftly as Doc covered this minute trail.

Things that showed him the trail were microscopic. One with faculties less developed than Doc's would have been hopelessly baffled. The slight deposit of dust atop leaves, scraped off by the fleeing Squint and his companion, would have escaped an ordinary eye. But such marks were all the clues Doc needed.

Squint and his aide had escaped from the factory grounds through a hole they had clipped in the high woven wire fence. Bushes concealed the spot. Doc Savage eased through.

The quarry was not far ahead. Neither of the two fleeing men had taken a bath recently. The unwashed odor of their bodies hung in the air. A set of ordinary nostrils would have failed to detect it, but here again, Doc Savage had powers exceeding those of more prosaic mortals.

Doc glided through high weeds. He reached a road, a little-used thoroughfare.

A score of yards distant, five men had just seated themselves in a touring car. The car engine started.

"How'd it go, Squint?" asked one of the five in the machine.

The man's words, lifted loudly because of the noisy car engine, reached Doc Savage's keen ears. And he heard the reply they received.

"Slick!" replied Squint. "Old Jerome Coffern is where he won't never give us nothin' to worry about!"

The touring car lunged away from the spot, gears squawling.

BEFORE the car had rolled two dozen yards, the ratty Squint looked back. He wanted to see if they were followed.

What he saw made his hair stand on end.

A bronze giant of a man was overhauling the car. The machine had gathered a great deal of speed. Squint would have bet his last dollar no racehorse could maintain the pace it was setting. Yet a bronze, flashing human form was not only maintaining the pace, but gaining!

The bronze man was close enough that Squint could see his eyes. They were strange eyes, like pools of flake gold. They had a weird quality of seeming to convey thoughts as well as words could have.

What those gleaming golden eyes told Squint made him cringe with fear. One of his companions clutched Squint's coat and kept him from toppling out of the car. Squint squealed as though caught in a steel trap.

At Squint's shriek, all eyes but the driver's went backward. The trio who had waited outside the factory grounds while Squint and his companion murdered Jerome Coffern were as terrified as Squint. Their hands dived down to the floorboards of the car. They brought up stubby machine guns.

As one crazed man, they turned the machine gun muzzles on the great bronze Nemesis overtaking them. The guns released a loud roar of powder noise. Lead shrieked. It dug up the road to the rear. It caromed away with angry squawls.

But not one of the deadly slugs was in time to lodge in the bronze frame of Doc Savage. As the first gun snout came into view, he saw the danger. His giant figure streaked to the left. With the first braying burst of shots, tall weeds already had absorbed him.

Squint and his companions promptly fired into the weeds. Doc, however, was dozens of yards from where they thought. Even his overhauling of the car had not made them realize the incredible speed of which he was capable.

"Git outa here!" Squint shrieked at the car driver.

Terror had seized upon Squint's rodent soul. He showed it plainly, in spite of a desire to have his companions think him a man of iron nerve. But they were as scared as Squint, and did not notice.

"W-who w-was it?" croaked one of the five.

"How do I know?" Squint snarled. Then, to the driver, "Won't this heap go any faster?"

The touring car was already doing its limit. Rounding a curve at the end of the factory grounds, it nearly went into the ditch. It turned again, onto the main highway. It headed toward New York, passing in front of the factory buildings.

The speeding machine flashed past a large, powerful roadster. Squint and his companions attached no significance to this car.

But they would have, had they seen the giant bronze man who cleared the factory fence with an incredible leap and sprang into the car. Doc Savage had simply cut back through the factory yard after escaping the machine guns.

Like a thing well trained, Doc's roadster shot ahead. The exhaust explosions came so fast they arose to a shrill wail. The speedometer needle passed sixty, seventy and eighty.

Doc caught sight of Squint and his four unsavory companions. Their touring car was turning into an approach to George Washington Bridge.

THE uniformed toll collector at the New Jersey end of the bridge stepped out to collect his fee. Directly in the path of Squint's racing car, he stood. He expected the car to halt. When it didn't, the toll collector gave a wild leap and barely got in the clear.

An instant later, Doc's roadster also rocketed past.

The toll collector must have telephoned ahead to the other end of the bridge. A cop was out to stop the car.

His shouts and gestures had as much effect as the antics of a cricket before a charging bull. Squint's car dived into New York City and whirled south.

Doc followed. He slouched low back of the wheel. He had taken a tweed cap from a door pocket and drawn it over his bronze hair. And so expertly did he handle the roadster, keeping behind other machines, that Squint and his companions did not yet know they were being followed. The killers had slowed up, thinking themselves lost in the city.

Behind them, a police siren wailed about like a stricken soul. No doubt it was a motorcycle cop summoned by the bridge watchman. But the officer did not find the trail.

Southward along Riverside Drive, the wide thoroughfare that follows the high bank of the Hudson River, the pursuit led.

Squint's touring car veered into a deserted side street. Old brick houses lined the thoroughfare. Their fronts made a wall the same height the entire length of the block. The entrance of each was exactly like all the others—a flight of steps with ornamental iron railings.

Swerving over to the curb before the tenth house from the corner, the touring car stopped. The occupants looked around. No one was in sight.

The floorboards in the rear of the touring car were lifted. Below was a secret compartment large enough to hold the machine guns. Into this went the weapons.

"Toss your roscoes in there, too!" Squint directed. "We ain't takin' no chances, see! A cop might pick us up, and we'd draw a stretch in stir if we was totin' guns."

"But what about that—that bronze ghost of a guy?" one muttered uneasily. "Gosh! He looked big as a mountain, and twice as hard!"

"Forget that bird!" Squint had recovered his nerve. He managed a sneering laugh. "He couldn't follow us here, anyway!"

At that instant, a large roadster turned into the street. Of the driver, nothing but a low-pulled tweed cap could be seen.

Squint and his four companions got out of their touring car. To cover shaky knees, they swaggered and spoke in tough voices from the corners of their mouths.

With a low whistle of sliding tires, the big roadster stopped beside the touring car. The whistle drew the eyes of Squint and his rats.

They saw a great form flash from the roadster; a man-figure that was like an animated, marvelously made statue of metal!

Squint wailed, "Hell! The bronze guy—"

"The rods!" squawled another man. They leaped for their guns in the secret recess below the touring car floorboards. But the bronze giant had moved with unbelievable speed. He was between them and their weapons.

SQUINT and his men gave vent to squeaks of rage and terror. That showed what spineless little bloodsuckers they were. They outnumbered Doc Savage five to one, yet, without their guns, they were like the rats they resembled before the big bronze man.

They wheeled toward the tenth house in the row of dwellings that were amazingly alike. It was as though they felt safety lay there. But Doc Savage, with two flashing sidewise steps, cut them off.

One man tried to dive past. Doc's left arm made a blurred movement. His open hand—a hand on which great bronze tendons stood out as if stripped of skin and softer flesh—slapped against the man's face.

It was as though a steel sledge had hit the fellow. His nose was broken. His upper and lower front teeth were caved inward. The man flew backward, head over heels, limp as so much clothes stuffed with straw.

But he didn't lose consciousness. Perhaps the utter pain of that terrible blow kept him awake.

Doc Savage advanced on the others. He did not hurry. There was confidence in his movements—a confidence that for Squint and his rats was a horrible thing. They felt like they were watching death stalk toward them.

No flicker of mercy warmed the flaky glitter of Doc's golden eyes. Two of these villainous little men had murdered his friend, Jerome Coffern. More than that, they had robbed the world of one of its greatest chemists. For this heinous offense, they must pay.

The three who had not committed the crime directly would suffer Doc's wrath, too. They were hardly less guilty. They would be fortunate men if they escaped with their lives.

It was a hard code, that one of Doc's. It would have curled the hair of weak sisters who want criminals mollycoddled. For Doc handed out justice where it was deserved.

Doc's justice was a brand all his own. It had amazing results. Criminals who went against Doc seldom wound up in prison. They either learned a lesson that made them law-abiding men the rest of their lives—or they became dead criminals. Doc never did the job halfway.

With a frightened, desperate squeak, one man leaped for the car. He tore at the floorboards under which the guns were hidden.

He was the fellow who had helped Squint murder Jerome Coffern.

Doc knew this. Bits of soft earth clinging to the shoes of that man and Squint had told him the ugly fact. The soft earth came from the grounds of the Mammoth factory.

With a quick leap, Doc was upon the killer. His great, bronze hands and corded arms picked the fellow out of the touring car as though he were a murderous little rodent.

The man had secured a pistol. But the awful agony of those metallic fingers crushing his flesh against his bones kept him from using it.

Squint and the others, cowards that they were, sought to reach the tenth house in the row along the street. Lunging and swinging his victim like a club, Doc knocked them back. He was like a huge cat among them.

Squint spun and sped wildly. The other three followed him. They pounded down the street, toward Riverside Drive.

The man Doc held got control over his pain-paralyzed muscles. He fired his gun. The bullet spatted the walk at Doc's feet.

Doc slid a bronze hand upward. The victim screamed as steel fingers closed on his gun fist. He kicked—tore at Doc's chest. One of his hands ripped open the pocket where Doc had placed the capsule of metal that had held the substance which dissolved the body of Jerome Coffern.

The capsule of strange metal flipped across the walk. It fell between the iron-barred cracks of a basement ventilator.

Chapter III
SHIP JUSTICE

DOC SAVAGE saw the metal capsule vanish. He wrenched at the hand of his victim. The pistol the man held was squeezed from the clawlike fist. The fellow had desperate nerve of a sort, now that he was in deadly terror of death. He seized the weapon with his other talon. He jammed the muzzle against Doc's side.

The life of a less agile man than Doc would have come to an end there. But Doc's bronze hand flashed up. It grasped the man's face. It twisted. There was a dull crack and the murderer fell to the walk. A broken neck had ended his career.

Doc could have finished him earlier. He had refrained from doing so for a purpose. Whatever weird substance had dissolved Jerome Coffern's body, a great, if demented scientific brain had developed it. None of these men had such a brain. They were hired killer caliber.

Doc had wanted to question the slayer and learn who employed him. No chance of that now! And Squint and the three others had nearly reached Riverside Drive.

To the iron-barred basement ventilator, Doc sprang. He could see the capsule of strange metal. His great hands grasped the ventilator bars. The metal grille was locked below.

Doc's remarkable legs braced on either side of the ventilator. They became rigid, hard as steel columns. His wonderful arms became tense also. Intermingled with Doc's amazing strength was the fine science of lifting great weights with the human body.

With a loud rusty tearing, the grille was uprooted. Loosened concrete scattered widely.

The feat of strength had taken but a moment. Doc dropped into the ventilator pit. He retrieved the crumpled metal capsule and pocketed it.

Squint and his trio had fled straight across Riverside Drive, dodging traffic. They vaulted the ornamental stone wall that ran along the lip of the high riverbank.

Running easily, but making deceptive speed, Doc pursued. He reached the showy stone parapet.

Below him sloped the nearly clifflike riverbank. It was so steep that grass and shrubs barely managed to cling. Some hundreds of yards down it and across a railroad track lay the Hudson River.

Squint and his three men were leaping and tumbling headlong in their mad haste.

At this point on the Hudson bank stood a couple of rickety piers. To one of these was anchored an ancient sailing ship. The vessel was quite large, a three-master. It was painted a villainous black color. The hull was perforated with numerous gun ports. From some of these, rusty old muzzle-loading cannon projected blunt snouts.

The old ship had a truculent, sinister appearance. Atop the deck house, a large sign stood. It read:

THE JOLLY ROGER
Former Pirate Ship
(Admission Fifty Cents)

Doc Savage vaulted the low stone wall. With prodigious leaps, he descended the precipitous slope.

Squint and his trio were racing for the old pirate vessel.

Doc knew from a Sunday newspaper feature story that the ancient craft had anchored at this spot recently. Curious persons strolling on Riverside Drive, young swains with their girls for the most part, were wont to pay half a dollar to go aboard the unusual ship.

The fiendish instruments of torture the old-time pirates had used on their captives was a chief attraction. The buccaneer craft was supposed to be replete with death traps. Among these was a trap-door which let an unwary stroller down a certain passage fall upon a bed of upturned swords. It was inoperative now, of course.

SQUINT and his men gained the pirate ship a dozen yards ahead of Doc. The last man aboard hauled in the rickety timber that served as a gang-plank.

But that inconvenienced Doc hardly at all. A great leap carried him up twice the height of a tall man to the rail. He poised there a moment, like a bronze monster.

Squint and the others were diving into the deck-house.

Doc dropped aboard.

A revolver cracked from the deckhouse door. Squint and his men had found weapons inside!

Doc had seen the revolver muzzle appear. Twisting aside and down, he evaded the whizzing bullet. A capstan, of hardwood and iron and thick as a small barrel, sheltered him momentarily. From that, a quick leap sent his bronze form down a gaping deck hatch.

He landed ten feet down, lightly as a settling eagle. Rough, aged planks were underfoot. Doc went aft.

The hold was a gruesome place. It had been fit-ted up as an exhibit of pirate butchery. Papier-mâché statues of whiskered buccaneers stood about, holding swords. Figures depicting victims sprawled or kneeled on the planking.

Some were beheaded, with puddles of red wax representing gore. Some were minus ears and arms. A likeness of a beautiful woman hung by chains from the ceiling.

Doc traversed a passage. Cutlasses and pikes reposed on pegs on the walls.

Seized with an idea, Doc grasped a pike and a cutlass. There was nothing fake about the weapons. They were genuine heavy steel. The cutlass was razor keen.

Doc retraced his route. He was in time to see one of his ratty quarry peering into the hatch. The villainous fellow got a glimpse of Doc's bronze form. He fired his revolver.

But Doc had moved. The bullet upset an image of a whiskered pirate. An instant later, the pike whizzed from Doc's long arm.

The steel-shod shaft found accurate lodgment in the gun fiend's brain. The man toppled headlong into the hold. His body, crashing to the floor, sent a gruesome papier-mâché head bouncing across the planks.

While the grisly head still rolled, Doc bounded to a spot below the hatch. Faint noises on the deck had reached his keen ears. One or more of the others were near the hatch.

Suddenly a thin claw shoved a revolver over the hatch lip. The gun exploded repeatedly, driving random bullets to various parts of the hold.

Doc's powerful form floated up from the floor. The razor-edged cutlass swished. The hand that held the revolver seemed to jump off the arm to which it belonged. It was completely amputated.

The maimed wretch shrieked. He fell to the deck.

With a second leap, Doc caught the hatch rim with his left hand. The by no means easy feat of flipping his heavy form outside with one hand, he accomplished easily. The handless man groveled on the deck.

The third of Squint's aides was running for the deckhouse entrance.

Squint himself was just diving into the temporary safety of the deck structure.

The running rat twisted his head and saw Doc. He brought his gun around. But the weapon was far from being in a position to fire when the sharp, heavy cutlass struck him. Doc had thrown it.

The blade ran the gangster through like a steel thorn. He convulsed his parasite life out on the deck.

Squint fired from within the superstructure. He was hasty and missed. As Doc's bronze form bore down upon him, he fled.

Across the first cabin in the deckhouse was a solid bulkhead and a door. Squint got through the door ahead of Doc. He closed the panel and barred it.

Doc hit the door once. The thick planks were too much for even his terrific strength. A great battle-ax reposed among the array of weapons in the first cabin. Doc could have chopped at the door with it. He didn't. He went back to the ratty fellow who had lost a hand.

THE man still groveled on the deck. Doc's golden eyes gave the fellow one appraising glance. Then the big bronze head shook regretfully.

Doc, above all his other accomplishments, was a great doctor and surgeon. He had studied under the masters of medicine and surgery in the greatest clinics until he had learned all they could teach. Then, by his own intense efforts, he had extended his knowledge to a fabulous degree.

Doc's father had trained him from the cradle for a certain goal in life. That goal was a life of service. To go from one end of the world to the other, looking for excitement and adventure, but always helping those who need help, punishing those who deserve it—that was Doc Savage's noble purpose in life. All his marvelous training was for that end. And the training had started with medicine and surgery. At that, of all things, Doc was most expert.

So Doc knew instantly the ratty man was dying. The fellow was a dope addict. The shock of losing the hand was ending a career that would have come to its vile termination within a year or two anyway.

Doc sank beside the man. When the fellow saw he was not to be harmed more, he quieted a little.

"You were hired to kill Jerome Coffern?" Doc asked in a calm, compelling voice.

"No! No!" wailed the dying man. But the expression on his pinched and paling face showed he was lying.

For a moment, Doc said nothing. He exerted the full, strange quality of his golden eyes. Those eyes were warm and comforting now. Doc was making them exert a command for the truth.

It was amazing, the things Doc could do with his eyes. He had studied with the great masters of hypnotism, just as he had studied with famous surgeons. He had even gone to India and the Orient to gain knowledge from the mystic cults of the Far East.

By the time Doc asked his next question, he had exerted such a hypnotic influence upon the dying man that the fellow replied with the truth.

"What is the strange substance that dissolved the body of Jerome Coffern?" Doc prompted.

"It is called the Smoke of Eternity," whimpered the dying man.

"Of what is it made?"

"I don't know. None of us know. None of us little guys, that is. The Smoke of Eternity is just given us to use. We never get more than one cartridge at a time. And—and we get—get orders of who to use it on."

The man was about gone. Swiftly, Doc questioned, "Who gives it to you?"

The thin lips parted. The man gulped. He seemed to be trying to speak a name that started with the letter "K."

But he died before he could voice that name.

OF the five who had gone to New Jersey to slay Jerome Coffern, only Squint was now alive.

A bronze giant of vengeance, Doc made for the stern of the strange old buccaneer ship. Squint was back there somewhere.

A time or two, Doc paused to press an ear to the deck planking. To his supersensitive ears, many sounds came. Wavelets lapped the hull. Rats scurried in the hold. Animal rats, these were.

Finally, Doc heard Squint skulking.

Doc reached a companionway. He eased down it, a noiseless metal shadow that faded into darker shadows below. He came upon a long, heavy timber. It was round, a length of an old spar. It weighed nearly two hundred pounds and was a dozen feet in length, thick as a keg. He carried it along easily.

The spar promptly saved him death or serious injury. He was thinking of what he had read in the Sunday paper. He never forgot things he read.

The article had said there was a trapdoor in a passage which let the unwary upon a bed of upturned swords. He figured Squint might put that death trap in operation again.

Squint had.

So, when a passage floor suddenly opened under his weight, it was not an accident that the twelve-foot spar kept Doc from dropping upon needle-pointed blades below. Probably some old pirate had constructed this trap to bring death to one of his fellows he didn't like.

With a deft swing, Doc got atop the spar. He ran along it to solid footing. Then he picked up the heavy spar again.

Squint had been waiting behind a door at the end of the passage. At the crash of the sprung trapdoor, he let out a loud bark of glee. He thought Doc was finished. Doc heard the bark.

To accommodate him, Doc emitted a realistic moan. It was the kind of a moan a man dying on those upturned swords might have given. It fooled Squint.

He opened the passage door.

Before the door could swing the whole way, Doc hurled the spar. He purposefully missed Squint. The spar burst the door planks with a resounding smash.

Squint spun and fled. He was so terrified he didn't even stop to use his gun.

He must have been surprised when Doc's powerful hands did not fall upon his neck. Probably he considered himself quite a master of strategy when he reached deck without seeing another sign of Doc.

He did not have the sense to know Doc had purposefully let him escape.

Almost at once, Squint quitted the pirate ship. He left furtively. He looked behind often. But not once did he catch sight of the terrible Nemesis of bronze.

"Gave him the slip!" Squint chortled, almost sobbing in his relief.

As he crept away, he continued to look behind. His elation grew. There was no sign of Doc.

Actually, Doc was *ahead* of Squint. Doc had reached the deck and gone ashore in advance of Squint. When the ratty man appeared, the bronze giant kept always ahead or to one side.

Doc hoped Squint would lead him to the sinister mastermind who had ordered Jerome Coffern slain.

Chapter IV
THE NEST OF EVIL

SQUINT climbed up to Riverside Drive. He dodged limousines and taxicabs across the Drive. Turning south a few blocks, he strode rapidly east until he reached Broadway, the sole street which runs the full length of Manhattan Island. A subway lies beneath Broadway nearly the whole distance.

Into this subway, Squint scuttled. He cocked a nickel into the entrance turnstile and waited on the white-tiled station platform. The light was dim. At either end, dark gullets of the tunnel gaped.

Squint felt safe. He had been listening to the entrance turnstile. The turnstiles always gave a loud clank when a customer came through. There had not been a single clank since Squint entered.

A subway train came howling down the tunnel, headlights like bleary red eyes. The roar it made, to which New Yorkers are accustomed, was deafening. At the height of the noise, the entrance turnstile clanked behind Doc Savage's giant, bronze form. Nobody saw him.

Doc saw Squint wait in a car door until the other doors in the train, operated automatically, had all closed. Squint held his own door open against the gentle pull of the automatic mechanism. When he was satisfied no bronze giant had boarded the train, he let the door close. The train moved.

Running lightly, Doc reached an open car window. He dived through it. The train plunged into the tunnel with a great moan.

Squint alighted at Times Square, which might easily be dubbed the crossroads of New York City. He mingled with the dense crowd. He went in one door of a skyscraper and out another. He changed taxis twice going back uptown.

Unseen, his presence even unsuspected by Squint, a great bronze shadow clung to Squint's trail.

Squint wound up on the street which had the long row of houses exactly alike.

Before the tenth house from the corner, a considerable crowd milled. Long since, an ambulance had taken away the body of the ratty man whose neck Doc had been forced to break. However, the police had found the cache of machine guns beneath the floorboards of the touring car. Curious persons were inspecting the vicious weapons.

A cop was getting the motor number of the car.

Squint chuckled. The officers would never trace that machine to him. It had been stolen in a Middle Western State.

"Let 'em try to figure it out!" Squint sneered.

Then his gaze rested on Doc Savage's big,

efficient roadster, and his ugly glee oozed. He could see the license number of the car. This was a single figure. Only personages of great importance in New York had such low license numbers.

Squint shivered, thinking of the fearsome giant of bronze. He wondered who that awesome personage could be.

Squint had never heard of Doc Savage, largely because he never read anything but the newspapers, and Doc Savage never appeared in brazen newspaper yarns. In truth, Squint's intelligence was not enough to rate a knowledge of Doc.

But some of the brainiest, most upright citizens of New York could have told Squint amazing things about the big bronze man. More than one of these owed Doc a debt of deepest gratitude for past services.

The leading political boss, the most influential man in the city government, owed his life to Doc's magical skill at surgery. An extremely delicate operation upon the very walls of his heart had taken him from the door of death.

SQUINT did not enter the tenth house from the corner. He sidled into another several doors distant. He felt his way up a gloomy succession of stairs. A trapdoor gave to the roof. He eased out. Quietly, he closed the trapdoor behind him.

He did not notice it open a fraction of an inch a moment later. He did not dream a pair of flaky gold eyes were photographing his every move.

Squint scuttled across rooftops to the tenth house from the corner. He entered through another hatch on that roof.

He had hardly disappeared when Doc's bronze form was floating over the roofs in pursuit. Doc pressed an ear to the hatch. His aural organs, imbued with a sensitiveness near superhuman, told him Squint had walked down a top-floor passage to the back.

A moment later, a window at the rear opened. Doc was poised above it in an instant. Squint's relieved whisper reached him.

"No chance of anybody listenin' from here!" Squint had breathed.

The window grated down.

With silent speed, Doc was over the roof edge. Even a bat, master of clinging to smooth surfaces, would have had trouble with the wall. Grooves between the bricks furnished the only handholds. Doc's steel-strong bronze fingers found the largest of these.

At the window, there was no perch. But Doc hung by little more than his fingertips. His tireless sinews could support him thus for hours.

A shade had been drawn on the other side of the window. But it was old and cracked. One of these cracks let Doc look into the room.

The window sash fitted poorly. It gaped open at the bottom. Through this space, conversation seeped.

More than a dozen men were assembled in the shabby room. Some were thick-necked and burly. More were thin, with the look of drug addicts in their vicious eyes. And every one had the furtive manner of the confirmed criminal.

They were as choice a devil's dozen as ever held unholy conclave.

Squint stood before them. He was swaggering and punctuating his talk with curses to cover his nervousness.

"Now you mugs pipe down while I call the big shot!" he snarled.

He strode to one wall. The old plaster was a network of jagged cracks. He pressed a certain spot. A secret panel, the edges cleverly disguised by the cracks, opened. Squint took out a telephone instrument.

The phone obviously was not a part of the regular city system, since Squint did not give a number, but began speaking at once.

"Kar?" he asked. "This is Squint."

Outside the window, Doc Savage's strong bronze lips formed the word "Kar." The dying man on the pirate ship, in trying to name the mastermind who had given them the mysterious dissolving substance called the "Smoke of Eternity," had started a name that began with a "K."

Kar was that name!

"Yeah," Squint was saying over the secret phone line. "We put old Jerome Coffern out of the way like you ordered." Squint paused to wet his dry lips nervously, then added, "We—we had a little tough luck."

Squint was surprisingly modest. His four companions had died violently and he had barely escaped with his life—and he passed it off as a little tough luck!

Replying to a sharp query from Kar, Squint reluctantly explained the nature of the insignificant misfortune.

The outburst the information got from Kar was so violent the rattling of the receiver diaphragm reached even Doc Savage's ears.

There followed what was evidently a long procession of orders. These were spoken in a low voice by Kar. Doc's ears, sensitive to the extreme, could not hear a single word.

SQUINT hung up at last and replaced the phone. He closed the secret panel. Lighting a cigarette, he drew deeply from it, as though seeking courage. Then he faced the assembled thugs.

"Kar says I'm to tell you guys the whole thing," he said, making his voice harsh. "He says you will work together better if you know what it's all about. He says it'll show you birds where your bread is buttered. I guess he's right, at that."

Squint paused to blow a plume of smoke at the ceiling. But the smoke apparently reminded him of the weird dissolving of Jerome Coffern's body. He made a face and flung the cigarette on the floor.

"This is the first time you guys have been here!" he told the men. "Each one of you got the word from me to come to this room. I sent for you. I know every one of you. You're regular guys. That's why I'm ringing you in on the best thing you ever saw."

"Aw, cut out the mush an' get down to talkin' turkey!" a thick-necked bruiser growled.

Squint ignored the contemptuous tone of the interruption.

"Sure, I'll talk turkey!" he sneered. "You just heard me jawin' to the big shot. His name is Kar. That phone leads to his secret hangout. I don't know where it is. I don't even know Kar."

"You dunno who the chief is?" muttered the thick-necked man.

"Nope."

"Then how'd you—"

"How'd I get hooked up with him?" Squint chuckled. "I got a telephone call from him. He said he'd heard I was a square shooter, and did I want to get in on the best thing in the world? I did. And I'm tellin' you it's good. This proposition is the best ever."

"What is it?" queried he of the beefy neck.

"How does a million bucks to each of you within a year sound?" Squint demanded dramatically.

Jaws fell. Eyes popped.

"A million—"

"That much anyway!" Squint declared. "Maybe more! The million is guaranteed. You draw fifty thousand of it tomorrow. Fifty grand for each guy! But before I say more, I gotta know if you're comin' in.

"I know you mugs can't afford to run to the police and talk. You're sure to be rubbed out if you do. And if you come in, you gotta take orders from me. And I get my orders from Kar. I'm sort of a straw boss, see!"

"Count me in!" ejaculated the thug with the ample neck.

Like flies to sugar, the others offered eager allegiance.

"Here's the lay!" announced Squint. "This fellow Kar has got something he calls the Smoke of Eternity. It's something nobody ever heard of before. A few drops of it will dissolve a man's body—make it turn into an ugly gray smoke. The stuff will dissolve brick, metal and wood—almost anything."

For some seconds the villainous assemblage digested this. It was too much for them to swallow. The big-necked fellow voiced the thoughts of the rest.

"You're crazy!" he said.

REDDENING, Squint swore and shook his fist. "I ain't nuts!" he ranted. "The Smoke of Eternity

works like that! I dunno what the stuff is. I only know it will dissolve a man. It will wipe the front right off the biggest bank vault there is. Enough of it, about a suitcase full, could turn the Empire State Building into that queer smoke."

The others were still skeptical.

"Don'tcha see what havin' such a thing as this Smoke of Eternity means?" Squint snarled. "It means we can walk right into any bank vault in town and take what we want. And listen, you apes! I ain't crazy—and I ain't lyin'!"

At this point, a newsboy's shout penetrated faintly to the room. The news hawker was crying his papers to the crowd of curious in front of the house.

"Body of famous chemist vanishes!" he was screaming. "Mystery baffles police!"

Squint laughed nastily. He leveled an arm at one of his listeners.

"Go buy a paper from that kid!"

The man left obediently. In a moment he was back with a pink tabloid newspaper.

Emblazoned in black scare-type was the story of the finding of Jerome Coffern's right hand and forearm on the grounds of the Mammoth Manufacturing Company plant in New Jersey.

"I guess you'll believe me now!" Squint sneered. "I used some of the Smoke of Eternity on old Jerome Coffern. It dissolved all of his body but the hand. Probably the hand didn't go because there wasn't quite enough of the stuff."

The expression on the evil faces surrounding Squint showed the thugs had changed their minds. They no longer thought Squint was lying or crazy.

"Why'd you rub out this Jerome Coffern?" one villain asked.

"Kar ordered it," said Squint. "Kar told me why, too. Kar believes in lettin' his men know why everything is done. The only thing Kar don't tell is who he is. Nobody knows that. Kar had Jerome Coffern killed because Coffern was the only man alive who might tell the police who Kar is."

"Jerome Coffern knew Kar, huh?" muttered a man.

"He must have." Squint fired another cigarette. "Now, I already got orders for you mugs. A shipment of gold money is goin' to Chicago tomorrow. Some banks out in Chi are hard up and need the jack. There's about two million dollars' worth goin'. A hundred miles out of New York, we jerk up the tracks. We use this Smoke of Eternity to wipe out the bullion guards and get into the armored express car. And out of that two million, each of you guys gets paid your fifty thousand. The rest of the gold coin goes into Kar's workin' fund."

A gasp of evil pleasure swept the group. Mean eyes glittered greedily.

Although Squint had proclaimed that Kar was letting them in on a great deal, they actually knew nothing but the existence of the Smoke of Eternity and the fact they were to rob a gold train.

Who Kar was—they had no idea. Should these men fall into the clutches of the law, they could help the police little even if they told all they knew. True, the gold robbery would be thwarted. But the master villain would still be free.

A FAINT buzz came from the secret phone. Squint hurried to the instrument. He received more orders from Kar. His thin, repulsive face was worried as he hung up and closed the hidden panel.

"Damn!" he groaned. "Kar has another job for us to do before the gold train thing!"

The others stared at Squint. They could see he was frightened.

"That big bronze devil who gimme such a lot of trouble!" Squint muttered. "Kar says we gotta get him like we did Jerome Coffern! The bronze devil's name is Doc Savage. Kar is plenty mad because I let Doc Savage get on my trail. He says it's the worst thing that coulda happened."

"One guy can't give us much trouble!" sneered the thick-necked thug.

"You wouldn't be so cocky if you'd seen this bronze man work!" Squint whined. "He ain't human! He moves quicker'n a tiger! He popped off my four pals just like you was snappin' your fingers."

"Baloney!" snorted the burly one. "Lead me to 'im! I ain't never seen the man I couldn't lick."

Squint passed a hand over his forehead.

"Beat it, all of you," he directed. "Go to wherever you live an' stay there. Kar knows where to get hold of each of you. I told him. Wait for orders from him, or from me."

As they started leaving, Squint added an afterthought.

"Remember, Kar has got guys besides you an' me workin' for him. I dunno myself who they are. But he's got more. And if one of you squawks to the cops, he's sure to be bumped off."

Then the villainous assemblage melted away. None of them would squeal.

Squint remained behind. When left alone, he went to the secret phone.

"I carried out your orders, boss," he told Kar.

Suddenly there impinged upon the ears of Squint a weird, soft, trilling sound, like the song of a mysterious jungle bird. It was a note without equal anywhere else in the universe, melodious, but possessing no definite tune. It had a unique quality of emanating from everywhere, as though the very air in the shabby room was giving birth to it.

The trilling sound struck terror into Squint's evil soul. He whirled, not knowing what he would see.

An awful scream tore through his teeth.

For the rickety window had lifted noiselessly.

Equally without sound, the shabby curtain had moved aside.

There, poised like some huge bronze bird of vengeance upon the windowsill, was Squint's doom.

"Doc Savage!" the rodent of a man wailed.

Convulsively, Squint clutched for the revolver he had secured aboard the pirate ship.

Doc's powerful bronze hands seized a table. The table drove across the room as though impelled from a cannon mouth.

Striking Squint squarely, it smashed his worthless life out against the wall. The man's body fell to the floor amid the table wreckage.

Doc Savage glided to the secret phone. The receiver came to his ear. He listened.

From his lips wafted the weird trilling sound that was part of Doc—the tiny, unconscious thing which he did in moments of absolute concentration. The strange note seemed to saturate and set singing all the air in the room.

Over that secret phone line cracked what sounded like a gulp of terror and rage. Then the receiver banged up at the other end.

It would probably be a long time before the evil Kar forgot that eerie, trilling sound! It was a thing to haunt the slumber hours!

Chapter V
JEROME COFFERN'S FRIEND

DOC SAVAGE replaced the receiver of the secret phone. He closed the hidden panel. Silently, he quitted the room as he had entered—through the window. He made his way to the street.

The crowd had thinned. Squint's scream had not been heard. Doc did not go near his roadster, although his sharp eyes detected no sign of Kar's men watching the machine.

Doc strode eastward. He reached the edge of Central Park—that rectangle of beautiful lawns and shrubbery two and a half miles long and half a mile wide which is New York's breathing place. Neat apartment buildings towered along the park.

An old woman held out, hopefully, a bundle of the late newspapers. She was almost blind. Her clothing was shabby. She looked hungry. Doc stopped and took one of the papers.

He looked at the old woman's eyes. His expert diagnosis told him their ailment could be cured by a few great specialists. He wrote a name and address on a corner of the paper, added his own name, and tore this off and gave it to the crone. The name was that of a specialist who could cure her ailment, but whose fee was a small fortune. But at sight of Doc's name scrawled on the note, the specialist would gladly cure the woman for nothing.

Doc added a bill he took from a pocket. For a long time after he had gone, the old, nearly blind woman stared at the bill, holding it almost against her eyes. Then she burst into tears. It was more money than she had ever expected to see.

The little incident had no bearing on Doc's troubles with Kar, except that Doc wanted the paper to see what had been published concerning Jerome Coffern's weird death—which proved to be nothing he did not already know.

It was such a thing as Doc did often. It was part of his creed, the thing to which his life was devoted—remedying the misfortunes of others.

It was a strange thing for a man to do who had just dealt cold and terrible justice to five murderers. But Doc Savage was a strange man, judged by the look-out-for-yourself-and-nobody-else code of a greedy civilization.

Doc turned into one of the largest apartment houses on that side of Central Park. He rode an elevator to the twentieth floor.

Here Jerome Coffern had lived alone in a modest three-room apartment which was filled almost entirely with scientific books.

The locked door quickly yielded to Doc's expert wielding of a small hook which he made by bending the tongue of his belt buckle. He entered. He paused just inside the door, bronze face grim.

His golden eyes noted a number of things.

Jerome Coffern thought a great deal of his books, and he had a habit of arranging them just a certain distance from the rear wall of the bookcase. Yet they had a different arrangement now.

He kept chemicals on his library table, also arranged in a certain fashion. Doc knew the arrangement well. To one who didn't know Coffern, they might look orderly now. But they were not in the right order!

The apartment had been searched!

Swiftly, Doc made a circuit of the place. His nimble fingers, his all-seeing eyes, missed little.

He found the evidence on the typewriter! Jerome Coffern had installed a new ribbon on the machine before starting an extensive document. The machine had written the complete length of the ribbon, then back a considerable distance. But where it had not overwritten, the lettered imprint of the keys was discernible.

Doc read:

STATEMENT TO THE POLICE.

In view of a recent incident when a bullet came near me, I have come to the conclusion an attempt is being made to murder me. Furthermore, I suspect my alleged assailant of being guilty of at least one other murder. I realize I should have gone to the authorities earlier, but the very fantastic, horrible, and ghastly nature of the thing led me to doubt my own suspicions.

Herewith is my story:

Nearly a year ago, I went on a scientific expedition to New Zealand with Oliver Wording Bittman, the taxidermist, and Gabe Yuder. From New Zealand, a trip to Thunder Island was—

And there, to Doc's disgust, it ended. The rest was illegible. But Jerome Coffern had obviously written it.

Doc continued his search. Jerome Coffern had been a man of few intimate friends. In his personal papers was no reference to anyone called Kar.

Oliver Wording Bittman, Doc recalled, was a taxidermist who made a specialty of preparing rare animals for museums. But the name of Gabe Yuder was unfamiliar.

Doc knew the address of Oliver Wording Bittman. It was an apartment house two blocks southward along Central Park.

Doc Savage, unable to find anything else of interest, hurried to interview Oliver Wording Bittman. There was a chance Bittman might have heard of Kar, through Jerome Coffern.

As Doc rode up in an elevator of Bittman's apartment building, he mentally assembled what he knew of the taxidermist.

The material his memory yielded was all favorable to Oliver Wording Bittman. The man's name was not unknown. He had a sizeable display of rare animal life in the Smithsonian Institution. Walls of several famous clubs and hostelries were adorned with trophies he had mounted.

Best of all, Doc recalled his father had once spoken favorably of Bittman.

The taxidermist himself opened the door.

Oliver Wording Bittman was a man nearly as tall as Doc. But he was thin—so very thin that he looked like a skeleton and a few hard muscles. If a prominent jaw denotes character, Bittman had plenty. His jaw was strikingly large.

Bittman had dark, determined eyes. His hair was dark. His skin had been burned by the wind and sun of many climes. He wore a brown, well-cut business suit. Lounging mules were on his bony, efficient feet.

The only jewelry he wore was a watch chain across his waistcoat front. One end of this secured a timepiece. To the other end was fastened a small implement which at first glance looked like a penknife. Actually, it was a razor-edged taxidermist scalpel for skinning specimens.

Bittman twirled this scalpel about a forefinger.

"You are Doc Savage!" he greeted Doc instantly. "I am indeed honored."

Doc admitted his identity, but wondered how Bittman knew him. Bittman must have guessed the question.

"You may wonder how I knew you," the taxidermist smiled. "Come into the library and I will show you the answer."

They moved through the apartment.

Oliver Wording Bittman certainly considered his own work decorative. And in truth, the fellow was an expert in his line. Many scores of rare animal trophies adorned the walls. A great Alaskan Kodiak bear stood in a corner, astoundingly lifelike. Skin rugs made an overlapping carpet underfoot. The workmanship on all these was fine.

They came to a large picture framed on the wall. In the lower left corner of the picture reposed a portion of a letter.

The picture was of Doc Savage's father. The resemblance between parent and son was marked.

Doc stepped nearer to read the letter.

It was a missive from his own father to Oliver Wording Bittman. It read:

To you, my dear Oliver, I can never express my thanks sufficiently for the recent occasion upon which you quite certainly saved my life. Were it not for your unerring eye and swift marksmanship, I should not be penning this.

Before me as I write, I have the skin of the lion which would surely have downed me but for your quick shooting, and which you so kindly consented to mount. It just arrived. The workmanship is one of the best samples of the taxidermist art I ever beheld. I shall treasure it.

I shall treasure also my association with you on our recent African expedition together. And may the best of the world be yours.

Sincerely,

CLARK SAVAGE, Sr.

The note moved Doc Savage deeply. The death of his father was still a fresh hurt. This had occurred only recently. The elder Savage had been murdered.

It had done little to assuage the pain when Doc himself took up the trail of the murderer, a trail that led to Central America, and ended in a stroke of cold justice for the killer, as well as perilous adventures for Doc and five friends who had accompanied him.

Doc offered his hand to Bittman.

"Whatever debt of gratitude my father owed you," he said feelingly, "you can consider that I also owe you."

Bittman smiled and took the hand in a firm clasp.

IN a very few minutes the conversation got around to Oliver Wording Bittman's acquaintance with Jerome Coffern.

"I knew Coffern, yes," said Bittman. "We went on that New Zealand expedition together. You say he is dead? What a shock! His murderers should be made to suffer!"

"Five of them have already done that," Doc

replied grimly. "But the mastermind who ordered Coffern's murder is still at large. He must pay the penalty!

"He is a man I know only as Kar. I was hoping you might yield some information. Or if not, perhaps you can inform me where Gabe Yuder, the other member of the expedition, can be found."

Oliver Wording Bittman toyed with the scalpel on his watch chain. His eyes were veiled in deep thought.

"Gabe Yuder!" he muttered. "I wonder—could he be the man? He was an unsavory chap. I have no idea what became of him after our return. He remained in New Zealand—intending to return here later."

"Will you describe Gabe Yuder?"

Around and around Bittman's finger flew the scalpel. He spoke in clipped sentences, giving an excellent description.

"Gabe Yuder was a young man, under thirty. He was robust, an athletic type. He had a red face. His mouth was big. The lower lip was cleft by a knife scar. His eyes were always bloodshot. They were a pale gray. They reminded you of a snake's undersides. His hair was sandy, a sort of mongrel color.

"Yuder had a loud, coarse voice. He had an overbearing manner. His knuckles were scarred from knocking people about. He would strike a native at the slightest provocation. And he was a combination of chemist and electrical engineer by trade. He went along with us to prospect for petroleum."

"He does sound rather villainous," Doc admitted. "Can you tell me anything about this Smoke of Eternity?"

"The Smoke of Eternity? What is that?" queried Bittman, looking puzzled.

Doc debated. There was no reason why he should not tell Bittman of the terrible dissolving compound that had destroyed Jerome Coffern. Besides, Bittman had been friend to Doc's father.

So Doc explained what the Smoke of Eternity was.

"Good heavens!" Bittman groaned. "Such a thing is incredible! No! I can't tell you the slightest thing about it."

"Did you note anything suspicious about Gabe Yuder's actions on the New Zealand expedition?"

Oliver Wording Bittman thought deeply, then nodded.

"Yes, now that I think of it. Here is what happened: Our expedition split in two parts when we reached New Zealand. I remained in New Zealand to gather and mount samples of the island bird life for a New York museum. Yuder and Jerome Coffern chartered a schooner and sailed with Yuder's plane to an island some distance away."

"A plane?" Doc interposed.

"I neglected to tell you," Bittman said hastily. "Yuder is also a flyer. He took a plane along on the expedition. Some American oil company was financing him."

"What was the name of the island to which Yuder and Jerome Coffern went?" Doc asked.

"Thunder Island."

THUNDER ISLAND!

Doc's bronze brow wrinkled as he groped in his memory. There were few spots in the world, however outlying, upon which he did not possess at least general information.

"As I recall," Doc continued, "Thunder Island is nothing but the cone of an active volcano projecting from the sea. The sides of the cone are so barren they support no vegetation whatever. And great quantities of steam come continually from the active crater."

"Exactly," corroborated Bittman. "Jerome Coffern told me he flew over the crater once with Yuder. The crater was a number of miles across, but the whole thing seemed filled with steam and fumes. They brought back specimens from the cone, however. Jerome Coffern turned them over to the largest college of geology in New York City."

"We're getting off the trail," Doc declared. "You said you noted something suspicious about Yuder's actions. What was it?"

"After he and Jerome Coffern returned from Thunder Island, Yuder was surly and furtive. He acted like he had a secret, now that I think back. But at the time, I thought he was in an ill temper because he had found no oil, although he scouted Thunder Island the whole time Jerome Coffern was there gathering specimens."

"Hm-m-m," Doc murmured.

"I'm afraid that does not help much," Bittman apologized.

"It's too soon to say."

Doc thought briefly. Then he nodded at the telephone.

"May I make a call from here?"

"Of course!"

Arising hastily, Bittman left the room. This politeness was to show he had no desire to listen in on Doc's phone talk.

Doc called a number.

"Monk?" he asked.

A mild, pleasant voice replied, "Sure thing, Doc."

That mild voice was a deceptive thing. A listener would not have dreamed it could come from the kind of a man who was at the other end of the wire. For the speaker was Lieutenant Colonel Andrew Blodgett Mayfair.

He was a two-hundred-and-sixty-pound human gorilla. He was one of the roughest and toughest and most likeable and homely men ever to live.

Monk was also one of the few chemists in the world who could be considered a greater expert in that line than poor, unfortunate Jerome Coffern.

Monk was one of five men who accompanied Doc Savage on his amazing jaunts in pursuit of adventure. These five, like Doc, were giving their lives to traveling about the world and righting wrongs and handing out their own brand of justice. Whatever excitement turned up in the course of that pursuit—and there was always plenty—they gobbled up and liked it. How they liked it!

"Monk," Doc suggested, "could you take on a little trouble right now?"

"I'm on my way!" chuckled Monk. "Where do I find this trouble?"

"Call Renny, Long Tom, Johnny and Ham," Doc directed. "All of you show up at my place right away. I think I'm mixed up in something that will make us all hump."

"I'll get hold of them," Monk promised.

DOC stood by the phone a moment after hanging up. He was thinking of his five friends, "Monk," "Renny," "Long Tom," "Johnny," and "Ham." They were probably the most efficient five men ever to assemble for a definite purpose. Each was a world-famed specialist in a particular line.

Renny was a great engineer, Long Tom an electrical wizard, Johnny an archaeologist and geologist, and Ham one of the cleverest lawyers Harvard ever turned out. The gorilla-like Monk, with his magical knowledge of chemistry, completed the group.

They had first assembled during the Great War, these adventurers. The love of excitement held them together. Not a one of the five men but owed his very life to the unique brain and skill of Doc.

With Doc Savage, scrapper above all others, adventurer supreme, they formed a combination which could accomplish marvels.

Doc went in search of Oliver Wording Bittman. He found the famous taxidermist in an adjoining room and thanked him for use of the phone.

"I must take my departure now," he finished. "I should like greatly, though, to discuss at some time your association with my father. And any service I can perform for you, a friend of my father's, a man who saved his life, I shall gladly do."

Oliver Wording Bittman shrugged. "My saving of your father's life was really no feat at all. I was simply there and shot a lion as it charged. But I would be delighted to talk at length with you. I admire you greatly. Where could I get in touch with you?"

Doc gave the address of a downtown New York skyscraper which towered nearly a hundred stories—a skyscraper known all over the world because of its great height.

"I occupy the offices formerly used by my father on the eighty-sixth floor," Doc explained.

"I have been there," Bittman smiled. "I shall look you up." He gestured at an extension telephone. "May I not call you a taxi?"

Doc shook his head. "I'll walk. I want to do some thinking."

Down on the street once more, Doc strode across traffic-laden Central Park West and entered the Park itself. He followed the pedestrian walk, angling southeast. He did not try to make haste.

His remarkable brain was working at top speed. Already, it had evolved a detailed plan which he would put in operation as soon as he met his five friends at the skyscraper office.

High overhead, a plane was droning. Doc looked up as a matter of course, for few things happened around him that he did not notice.

The craft was a cabin seaplane, a monoplane, single-motored. And it was painted green. It circled, seemingly bound nowhere.

Doc dismissed it from his thoughts. Planes circling over New York City were a more common sight than the discovery of an ordinary horsefly.

The walk he traversed descended steeply. It crossed a long, narrow bridge over a Park lagoon. The bridge was of rustic log construction.

Doc reached the bridge middle.

Unexpected things then happened.

With a loud bawl of exhaust stacks, the seaplane above dived. Straight down it came. There was murderous purpose in its plunge.

Doc Savage did not have time to race to the end of the bridge. Had he done so successfully, there was no shelter to be had.

A bronze flash, Doc whipped over the rustic railing. He slid under the bridge.

An object dropped from the plane. It was hardly larger than a baseball.

This thing struck the bridge squarely above where Doc had gone over.

A gush of vile grayish smoke arose. With incredible speed, the bridge began dissolving!

Chapter VI
THE MISSING MAN

THE weird phenomenon, as the rustic bridge was wiped out by the fantastic Smoke of Eternity, was even more striking than had been the dissolution of Jerome Coffern's body.

The metallic capsule bearing the Smoke of Eternity had splashed the strange stuff some distance in bursting. A great section of the bridge seemed to burn instantly. But there was no flame, no heat.

The play of electrical sparks was very marked,

however. In such volume did they flicker that their noise was like the sound of a rapidly running brook.

The Smoke of Eternity, after passing through and destroying the bridge, next dissolved the water below. So rapidly did the eerie substance work that a great pit appeared in the surface of the lagoon.

Water rushing to fill this pit formed a current like a strong river.

It was that current which offered Doc Savage his only real threat. For Doc had not lingered under the bridge. With scarcely a splash, he had cleaved beneath the surface. Guessing what was to come, he swam rapidly away.

Doc's lungs were tremendous. He could readily stay under water twice as long as a South Sea pearl diver, and such men have been known to remain under several minutes. He swam rapidly down the lagoon, keeping close to the bottom and stroking powerfully to vanquish the current.

Overhead, the seaplane circled again and again. The only occupant, the pilot, peered out anxiously.

"Got him!" the vicious fellow chortled. "Easy money, the twenty grand Kar is payin' me for this!"

The murderous pilot did not dream Doc Savage could have escaped. He had no comprehension of Doc's physical powers.

But he had been warned to make absolutely certain. He circled continuously above the lagoon, eyes roving like a vulture's.

Under an overhanging bush, a full hundred yards from the bridge, Doc's bronze head broke water. He came up so smoothly that there was no splash.

The killer pilot of the seaplane did not see Doc glide into the shrubbery, although he was staring mightily.

An onlooker would have remarked a striking thing about Doc as he came out of the water. Doc's straight bronze hair showed no traces of moisture. It was disarrayed. It seemed to shed water like the proverbial duck's back. Nor did moisture cling to Doc's fine-textured bronze skin.

This was but another of the strange things about this unusual metallic giant of a man.

Nearby stood a Park policeman. The officer was goggling at the spiraling plane. He had seen the baseball-sized bomb drop. He had witnessed the upheaval of queer gray smoke.

The cop was trying to think what to do about it! Nothing like this had ever happened before.

The officer fingered the grip of his revolver. Then the revolver was spirited from under his fingers. He had heard no one come near. Wildly, he turned.

Even as he spun, the revolver banged itself empty of cartridges. The shots camc so rapidly as to be a single thunderous *whurr-r-ram!*

The circling seaplane gave a wild lurch. A wing sank. It nearly crashed. The pilot was wounded. But he fought the ship to an even keel. The plane scudded away like a shot-splattered duck.

The policeman suddenly found his warm, smoking gun back in his hand. He had a dizzy vision of a great bronze form in dripping clothes. He even noted the bronze man's face and hair seemed perfectly dry, although his clothing was saturated.

Then the giant was gone into the shrubbery. And there was no sound to show from whence he had come, or where he had betaken himself.

The cop looked into the bushes and saw nobody. He gulped a time or two and wiped sweat off his brow.

"Goshamighty!" he managed to croak at last.

AT the Fifth Avenue side of Central Park, Doc Savage got into a taxicab. It hurried him southward. Before a towering, gleaming spike of brick and steel, the machine let him out. Streets here were walled by buildings so tall the sunlight only reached the sidewalks at high noon.

An elevator raced Doc up to the eighty-sixth floor. He entered a sumptuously furnished reception room. No one was there. He went to the next room. This was a library, a chamber which contained thousands of the finest technical tomes.

Into another and much larger room, Doc went. This was the laboratory. Marble and glass-topped worktables were everywhere. Scores of huge steel-and-glass cases held chemicals, rare metals, test tubes, siphons, mortars, retorts, tubing and apparatus of which only Doc knew the use. No one was there.

This laboratory was exceeded for completeness by only one on earth—the one which Jerome Coffern had told his fellow chemists that Doc must visit to conduct his great experiments uninterrupted. Jerome Coffern's guess had been right.

Doc had another laboratory, vaster even than this. It was at the spot he called his "Fortress of Solitude." This was built upon a rocky island far within the Arctic Circle. No one but Doc knew its location. And when he was there, no word from the outside world could ever reach him. It was to his Fortress of Solitude that Doc retired periodically to study and experiment and increase his fabulous store of knowledge.

Convinced none of his five friends had as yet arrived, Doc returned to the reception room. He stripped and donned dry clothes which he got from a cleverly concealed locker.

Doc's frame, stripped, was an amazing thing. He had the muscles of an Atlas. They were not knotty, but more like bundled piano wire lacquered a deep bronze color. The strength and symmetry of that great form was such as to stun an onlooker.

Suddenly there came an interruption.

Wham!

The report was loud. With a rending of wood, the thick panel of the outer door caved inward, propelled by an enormous fist. That fist was composed of an ample gallon of knuckles. They looked like solid, rusty iron. And it would have taken a very big and violent mule to do as much damage to that door as they had done.

The fist withdrew.

A man now opened what was left of the door and came in. He was at least six feet four in height, and would weigh two fifty. The man resembled an elephant, with his sloping, gristle-heaped shoulders.

He had a severe, puritanical face. His eyes were dark, somber and forbidding. His mouth was thin and grim and pinched together as though he disapproved of something.

This was Colonel John Renwick. Everyone called him "Renny." He was honored throughout the world for his accomplishments as a civil engineer.

Renny looked like he was coming to a funeral. Actually, he was literally rolling in joy. His popping out the panel of the door showed that. It was a trick Renny did when he felt good. And the better he felt, the more sour he looked.

"Where's this trouble you was tellin' Monk about?" he asked Doc.

Doc Savage chuckled. "It'll keep until the others get here. I'll tell you all together."

SOON two men could be heard haranguing each other loudly in the corridor.

"You can't tell me nothing about electronic refraction, you skinny galoot!" shouted a belligerent voice. "Electricity is my business!"

"I don't give a snap if it is!" retorted another voice. "I'm telling you what I read about electronic refraction. I know what I read, and it was in an article you wrote. You made a mistake—"

There was a loud slamming noise. A man came flying into the room, propelled by a vigorous toe.

This man was tall and gaunt, with a half-starved look. His shoulders were like a clothes hanger under his coat.

He was William Harper Littlejohn. The year before, he had won a coveted international medal for his work in archaeology.

"What's the trouble now, Johnny?" Doc inquired.

Johnny got up from the floor, laughing.

"Long Tom wrote an article for a technical magazine and he made a mistake any ten-year-old kid could catch," Johnny chuckled. "He hasn't seen the article since it got in print, and he won't believe me."

Snorting loudly, an undersized, slender man came in from the corridor. He had a complexion that was none too healthy. His hair was pale, his eyes a faded blue. He looked like a physical weakling. He wasn't, though. It had taken a lusty kick to propel Johnny inside.

The undersized man was Major Thomas J. Roberts on the official records, but Long Tom to everybody else. He had done electrical experiments with Steinmetz and Edison. He was a wizard with the juice.

"Where's Ham and Monk?" Long Tom asked. "And where's this trouble? I'm gonna tear an arm off Johnny if I don't get some excitement pretty quick."

"Here comes Ham," Doc offered.

Brigadier General Theodore Marley Brooks now appeared. He was a waspish, swift-moving, slender man. Of all the lawyers Harvard had sent forth from its legal department, it was most proud of Ham. He was an amazingly quick-witted man.

Ham's dress was the ultra in sartorial perfection. Not that he was flashily clad, for he had too good taste for that. But he had certainly given his attire a lot of attention.

Ham carried a black, severe-looking cane with a gold band. This was in reality a sword cane, a blade of keenest Damascus steel sheathed within the black metal tube.

Ham also was eager for action.

They waited for Monk to appear.

Monk was the fifth of Doc's friends. He had a penthouse chemical laboratory and living quarters downtown, near Wall Street. He should have arrived by now.

They were remarkable men, these adventurers. A lesser man than Doc Savage could never have held their allegiance. But to Doc, they gave their absolute loyalty. For Doc was a greater engineer than Renny, a more learned archaeologist than Johnny, an electrical wizard exceeding even Long Tom, a more astute man of law than Ham, and he could teach Monk things about chemistry. Too, each of the five owed his life to Doc, thanks to some feat of the bronze man on the field of battle, or the magic of Doc's surgery.

As time passed, they began to exchange uneasy glances.

"Now I wonder what has happened to that ugly ape, Monk?" Ham muttered.

Doc called Monk's downtown penthouse place. Monk's secretary—she was one of the prettiest secretaries in New York City—informed him that Monk had left some time ago.

Doc hung up.

"I'm afraid, brothers, that Kar has got his hands on Monk," he said slowly.

Chapter VII
THE UNDERWATER LAIR

DOC was right.

Monk wasted little time after receiving Doc's call. He shucked off his rubber work apron. He had a chest fully as thick as it was wide. He put on a coat especially tailored with extra long sleeves. Monk's arms, thick as kegs, were six inches longer than his legs. Only five feet and a half in height, Monk weighed two hundred and sixty pounds.

His little eyes twinkled like stars in their pits of gristle as he gave his secretary a few orders about his correspondence. Monk knew he might be away six months—or only an hour.

An elevator hurried him down from his penthouse establishment. The elevator operator and the clerk at the cigar stand both grinned widely at the homely Monk. They admired and liked him.

Each carried a pocket piece presented by Monk. These were silver half dollars which Monk had folded in the middle with his huge, hairy, bare hands.

Monk purchased a can of smoking tobacco and a book of cigarette papers. He rolled his own. Then he left the building.

He headed for a nearby subway. The subways offer the quickest, most traffic-free transportation in New York City.

A slender, sallow-skinned weasel of a man fell in behind Monk. The fellow was foppishly clad. He kept a hand in a coat pocket.

Monk's forehead was so low as to be practically nonexistent. This characteristic is popularly supposed to denote stupidity. It didn't in Monk. He was a highly intelligent man.

Monk's sharp eyes noted the foppish man trailing him. He saw the weasel-like fellow's reflection in a plate-glass window of a store.

Monk stopped sharply. His monster hand whipped back. It grasped the knot which the weasel man's claw made in his coat pocket. Monk twisted. The weasel man's coat tore half off. Skin was crushed from his hand. And Monk got the long-barreled revolver which the fellow had been holding in the pocket.

The foppish man staggered into a deserted entryway, propelled by a hirsute paw. Monk crowded against him and held him there.

Both Monk's great hands gripped the revolver barrel. They exerted terrific force. Slowly, the barrel bent until it was like a hairpin.

Monk gave the weasel man back his gun.

"Now you can shoot!" he rumbled pleasantly. "Maybe the bullet will turn around and hit the guy it oughta hit!"

Monk was something of a practical jokester.

The weasel man threw down his useless weapon. He tried to escape. He was helpless in the clutch of this human gorilla.

"Guess I'll take you along and let Doc Savage talk to you," Monk said amiably.

Monk hauled his prisoner out onto the walk.

"Hold it, you missin' link!" snarled a coarse voice.

Monk started and stared at the curb.

A sedan had pulled up there. Four villainous looking men occupied it. They had automatic pistols and submachine guns pointed at Monk.

"Get in here!" rasped one of them.

MONK could do two things. He could put up a fight—and certainly get shot. Or he could enter the car.

He got in the sedan.

The instant Monk was seated in the machine, manacles were clicked upon his arms and legs. Not one pair—but three! His captors were prepared to cope with Monk's vast strength.

Monk began to wish he had taken his chances in a fight.

The sedan wended through traffic. It passed a couple of cops. Monk kept silent. To shout an alarm would have meant the death of those policemen, as well as his own finish. Monk knew men. This was a crew of killers which had him.

The weasel man whose gun Monk had bent was in the car. He cursed the big prisoner and kicked him. Monk said nothing. He did not resist. But he marked the weasel man for a neck-wringing if the opportunity presented.

Rolling on a less-used street, the sedan reached the waterfront. The district was one of rotting piers and disused warehouses on the East River.

The motor of an airplane could be heard out on the river.

The sedan halted. Monk was yanked out.

He saw the plane now. A seaplane, it was painted green.

The seaplane pilot tossed a line. His craft was hauled carefully to one of the old piers.

They dumped Monk in the plane cabin.

The pilot, Monk saw now, had a crimson-soaked bandage about his forehead, and another around his left arm. He was a squat fellow, much too fat. He had mean eyes.

Monk's captors looked curiously at the pilot's wounds.

"How'd you get plinked?" one asked.

The pilot vented a snarl of rage. He pointed at several bullet holes in the control compartment.

"Doc Savage!" he gritted. "The bronze devil popped up after I thought I'd finished him! He nearly got me!"

Monk grinned at this. He had iron nerves. If Doc Savage was after this gang, the villainous fellows were in for a brisk time indeed. Monk tested his strength against his manacles. They were too much for him.

"Take the big guy to—you know where!" directed one of the men who had occupied the car.

The pilot indicated a radio receiving set in the plane.

"Sure," he said. "I know where he's goin'. Kar gimme my orders over the shortwave radio set."

He opened the throttle. With a moan from the exhaust pipes, the seaplane taxied about. It raced across the river surface and took the air.

MONK was prepared for an extensive air journey. He was fooled. The seaplane circled over Brooklyn, then across the harbor. It went nearly as far south as the Statue of Liberty. Banking north, it flew up the Hudson River.

The craft descended to the water near the beginning of Riverside Drive. It taxied slowly along the surface, close inshore.

Rearing up in the cabin, Monk was able to peer through the windows.

Nearby and directly ahead stood a couple of rickety piers. To one of these was anchored a large, ancient three-masted sailing ship. The black, somber hull of this strange craft was pierced with cannon ports.

On top of the superstructure reared a big sign, reading:

THE JOLLY ROGER
Former Pirate Ship
(Admission Fifty Cents)

It was the same craft upon which Doc Savage had cornered Squint and his companions. Monk, however, had no way of knowing this.

From the smokestack of the cookhouse, or galley, poured dense black smoke. This smudge was rapidly settling to the water about the old corsair craft.

Soon the vessel was completely hidden. The darksome pall spread to cover the river out a considerable distance from the ship.

Directly into this unusual smoke screen taxied the seaplane.

The floats of the craft were suddenly seized and held. Monk perceived several men had grasped the plane. These men were standing upon something. Monk craned his neck to see what it was.

His little eyes popped in astonishment.

Under the concealment of the smoke screen, a great steel tank of a thing had come up from the deep riverbed. This was in the nature of a submarine, but without conning tower or engines and propellers.

A steel hatch gaped open in the middle of the tank. Into this hatch Monk was hauled.

The seaplane taxied away. The hatch closed. The tank of a submarine sank beneath the surface, submerging after the fashion of a genuine U-boat.

The whole operation had been blanketed by the smoke screen. An observer would not have dreamed a man had been shifted from the plane to a strange underwater craft which now rested on the riverbed.

Kar's men dragged Monk into a tiny steel chamber.

For a minute or two, the loud, sobbing gurgling of water entering the ballast tanks persisted. The submersible rolled a little, then settled solidly on the river bottom. One of the gang now spun metal wheels. These, no doubt, controlled valves.

The interior of the strange craft became quiet as a tomb, except for a monotonous *drip-drip-drip* of a leak somewhere.

The men were taking no chance on Monk's escape. Three of them stood apart and kept pistols pointed at him.

One fellow picked up an ordinary telephone. This obviously was connected to a wire that led ashore, probably along the cable which must anchor this unusual vessel.

"Kar," he said into the mouthpiece. "We got the big guy here now."

So quiet was the interior of the steel cell that the metallic voice from the receiver diaphragm was plainly audible to everyone.

"Let me talk to him," Kar commanded.

THE receiver was jammed against Monk's scarred ear, but tilted so the others could hear. They held the mouthpiece a few inches from his lips.

"Well, say your piece!" Monk roared.

"You will speak with civility!" snarled the voice from the phone.

Monk blew air out between his lips and tongue, making a loud and insulting noise known variously as the Bronx cheer and the razzberry.

He was kicked in the barrel of a chest for his performance.

"I fear you are going to come to an unfortunate end very soon," Kar sneered silkily.

Monk's brain was working rapidly, despite his rowdyism. This voice had an ugly, unreal rasp. He knew Kar must be pulling his mouth out of shape with a finger as he spoke, thus disguising his voice.

"What d'you want?" Monk demanded.

"You will write a note to your friend and chief, Doc Savage. The note will tell him to meet you at a certain spot."

Monk snorted. "You want me to lead Doc into your trap, eh? Nothin' stirrin'!"

"You refuse?"

"You guessed it!"

There ensued a brief silence. Kar was thinking.

"Give me the addresses of the men you call Renny, Long Tom, Johnny, and Ham!" he commanded.

"I learned from a chemical supply firm where you lived. That is how my men came to be waiting for you to appear. But I could not find where the other four of your friends reside. You will give me that information!"

"Sure," Monk growled. "Just watch me do it!"

Then his pug nose wrinkled as he thought deeply. He asked a question: "How did you know our names? How did you find Renny, Long Tom, Johnny, Ham, and I always join Doc Savage when he tackles trouble?"

Kar's voice rattled an ugly laugh.

"The information was simple to obtain!"

"I'll bet it was!" Monk snorted. "Not many people know we work together!"

"I already knew that Doc Savage has his New York headquarters on the eighty-sixth floor of a skyscraper," Kar rasped. "I simply sent one of my men to strike up a conversation with the elevator operators of that skyscraper. My man learned you five men were often with Doc Savage. He wormed your nicknames from the elevator operators."

"What's behind all this?" Monk questioned.

Monk did not, of course, know anything about Kar's sinister purpose. He did not even know of the existence of the weird and horrible Smoke of Eternity.

"Doc Savage has interfered with my plans!" Kar gritted. "He must die! You five who are his friends would try to avenge his death. So you also must die!"

"You don't know what you're tryin' to do!" Monk declared.

"I do!"

"Oh, no, you don't! You'd be runnin' like hell if you knew what a terror Doc Savage is when he gets on the trail of a snake like you!"

This drew a loud snarl from Kar. "I do not fear Doc Savage!"

"Which shows you ain't got good sense!" Monk chuckled.

"Put him in the death chamber!" Kar commanded angrily.

The telephone was plucked from Monk's furry hands. He was hauled aft.

Evidently Kar was enough of a judge of character to realize he could never force Monk to lead Doc Savage into a death trap. So he was going to get rid of Monk immediately.

ONE of the men twisted metal dogs which secured a hatchlike steel panel in a wall of the submerged tank. This swung back. It revealed a box riveted to the hull. The box had the dimensions of a large trunk. It barely accommodated Monk's bulk as he was jammed inside.

At the end of the box was another steel hatch. But this was obviously secured tightly on the outside.

A small petcock protruded from the box ceiling. One of Kar's men opened this with a key. He fitted a grille over it.

A thin stream of water entered.

The hatch into the tank-like craft clanked shut. The dogs rattled loudly as they were secured.

Monk flounced about, wrenching at his manacles. He could not snap them with all his prodigous effort.

He tried to stop the inrush of water through the petcock. He failed. The petcock construction was such that he could not block it, due to the grille covering.

The water had risen above his ankles by now. The clammy wetness was like the creep of death.

Monk beat the steel plates of the outer hatch with his shackled legs. They held. Nothing less than nitroglycerin could shatter them.

Steadily, the water crawled upward. The minutes were passing with agonizing speed for Monk. He perspired. His brain raced. He could evolve no possible scheme of escape.

The river water now covered his mouth. He had his head rammed tightly against the roof plates. It could go no higher. Over his upper lip, the deadly liquid sloshed.

After the fashion of a diver, Monk determined to take a couple of quick inhalations, then draw in a lungful of air. He was going to hang on as long as he could.

But with the first indraw of air, water was sucked into his lungs.

Gagging, choking, he sank helplessly to the bottom plates.

Monk was drowning! There was nothing he could do to save himself; no way to inform Doc to get aid.

However, while Monk had been taken captive, during the time required for the trip up the river, Doc Savage was not idle. Monk's failure to appear was evidence that something was wrong—and Doc never let anything stay wrong for long!

Chapter VIII
THE TRAIL

"I'M afraid, brothers, that Kar has got his hands on Monk," Doc Savage said slowly.

"Nothing less could have kept the big ape from showing up here," agreed Ham, the waspish, quick-thinking lawyer. He made an angry, baffled gesture with his innocent-looking black sword cane.

Below the eighty-sixth floor window of the skyscraper office, the inspiring panorama of New York City spread. They were beautiful, impressive things, those gigantic, gleaming spires of office buildings. From that height, automobiles on the street looked like little, sluggish bugs moving along.

Doc lifted a bronze hand. He got instant attention. Ham, Renny, Long Tom, and Johnny knew this signal meant Doc was about to start his campaign of action.

To Long Tom, the electrical wizard, came the first commands.

Doc gave Long Tom the address of that tenth house in a row of dwellings that were all alike. He told the exact location of the secret wall recess.

"I want you to trace that phone wire," Doc explained. "It was not installed by the regular telephone company. Kar must have put it in himself. It leads to some secret lair of Kar's. I want you to follow it to that lair."

"Sure," said Long Tom. "I'll use a—"

"I know what you'll use," Doc interposed. "The apparatus is right here in my laboratory. You can find it!"

Long Tom hurried into the great laboratory room. He selected two boxes. They were replete with vacuum tubes, dials and intricate coils. They might have been radio sets, because one was equipped with headphones. But they weren't.

One box held an apparatus which created a high-frequency electric current. When this current was placed upon a telephone wire, it would make no sound audible to the human ear. But it would throw an electrical field about the wire. This field extended a considerable distance.

The other box was an "ear" for detecting this field. Using it, Long Tom could walk about with the headphones upon his head. The phones would give a loud squeal when he brought the "ear" within proximity of the wire charged with his peculiar current.

The wire might be buried yards underground, but the "ear" would detect its presence anyway. Nor would brick walls interfere with the sensitive detector.

Long Tom hurried out with his equipment. He took a taxi for the tenth house in the row of similar houses uptown.

"NEXT, Johnny!" Doc addressed the tall, emaciated geologist and archaeologist. "There is an island in the South Seas, some distance from New Zealand. It is known as Thunder Island."

Johnny nodded. He took off the glasses he wore and fiddled with them excitedly. These glasses were peculiar in that the left lens was extremely thick. This left lens was in reality a powerful magnifying glass which Johnny carried there for convenience. Johnny's left eye was virtually useless since an injury he had received in the World War.

"Go to the largest college of geology in New York City," Doc directed Johnny. "You will find there a collection of rock specimens from Thunder Island. They were turned over to the institution by Jerome Coffern, after an expedition he recently made to Thunder Island. I want those specimens."

"Mind telling me why you want them?" Johnny inquired.

"Of course not!"

In a few quick sentences, Doc Savage told of the existence of the horrible stuff called Smoke of Eternity.

"I am not sure what the Smoke of Eternity is," Doc explained. "But I have an idea what it could be. When the substance dissolves anything, there is a weird electrical display. This leads me to believe it operates through the disintegration of atoms. In other words, the dissolving is simply a disruption of the atomic structure."

"I thought it was generally believed there would be a great explosion once the atom was shattered!" Johnny murmured.

"That was largely disproved by recent accomplishments of scientists who have succeeded in cracking the atom," Doc corrected. "I have experimented extensively along that line myself. There is no explosion, for the very simple reason that it takes as much energy to shatter the atom as is released."

"But why the specimens from Thunder Island?" persisted Johnny.

"The basis of this Smoke of Eternity must be some hitherto undiscovered element or substance," Doc elaborated. "In other words, it is possible Gabe Yuder discovered on Thunder Island such an element.

"The man is a chemist and electrical engineer. From that element, he might have developed this Smoke of Eternity. I want to examine the rock specimens from Thunder Island in hopes they may give me some clue as to what this unknown element or substance is."

"I'll get the specimens!" Johnny declared.

He hurried out.

"Ham—Renny!" Doc addressed his other two friends. "I want you two to hurry down to Monk's penthouse place. See if you can find him."

These two also departed, Renny moving lightly as a mouse in spite of his elephantine bulk; Ham twirling his sword cane.

Doc Savage tarried only to enter the laboratory. From his clothing he removed the crumpled capsule of metal that had contained the Smoke of Eternity which had wiped out the body of poor Jerome Coffern.

Doc concealed the capsule by sticking it to the bottom of a microscope stand with a bit of adhesive wax.

Quitting his headquarters, Doc journeyed the eighty-six floors downward in an elevator. He got into a taxicab. The driver, he directed to take him to a point on Riverside Drive near where an ancient pirate ship was tied up.

Doc Savage intended to examine the old corsair bark at his leisure. His suspicions were aroused. The fact that the ill-savored Squint and his companions had found modern guns aboard, the familiarity they had shown with the strange craft, indicated they had been there before.

Aboard the buccaneer vessel, Doc hoped to find something that would lead him to the master fiend, Kar.

THE moment he came in sight of the *Jolly Roger,* Doc's golden eyes noted something a bit puzzling.

Some distance down the river drifted a smudge of particularly vile black smoke. No factory smokestacks along the river were disgorging such stuff. Nor were any water craft, which might have thrown it off, to be seen.

The slight breeze was such that this darksome pall might have been swept from the vicinity of the *Jolly Roger.*

Too, far up the river, was a seaplane. It taxied along the surface, receding.

Doc strained the telescopic quality of his vision. He recognized the seaplane as the same which had attempted his life in Central Park!

Doc was thoughtful. His suspicions were now stronger.

But he had no way of knowing he was viewing the after-signs of Monk's being taken aboard the submersible tank hiding place!

Down to the pirate vessel, Doc hurried. A springy leap from the ramshackle wharf put his bronze form aboard. A leaf settling on the deck planks would have made more noise than he did in landing.

Doc glided to the superstructure. Poising, he listened. A stray rope end, swinging in the breeze, made brushing noises up in the labyrinth of rigging.

Another sound, too! A man muttering in the vicinity of the galley!

Doc backed a pace. His sharp gaze rested on the galley stovepipe. The faintest wisp of dark smoke drifted out. The smoke was like that pall hanging downriver.

Instantly, Doc became a wary, stalking bronze hunter. He slid aft, then went down a companionway. He made for the galley. He was shortly framed in the galley door.

Beside a rusty old cook oven stood a strange contrivance.

This was larger than the oven, but built along similar lines. It seemed to be a furnace for burning resinous, smoke-making material. A big pipe from this led the smoke to the galley flue.

A printed sign above the contraption read:

OLD-TIME PIRATES
USED SMOKE SCREENS

Modern warships were not the first to employ smoke screens! Below is an apparatus used by the rovers of the Spanish Main to throw off clouds of smoke intended to baffle the aim of pursuing men-of-war.

If visitors desire to see this smoke-maker in performance, an attendant will put it in operation.

There is a small charge of one dollar for this.

Doc Savage's mobile, strong lips made the slightest of appreciative smiles. Whether old-time corsairs had actually used smoke screens was immaterial. This was probably faked, like most of the other stuff aboard the ship.

But if it was desired to lay a smoke screen over this part of the river without attracting suspicion, here was an ingenious method. If anybody asked questions, the proprietors of the pirate exhibit could claim somebody had paid them a dollar to make the smoke.

BESIDE the smoke-maker stood a man. He had not yet become aware of Doc's presence. The man was cleaning ashes out of the smoke-maker.

The fellow was tall and thin. His pasty complexion, his shaking hands, his inarticulate mumbling, marked him as a drug addict.

"Well?" said Doc.

The man whirled. His mean eyes goggled. His teeth rattled as a great terror seized him.

He was one of the unsavory crew assembled by Squint in that tenth house of the row of similar dwellings.

Suddenly, he leaped across the galley, pitched through a door. His feet hammered down a passage.

"Stop!" Doc rapped.

The terrified man never heeded. He was not long on nerve. And he had heard enough about Doc to know the giant bronze man was Nemesis to his kind.

Doc pursued. He put a great deal of effort in his flashing lunge. He wanted to question this rat. And he knew he would have to get the fellow before—

It happened!

Came a piercing shriek! It ended in a ghastly thunking sound and a horrible gurgling.

The man had fallen through the death trap in the passage—the trap from which the spar had saved Doc.

The upended swords in the pit under the trapdoor had thorned out the life of the fellow before Doc reached him!

Doc slowly returned to the deck. He had hoped to learn why the smoke screen had just been placed. His chance for that was gone with the thin man's death.

Thus also had vanished whatever chance Doc

might have had of learning that Monk was in a submersible barge under the river nearby.

Chapter IX
THE COLD KILLER

DOC SAVAGE moved toward the bows of the corsair craft. He desired to ascertain what had become of the bodies of Squint's unlucky companions. He had noted that the one who had died from the shock of a dismembered hand no longer reposed upon the deck.

The bodies had been added to the grisly exhibits of pirate butchery in the hold. A few garments of

... at times Doc was forced to tear up the planking ...

the seventeenth century had been drawn carelessly upon the bodies. So realistic was the rest of the exhibit that the real corpses fitted in perfectly with the ghastly scene. They could hardly be told from the papier-mâché victims of corsair lust.

Doc began at the bows and searched the buccaneer craft minutely.

He soon found a twisted pair of insulated wires of a telephone line. These came aboard inside one of the rope hawsers that moored the vessel to the wharf. So cleverly were they concealed that they would have escaped any but an unusually intent inspection.

Doc traced the wires. They descended to the very keel, near the limber board. Here they were covered with rubber for protection from the bilge water. They progressed aft. At times Doc was forced to tear up planking to keep track of them.

Near the stern, the wires suddenly passed through the hull into the water.

Doc returned to the deck. He stood near the taffrail. His golden eyes roved the river surface.

Entering the deckhouse, he removed his outer clothing and shoes. An amazing figure of bronze, he returned to the stern. He poised at the taffrail.

But he did not dive overboard immediately to follow the wires underwater.

A great bubble arose a few yards out in the river. A second came. Then a *blub-blub-blub* series of them!

This was air leaving the underwater cell in which Monk was imprisoned. The escaping air made room for the water that was drowning Monk.

But Doc knew only that the phenomenon was something suspicious. He waited to see what would happen next. Nothing did, except that the bubbles ceased to arise.

Doc dropped into the river. He drew plenty of air into his lungs before he struck. He swam, beneath the surface, out to the spot where the bubbles arose.

His powerful hands soon touched the steel tank-like submersible which lay on the river bottom. He explored along it. He found a box of a protuberance. This was the size of a very large trunk.

He heard faint struggle sounds from within the box.

Instantly, his great fingers went to work on the hatch which gave admission to the box. He got it open.

Monk toppled out.

MONK was a mighty distressed man, but far from dead. Opening his eyes, he could see Doc faintly in the water.

Monk's ill-timed bark of pleasure expelled the last vestige of air from his lungs. As a result, his drowning was nearly finished before Doc could get him to the surface.

"Imagine finding you here!" Doc chuckled. "You pick the strangest places to visit!"

Monk spouted a prodigious quantity of river water. He held up his manacled arms.

"Get these off, Doc!" he roared. "I'm gonna dive back down there and give them babies a taste of their own medicine! I'll tear a hole in the thing if nothing else!"

Doc Savage grasped the first of the three handcuffs on Monk's wrists. He brought the manacle close to his great chest and pulled.

Monstrous muscles popped out on his arms and shoulders. The handcuff chain snapped apart.

With successive duplications of this remarkable feat, Doc shattered the other cuffs securing Monk's wrists and ankles.

Monk immediately prepared to dive to the tank of a submarine on the river bottom. His pleasantly ugly face sank. He was thirsting for vengeance on the men who had tried to murder him.

Doc Savage followed him down.

Doc it was who found a way to attack those inside the sunken tank of the craft. He discovered that the dogs which held the entrance lid could be worked from the outside as well as the inside. They operated on the principle which is occasionally applied to the hatches of regulation submarines.

With a twist, Doc threw them. His powerful arms wrenched up the lid. With a great rush, water poured in.

Doc stroked back to the surface. Monk sputtered and splashed there, his simian face disappointed.

"I had no luck!" he growled.

"Watch it!" Doc called. "They'll be swimming out!"

Hardly had the warning been voiced when a streaming head broke water. Monk's fist swung like a sledge. The victim would have drowned had Monk not seized and held him.

A second of Kar's men came up from the tank-like craft, which, no doubt, was already filled with water. Doc captured that one. For the next few seconds, half-drowned villains bobbed on all sides.

Snorting and chuckling uproariously, Monk laid about briskly with his long, furry arms. He sounded like a porpoise disporting atop the water. Monk liked plenty of noise when he fought.

Monk kept count of their bag.

"That's all of 'em!" he announced at length. "Every rat of them got to the top."

The conquest had not been a difficult one. Kar's men were all but unconscious as they reached the surface. It became a matter of simply stunning each one, a simple process for such fists and strength as Doc and Monk possessed.

They made a human raft out of their captives and shoved them to the *Jolly Roger.* Monk held them there, keeping them afloat. He administered a judicious belt with a hairy fist when one showed signs of reviving. He grinned, "How I like this job!"

Doc stroked to a wharf pile. He climbed it with a rapidity that made the feat seem ridiculously easy.

COILED on the afterdeck, Doc Savage found a rope which would support the weight of a man. He lowered the end. Monk looped it under a prisoner's arms.

They had all the captives on the afterdeck of the *Jolly Roger* within a few seconds.

"What do we do with 'em?" Monk inquired.

"See what they know of Kar," Doc explained. He inspected the array of prisoners. "They may know something. None of them was with the group who met Squint."

"Squint—who's he?" Monk inquired. "Say, Doc, I still don't know what this is all about!"

Doc began with the fiendish murder of Jerome Coffern by the Smoke of Eternity and sketched briefly what had occurred.

"Whew!" muttered Monk. "And you think this Smoke of Eternity is a substance which shatters the atom! In that case, it certainly must have something new and hitherto undiscovered for its basic ingredient!"

"Exactly," Doc agreed. "It is possible Gabe Yuder discovered this new element, or whatever it is, on Thunder Island. He may be Kar."

They relieved their prisoners of arms, throwing the water-logged weapons into the river. The pockets of the men disgorged nothing that might lead to Kar.

One by one, the villainous group regained consciousness. One or two tried to escape. They didn't have a chance against Doc's flashing speed. And Monk, for all his anthropoid appearance, was a hairy blur when he wanted to move quickly.

The prisoners were herded forward. Doc forced them down in the fore hold, which held the unnerving display of pirate bloodthirstiness. He wanted them to have a good look at the three of Kar's men who were already dead there. The sight might loosen their tongues.

The gruesome exhibit proved to be potent medicine. The captives shuddered. They became pale.

"Where can Kar be found?" Doc demanded, his powerful voice holding a ring of command.

He got no answer. He had not expected one yet.

Monk picked up a big, gleaming cutlass. He whetted it suggestively on a soggy shoe sole, then whacked an ear off a papier-mâché likeness of a bearded pirate, just to show Kar's men how it might go.

"Only say the word, Doc!" He slanted a great arm at a wizened fellow who looked the most cowardly of the lot. "I'll start on the little one, there!"

The man in question whimpered in fright.

Doc's golden eyes came to rest on the cowardly one. The play of flaky gleamings within those orbs seemed to increase. The golden eyes gathered a compelling, hypnotic quality. They searched the very soul of the quailing captive.

"I—I—" the fellow frothed.

There was no question but that in a very few minutes he could have been made to tell all he knew.

But he never got the chance.

A DECK planking creaked above their heads. Someone lurked up there!

"Duck!" Doc breathed.

He and Monk faded into shadowy corners of the hold with the speed and silence of men accustomed to danger.

The man at the deck hatch must have caught a fleeting glimpse of Doc's bronze form.

A machine gun erupted down the hatch. The reports of the weapon were surprisingly mild—it was fitted with a silencer of some sort. The hosing metal torrent tore great, splinter-edged rents in the floor planks. It reduced a papier-mâché replica of a corsair victim to a chewed pile of paper-and-glue pulp.

Sudden silence fell.

Kar's men milled under the hatch, not knowing what to do. They looked up.

"Kar—"

The cowardly man of the group had started to speak. But he got no further than that one word.

Bur-r-rip! A machine-gun volley poured into him. His wizened body seemed to lose all its shape under the murderous leaden stream.

The rapid-firer did not stop with his death. It ripped into the other members of Kar's gang.

Doc Savage knew that the first man to die had seen Kar at the hatch above. Kar was slaying the whole group so none of them could give information concerning him.

It was one of the most cold-blooded, fiendish things Doc had ever witnessed.

In a half dozen ticks of a stopwatch, every man of Kar's in the hold died under the gobbling machine gun.

Then Kar ran wildly away from the hatch, across the deck. Both Doc and Monk heard the master murderer's leap to the wharf.

Doc's bronze, giant form flashed from the shadows. It seemed to slide upward on invisible wires. Powerful fingers seized the hatch rim. Doc looked out.

A man raced furiously shoreward along the wharf. He wore a dark raincoat. It enveloped his form down to the ankles. He had a large, nondescript, concealing hat.

Kar—for he it must be—still carried his submachine gun. He whirled suddenly and let fly a volley of bullets.

Doc dropped back into the hold an instant before slivers flew from the hatch edge. But he had seen that Kar's face was wrapped in a great mask of dark cloth. It covered even his neck.

Whether Kar was Gabe Yuder it was impossible to tell. The fleeing figure *could* be Gabe Yuder, though.

Doc did not try to leave by the hatch again. He raced aft. Monk trailed him.

"What a cold killer!" Monk grated.

"There should be guns in the deckhouse!" Doc breathed.

They found the guns. A rack held quite an arsenal of modern weapons. Kar had prepared well. They sprang out on deck.

But Kar was something of a sprinter. Already, he had scampered well up the bluff which was surmounted by Riverside Drive. He kept to the concealment of scrawny shrubbery.

Doc saw a bush shake and fired into it. Machine gun missiles came screaming back in a second. They forced Doc to cover.

Kar reached the low stone wall at the bluff rim. He dived over it.

Doc and Monk found no trace of the fiendish killer when they reached Riverside Drive.

Chapter X
HOT PURSUIT

"KAR must have had an automobile waitin' here on the Drive," guessed Monk. "Did you get a look at his face, Doc?"

"No," Doc replied slowly. "He was quite thoroughly masked. Whoever he is, he is taking pains that his face does not become known."

Monk and Doc soon found themselves the object of many eyes. A crowd began to gather.

Monk's clothing was still wet and clung to his great, beamlike limbs, making their anthropoid nature more prominent. He looked like a monster gorilla beside Doc.

Doc Savage had not donned the garments he had removed to dive from the *Jolly Roger* into the river. He stood clad only in shorts. Pedestrians on Riverside Drive got a glimpse of Doc's amazing bronze form and stopped to stare in awe.

That giant, metallic figure was a sensation. A passing motorist sighted the bronze man and was so held that he forgot his driving and let his car jam into another.

"We better clear out before we start a panic," Monk snorted.

Hailing a taxi, they got inside. Doc directed the chauffeur to turn into the street which held the row of houses, each of which was so closely like all the others.

Doc entered the tenth house quickly. He soon found Long Tom's electrical apparatus which put the high-frequency current on the secret telephone line.

Glancing from the rear window at which he had listened, Doc discovered Long Tom working along the back of the houses with his sensitive electrical "ear" mechanism.

Doc tarried to note that the body of Squint had not been removed from the room. Evidently the other rooms in the house were untenanted.

Then Doc slid through the window, descended the wall as easily as a fly, and consulted with Long Tom.

"There is a telephone line from a tank-like submersible sunken near that old pirate exhibition vessel," he explained. "The line enters the pirate ship, then leaves inside a mooring cable. When you trace this line down, you might trace that one also."

"O. K.," said Long Tom.

"And watch out for Kar. The man is a devil."

Long Tom nodded and drew back his coat to show that he had donned a bulletproof vest. Belted to his middle, he also wore a singular pistol. This gun was fitted with a cartridge magazine of extra capacity, curled like a ram's horn for compactness. The weapon was one of Doc's invention. In operation, it was what is known as continuously automatic—actually an extremely small machine gun.

"I'm prepared," Long Tom said, his rather unhealthy looking face set grimly.

Retracing his steps to the taxi, Doc directed the machine to his skyscraper headquarters downtown. He and Monk went inside in haste to avoid attracting undue attention. An elevator wafted them up to the eighty-sixth floor.

They entered Doc's office. Surprise stopped them.

Oliver Wording Bittman, the taxidermist, sat waiting!

AROUND and around his forefinger, the taxidermist was spinning the skinning scalpel which he wore on his watch chain. He leaped erect. A strange, worried light filled his dark, determined eyes. His rough, weather-darkened skin seemed a little pale. His large jaw had a desperate tightness.

"I am paying my visit to you rather sooner than expected," he said. He tried to smile. The smile didn't quite jell.

Doc knew there was something behind the perturbation of this man who had saved his father's life.

"You are in trouble?" he inquired curiously.

Bittman nodded violently.

"I certainly am!" He unbuttoned his vest and shirt with thin fingers. He lifted a bandage below.

There was a shallow scrape of a wound across the man's ribs. It resembled the mark of a bullet.

"I was shot at," Bittman explained. "You can see

how narrowly the bullet missed being my finish. This occurred only a few minutes after you left my apartment."

"Did you see who fired?"

"It was Yuder!"

"Gabe Yuder?"

"It was!" Bittman said fiercely. "He escaped in an automobile. But not before I saw his face. The man you call Kar is Gabe Yuder!"

Violent flickerings were in Doc's flaky eyes as he spoke to Bittman.

"In some mysterious manner, Kar learned I visited you, Bittman. One of his men, piloting a seaplane, made an unsuccessful attempt on my life soon after I left your apartment."

"This means Kar has marked me for death," muttered Oliver Wording Bittman. He juggled the watch-chain scalpel nervously. "I—I wonder—if—could I—join you for my own protection? To be frank, I do not believe the police would be equal to a thing such as this."

Doc Savage hesitated not at all. Although he and his five remarkable men worked best alone, unimpeded by the presence of one of lesser ability, he could not refuse Bittman. The man had done Doc's father a supreme favor, as evidenced by the picture and the letter Bittman possessed.

"Of course you can join us," Doc replied generously. "But perhaps I had better warn you that being with us will not be exactly safe. We seem to draw death and violence like honey draws bees. You might be more secure from danger if you went into hiding somewhere."

Bittman's large jaw set firmly. "I am not a coward who runs to a hiding place! I wish to assist you in my feeble way. Jerome Coffern was a friend of mine! I beg you to permit me to do my bit to bring the man who murdered him to justice! That is all I ask. Will you not grant it?"

This speech moved Doc Savage. Bittman had voiced Doc's own motives in pursuing the devilish Kar.

"You shall become one of us," Doc declared.

He knew, however, that in accepting Bittman's presence, he was taking on added responsibilities. Bittman's life would have to be guarded.

JOHNNY, the elongated, gaunt geologist and archaeologist, now appeared. He came in bearing a sizeable box. It seemed quite heavy.

"The rock specimens from Thunder Island," he announced. "There's a lot of them. Jerome Coffern made a complete collection."

Doc Savage gave the specimens a swift inspection. But he did not put them under a microscope or start analyzing them.

"No time right now to examine them intensively," he explained. "That can come later."

He locked the specimens in a safe which stood in the outer office. This safe was rather large. In height, it came above Doc's shoulder.

Taking fresh clothing from the concealed locker, Doc put it on.

He got from the laboratory a large sheet of cardboard such as artists use to make drawings upon. A cabinet yielded pencils.

"If you'll just lend me some assistance," he requested Oliver Wording Bittman, "I am going to make a sketch of Gabe Yuder, as you described him. I want you to watch me and point out any differences between my sketch and Yuder's features."

Doc's steady, sensitive bronze fingers moved with a rapidity that defied the eye. On the cardboard took form, as though by magic, the features of a man.

"A little fuller in the cheeks," said Bittman, "and a smaller jaw."

The work came to an end.

"That is a remarkable likeness!" said Bittman.

"This is for the police," Doc told him. "We will have them put out an alarm for Gabe Yuder. If we get him—we will—"

"We will have Kar!" Bittman said fiercely.

Calling a messenger, Doc dispatched the drawing to the nearest police station.

Soon after, the voices of Renny and Ham were heard in the corridor.

"Poor Monk!" Renny's voice rambled. "We found nothing but a bootblack who saw Monk forced into a car. That means those devils took him for a ride. He's done for!"

There was the trace of a sob in Ham's reply.

"I'm afraid you're right, Renny. It's a terrible thing. Monk was one of the finest men who ever lived. I actually loved Monk!"

Monk heard this. Devilment danced in his little, starry eyes. He looked like he was going to explode with mirth.

For Ham, the waspish, quick-thinking lawyer, had never before expressed such sweet sentiments. He was wont to call Monk the "missing link" and other things even less complimentary. To hear the sharp-tongued Ham talk, one would think nothing would give him more pleasure than to stick his sword cane in Monk's anthropoid form.

This peeve of Ham's dated back to the Great War, to the incident which had given Ham his nickname. As a joke, Ham had taught Monk some French words which were highly insulting, telling Monk they were the proper things to flatter a Frenchman with. Monk had addressed the words to a French general, and that worthy promptly had Monk clapped in the guardhouse for several days.

But within the week after Monk's release, Ham was haled upon a charge of stealing hams.

Somebody had planted the evidence. Ham had never been able to prove it was Monk who framed him, and it still irked him to think of it. He blamed Monk for the nickname of Ham, which he didn't particularly care for.

HAM and Renny entered. They saw Monk.

"Haw, haw, haw!" Monk let out a tornado of laughter. "So you love me, eh?"

Ham carefully wiped from his face the first flash of joy at seeing Monk.

"I'd love to cut your hairy throat!" he snapped angrily.

Doc advised Ham and Renny what had happened to Monk. As he finished, the telephone rang. Long Tom's voice came over the wire.

"I've traced the phone wire from that tenth house," he advised. "And also the one from the *Jolly Roger.*"

"We'll be right up!" Doc declared.

Monk, Renny, Ham and Johnny were plunging through the door as Doc hung up. They had buckled on bulletproof vests. They had seized the small, deadly machine guns which were Doc's invention.

Oliver Wording Bittman seemed dazed by the suddenness with which these men went into action. Swallowing his astonishment, he dived in their wake.

Doc summoned an elevator.

"Better take two taxicabs!" he advised when they were on the street. "If Kar should turn that Smoke of Eternity on one carload, it wouldn't get us all."

"Pleasant thought!" Monk grinned.

The two cabs wheeled up Fifth Avenue. Doc rode the running board of the foremost machine. He habitually did this, for his very presence was a charm which magically gave him right of way through all traffic. New York City's traffic policemen had been instructed by their chiefs to give every assistance to this remarkable man of bronze.

Too, Doc preferred to be outside where his keen eyes missed nothing. For this reason also, Doc's personal cars were always roadsters or convertibles, the tops of which could be lowered.

The trip uptown turned out to be uneventful.

Long Tom, thin and sallow and looking like an invalid, but in reality as tough as any of Doc's entourage, stood at a corner on Riverside Drive. His two boxes of apparatus were at his feet.

Doc had his cab pull up beside Long Tom.

"Where'd the wires go?" he asked.

Long Tom made a wry face. "I'm afraid we're out of luck. The wires led from that tenth house, along the rear of other houses and went under Riverside Drive through a culvert. From there, they led underground down to that pirate ship, the *Jolly Roger.* They went aboard through a hawser, down to the keel, then into the water to—"

"To the tank-like submersible!" Doc said disgustedly. "So the wires in the room and on the boat were one circuit!"

"That's it," Long Tom agreed.

DOC SAVAGE now shook his bronze head. "This is strange, Long Tom! When Kar talked to Monk, the fellow would hardly have been reckless enough to have done so from that room. He knew I had discovered the place."

"The secret phone circuit didn't branch off anywhere," Long Tom said with certainty. He pointed at his instruments. "My thingamajig would have shown it if the wires were tapped anywhere."

Doc's golden eyes ranged along the landward side of Riverside Drive. Apartment houses fronting the Drive were new and tall, although those on the side streets were not nearly so opulent. The Drive apartments commanded a view of the Hudson. They brought neat rentals.

Doc's low, strange, trilling sound abruptly came from his lips. It was hardly audible now. Probably no one but Long Tom heard it. And Long Tom grinned. He knew this sound presaged some remarkable feat of Doc's, for it came at the bronze man's moments of greatest concentration. The sound with the weird, melodious quality of some weird jungle bird always precursed a masterstroke.

"Let us do some investigating, brothers," Doc said softly.

He led them into the tenth house from the corner, which held in an upstairs room the end of the secret phone line. But Doc did not go upstairs. He guided the group out through a rear door.

Here was a long, narrow court. The place was untidy. Rickety old wooden fences marked off backyards hardly larger than good-sized bedspreads. Rusty clotheslines draped like old cobwebs.

The court resembled little else than a brick-walled pit. At the Riverside Drive end, the rear wall of a great apartment house towered many stories. At the opposite end was a lesser building. And on either side, the shabby sterns of old tenements buttressed each other solidly.

Evening was near. The hulking buildings threw shadows into the pit of a court.

Doc moved along the court, toward Riverside Drive. His sharp eyes soon located the secret phone wires. These followed the chinks between bricks for the most part. They had been coated with a paint the exact color of the brickwork.

They reached the wall of the immensely larger building which fronted Riverside Drive. Turning here, the thin, hardly visible strands traced along the rear of the structure.

At one point, a loop abruptly dangled out—a very small loop.

Doc pointed at this. "Notice anything peculiar about that?"

Long Tom stared.

"The insulation is gone at that point!" he ejaculated. "The naked copper of the wires shows!"

"Exactly. Note also that there are many windows directly above the spot."

"You mean Kar tapped them there and—"

"By reaching down and clipping the ends of other wires to them," Doc replied. "That means he did it from the window immediately above! Those loops are too small to be fished for from a greater distance."

To Renny and Johnny, Doc breathed a command. "You two stay here. Watch that window. Shoot at the slightest hostile move.

"The rest of you come with me!"

He led them swiftly around to the front of the apartment building which overlooked Riverside Drive.

THEY shoved past a bewildered doorman. The foyer was decorated elaborately. Deep carpet swathed the floor. It seemed quite a high-class establishment.

Doc described to the doorman the location of the apartment they suspected.

"Who lives there?" he asked.

"No one, yet," replied the doorman. "It was rented some time ago, but the tenant has not yet moved in."

Doc, Monk, Ham, Long Tom and Oliver Wording Bittman hurried up the stairs. Luxurious carpet made their footsteps noiseless. They reached the suspicious apartment.

Halting the others with an uplifted arm, some yards from the door, Doc advanced alone. He did not want them near enough that the sound of their breathing would interfere with his listening. For Doc's ears were keen enough that he could detect the faintest respiration noises of men within the apartment.

He listened. Lowering close to the threshold, where there gaped a small crack, he used his nostrils. The olfactory senses of the average man are underdeveloped through insufficient use. He has no need for a super-keen organ of smell. Indeed, city life is more comfortable if the multitude of odors present go unnoticed. But Doc Savage, through unremitting, scientific exercise, had developed an olfactory sense far beyond the common.

Doc's ears and nostrils told him no one occupied the apartment. He tried the door. Locked! He exerted what for his great muscles was moderate pressure. The door swished inward, lock torn out.

Not only was the place untenanted, but it held no furniture. The bare, varnished floor glistened faintly in the light of approaching evening.

Doc glided to the window. He waved at Renny and Johnny in the brick-sided pit of a courtyard below. His gesture advised them to stay where they were.

Back to the door, Doc whipped. His movements seemed effortless for all their speed.

Although there was no sign of a wire by which the secret phone line had been tapped, Doc was not satisfied. His trained brain told him where to look.

He tugged at the corridor carpet immediately outside the door. It came up readily.

The ends of two fine wires were revealed.

"They used a splice long enough to reach from these through the window!" Doc told the others.

Wrenching up the carpet, he followed the wires down the corridor.

Oliver Wording Bittman was white-faced. The flesh on his big jaw looked hard as rock. But he was not trembling.

"I am unarmed," he said jerkily. "C-can one of you loan me a gun? One of those c-compact machine guns! I want to do my part to wipe out those fiends!"

Doc reached a quick decision. It was his duty to take care of Bittman's life, a repayment for the man's service to his father.

"We neglected to bring along an extra gun," he said. "If you wish to help, you might hurry down and call the police."

Bittman smiled. "I see through your ruse to get me out of harm's way. But, of course, I will call the officers."

He retreated down the wide stairway.

Doc continued to follow the wire. It terminated at a door of a front apartment.

Hardly had he determined that fact when a storm of bullets crashed through the door.

ONLY Doc's instinct for caution, which had urged him to keep clear of the door, saved his life.

"They're inside!" Monk howled. "Now for a rat killin'!"

Monk's compact machine gun coughed a blatting roar of sound. He literally cut the door off its hinges. It fell inward.

More lead came out of the apartment of the besieged. The slugs hit nobody. But they gouged plaster off the walls. The plaster dust became a blinding cloud. A machine gun equipped with a silencer was doing most of the shooting from within the apartment.

"That sounds like Kar's typewriter!" Monk bellowed. "He's in there!"

Doc abruptly backed from the door.

"You handle this end!" he directed.

He glided down the stairs to the foyer.

Oliver Wording Bittman stood in a telephone booth, speaking rapidly into the instrument.

"Yes! Send a riot squad!" he was saying.

Doc's bronze form slid outside. Excitement had gripped the street. A cop was coming from the corner, tweedling vigorously on his whistle. Upon the thoroughfare, the shots within the apartment building sounded like clamoring thunder.

To the apartment window, Doc's golden eyes flashed. What they saw was about the most disappointing thing possible.

A rope made of knotted bedclothing dangled from the open window! This makeshift cord hung to within ten feet of the walk.

Doc's gaze raked right and left. They ranged far up and down Riverside Drive. Nowhere did they detect trace of anyone who might have escaped down that rope.

Running lightly and leaping, Doc grasped the rope end. Powerful fingers clamped an ornamental fresco and helped the bedclothing support his weight. He went up rapidly.

An ugly face poked out of the window. A pipestem arm brought an automatic pistol into view. But before the weapon had a chance to discharge, an incredible vise of bronze fingers clamped the killer's scrawny neck. They jerked.

The man came out of the window with a snap. Screeching, he fell to his death far out in the street.

An instant later, Monk, Long Tom and Ham charged the room. Their compact guns stuttered briefly. Two of Kar's men collapsed. They had been among those assembled by Squint. One fell and leaked crimson over the muffled machine gun which had been used by Kar at the pirate ship, *Jolly Roger.*

Of Kar, there was no sign.

"He got away—down the rope of bedclothing," Ham declared regretfully. "Although it is possible he was never in the room!"

A brief examination showed the secret phone line terminated in the apartment of death. Glancing from the window, Doc also ascertained another thing.

"You can see the *Jolly Roger* from here," he informed Monk. "That accounts for Kar's appearance. He saw us capture those men of his from the underwater tank."

DOC returned with his friends to his skyscraper office downtown.

The police received from Doc Savage an account of what was happening. Doc, however, withheld all reference to the plan to steal the gold destined for the Chicago banks.

This puzzled Ham.

"We'll stop that robbery ourselves," Doc explained. "Kar will use his infernal Smoke of Eternity. The police have no defense against it. Many of them would be killed."

"Well, won't Kar use it on us, too?" Monk snorted.

"If he applies it to you, I want to be watching!" the sharp-tongued Ham told Monk. "I'll bet the cloud of smoke it turns you into will have a spike tail, horns and pitchfork!"

"Maybe. But it won't make a noise like this!" And Monk gave a boisterous imitation of a pig grunting.

Ham reddened and shut up. All Monk had to do to get Ham's goat was make some reference to a porker. Monk often made those piggy, grunting noises just to see Ham swell up with rage.

Long Tom suddenly emitted a howl of surprise. Wandering about the office nervously, he had chanced to look behind the safe.

A large hole gaped there! The solid steel had simply been wiped away!

Doc hurriedly opened the safe.

The rock specimens from Thunder Island were gone!

"Kar, or one of his men, opened a hole in the rear of the safe with that Smoke of Eternity, and got the specimens!" Doc declared.

"But how did he know they were there?" Monk muttered.

It was Oliver Wording Bittman who suggested an answer. He indicated the spire of a skyscraper some blocks distant. From an observation tower which topped this, it was possible to see into Doc's office.

"They must have had a man watching from there!" he offered.

Doc drew the shades, saying, "It won't happen again."

"Doc, that shows you were on the right trail with those specimens," Johnny, the geologist, spoke up excitedly. He adjusted his glasses which had the magnifying lens on the left side. "Otherwise, Kar would not have taken so much trouble to take them away."

Night had fallen. In the great buildings surrounding Doc's high perch, only a few glowing freckles marked lighted windows.

The police commissioner of the City of New York paid Doc Savage's office a call in person to express his appreciation for Doc's services thus far in wiping out the fiendish Kar and his gang. Shortly after this, Doc received a telegram, also expressing thanks, from the New Jersey police official in whose jurisdiction the murder of Jerome Coffern had occurred.

And the tabloid newspapers ranted at the cops for not telling their reporters what was happening. The police were keeping secret Doc's connection with the sudden epidemic of death among criminals, at his request.

Doc now locked himself in his laboratory. He retrieved from the bottom of the microscope, where he had hidden it, the tiny capsule which had held the Smoke of Eternity. With all the resources of his great laboratory and his trained brain, he set to work to learn the nature of the strange metal.

It was nearly midnight when he came out of the laboratory.

"You fellows stick here," he told Monk, Ham, Renny, Johnny, Long Tom and Oliver Wording Bittman.

He departed without telling the six men whence he was bound or what nature of plan his profound mind had evolved.

Chapter XI
DOC SPRINGS A TRAP

THREE o'clock in the morning!

A black ghost of a night seemed to have sucked the city into its maw. There was fog, like the clammy breath of that night ghost. Out on the bay, a night owl ferry to Staten Island hooted disconsolately at some fancied obstruction in its path.

The financial district was quiet. The silence in Wall Street was like that among the tombstones in Trinity Churchyard, which lies at the uphill end of the street.

The big feet of occasional policemen made dull clappings on the deserted sidewalks. Periodic subway trains rumbled like monstrous sleepy beasts underground.

Things more sinister were impending around the bank, the vaults of which held the gold coin that tomorrow was to go to the aid of hard-pressed Chicago financial institutions.

The watchman didn't know it, as yet. He was a thick-headed chap, honest, but inclined to do things suddenly and think about it later.

"When I see somethin' suspicious, I shoot and ask questions afterward," he was wont to say. He was proud of this. So far, it had miraculously failed to get him into serious trouble. The only people he had shot were those who happened to need it.

The watchman noted a strange grayish haze which seemed to hang in the bank. He passed this off as fog. He would have thought differently, had he seen an enormous hole which gaped in one wall of the building. But he failed to see this, because most of his attention went to the doors and windows, where crooks usually tried to enter.

Nor did the watchman see a ratty man who slid out of the gloom of a cashier's cage. This marauder raised an air pistol. He pointed it at the man's back.

Suddenly a mighty bronze form flashed from the adjacent cage. A powerful hand clapped upon the air pistol. Another terrible hand covered all the ratty man's face, drawing the loose skin, lips and nostrils into a tight bunch from which no outcry could escape.

There ensued a brief flurry. The air pistol went off with a dull *chung!*

Only then did the watchman wake up. He spun, instinctively tugging at his hip pocket for his gun. His jaw fell in horror.

The ratty man had taken the missile from the air pistol. The fellow lay on the floor. That is—his upper body lay there! His legs had already dissolved in a grisly grayish smoke, shot through and through with weird electrical flashes.

The air-pistol slug of Smoke of Eternity had hit the man in the foot. The discharge of the thing was an accident.

Over the dissolving form towered an awesome man-figure that looked like solid, tempered bronze. It was such a figure as the watchman had never seen.

The watchman went wild. He tried to put into effect his shoot-first-and-question-later creed. He got his gun out.

But about that time, a ton of dynamite seemed to explode on his jaw. He never even saw the great bronze fist which had hit him.

Doc Savage swept the watchman up. He glided silently across the floor. The gloom behind a vice president's desk swallowed him and his burden.

INTO the bank now came more than a dozen furtive men. They carried automatic pistols and submachine guns.

One man alone had an air pistol. "C'mon!" he snarled. "Kar's orders was to push this right through!"

"Hey, Guffey!" called one. "Didja fix the watchman?"

When there was no answer from their companion, they muttered uneasily. Then they advanced.

"Gosh, look!" a man choked.

On the floor, just turning into the horrible gray vapor, lay a human head.

"It's Guffey!"

For a moment, it looked like they were going to flee. The sight of the fantastic thing happening to Guffey's head drained whatever courage they had.

"Aw, get next to yourselves, you mugs!" sneered the man who carried the only other air pistol. "You don't see the watchman around, do you? Guffey just had a little accident. The Smoke of Eternity dissolved both him and the watchman."

After a few more mutters, the explanation of the watchman's absence and Guffey's demise was accepted. The men set to work. They advanced on the vault. The man with the air pistol fired it at the vault door.

Instantly, the thick steel began dissolving into the strange smoke.

Over in the shadow of the vice president's desk, Doc Savage's sensitive bronze fingers explored the air pistol, the slug from which had finished Guffey. He was disgusted to learn it held no other capsule cartridge of the Smoke of Eternity.

Doc recalled the words of the man dying from a lopped-off hand aboard the *Jolly Roger*. The fellow had said that Kar never gave one of his men more than a single cartridge of the Smoke of Eternity. Kar feared, probably, that his men would launch out on a robbery campaign of their own if supplied with a quantity of the stuff.

The dissolving of the vault door had now ceased, the potency of the missile of Smoke of Eternity exhausted.

Kar's men were reluctant to go near the opening, at first. They were like boys playing with a mad dog. They didn't know but what the fearsome dissolving substance might do them harm.

But one finally entered the vault. The others followed. In a moment, they reappeared weighted down with sacks of clinking gold coin. Gone was their hesitation now. The gold had affected them like potent liquor. They were drunk with the thought of such wealth.

In the shadow of the desk, Doc's mighty bronze form remained motionless. The numbskull guard slept silently at his feet. Doc was letting the robbery go forward!

But it was for good purpose. He wanted to trail the loot to Kar!

The thieves were stacking the swag near the hole they had opened in the bank building.

Doc's golden eyes missed no move. He reasoned they would haul it away in one or more trucks. Two million dollars in gold weighed a great deal.

His reasoning was right—just as right as had been his guess that Kar might try to get his hands on this gold without waiting for it to leave New York by train. For Kar was clever enough to realize the train plot might have been overheard by Doc.

A large truck rolled up in the dark side street beside the hole in the bank wall. Into this, the thieves heaved sacks of gold coin.

At this point, the watchman began to revive. With his first move, he was pinned helplessly by hard bronze arms. He could not have been held more solidly had he been dressed in a block of solid steel. Nor could he cry out, or use his eyes.

The last bag of gold was hoisted into the truck by tired arms that were very unused to anything that smacked of work. The truck was large. It held all the gold.

The thieves piled in. The truck rolled away.

DOC'S impressive voice throbbed against the ear of the helpless watchman. It was pregnant with command.

"Call the police! Tell them the bank was robbed by Kar's men. They will know who is meant by Kar's men. Do you understand?"

The watchman started to swear at Doc, but desisted quickly when he felt the power of those great bronze fingers.

"I understand," he mumbled.

"You are to tell them nothing else until they

arrive," Doc continued. "Then you can tell them of me. Tell them Doc Savage was here. They will keep it out of the newspapers. And, most important of all, you are not to tell the newspapers of me, understand?"

The watchman snarled that he did. Doc had saved his life, but the man was far from grateful.

Doc Savage glided for the door.

Instantly, the watchman made a dive for his gun, which lay on the floor near the spot where the body of Guffey had dissolved. The man's fingers clenched the weapon.

But when he lifted the muzzle, no bronze man could be seen. This reminded the watchman of the horrible dissolving of a human body he had witnessed. He got an attack of the jitters. His knees shook so he had to sit down on the floor and recover his nerve.

Doc Savage followed the truck. He had expended only a few minutes with the watchman. The truck had rolled slowly, so there would be less noise. Three blocks only, it had covered.

Doc ran. He haunted the gloom next to buildings. The truck headed uptown. Doc kept pace easily.

After fifteen blocks or so, the big bronze man hailed a nighthawking taxi. His physical condition was so perfect that he was breathing no more swiftly than normal when he entered the taxicab.

"Follow that truck," Doc directed. He noted the taxi driver had an honest face and frank manners. He displayed a bill.

The denomination of the bill made the driver gulp.

"This can't be honest money!" he grinned.

"Stop and take aboard the first cop you see, if you think it's not honest," Doc invited.

"You win!" the driver chuckled.

The hackman knew his business. He drove ahead of the truck, haunted side streets parallel to its course, and remained behind, where he might arouse suspicion, only at rare intervals.

Keeping to the East Side, where fish trucks were already beginning to rumble on the streets, the thieves drove far uptown. Near the northern end of Manhattan Island, they turned west and crossed the isle. Then they came down the other side. They had simply gone out of their way to mislead the police, should the officers get a description of the vehicle.

The thieves' destination was the *Jolly Roger!*

The truck pulled down the bluff from Riverside Drive on a rutty old road used by dump vehicles.

Doc dismissed his taxi at the top of the bluff. The shadows gobbled him up. He reappeared near the ancient corsair craft, to lurk in the shelter of a tangled bush.

He watched the thieves consign the bags of gold coin to a hiding place. The simplicity of that hiding place surprised him.

They merely dumped the gold off the ramshackle wharf!

THE spot they chose for the dumping was out in deep water, near the stern of the *Jolly Roger,* but between the hull of the old craft and the wharf.

"Drop it close to the hull, you fool!" Doc heard one of the thieves order another. "Be sure it lands on the shelf fastened to the hull!"

So that explained it!

Far enough beneath the river surface that no one would ever notice, there was a shelf affixed to the *Jolly Roger.* Considering that the police now knew Kar had used the old corsair ship, it was a daring move to conceal the loot here. But perhaps the safer for that! Searchers would hardly suspect so prominent a spot.

It was far from what it seemed—this old buccaneer vessel.

Doc waited patiently for some sign of Kar.

Another man appeared unexpectedly, running from the direction of the bluff. He made a good deal of noise in the darkness.

Guns were clutched uneasily. Then the thieves hailed the newcomer as one of their number. "We nearly let you have it!"

Conversation followed, the new arrival speaking rapidly. The words were pitched too low to reach Doc, who was some distance away.

Then tones were raised.

"All but four of you clear out!" commanded the late arrival. "That's Kar's orders. I'm to take the four who stay to Kar."

Several loud grumbles wafted to Doc's sharply tuned ears. But whatever the dissension was, the thieves accepted the command of their leader. Probably they were complaining about leaving the gold unwatched.

The last of the coin plunked overside to land on the shelf fastened to the *Jolly Roger* hull. All but four of the looters got in the truck. The big machine rumbled away.

The four who had remained stood on the wharf with the man who had brought them their orders. Several minutes passed. Noise of the truck died away.

"C'mon!" said the messenger loudly. "I'll take you to Kar now!"

The man turned toward the old pirate ship.

"Kar is on the *Jolly Roger*?" ejaculated one of the gang.

"Sure! What'd you think?"

The men disappeared aboard the corsair vessel.

Little more than a darker blur in the murk, Doc's bronze figure flashed to the *Jolly Roger*. He scaled the rail with a catlike leap.

Shuffling footsteps located his quarry. They

were aft. Down a companion, they went. Doc trailed. He had not visited this part of the craft, despite the number of times he had been aboard. The weird vessel was a labyrinth of narrow passages and tiny cubicles. Evidently every old-time pirate had had to have his individual cabin.

The police, Doc knew, had searched the *Jolly Roger* from stem to stern when they removed the bodies of Kar's mobsters to the morgue. Had Kar been hiding aboard, they would have found him.

Doc kept only a few yards behind the five he followed. He entered the third of a series of cramped passages.

A door slammed behind him, barring the passage.

He flung forward. But even his marvelous fleetness could not get him to the passage end before that, too, was blocked by a closing door.

Then the entire ceiling of the passage descended with a crash upon his head!

THE dropping roof would have crushed the life from a body a whit less like springy steel than Doc's. The mass of monster timbers must have weighed a full ton. The innocent-looking up-and-down beams at the passage sides formed guides upon which the ugly trap operated.

Doc caught the tremendous weight on broad, arched shoulders. He put forth gigantic effort. He broke the deadly force somewhat. But the shock bore him to hands and knees.

Instantly, the door in front of Doc opened. A flashlight sprayed blinding luminance into his golden eyes.

"Got him!" chortled the man who had brought the message to the thieves. "We outsmarted him slick as could be!"

An air-pistol snout poked into the flash beam. It leveled at Doc's perfectly formed bronze features.

Chung! It discharged.

The flashlight promptly went out as the man who held it leaped back. Obviously, he was fearful some of the ghastly Smoke of Eternity would be splashed upon his person.

From a distance of several yards, the men waited.

"How did Kar get wise the bronze guy was followin' us?" one asked the messenger.

"Simple" was the chuckled reply. "The watchman at that bank telephoned the morning newspapers a big bronze bird had attacked him and robbed the vault. Guess he phoned the papers before the police. Probably wanted to see his name in print.

"Anyway, it caught the newspapers just at the deadline. They came out with it on the front page. Kar has men watching every paper to grab the editions as they hit the street. He does that to keep track of things. Sometimes the papers have news ahead of the police. Anyhow, the minute Kar got his dope, he reasoned the bronze guy was trailin' the loot in hopes it would lead him to the chief's hangout."

"So he sent you—"

"So he sent me here to make that loud talk about leadin' you guys to him." The speaker laughed nastily. "Kar knew Doc Savage would follow us right into this trap!"

"Kar is pretty slick," said one of the group, smitten with evil admiration.

"You said it! Slickest of all is how he keeps anybody from ever seein' him, or even of learnin' what his real name is."

"We were in luck that the watchman called the papers!"

The flashlight spilled glare onto the passage deadfall.

Vile gray smoke had made a sizeable smudge. Eerie electrical sparks played in a pronounced fashion.

The heavy timbers of the deadfall were dissolving!

"That," leered one of the men, "fixes the bronze guy!"

But, whether the bronze man met his end or not, his companions were still at his office headquarters; while Doc was out on his errand, they were waiting for the next move.

Chapter XII
THE TERRIBLE DESTROYER

IN Doc Savage's skyscraper office, six men were waiting the night out, obeying Doc's command to wait as he made his hurried exit the previous night.

Dawn was not far off. Over on the Sixth Avenue Elevated, trains were beginning to rattle past more often. In another hour, the city would awaken in earnest.

On a table in the office lay the last edition of a morning newspaper. Emblazoned in scare type on the front page was the story the stupid watchman had turned in. The scream heads read:

MYSTERIOUS BRONZE MAN
ROBS BANK

"I wonder if we should do something about that?" Johnny, the geologist, murmured anxiously, wiping his glasses with the thick left lens.

"Doc knows what he is about!" declared Long Tom, who had his nose buried in a highly technical pamphlet on advanced electrical research. "Shut up and let me read."

"Yes, do shut up!" Ham echoed. "I want to listen to this remarkable music!"

Monk and Renny, with the innate calmness of men huge physically, were sleeping. Monk snored. His snores had the peculiar quality of no two sounding remotely alike.

Ham, the waspish, quick-thinking lawyer, sat near Monk, listening with great interest to the variety of snore noises in Monk's repertoire. His sword cane was between his knees.

"Can you imagine!" Ham jeered. "Not only is Monk the homeliest bird on earth, but he makes the awfulest noises!"

Of the six men present, only Oliver Wording Bittman betrayed nervousness. He got up from his chair often. He paced the floor.

"Aren't you worried about Doc Savage?" he inquired wonderingly. "He left near midnight. Now it is almost dawn, and no word."

Long Tom repeated his previous declaration. "Doc knows what he is doing. Long ago, we learned not to worry about him."

Bittman made a move to return to his chair. His fingers sought the scalpel on his watch chain. Twirling the thing seemed to give him nervous surcease.

Suddenly he leveled an arm at the door.

"Listen!" he breathed. "Did you hear something?"

Monk promptly awakened—although the words were far less loud than others he had slept through. One had a suspicion Monk had been pretending sleep so as to annoy Ham with his snoring.

Renny's gigantic fist had ruined the door panel, but temporary repairs had been effected with rough boards.

A faint sound came from the other side of the door. Feet scuffing the corridor floor! Someone in flight!

Monk kicked over the chair in which Renny slept. In a thundering avalanche, Doc's five friends hit the door. They volleyed through. Oliver Wording Bittman jumped out of their path as though getting clear of a stampede.

A man was just wedging into one of two waiting elevators.

Doc had described all of the recruits assembled to Kar's cause by Squint. This was one of them!

The man got the elevator door shut before Doc's friends reached it. The cage sank swiftly.

But directly beside the lift the sneak had used, stood another car, open.

In the office, Oliver Wording Bittman searched about wildly, calling, "Where are the guns?" He was not going to barge into trouble unarmed, it seemed.

Renny, Long Tom, Johnny, and Monk dived into the open elevators. Monk stamped the button which started the doors sliding shut.

Quick-thinking, waspish Ham threw himself against the closing panels, halting them.

"Hold on a minute!" he clipped. "That man deliberately let himself be heard! And there is no attendant in this elevator!"

THE others stared at Ham, not comprehending what he was driving at.

"Scat!" rumbled Monk. "If you don't wanta see action, get out of the way of somebody who does! You can stay and guard Bittman. He still ain't got no gun."

"Shut up!" Ham rapped. "Come out of there! All of you!"

"But what—"

"Come out and I'll show you what I suspect!"

The conversation had occurred rapidly. Renny, Monk, Long Tom, and Johnny erupted from the elevator door as tumultuously as they had entered.

Reaching into the cage gingerly, using his sword cane for a prod, Ham threw the lift control lever to the point marked, "Down."

Nothing happened.

Ham let the doors slide shut, closing the master circuit of the hoist machinery. Ordinarily, the cage would have departed with a gentle acceleration.

But this time it fell!

The dull report of a blast echoed from high overhead. An explosive had been placed in the lift mechanism!

"Aw—" Monk muttered. He was not affected as much by the narrow escape from death as by the thought he would have to thank his roasting mate, Ham, for saving his life.

Ham's quick thinking had saved them from Kar's death trap!

"We'll use Doc's scooter!" Renny barked.

They ran down the battery of elevators. The metal-paneled last door was shut. Apparently no cage stood there.

Renny's monster hand found a secret button and pushed it. The doors cracked open. A waiting cage was revealed.

This was Doc Savage's private lift, to be used in reaching the street in moments of emergency. Doc's friends called it his "scooter." It operated at a far greater speed than any other cage in the huge skyscraper. It always waited here on the eighty-sixth floor for Doc's use.

Oliver Wording Bittman now came dashing out of the office. He had apparently reconciled himself to going into action without a gun.

"Wait for me! I want in on this!" he called.

He sprang into the elevator with the others, Monk hit the control lever. The cage floor seemed to hop out from under their feet. So swift was the descent that the sensation of falling persisted for some seventy stories. And the stopping piled them down on all fours.

"Golly!" grinned Monk. "I always get a wallop out of ridin' in this thing!"

They hurried out to the street.

"There he goes!" declared Long Tom.

Their skulking visitor stood beside the curb half a block distant. Parked at this point was a cream-colored taxi. The man drew a taxi driver's uniform cap from the cab, donned it. Evidently this was his masquerade.

Suddenly he discovered Doc's men.

He bounded into the cab. The machine jumped from the curb, turned in the street like a dog chasing its own tail, and hooted away.

Fortunately, Renny had his own car parked near. It was a tiny sedan, ill befitting Renny's immense bulk. Into it, Doc's men piled.

The chase was on!

FEW vehicles other than an occasional milk wagon moved on the streets. That was lucky. The headlong pace the pursuit set allowed for no niceties of traffic dodging.

Up Broadway they thundered, leaving a trail of bleating police whistles behind.

Renny's peewee limousine proved a surprise. It ran like a racer. And Renny was something of a Barney Oldfield at the wheel. The fleeing cab was slowly, steadily overhauled.

Desperate, the machine dodged, doubled back. It only lost ground.

Finally, the taxi veered over to Riverside Drive, then off the Drive and down a rutty workroad—the same road followed by the gold truck Doc Savage had trailed.

Renny steered his machine in pursuit.

Behind them, a police squad car caterwauled along the Drive, but missed seeing them. It wandered off, wrapped in the bedlam of its own siren, vainly searching for the two automobiles which had used the early morning streets of New York for a racetrack.

The fleeing thug drove almost to the tumble-down pier where lay anchored the *Jolly Roger*. He hopped out, kept behind the taxi and scuttled for the pirate vessel.

A pistol flamed desperately from his hand as he caught sight of Renny's little sedan bucking down the rutty road. The murk was thick, so he missed.

Renny instantly leveled one of the compact little machine guns Doc had devised.

"It would be better if we could question the fellow!" Ham suggested. "Maybe we can make him lead us to Kar!"

Realizing the truth of that, Renny withheld his fire. He braked to a stop. Monk all but tore a door off the tiny sedan in getting out. They pounded after the fleeing rat.

Hollow clatterings arose as the rat ran across the wharf timbers, then a rowdy thunder as Renny and the rest arrived. The would-be killer had no time to draw in the gangplank. Wildly, he sprang for the first shelter handy—the forward deck hatch. His body plummeted straight into the black hold interior.

The fellow made a bad landing. Monk nearly overhauled him there, his great, anthropoid hulk descending with a loud crash into the hold, and his hairy fingers trapping the quarry's coat.

But the Kar rodent twisted and tore out of his coat. He fled sternward.

It was Renny who winged the man with a quick shot. The fellow plunged down, a leg shattered by the bullet.

In a moment, Doc's five men and Oliver Wording Bittman had surrounded the captive. They prepared to ask questions.

Not even the first query was put, however.

Several flashlights suddenly popped blinding beams upon them. The glare came from the hatchway above, and from the door in an aft bulkhead. The ugly nozzles of machine guns appeared in the luminance.

Doc's men stood helpless. They had pocketed their own compact and deadly weapons while they examined the prisoner.

"Let 'em have it!" snarled a voice from the hatch rim.

Another rat suggested: "Maybe Kar will want—"

"Sure—he wants 'em dead! We got the bronze guy! We'll get these fellows and finish the job! Let's have it!"

Oliver Wording Bittman gave a shrill cry and sprang to one side, seeking madly to evade the incandescent blaze of the flashlights held by Kar's killers.

On the hatch rim, a machine gun in the hands of one of Kar's men released an awful hail of bullets.

While Doc was seemingly in the grip of death due to Kar's planning, Doc's friends, too, had fallen in a trap of the evil Kar!

Chapter XIII
HIDING PLACE!

DOC SAVAGE, as he braced himself on all fours with the terrific weight of the deadfall crushing down upon his back, knew the fate intended for him. He saw the slight steadying of the air gun which presages a trigger being pulled. He saw the finger of Kar's hired killer snug to the trigger.

The many hundreds of pounds atop him prevented even his mighty bronze body from negotiating a leap. He could not possibly reach the air gun muzzle and knock it aside.

Nor did he attempt to!

Doc had another plan. Inside his buttoned coat, he wore a metal plate which covered most of his chest. It was no ordinary metal, that plate. It was composed of the same material as the capsule missiles which held the Smoke of Eternity.

Not without results had Doc consigned himself to his locked laboratory to analyze the capsule. The metal was a rare alloy, but its nature had soon been revealed by a searching analysis.

As a matter of precaution, in case he was shot at with the Smoke of Eternity, Doc had fashioned himself a body armor from the rare alloy, a supply of which could be assembled from the absolutely complete stock of little-known medicals and chemicals which his laboratory held.

Hence, the instant Doc saw the air gun about to discharge, he put forth a Herculean effort and managed to get his armor before the muzzle. The capsule containing the terrible dissolving compound shattered on the armor.

Doc had saved himself!

Supporting the vast weight on his back with one hand, Doc used the other to tear off the armor and the front of his coat. The Smoke of Eternity was very potent—it might creep around the armor.

Some of the weird stuff spilled on the deadfall. The ponderous timbers began dissolving.

Not without effort, Doc moved rearward along the passage a few feet, being careful the while not to permit the heavy roof to crush him lower.

He listened to the elated conversation of his attackers.

"That," said one of the men, "fixes the bronze guy!"

"Hey!" barked another an instant later. "What's the noise?"

Men could be heard, charging wildly onto the *Jolly Roger!*

"We gotta look into this!"

Doc's assailants hurried away.

The moment they were gone, Doc employed the full power of his huge muscles and lifted the deadfall. He worked clear, afterward easing the deadfall down so as not to make a thump.

Doc crept out on deck. Forward, a man was snarling.

"Let 'em have it!" were his words.

The man never heard the mighty bronze Nemesis that towered up behind him.

DOC SAVAGE took in the scene. Renny, Long Tom, Ham, Johnny, Monk, and Oliver Wording Bittman were all in the hold, brightened by flashlight beams.

The fellows who thought they had just killed Doc were gripping machine guns.

Also gathered about were the other members of the gang who had robbed the bank.

All the thieves had returned!

Doc's eyes searched for Kar. No sign of the mastermind did he discern.

The machine gunners were preparing to fire. The leader of the gang would be the first to kill. He hissed, *"Now!"*

But the fellow's trigger finger did not discharge a single shot! The rapid firer was whisked out of his clutch by a grip of such strength there was no resisting it.

The weapon erupted a loud squawl of reports. A ghastly lead storm struck Kar's assembled slayers. Dying men toppled over the hatch rim, to fall into the hold like ripe fruit.

"Doc!" howled Monk, down in the hold. "It's Doc!"

The respite furnished by their bronze leader gave the besieged men time to unlimber their compact guns.

Kar gunmen who had been covering them from the bulkhead door now tried to shoot. They were too late. A hot wind of bullets wilted them.

The captive Doc's friends had been about to question tried to escape. Johnny knocked him cold with a set of bony knuckles.

With powerful leaps, Renny and Monk sailed upward and grasped the hatch rim.

"We'll help Doc!" Renny clipped.

Doc needed little help, though. By the time Renny and Monk pulled themselves outside, a Kar killer flung down his weapon.

"Don't croak me!" he blubbered.

"The rest of you—drop your guns!" Doc's powerful voice dominated the uproar.

Weapons clattered on the deck. Arms flew skyward. The bleating pleas for mercy made a bedlam like a yelping coyote pack.

"What a brave gang!" sneered waspish, quick-thinking Ham. He kicked a dropped submachine gun. "Only take these toys away from them and they are helpless!"

"Tie them up," Doc directed. "I'm going to have a talk with the one who seems to have taken Squint's place as straw boss."

Doc collared the man who led him into the deadfall trap in the passage—the fellow who had fired the dissolving compound at Doc only a few minutes before.

A WHINE of fear escaped the man. He looked at Doc's golden eyes, gleaming in the luminance of flashlights, and the whine became a screech.

"Lemme go!" he slavered. He was afraid he would be killed on the spot.

"He don't want much!" Monk chuckled fiercely.

Doc held the man, forcing their eyes to meet. "Where's Kar?"

"I don't know anybody by that—" The lie ended in a loud wail as Doc's amazing hands tightened a trifle.

"Do you want to die?" Doc's voice was like the knell of doom.

The man obviously didn't. And his resolution not to talk was rapidly evaporating.

"I dunno where Kar is," he whimpered. "Honest, I don't! He's got a new hangout that nobody knows about but himself. He calls me whenever he's got orders. I don't even know who he is. I ain't never seen him! That's the truth—honest, it is!"

"Ever hear of a man named Gabe Yuder?" Doc inquired.

The captive wriggled. "I dunno!"

Doc's tone commanded the truth. "Have you?"

"I guess so. I seen that name on a packin' box, once. I think it was a box the Smoke of Eternity was shipped in."

"Is he Kar?"

"Huh?" The captive considered the matter. "He might be."

"Where does Kar keep his supply of the Smoke of Eternity?"

A mean, foxy look came into the prisoner's face. He glanced to one side, then hurriedly back. "What do I get for telling?"

"Plenty!" said Doc. "Your life."

"You gotta promise to turn me loose," whined the captive. "It's worth that to you, too. I'll tell you why! Kar has only got so much of the Smoke of Eternity. It's all in the hidin' place. Kar can't make any more until he goes way off to an island somewhere an' gets the stuff to make it out of. You destroy his supply and you've got him."

"No." Doc's bronze mouth was grim. "You will remain my prisoner. I will not free you."

"Then I don't tell you where the Smoke of Eternity is!"

"You don't have to."

"Huh?" The man's eyes moved slightly—toward the same spot at which he had looked at first mention of the Smoke of Eternity hiding place.

That eye-play had shown Doc where the horrible dissolving compound was stored!

"I know where it is!" Doc's voice had a triumphant ring.

"Where?" Monk demanded eagerly. "If we destroy the supply, and Kar can't make anymore, we've fixed him."

"Until he goes to Thunder Island and gets whatever unknown element or substance is the basis of the weird stuff," Doc pointed out. "I'll show you where the cache is in a short while. First, we'll do a couple of things. No. 1 is, tie up these prisoners."

The binding was effected in short order.

"Now we get the gold ashore," Doc directed.

This took considerably longer. Doc and Renny did the diving. They looped ropes around the sacks. The others hauled the coin to the wharf.

"Carry it to shore," Doc commanded, to their puzzlement.

The sun was well up before the task was completed.

Doc now took care that all the prisoners were clear of the *Jolly Roger,* and the wharf as well, by some hundreds of feet.

He dived overboard near the stern. As he had suspected, he found the shelf on which the gold coin had been hidden was not the only one fixed to the *Jolly Roger* hull below the water line. On the opposite side was another.

The Smoke of Eternity cache was here. It consisted of a single large canister of the rare metal which was impervious to its effects. This had a capacity of perhaps five gallons.

Doc brought the canister to the deck. He placed it in plain view atop the deckhouse.

Going ashore, he used a pistol to perforate the canister.

The result was awesome to the extreme. The earlier phenomena when the Smoke of Eternity was released were pygmy in relation. It was like comparing a match flame to an eruption of Vesuvius. In the space of seconds, the *Jolly Roger,* the ramshackle wharf, and a sizeable bite of the shore were wiped out.

It was impossible to tell how deep into the bowels of the earth the annihilation extended. But it must have been a respectable distance, judging from the terrific rush of water to fill the hole. Anchored ships far down the Hudson snapped their hawsers, so great was the pull of water. A Weehawken ferry gave its passengers a hair-raising ride as it went with the current.

The gray, vile smoke arose in such prodigious quantity as to make a pall over all the midtown section of New York. The play of strange electrical sparks created a sound like a hurricane going through a monster forest.

But, beyond a general scare, no harm to anybody resulted.

Chapter XIV
THE RACE

ONE week had passed since the incidents on the *Jolly Roger*. The nearly two million dollars in gold coin, which Doc had recovered, had been restored to the bank. One noteworthy incident accompanied the return of the wealth.

The officials of the bank learned Doc was a great benefactor of mankind, that his purpose in life was the righting of wrongs. So they offered a generous reward of one hundred thousand dollars, thinking Doc would decline to accept, and that the bank would get a lot of good publicity.

Doc fooled them. He took the money. And the next day ten restaurants began supplying free meals to deserving unemployed.

The police never received a single one of Kar's villains for trial and sentence to the penitentiary. Instead, Doc sent his prisoners to a certain institution for the mentally imperfect, in a mountain section of upstate New York.

All criminals have a defective mental balance, otherwise they would not be lawbreakers. A famous psychologist would treat Kar's men. It might take years. But when released, they would be completely cured of their criminal tendencies.

"Which is what I call taking a lot of pains with 'em!" Monk had remarked.

Of Kar, there had been no sign. The man had gone into hiding, probably far from New York, Doc rather suspected.

Despite the absence of any hostile move by the master villain, Oliver Wording Bittman had remained close to Doc and his men. This was a privilege Doc could not deny the man, in view of the debt of gratitude the elder Savage had owed him.

"You can play safe," Doc said. "Although it is hardly likely Kar will tackle us again, now that his supply of the Smoke of Eternity is gone. We have him checkmated—until he can replenish himself with the ghastly stuff."

"You think he will try to do that?" Bittman inquired.

"I hope so."

Bittman was puzzled.

"I have put Ham to checking on the passports issued all over the country," Doc explained. "The moment Kar leaves the United States for the South Seas, we will know it."

"You think Kar must go to Thunder Island for the unknown element or substance which is the main ingredient of the Smoke of Eternity?"

"I am sure of it. The fact that Kar stole the rock samples from Thunder Island proves it. By stealing the samples from my safe, he told me what I hoped to learn by analyzing the rocks."

Doc Savage was even now waiting for Ham to appear with an early morning report on the passports he had examined. Ham was having the pictures from all passports sent by telephoto from the West Coast.

While waiting, Doc Savage was taking his remarkable two-hour routine of exercise. They were unlike anything else in the world. Doc's father had started him taking them when he could hardly walk, and Doc had continued them religiously from that day.

These exercises were solely responsible for Doc's amazing physical and mental powers. He made his muscles work against each other, straining until a fine film of perspiration covered his mighty bronze body. He juggled a number of a dozen figures in his head, multiplying, dividing, extracting square and cube roots.

He had an apparatus which made soundwaves of frequencies so high and low the ordinary human ear could not detect them. Through a lifetime of practice, Doc had perfected his ears to a point where the sounds registered. He named several score of different odors after a quick olfactory test of small vials racked in the case which held his exercising apparatus, and which accompanied Doc wherever he journeyed.

He read a page of Braille printing—the writing for the blind which is a system of upraised dots—so rapidly his fingers merely seemed to stroke the sheet. This was to attune his sense of touch.

He had many other varied parts in his routine. They filled the entire two hours at a terrific pace, with no time out for rest.

HAM suddenly appeared, twirling his sword cane. He had an air of bearing important news.

"You had the right dope, Doc!" he declared. "Look at this set of pictures which were telephotoed from San Francisco!"

He displayed four reproductions, still wet from the developer bath of the telephoto apparatus. Doc examined them.

"Four of Kar's men!" he declared. "They're part of the group Squint assembled!"

"They sailed on the liner *Sea Star,* bound for New Zealand," Ham explained.

"Sailed!"

"Exactly. The vessel put out to sea yesterday."

Long Tom

Doc swung to the telephone. He called the number of one of New York's most modern airports. He instructed: "My low-wing speed plane, the large one—I want it checked over and fueled to capacity at once!"

"There was no passport issued to Gabe Yuder," Ham pointed out.

"Gabe Yuder may not be Kar!" Doc declared. "Kar would fear to monkey with a passport. Possibly he stowed away on the *Sea Star,* in the cabin of one of his men. At any rate, it's up to us to stop that gang from securing from Thunder Island the element that is the basic ingredient of the Smoke of Eternity."

Doc now called the large banking house with which he did business.

"Has it arrived?" he inquired of the firm president.

"Yes, Mr. Savage" was the answer. "The sum was exactly six million dollars. It was cabled by the National Bank of Blanco Grande, in the Central American Republic of Hidalgo, exactly on schedule."

"Thank you," said Doc, and hung up.

This fabulous sum was from Doc Savage's secret reservoir of wealth—a lost valley in the impenetrable mountains of Hidalgo, a valley inhabited by a race of golden-skinned people who were pure descendants of the ancient Mayan nation. In the valley was a great treasure cavern and a fabulous mine of gold—the treasure trove of ancient Maya.

It was from this amazing spot that Doc's limitless wealth came. But the money was in a sense not his—he must use it in the thing to which his life was devoted, in traveling to odd ends of the world in search of those needing help and punishment, and administering to them.

His method of letting the Mayans know when to send him a mule train laden with gold was as strange as the rest—he broadcast from a powerful radio station on a certain wavelength at high noon on a seventh day. The chief of the Mayans listened in at this hour.

"We don't need to worry about cash," Doc told Ham.

At this point Oliver Wording Bittman, the taxidermist, spoke up.

"I hope you may consider my assistance of some value."

"You mean you wish to accompany us?" Doc inquired.

"I certainly do. I must confess my contact with you thus far has been very enjoyable and the excitement highly exhilarating. I should like to continue in your company. My experience on the expedition which I took to New Zealand with Jerome Coffern should render me of some value."

"You speak any of the native dialects?"

"One or two."

To Doc's lips came words of a language native to the South Seas. Bittman replied, although rather uncertainly, in the same tongue.

But Doc still hesitated. He did not want to lead this man into danger, although the fellow seemed pathetically eager to go along.

"Perhaps I can assist in finding natives who accompanied Jerome Coffern and Kar to Thunder Island," Bittman said hopefully. "Talking to those men should help us."

That decided Doc.

"You shall go with us if you wish," he said.

PREPARATIONS were pushed swiftly. Doc's five men knew what they might possibly need.

Monk took a unique, extremely portable chemical laboratory which he had perfected.

Long Tom took some parts from which he could create an astounding variety of electrical mechanisms.

Renny, the engineer, took care of charts and navigation instruments, as well as machine guns—for Renny was a remarkable rapid-firer marksman.

Johnny posted himself on the geology and natives of the district they were to visit, while Ham cleared up aspects of law.

"We'll have to wait two days on a liner from the Pacific coast," Renny complained.

"I have a scheme to remedy that!" Doc assured him.

The afternoon was young when they took off in Doc's speed plane. This craft was a latest design, trimotored, low-wing job. The landing gear folded up into the wings, offering little air resistance. It had a cruising speed of about two hundred miles an hour.

It was the final word in aircraft.

The ship climbed rapidly. At sixteen thousand feet, it found a favorable air current. The Appalachian Mountains squirmed below. Later, clouds cracked open to give a sight of Pittsburgh.

The passengers rode in comfort. The fireproof cabin permitted them to smoke. The cabin was also soundproofed. The all-metal ship had a gasoline capacity that, in an emergency, could take it nonstop across the Atlantic.

Doc flew. He was as accomplished at flying as at other things. His five friends were also pilots of better than average ability.

At Wichita, Kansas, Doc landed to refuel, and to telephone long-distance to the San Francisco office of the shipping firm which owned the *Sea Star,* the liner which Kar's men had boarded.

The *Sea Star* was already some hundreds of miles offshore, the owners informed him.

It was night when they swooped down upon an airport near Los Angeles.

"This is what I call traveling!" Oliver Wording Bittman said admiringly.

They took on sandwiches. Monk purchased a can of tobacco and cigarette papers. The fuel tanks were filled to capacity with high test. Bittman went off with the word he was going to shop for some medicine effective against air sickness.

In the meantime, workmen had been supplanting the plane's wheels with long floats. A tractor hauled it to the water. Doc had purposefully selected a flying field near the shore. The whole thing required less than two hours.

Taking the air, Doc nosed straight out into the Pacific.

"Good Lord!" Bittman gulped. "Are we going to fly the ocean?"

"Not unless Renny has forgotten how to navigate, and Long Tom can't take radio bearings," Doc replied. "We're overtaking the *Sea Star.*"

"But the plane—"

"The owners of the *Sea Star,* at my request, radioed the captain to lift the plane aboard his craft."

Long Tom worked continuously over the radio equipment, his pale fingers flying from dial to dial. Periodically, he called to Renny the exact direction from which the *Sea Star*'s radio signals came, as disclosed by the directional loop aerial he was using. It was ticklish business, flying directly to a ship so far out to sea.

DAYLIGHT had come again before they sighted the *Sea Star*. The liner was steaming in a calm sea.

Doc landed nearby. He taxied expertly into the lee of the massive hull. A cargo boom swung over. Lines dropped from its end. Doc secured these to stout steel eyes which had been built—with thought of this very purpose—into the speed plane.

Passengers crowded the rails and cheered as the plane was hoisted aboard the liner. Curious speculation was rife. Doc's bronze, giant figure created the sensation it always did.

After seeing his plane lashed down on the forward deck, Doc closeted himself with the *Sea Star*'s master.

"You have four desperate men aboard," he explained. "Here are their pictures." Doc exhibited the telephoto copies of the passport photographs of Kar's four men.

The ship captain eyed them. He gave a gasp of surprise.

"Those four men transferred to a small, but very speedy and seaworthy yacht which overhauled us yesterday!" he declared.

"Then we're out of luck for the time being," Doc murmured, his powerful voice showing none of the disappointment he felt.

Doc now described Gabe Yuder—repeating Bittman's word-picture of the man. "Is such a fellow aboard?"

"I do not believe so," replied the commander. "There is no one by the name of Gabe Yuder, or Kar, and no one answering the description you have just given me."

"Thank you," replied Doc.

He left the captain's cabin slowly and conveyed the bad news to his companions.

"But how on earth did they know we were coming?" Oliver Wording Bittman murmured, twirling the watch-chain scalpel about a forefinger.

"Yes—how did they know?" Monk growled.

"Kar must have had someone in New York shadowing us," Doc offered. "When we took off by plane, Kar received the news and put two and two together. Possibly the fast yacht which took his men off was a rum-running vessel he got in contact with through underworld channels."

"Well, what do we do about it?" Renny inquired.

"The only thing left to do—tangle with Kar on Thunder Island."

THE following days aboard the *Sea Star* were nothing if not monotonous. Doc and his friends had rambled the world too much for an ordinary ocean voyage to prove interesting.

They did not know what Kar might be doing. Further conversation with the master of the *Sea Star* convinced Doc the yacht which had taken Kar's men aboard was very fast indeed—speedier even than the liner!

"The fiend may be ahead of us!" Bittman wailed.

"Probably is," Doc admitted.

When some hundreds of miles from New Zealand, Doc could have taken a shortcut by transferring to the air. But at the moment the *Sea Star* was bucking a South Sea gale, a thing of whistling winds filled with shotty spray, and gigantic waves which all but topped the bridge.

The plane was fortunate to exist, lashed down on the forward deck. It could not possibly have been lowered over-side, so as to take off. And the *Sea Star* was not equipped with catapults for launching planes, as are some modern ocean greyhounds.

So Doc remained aboard.

Auckland, the *Sea Star*'s port of call in New Zealand, was a welcome sight. The water was calm enough in the harbor to permit the unloading of Doc's plane, although the gale still raged.

Johnny, the geologist, visited various local sources of information and dug up what he could on Thunder Island.

"It's a queer place," he reported to Doc. "It's the cone of a gigantic active volcano. Not a speck of vegetation grows on the outside of the cone. It's solid rock."

Johnny looked mysterious.

"Here's the strange part, Doc," he declared.

"That crater is a monster. It must be twenty miles across. And it is always filled with steam. Great clouds of vapor hang over it. I talked to an airplane pilot who had flown over it some years ago. He gave me an excellent description."

"That's fine," Doc smiled.

"He says there's another island, a coral atoll, about fifty miles from Thunder Island," Johnny continued. "This is inhabited by a tribe of half-savage natives. He recommended that for our headquarters."

"Not a bad idea," agreed Doc.

Oliver Wording Bittman had been away in search of the native New Zealanders who had taken Jerome Coffern and Kar to Thunder Island months ago. He returned shaking his head.

"A ghastly thing!" he said hollowly. "Every man who accompanied Jerome Coffern and Kar has mysteriously disappeared in recent months."

Doc Savage's golden eyes gave off diamond-hard lights. He saw Kar's hand here, again. The man was a devil incarnate! He had callously murdered everyone who might connect him with Thunder Island. His only slip had been when his two hired killers slew Jerome Coffern almost in the presence of Doc Savage!

"I hope I get my hooks on that guy!" Renny said grimly. His great hands—hands that could squeeze the very sap from blocks of green timber—opened and shut slowly.

"We'll do our best to get you that wish." Determination was uppermost in Doc's powerful voice. "We're hopping off for Thunder Island at once!"

Chapter XV
THE FLYING DEVIL

THUNDER ISLAND!

The great cone projected high enough above the southern seas that they sighted it while still more than a hundred miles distant. The air was clear; the sun flamed with a scintillant revelry. Yet above the giant crater, and obviously crawling out of its interior, lurked masses of cloud.

"The dope I got from that pilot was right!" Johnny declared, quickly removing his glasses with the magnifying lens to the left side so he could peer through high-magnification binoculars. "Note the steam which always forms a blanket above the crater."

"Strange lookin' place!" Monk muttered, his little eyes taking in Thunder Island.

"Not so strange!" Johnny corrected. "Steam-filled volcanic craters are not so uncommon in this part of the world. It is a region of active craters. There is, for instance, Ngauruhoe, a cone in New Zealand which emits steam and vapor incessantly. And for further example of unusual earth activity, take the great region of geysers, strange lakes of boiling mud and hot springs, which is also in New Zealand. Like the phenomena in the Yellowstone Park, in the United States, this region—"

"You can serve that geology lecture with our supper," snorted Monk. "What I meant was the shape of that cone. Notice how steep it gets toward the top? Man alive! It's a thousand feet straight up and down in more than one spot!"

"The cone rim is inaccessible," said Johnny, peevishly.

"You mean nobody has ever climbed up there and looked over?"

"I believe that is what inaccessible means!"

"You're gettin' touchy as Ham!" Monk snorted. "Hey, fellows! There's the little atoll that is inhabited! We make our base there, don't we?"

The atoll in question was much smaller than Thunder Island. Of coral formation, it was like a starved green doughnut with a piece of mirror in the center. This mirror was, of course, the lagoon.

Doc banked the plane for the atoll.

As they neared the green ring, they saw the vegetation was of the type usual to tropical isles. There was *noni enata,* a diminutive bush bearing crimson pears, ironwood, umbrella ferns which grew in profusion, candlenut trees, and the paper mulberry with yellow blossoms and cottony, round leaves. Hibiscus and pandanus spread their green and glossy flowers, and there were many *petavii,* a kind of banana, the fronds of which arched high.

"It's inhabited, all right!" announced Monk. "There's the native devil-devil house on top of the highest ground!"

Johnny used his superpower binoculars on the structure of pagan worship, then gasped, "The inhabitants must be near savages! The devil-devil house is surrounded by human skulls mounted on poles!"

"Not an uncommon practice," began Johnny. "Formerly—"

"There's the village!" barked Long Tom.

The cluster of thatched huts had been lost among the coconut palms at the lagoon edge. They looked like shaggy, dark beehives on stilts.

Natives dashed about, excited by the plane. They were well-built fellows, gaudy *pareus* of *tapa* cloth, made from the bark of the paper mulberry, girded about their hips. Many had tropical blooms in their hair, a number of the women wearing a blossom over an ear. Some of the men had scroll-like designs in blue *ama* ink upon their bodies, making them quite ugly, judged by civilized standards.

Several *prahus* appeared on the lagoon, each boat filled with perturbed natives. The brown men grasped spears, and knives of bamboo as sharp as a razor, which could be sharpened again simply by splitting a piece from the blade.

"They seem kinda excited!" Monk grunted.

"Yes—entirely too excited!" Doc replied thoughtfully.

DOC'S big plane wheeled over the atoll as gracefully as a mighty gull. It dipped. With a *swis-s-s-h* of a noise, the floats settled on the glass-smooth lagoon.

The *prahus* filled with natives fled as though the very devil was after them. Thousands of *koi*, a black bird which travels in dense flocks, arose from the luxuriant jungle. As Doc cut the motors, they could hear the excited notes of cockatoos.

"I don't like the way they're acting," Doc warned. "We'd better keep our eyes open, brothers!"

He grounded the plane near the cluster of thatched huts. Tall palm trees showed evidence of being cultivated for coconuts—at least, they were fitted with the ingenious native traps for the destructive *tupa* crab.

The traps consisted of a false "earth" well up the tree. The crabs, wont to descend the palms backward, upon touching these "earths," would release their grip on the tree under the impression they were on the ground, thus falling to destruction.

Suddenly Ham gave a startled yelp, and dropping his sword cane, clapped a hand to his leg. An instant later, the fiendish, chuckling echoes of a rifle shot leaped along the lagoon.

Someone was sniping at them!

More bullets buzzed loudly near the plane.

Ham was barely scratched. He was the first to dive out of the plane and take shelter among the palms. The others followed, guns ready.

Doc's golden eyes noted a surprising thing. The shot seemed as much of a shock to the natives as to the flyers!

After a moment, Doc's perceptive ears caught a word or two of the native language. He recognized the lingo—it was one of the myriads of vernaculars in his great magazine of knowledge.

"Why do you treat peaceful newcomers in this fashion?" he called in the dialect.

The natives were impressed by hearing their language spoken in such perfect fashion by the mighty bronze man. Soon they replied.

For some minutes, strange words clucked back and forth. The tension subsided visibly. The very power of Doc's pleasant voice seemed to spread good will.

"This is strange!" Doc told his fellows, none of whom comprehended the native tongue. "They don't know who fired that shot. They're trying to tell me they thought there were no rifles on the island!"

"They're liars!" Monk grinned. "Or else the bumblebees here are made out of lead."

"They're wrong, of course," Doc replied thoughtfully. "But I'm sure they did not know there was a rifle here. There was apparently but one gun, at that."

"We'd better stop gabbing and hunt for the sniper!" Ham clipped waspishly. "In case you've forgotten, he nearly winged me!"

"Keep your shirt on, Ham." Doc indicated natives who were prowling off through the tropical growth. "They're instituting a search for the hidden marksman."

THE sniper was not located, though. The natives searched briskly for a time, but the natural languidness common to tropical folk soon caused them to lose interest when they found nobody. Standing around in groups and staring at the white men, especially their mighty leader of bronze, was much more interesting.

"It never fails!" Monk chuckled. "Doc is a sensation wherever he goes!"

Ham cast his eyes over the crowd surrounding Monk. This was only slightly smaller than the group about Doc. Monk's incredible homeliness and titanic, apelike frame had them utterly agog.

"You don't do so bad!" Ham jeered. "They figure you're the missing link!"

But he regretted the insult a moment later when Monk cornered a native and gravely explained, by gestures, that the tribe must watch the many pigs running about, or Ham would steal them. It didn't help matters when fully thirty natives ran up with squealing porkers in their arms and tried to thrust the gifts onto Ham.

Renny was entertaining and overawing the islanders by the amazing feat of crushing hard coconuts in one vast hand.

Johnny and Long Tom, well-armed and alert, moved into the jungle to get breadfruit which weighed several pounds apiece and was pitted on the surface like a golf ball. Delicate, beautiful orchids were like varicolored butterflies in the shadowed, luxuriant growth. The hunters also gathered coconuts, so as to make *feikai*, or roasted breadfruit mixed with coconut-milk sauce.

Oliver Wording Bittman wandered alone into the jungle, but returned soon and kept close to Doc, as though for protection.

Doc busied himself performing a minor operation upon an ill native. He was thus engaged when an exciting development occurred.

A machine gun blatted a procession of reports. By the terrific swiftness of the shots, Doc knew it was one of the guns he had himself invented.

A man screamed with a mortal wound.

Kar-o-o-m!

A tremendous explosion brought a tremor to the

hut in which Doc was operating upon the native. He and Bittman rushed out.

Near the plane, a sooty cauliflower of smoke had sprouted. Bits of débris still swirled in the air. It fell about a gruesome, torn thing upon the lagoon edge. The dismembered body of a man!

"It was one of Kar's gunmen!" Renny called. Renny held a smoking machine gun. "The fellow had a bomb, with the fuse already lighted! He was running to throw it in the plane when I saw him and shot."

"Sure it was one of Kar's men?" Doc inquired.

"You bet. One of the four we hoped to trap on the *Sea Star*!"

"That is too bad," Doc declared regretfully. "It means the yacht which took them off the *Sea Star* was speedy enough to get here ahead of us."

"You think Kar is right here on this coral atoll?"

Instead of replying, Doc proceeded to question what his accurate judgment told him were the most intelligent of the natives. What he learned cast an important light on the situation.

"Listen to this!" he translated for his friends. "I asked the natives if they had seen a ship, but they haven't. Then I asked them if they had sighted a man-made bird that flies, such as ours. And the answer explains their terror at our arrival."

"You mean Kar came around in a plane and bombed or machine-gunned them?" Ham queried.

"Nothing so simple as that! The reply they gave me was utterly fantastic. They claim great, flying devils nearly as large as our plane sometimes come from Thunder Island to seize and devour members of the tribe. They thought we were such a flying devil."

"They must drink caterpillar liquor!" Monk snorted.

"Eh?" said Ham.

"Two drinks and the birds are after you!"

"Furthermore," Doc continued, "they claim they sighted such a flying devil only yesterday. Questioned closely, they admit it did not flap its wings, and that it made a loud and steady groaning noise. That means they saw a plane. And what craft could it be but Kar's?"

Renny growled, "Kar is—"

"Already at Thunder Island! The man you just wiped out was landed here by Kar for the specific purpose of stopping us in case we visited this atoll. He has been hiding from the natives. No doubt, Kar intended to pick him up later."

"But where did Kar get a plane—"

"Honolulu, New Zealand, or even Australia. They had time. Remember, the storm delayed the *Sea Star* on which we came. It is possible Kar evaded that storm, and his boat was faster."

Ham slanted his sword cane at the sun. "What do you say we fly over and have a look at Thunder Island? There's barely time before dark."

"We'll do that very thing, brothers," Doc said swiftly. "Every one of you will put on parachutes. Kar's plane might attack us and have the good luck to slam an incendiary bullet into our gas tank. In such event, 'chutes would be pretty handy."

PREPARATIONS were quickly completed. The big speed plane skimmed down the glassy lagoon and took the air, watched by an awed crowd of natives. Doc opened the throttles wide and boomed for Thunder Island at better than two hundred miles an hour. Night was not far off.

The volcanic cone gathered majestic height as they flew nearer. Its vast size was astounding, impressive. The steaming clouds piled like cotton above it. It was as though the world was hollow and filled with foam, and the foam was escaping through this gigantic vent.

"One of the most striking sights of my life!" said the artistic Ham.

Even the prosaic Monk was impressed, agreeing, "Yeah—hot stuff!"

Doc's mighty bronze hand guided the plane around the stupendous cone of bleak stone that was Thunder Island. Nowhere was there a blade of green growth. The titanic, rocky cliffs could not have been more denuded had they been seared with acid. The lifeless aspect, the baldness of the waste, was depressing.

"Even a goat couldn't live there!" Renny muttered.

"Unless he formed an appetite for rocks," snorted the irrepressible Monk.

Nowhere did they see sign of Kar!

"That's queer!" Ham declared. "There are no canyons or great caves in which he could hide his plane. If he was here, we certainly would have seen him."

"Do you think he has secured a fresh supply of the element from which the Smoke of Eternity is made, and gone back to civilization?" asked Oliver Wording Bittman. "He most naturally wouldn't tarry here."

"Impossible to tell—except that I doubt he would have deserted his man on the atoll," replied Doc. "There is one chance—we'll try the crater."

"Into that terrible steam!" Bittman wailed. "We shall perish!"

Bittman looked terrified at the prospect. He even moved for the plane door as though to take to his parachute. But Renny's great hand restrained him.

"You'll be safe enough with Doc," Renny said confidently.

"We shall be scalded—"

"I think not," Doc assured him. "The top of that cone is many thousands of feet above sea level. Indeed, you will notice traces of snow near the rim.

At that height, it takes little more than moist, warm air to make a cloud like this 'steam' over the crater."

"You mean we may be able to fly down into the crater?" Monk asked.

"We're going to try just that," Doc smiled.

UP and up climbed the powerful speed plane, motors moaning an increasing song of effort. The first wisps of steam whipped grizzled pennants about the craft. Doc opened the cockpit windows and kept an accurate check on a thermometer.

"This is nothing but cloud formation caused by very warm and moist air lifting out of the crater!" he called, raising his voice over the motor howl—for opening the windows nullified the soundproofing of the cabin.

The vapor thickened. It poured densely into the cabin. The very world about them seemed to turn a bilious gray hue. Visibility was wiped out, except for a few score yards, beyond the wing tips.

"Long Tom," Doc's energetic voice had little trouble piercing the engine clamor, "set the danger alarm for five hundred feet!"

Long Tom hastily complied. This danger alarm was simply an apparatus which sent out a series of bell-like sounds very distinctive from the motor uproar, and another sensitive device which measured the time that ensued until an echo was tossed back by the earth. If this time interval became too short, an alarm bell rang.

With it in operation, if the plane came blindly within five hundred feet of the crater bottom or sides, an alarm would sound. Doc had perfected this device. It was little different from the apparatus all modern liners use to take depth measurements.

Deeper into the crater moaned the plane. It spiraled tightly, as though descending the thread of an invisible screw in the crater center. It might have been a tiny fish in a sea of milk.

"Let's go back!" wailed Oliver Wording Bittman. "This is a horrible place!"

"It does kinda give a guy the creeps!" Monk muttered. *"Ye-e-ow-w! Look at that thing!"*

Monk's squawl of surprise was so loud it threatened to tear the thin metal sides off the plane. Every eye focused in the direction both his great, hairy arms pointed. What they saw was little, but it chilled the blood in their veins.

A black, evil mass seemed to bulk for an instant in the gray domain of vapor. It might have been a tortured, sooty cloud from the way it convulsed and changed its shape. Then it was gone, sucking after it a distinct wake of the pigeon-colored vapor.

"I c-couldn't h-have s-seen what I d-did!" Monk stuttered.

"What was it?" Ham shouted. "What was that thing in the cloud? It looked big as this plane!"

Monk panted like a runner. His eyes still protruded.

"It wasn't quite that b-big!" he gulped. "But it was the ugliest thing I ever saw! And I've seen plenty of ugly things!"

"If you own a mirror, you have!" Ham couldn't resist putting in.

Monk made no reference to pigs—which was in itself demonstration of what a shock he had just received.

"I saw one of them flyin' devils the natives on the atoll told Doc about!" Monk declared. "And what I mean, flyin' devil is the name for it."

"You must have had a swig of that caterpillar liquor," Ham jeered.

"Quick!" Doc Savage's mighty voice crashed through the plane. "The machine guns! Off to the right! Get that thing! *Get it! Shoot it!"*

Everyone gazed to the right.

"It's comin' back—the flyin' devil!" Monk bawled.

The black, evil mass had appeared in the misty world again. It convulsed and altered its shape, as before. But now the aviators had the opportunity to see what it really was—they could drink in the awful horror of the monster with their eyes.

THE thing was flying along—keeping pace with the plane! Terrible eyes appraised the ship, as though deciding whether to attack.

It had a ghastly set of jaws—nearly as long as a man's body, and spiked full of foul, conical teeth. The body had neither hair nor feathers—it was like the skin of a dog denuded by the mange.

Most awesome of all were the wings, for they were membranous, like those of a bat. As they folded and unfolded in flight, the membrane fluttered and flapped like unclean gray canvas. On the tip of the first joint of the wings were four highly developed fingers, armed with fearful talons.

The appalling monster suddenly gave vent to its cry. This was an outrageous combination of a roaring and gargling, a sound of such volume that it reduced the pant of the plane motors to insignificance. And the noise had an ending as ghastly as its note—it stopped in a manner that gave one the sickening impression that the noise itself had choked to death the gruesome thing.

"A prehistoric pterodactyl!" screamed Johnny. "That's what it is!"

"A what?" grunted Monk.

"A pterodactyl, a flying reptile of the Pterosauri order. They were supposed to have become extinct near the end of the Mesozoic age."

"They didn't!" snorted Monk. "You can look for yourself!"

"Use those machine guns!" Doc directed. "The thing is going to attack us!"

The hideous flying reptile was slowly opening its huge, tooth-armed jaws!

Rapid-firer barrels poked through the plane windows. They spewed. Empty cartridges rained on the floorboards. Bullets found their mark.

The aerial reptile started its bloodcurdling cry. The sound ended in a drawn, piercing blare. The thing fell, bones broken, foul canvas-like wings flapping. It was like a dirty gray cloth somebody had dropped.

Monk grinned. "What a relief that it—"

The plane lurched madly as Doc whipped the controls about.

A second of the prehistoric pterodactyls had materialized out of the vapor. A gigantic, eerie thing reminiscent of a mangy crocodile clad in a great gray cape, it plunged at the plane.

Its horrid, conical teeth closed upon the left wing. A wrench, a gritty scream of rending metal—and the plane wing was ruined! The ship keeled off on a wing tip and began a slow spin.

The pterodactyl hung to the wing it had grabbed, like a tenacious bulldog.

"The parachutes!" Doc barked. "Jump! We may crash any instant!"

Chapter XVI
THE AWFUL NIGHT

IN quick succession, Doc's five men piled through the plane door, hands on the ripcord rings of their backpack parachutes.

Renny was first to go. Monk paused to grab his can of tobacco out of a seat, then followed. Long Tom, Ham and Johnny dived after him.

Only Oliver Wording Bittman held back, trembling.

"I don't want—" he whined.

"Neither do we!" Doc said firmly. "There's no choice!" Then, before it should be too late, Doc swept Bittman up in bronze arms of vast power and sprang with him into space.

As calmly as though he were on solid ground, Doc snapped open Bittman's 'chute, then dropped down a few hundred feet and bloomed his own mushroom of silk. A jerk, and he floated gently. He had time to view the astounding domain about him.

The vapor, as he had half suspected would be the case, was becoming less dense. At the same time, the warmth increased. The hot, moist air, suddenly striking the cool strata above the crater, formed the steamlike clouds, which had curtained whatever additional shocking secrets the place held.

A stutter of machine-gun shots below drew Doc's golden eyes. He hastily plucked his own compact rapid-firer from its belt holster.

The pterodactyl had released its silly hold on the falling plane and had attacked Johnny. The lanky archaeologist's bullets had driven its first dive aside. But it was coming back. The repellent jaws were widely distended. Each of the many odious, conical teeth could pierce through a man's body.

Doc's machine gun clattered. He knew where to aim. Greater even than the learning of Johnny, whose profession was knowing the world and all its past, was Doc Savage's fund of knowledge on prehistoric reptiles and vegetation. Doc realized this pterodactyl probably had little or no brain. He shot for the neck bones and shattered them.

The air reptile tumbled away. Johnny lifted a grateful face.

"My shots didn't seem to do much good!" he called.

"Try for the neck or eyes!" Doc replied.

Strong air currents now made themselves felt. The parachutes were swept rapidly to one side, away from the edge of the crater.

Directly below, Doc's gaze rested upon a remarkable sight. It would have been a fearsome sight, too, except that his practiced eye told him they were going to be carried clear of danger by the wind.

A mud lake, narrow, but spreading for thousands of rods along the crater side, was below. A crust, resembling asphalt and apparently very hard, covered the lake. This must be nearly red-hot, judging from the heat of the moist air which rushed upward.

Probably this amazing mud lake reached in a horseshoe shape halfway around the crater. Certainly, the ends were lost to sight.

A natural lava wall confined it to the crater side, well above the floor.

The ruined plane fell into the mud lake. Its weight broke the crust. Instantly, there was a great eruption at that point. A geyser column of scalding, lava-like mud shot hundreds of feet upward, driven by steam pressure gathered beneath the crust. Steam itself now exuded. It made a deafening roar.

A thunderous crackling swept over the mud lake as the crust settled. From countless points came minor eruptions. The steam, squirting outward and upward, enveloped the falling parachutes.

They could not see where they were landing!

THE parachutes pitched like leaves in the disturbed air. Not only did the gushing, superheated winds carry them clear of the mud lake, but they were flung far out on the crater floor.

Doc, compact machine gun in hand, waited. His golden eyes sought to pierce the steamy world. The air was so hot as to be near sickening. It possessed a weird, unusual fragrance.

It was like the atmosphere within a greenhouse—impregnated with the odor of rankly growing plants.

The thunderous crackling from the mud lake subsided as quickly as it began.

Suddenly a shocking din arose below. A piercing,

trumpet-like cry quavered. A coarse, beastly bawling joined it. Tearing of branches, the hollow pops of green timber breaking, the dull reverberations of great bodies thumping the earth, made a nightmarish discord. It was a sound to make the flesh creep.

"Renny! Monk! The rest of you!" Doc's resonant tones pealed through the hobgoblin clamor. "Spill air from one side of your 'chute and try to avoid the vicinity of that noise!"

From below the abyss of steam, where his men were lost from view, came replying shouts. But there was little time to comply.

So great was the weight of the thing that its feet sank into the earth ...

The frond of an immense plant brushed past Doc's mighty bronze form. The plant was of colossal size. It seemed to be something on the order of a tree fern. So towering was it that there elapsed a distinct interval before the parachute reached the ground.

Doc landed in a tangle of creepers and low trees which looked like ordinary evergreens. More ferns, these much smaller, made a spongy mat of the whole. It was like descending in a pile of enormous, coarse green cobwebs.

Shucking off the parachute harness, Doc sprang to less tangled footing. The ground was a soft mulch underfoot—as though fresh plowed.

The hideous uproar they had heard from the air had subsided! A low rumble had replaced it. This rumble seemed to be some great monster in flight! The sound was already some distance away, and departing like an express train.

Of a sudden, there came into the surrounding air the low, trilling note that was part of Doc. Now, more than ever, was that sound suggestive of a strange bird of the jungle. It might have been a wind filtering through the ghostly, fantastic forest around about.

And as always, that inspiring sound conveyed some definite meaning. This time it was—be silent! There is danger near!

Doc knew that grisly, caterwauling concert he had heard while in the air meant a fight between behemoths of a prehistoric reptilian world. He recognized the plant forms about him. Some had been extinct for ages.

Doc had dropped into a land which was very much as it had been countless ages ago. A fearsome, bloodcurdling land where survival of the fiercest was the only law!

Doc's strange sound trailed away in echoes that, although they possessed no definite tune, were entrancingly musical in their quality.

Now he could hear some gigantic horror breathing nearby! The breathing was hurried, as though the terrible thing had been engaged in strife. The sounds were hollow, very loud—almost like the pant of an idling freight locomotive!

Suddenly vegetation swished and crashed as the monster got into motion.

It was charging Doc!

Doc's mighty bronze figure flashed sidewise, moving with a speed such as it possibly had never before attained. But as he changed position, his golden eyes were sharpened for sight of the peril that rushed him.

He saw it—as fearful and loathsome a sight as human eyes ever beheld!

THE shocking size of the horror was apparent. It bulged out of the steam like a tall house. It hopped on massive rear legs, balancing itself by a great tail, kangaroolike.

The two forelegs were tiny in proportion—like short strings dangling. Yet those forelegs that seemed so small were thicker through by far than Doc Savage's body!

The revolting odor of a carnivorous thing accompanied the dread apparition. The stench was of decaying gore. The hide of the monster had a pebbled aspect, somewhat like a crocodile. Its claws were frightful weapons of offense, being of such proportions as to easily grasp and crush a large bull.

Perhaps the most ghastly aspect of the thing was its teeth. They armored a blunt, revolting snout of a size as stupendous as the rest of the hopping terror.

So great was the weight of the thing that its feet sank into the spongy earth the depth of a tall man at each step.

"What is it, Doc?" Monk shouted.

"Tyrannosaurus!" Doc answered him. "Look lively!"

The monster reptile, after bounding past Doc, stopped. An instant following Monk's called words, the beast charged the sound of his voice.

"Dodge it, Monk!" Doc barked. "Dodge it! The thing probably has a very sluggish brain. That has always been supposed to be a trait of prehistoric dinosaurs. Get out of its path, and several seconds will elapse before it can make up its mind to follow you!"

Shrubs ripped. A stream of shots erupted from Monk's compact machine gun. Bushes fluttered again. Monk gave a bark of utter awe.

"Monk!" Doc called. "You shouldn't have tried to shoot it! Nothing less than a cannon can even trouble that baby!"

"You're tellin' me!" Monk snorted. "Man! Man! The bat of a thing that chewed the wing of our plane was a pretty little angel alongside this cuss! *O-o-op!* Here it comes again!"

The noisy charge, and Monk's dodging, was repeated. Monk did not fire this time. He knew Doc was right. The little machine guns, efficient though they might be, would bother this reptilian monster less than beans thumbed at an alligator.

"Made it!" Monk called.

"Then keep that noisy mouth shut!" snapped the waspish Ham. "It rushes the sound of your voice!"

The steam—it had come from the eruption of the mud lake—was rapidly disappearing. The ferocious tyrannosaurus would soon be able to search them out with its eyes!

"All of you get over with Monk!" Doc shouted.

He nimbly evaded the great reptile as it sought his voice, then worked over until Monk's anthropoid figure loomed in the dispersing steam.

Oliver Wording Bittman was there. The taxidermist's face was the color of a soiled handkerchief. His jaw jerked up and down visibly, but he had his tongue thrust between his teeth, fearful lest their chattering attract the awful bounding reptile.

Doc felt surprise. Bittman had turned into a craven coward! But this direful world in which they found themselves was enough to reduce the valor of even the bravest.

Johnny, Long Tom and Ham were with Monk. They, too, were pale. But the light of a magnificent courage glowed in their eyes. They were enthralled. They lived for adventure and excitement—and it was upon them in quantities undreamed of.

"Where's Renny?" Doc's tone was so low the odious tyrannosaurus, still prowling about, did not hear.

Renny was not present!

Doc's shout pealed out like a great bell. "Renny! Renny!"

That drew the giant reptile. With frantic dodging, they evaded it.

But there came no answer from Renny!

"That—that cross between a crocodile, the Empire State Building and a kangaroo must have got him!" Monk muttered in horror.

"A terrible fate!" gulped Johnny, the geologist. "The tyrannosaurus is generally believed to be the most destructive killing machine ever created by nature! To think that I should live to see the things in flesh and blood!"

"If you wanta live to tell about it, we gotta get away from the thing!" Monk declared. "How'll we do it, Doc?"

"See if we cannot leave the vicinity silently," Doc suggested.

AN attempt to do this, however, nearly proved disastrous. The monster tyrannosaurus seemed to have very sensitive ears. Too, it could see them for a distance of many yards, now that the steam had nearly dissipated. It rushed them.

Doc, to save the lives of his friends, took the awful risk of decoying the reptile away while the others fled. Only the power and agility of his mighty bronze body saved him, for once he had to dodge between the very legs of the monster, evading by a remarkable spring snapping, foul, fetid teeth that were nearly as long as a man's arm.

Gliding under a canopy of overlapping ferns, Doc evaded the bloodthirsty reptile.

Darkness was descending swiftly, for the steam above the pit, although it let through sunlight, kept out the moonbeams and made the period of twilight almost nonexistent.

While the days within the crater were probably as light as a cloudy day in the outside world, the nights were things of incredible blackness.

Doc found his companions in the thickening murk.

"We'd better take a page out of the life of Monk's ancestors and climb a tree for the night!" suggested Ham.

"Yeah!" growled Monk, goaded by the insult. "Yeah!" He apparently couldn't think of anything else to say.

"We can tackle that tree fern!" Doc declared, pointing.

The tree fern in question was on the order of a palm tree, but with fronds all the way up. In height, it exceeded by far the tallest of ordinary palms. Doc and his men climbed this.

"Remarkable!" Johnny murmured. "Although this species is closely related to fern growths found in fossilized state in certain parts of the world, it is much larger than anything—"

"You must consider the fact that this crater is merely a spot left behind in the march of time," Doc interposed. "Some changes are bound to have taken place in the countless ages, however. And after all, science has but scratched the surface in ascertaining the nature of prehistoric fauna and flora. We may; indeed, we surely should, find many species undreamed of hitherto—"

"How we gonna sleep up here without fallin' off?" Monk wanted to know.

"Sleep!" jeered Ham. "If you ask me, there won't be much sleep tonight. Listen!"

In a distant part of the crater, another ferocious fight between reptilian monsters was in progress. Although the sound was borne to them muffled, it had a fearsome quality that brought a cold sweat to each man.

"What an awful place!" Oliver Wording Bittman whimpered. Terror had literally frozen the taxidermist to the limb to which he clung.

IT was a ghastly night they spent. No sooner did one titanic struggle of dinosaurs subside, than another arose. Often more than one noisy, bloodcurdling fight was in progress at the same moment.

Vast bodies sloughed through the dense plant growth, some going with great hops as had the tyrannosaurus, others traveling on all fours.

Sleep was out of the question. Doc and his friends felt safe in their fern top—until some monstrous dinosaur came along and browsed off the crest of a fern which they could tell by the sound was nearly as tall as their perch. After this, throughout the night, they rested in momentary expectation of meeting disaster.

But, had they been in perfect safety, they would not have slept. Slumber was unthinkable. There was too much to hear. For they were wayfarers in another world!

They might as well have stepped back in time a thousand ages!

Daylight returned as suddenly as it had departed. With the appearance of the sun, a heavy rain fell, a tropical downpour that lasted only a few minutes. But as the water hit the red-hot surface of the mud lake up on the crater side, tremendous clouds of steam rolled.

The day was about as bright as a very cloudy winter afternoon in New York City, due to the "steam" clouds always above the crater.

It was at once evident that the ferocious dinosaurs preferred to prowl at night. For with dawn, the hideous bloodshed within the crater subsided to a marked degree.

Doc at once led his friends—with the exception of the whimpering Oliver Wording Bittman, who would not desert his perch in the fern tree—to see what had happened to Renny.

They found Renny's collapsed parachute at last. The spot where it lay was some hundreds of yards from the nearest giant fern which would offer safety to a man.

Monk had been making himself a cigarette. But at sight of what lay near Renny's parachute, his big and hairy hands froze, can of tobacco in one, papers in the other.

For all about Renny's 'chute was torn and ripped turf. And blood! Amid the gore lay Renny's hat.

It looked like a dinosaur had devoured Renny!

"Maybe—he got away?" Long Tom mumbled hopefully.

But Doc, after a quick circle of the spot, replied: "There is no human trail away from this place! I'm sure of that! The soft earth would take the prints. Renny never walked away from here!"

Monk slowly stuffed the tobacco can in a pocket. He had no appetite for a smoke now.

A reverent, sorrowful silence prevailed, dedicated to the memory of Renny.

This was broken in a frightful fashion.

"Over there!" Ham's voice cracked. "What—"

They looked, as one man, at first hoping Ham had sighted Renny. But it was not that.

OUT of the unhealthy rank jungle growth had come an amazing animal. In appearance, the thing was a conglomerate of weasel, cat, dog and bear. It was remarkable because it seemed a combination of most animals known to the twentieth-century world.

But it was approximately the size of a very large elephant!

Monk gulped, "What the—"

"A creodont!" breathed Johnny, awed. "The ancestor of a great many of our modern animals!"

"Yeah?" muttered Monk. "Well, from right now on, you don't catch me out of jumping distance of a tree!"

These words brought home to the others the shocking fact that they were helpless before the nondescript but fierce creodont. This animal could not be dodged as they had evaded the tyrannosaurus. It could turn too quickly! And its jaws were full of great teeth; its claws long and sharp. And no safety lay within reach!

The creodont abruptly charged!

Their guns cracked. But the gigantic animal came on as fast as ever. The thing had its head low—they could not locate its small eyes for an effective target.

The men spread apart. But that could help but little. The monstrous creodont would lay about among them, crushing and mangling. They could not hope to outrun it!

Only a few yards distant, the creodont reared and separated its great, frothing jaws. It sprang with a hideous snarl.

It looked like the end for Doc and his men—an end as terrible as they supposed Renny had suffered.

Chapter XVII
RENNY, THE HUNTED

WHILE Doc and his friends faced the dangers of this weird place the first night, Renny, lost from the others, had difficulties of his own.

When Renny's parachute lowered him to the spongy floor of the vast crater, he landed in the midst of such a scene as his wildest nightmares had never produced.

He dropped squarely into the fight which was heard from the air. This was a ferocious battle between the same tyrannosaurus which had pursued Doc and the others, and a three-horned rhinoceros of a monster.

Renny's parachute spilled over the revolting face of the terrible tyrannosaurus. Renny instantly squirmed out of the 'chute harness and dropped to the cushionlike earth.

The tyrannosaurus, pitching about like a tall house caught in a tornado, soon got the silken folds out of its face.

But Renny had no time to witness that. The other beast came thundering straight for Renny.

The iron-fisted engineer had inspected the pictures of a few of the genus triceratops in textbooks, and had gazed without particular interest at a skeleton of one as displayed in a great museum. Beyond that, his knowledge did not extend.

He recognized the thing as a triceratops, for Renny had an excellent memory. But he didn't know it was a herb eater. He wouldn't have believed that at the moment, anyway. The thing looked like it was bent on making a meal out of Renny.

The monster dinosaur came at him with all the

noise and impressive size of a snorting locomotive. Renny didn't have time to clutch for his gun. It was just as well. He could not have stopped the triceratops.

The huge reptile possessed three rhinoceros-like horns. Two jutted straight forward, one above each eye. These were fully as long as Renny's by-no-means-short body. The third horn was much smaller, and set down on the nose, as though for rooting purposes.

The striking thing about the triceratops was the great bony hood extending back from the head. This natural armor protected the neck and forepart of the body.

The armor was marked with great, fresh gouges. The fearful tyrannosaurus had been engaged in slaying this armored, three-horned vegetation eater for supper. Only the armor had saved the triceratops.

The three-horned dinosaur was now fleeing madly for its life! But Renny had no way of knowing that. He happened to be directly in the path of the thing. There was no time for a leap sidewise.

"Only one chance!" Renny gritted—and sprang high into the air, flinging his two-hundred-and-fifty-pound frame directly between the two massive horns set over the dinosaur's eyes.

Renny's hands, each one a gallon of knuckles, clasped the horns. They clung tightly.

When the hulking beast ran straight forward, not even shaking its vast head, Renny merely hung on. The space between the horns was ample to accommodate him. The smaller lower horn furnished a footrest.

"If I get off, the thing will turn on me!" Renny reasoned—wrongly.

This particular dinosaur was a peace lover, despite its formidable looks. Its only idea now was to get away from the terrible tyrannosaurus. Such a small object as Renny clinging to its head bothered it not at all for the time being.

The steam was dissipating now, and Renny could take in his surroundings. His amazing steed had a bald skin. It reminded Renny of an elephant's hide, although rougher and thicker. It was hard as sole leather to his touch.

"A bullet wouldn't faze the thing!" he decided.

RENNY'S scant knowledge was sufficient to inform him the major portion of this creature's brain probably lay in its spine. It was even likely the spinal cord served as a brain, a function not uncommon in the prehistoric members of the dinosaur tribe.

The stampeding beast wallowed through a small body of water without slackening pace. Renny was drenched. He noted the water was very warm, like piping hot coffee. It did not scald, though.

The breathing of Renny's conveyance was becoming labored. The thing was short of wind. Renny began to have an unpleasant feeling it would soon stop. He wondered how he would dismount without meeting disaster.

The problem solved itself.

Blindly, as unvarying in its wild course as a bullet, the triceratops hit a great tangle of lianas and ferns and small coniferous trees. It gouged through by main strength.

Renny was left behind, hanging over a vine!

To this vine Renny clung for a time. He listened. The ground was about seven feet below. Renny didn't know but what other predatory monsters might be about. He glanced up nervously, fearing sight of the gruesome, batlike flying reptiles.

Exploring, Renny found he still had his pistol-like machine gun.

"Wish I had a pocketful of hand grenades too!" he muttered.

He dropped down from the liana and set out on the triceratops's back trail. He found traveling difficult. Clinging creepers and packed ferns interfered.

Renny had penetrated the thick jungles of the upper Amazon. He had explored in rankest Africa. But he had never seen a jungle which approached this for denseness. Without the path the dinosaur had opened, Renny would have been baffled.

As it was, he had to be alert steadily, lest he stumble into the waist-deep tracks of the monster.

He soon noted the unusual character of the growth. Many of the trees were of a type he had never seen before. But others had a familiar look.

"The ones I don't recognize became extinct ages ago," he concluded. "The others, more fitted to changing conditions in the outside world, survived."

Renny chuckled. He felt exhilarated, now that he had escaped with his life.

"What I mean, this is a sure-enough example of how evolution has worked on the rest of the world!"

Suddenly came the dismaying knowledge that night had almost arrived.

Renny was conservative. He knew the safe thing to do.

"I'll hunt a tree for the night!" he concluded.

But he was not fortunate enough to be in a region of tall growth. He saw that climbing any of the small ferns or evergreen trees about him would not give him safety from the hulking dinosaurs.

He began to run, hoping to reach Doc before darkness. But, as though the very moist, depressively hot air were turning a jet-black ink, night started closing in.

Sprinting, Renny reached the body of water through which his huge steed had plowed. About to plunge in, he hesitated. A great gurgling arose beyond the enormous rushes that edged the shore. The sound was like huge tanks of water emptying in succession. Then a vast body, which was apparently dunking up and down and making the noises, must have rolled over.

A miniature tidal wave came boiling inshore. It reached above Renny's knees! What a monster this prehistoric beast must be!

Over the rushes suddenly projected what Renny at first took to be the head and neck of a snake. A workaday world serpent magnified a thousandfold! A large barrel could not have held the head!

For all its snaky look and fantastic size, the head had a peaceful look, though. A repetition of the loud water noises showed that the long, lithe neck was attached to a monster body.

Slowly, the weird beast came dragging out of the water.

RENNY felt a ticklish sensation in his scalp, which might have been his hair standing on end.

The thing was longer than a freight car!

"Good—" Renny spun and fled.

He knew he had just looked at a member of the family of largest creatures ever to tread the earth. Even the ferocious, meat-eating killer, the tyrannosaurus, was eclipsed by the bulk of this colossus.

The great reptile he had just seen was a "thunder lizard," or brontosaurus.

Renny recalled they were popularly supposed to be peaceful giants, haunting the water and feeding on lake plants and shore growth. The theory held by scientists is that they were not meat devourers.

Renny had no desire to test the accuracy of that theory. Compared to the thunder lizard in size, he was like a mouse beside a fat hog. He didn't know but what the beast might decide to try a man for a change of diet.

So Renny ran for all he was worth. The thunder lizard, apparently curious or playful, lumbered after him. The earth shook in a pronounced manner under its incalculable weight.

Quitting the trail opened by the armor-plated monster which had brought him here, Renny dived into the tangled vegetation. He lost his hundreds of tons of gamboling pursuer.

"Whew!" He mopped his forehead with both sleeves. "Whew!"

He felt his way onward, machine gun ready in one hand. So dark had become the night that he could not even see the weapon he held. He halted often to listen to the awful uproar of the night.

Once a nocturnal fray broke out nearby, and the course of the battle brought it directly for Renny! He fled madly. Strong in his nostrils was the fetid, near-suffocating odor of a great carnivore. He knew here was genuine danger! It was another of the monster killers of prehistoric ages, a tyrannosaurus. His parachute had fallen upon one of those!

Renny crept away, marveling at the variety of ear-splitting sounds emitted by the weird beasts of the crater. He reasoned the things could see somewhat in the darkness. He had noticed the eyes of the reptiles were particularly fitted for vision in restricted light. But in darkness such as this, it was impossible for them to see much. They must hunt largely by the sense of hearing, perhaps some of them with the organ of smell.

"What a place to have to live in!" he muttered.

It was only a moment later that fresh disaster overtook him.

Came a great fluttering sound from above his head! It was as if someone were shaking a large carpet up there.

"What the—" Then Renny knew what it was. One of the flying reptiles! A pterodactyl—one of the horrors which had disabled their plane!

Wildly, Renny flung up his gun.

But before he could pull the trigger, the gruesome marauder was upon him!

RENNY now got one of the few pleasant surprises of the night. He realized this aerial, batlike thing was much smaller than the one which had assailed the plane. Probably it was a chick of the species!

Evading the snapping, toothed beak, Renny clutched with his powerful hands. He got fistfuls of the revolting, membranous wings. The stuff felt like rubber. It was clammy. And a noisome stench accompanied the reptile.

The beak crunched. It took off the entire back of Renny's coat!

Grasping again, Renny secured a hold on the fearsome head. The body of this pterodactyl was about the size of an ostrich's. Renny put forth a superhuman effort, tossing himself about violently. He succeeded at last in what he was trying to do. He wrung the neck of the flying reptile!

But the thing did not die immediately! It whipped about, as tenacious of life as the tail of a snake. But Renny had at least stopped its attack. The slow death meant the creature scarcely had a definite brain center. Possibly it depended on its brain so little that it could even go on living for a time with that organ entirely removed!

"What a place this is!" Renny muttered.

He lifted the expiring pterodactyl. Its lightness was astounding.

"Bones hollow and filled with air!" decided Renny, drawing on his scant knowledge of prehistoric life-forms.

He tossed the flying reptile away, took a step sidewise—and froze in horror!

Another specimen of monster dinosaur was

approaching. The struggles of the dying air monster were attracting it!

Renny retreated hastily. He tried to be silent. But this was impossible in the abyss of darkness.

He heard the heavy steps of the approaching giant. They sank noisily into the spongy earth, so vast was the weight upon them. At the dying pterodactyl, the steps stopped.

A ghastly crunching of flesh and popping of chewed bones indicated the flying reptile was being devoured.

Renny quickened his pace, thinking to escape while the beast was occupied. But he had the misfortune to stumble. His shoulder brushed a bush. There was considerable noise.

The beast charged!

The rapidity with which it came showed Renny he could not hope to outrun it. He tried a desperate experiment. Halting, he quickly wrenched off what of his coat had remained after the bite delivered by the gargantuan aerial reptile.

Renny carried a waterproof cigarette lighter, although he did not smoke. It was handier than matches. He plucked it out of a pocket. Its tiny flame sprang up. He set fire to his fragment of coat.

Whirling the coat around his head speeded the fire. In an instant it was a sizeable brand.

He flung it in the face of the charging monster!

AS the flaming cloth gyrated through the air, Renny got a fleeting view of the repellent dinosaur stalking him.

It had a lizardlike body, armored with great bony plates. It traveled on all fours. Its head was uncouth as that of a mud turtle, but more than a yard in length. The low-slung carcass of the creature, although thin from side to side, was very high.

Most striking of its characteristics was the double row of huge, horny plates standing on edge down its back. These looked like two lines of monster sawteeth.

The name of the thing—stegosaur—escaped Renny. Anyway, what interested him at the moment was its reaction to the fire. Would it flee?

It didn't!

Renny realized the colossal reptile did not have the brains to recognize the fire as danger. Pivoting, he ran with all his speed.

Ferns whipped him. The needled tips of coniferous shrubs gouged at his eyes. Lianas held him back. He tore at the growth with his powerful hands. Suddenly, penetrating that jungle became like burrowing through a stack of green, wet hay.

Behind him thundered the Leviathan of the reptilian world. It seemed to gain as though he were standing still. Great knots of the soggy earth, dug up by its churning feet, fell noisily.

Renny had been in few tighter spots in his eventful life. He could not outrun this thing. In the darkness, he could not hide effectively—it would smell him out.

It was now no more than twice Renny's own length behind him!

And Renny stumbled and fell!

That fall was his salvation. A deep trench had brought him down. Evidently it had been opened by the snout of some tremendous rooting dinosaur.

Renny rolled into the trench!

The pursuing reptile passed over him! It was as though an earthquake had laid upon the surrounding ground. The earth walls of the trench gave under the vast weight. They caved.

Renny was buried by the earth!

He was drawing in a breath of relief when the cave-in came. So he had a quantity of air in his lungs. He held it there. Not a muscle did he move.

The clumsy reptile turned slowly and came back. The stupid thing did not know what had become of its quarry. It tramped the vicinity for a time, searching.

Earth pressed in more tightly as it strode somewhere near Renny.

The big-fisted engineer had held his breath about as long as he could. His lungs felt lead-filled. His ears sang.

The giant dinosaur lumbered majestically away. It had given up. The earth covering Renny had kept the reptile from scenting him.

In a near frenzy, such torture was he suffering, Renny squirmed about. He threshed in the soft earth. For a moment he thought he was entombed alive. But the convulsive effort this belief made him put forth, brought him near the surface.

His head came out into the warm, damp, crater air.

A ferocious bedlam of snarling and growling greeted him.

Sharp teeth sank into his body!

Chapter XVIII
WHERE TIME STOPPED

MEANWHILE, Doc and his men stood before the charge of the giant creodont, not knowing what strange thing would happen next.

The thing sprang for Monk. It missed, thanks to Monk's great leap to one side. Monk's machine gun hosed a stream of bullets into the side of the animal. This gave them an instant respite. The huge creature turned to bite itself where the bullets had hit, as though it had been jabbed there by thorns.

The beast was a fierce, deadly killer, even though it did look like a combination of weasel, dog and bear, with possibly a little long-haired elephant for good measure.

"Beat it, the rest of you!" Monk rapped. "Maybe

I can delay the thing long enough for you to reach safety!"

Monk made a move to step in the path of the charging animal. He was willing to sacrifice himself, if only it would help his friends. This looked like the only thing that would save them.

"Wait!" Doc's strong bronze hand stopped Monk.

"But Doc—" Monk started to object.

"Dry up—you homely ape!" Doc was actually chuckling in the face of the frightful danger! His tone was calm. His movements, although lightning-like, seemed unhurried.

"Let's have your tobacco, Monk!" Doc's hand suddenly possessed the can of smoking tobacco. So swiftly had it been taken that Monk hardly saw the gesture.

"Now—pick 'em up and lay 'em down!" Doc's powerful arm propelled Monk in the direction of the nearest tree large enough to furnish safety.

"Good—good luck, Doc!" Monk muttered. Then he sprinted away at full speed. Monk didn't see how even Doc's sovereign powers could prevail over this prehistoric monster.

Emitting a loud, fierce noise, a combined bark and squeal and snarl, the hybrid behemoth sprang.

Doc's sinewy fingers had tweaked open the tobacco tin. In a trice, he had the tobacco clutched, half in either palm. He sprang forward to oppose the giant beast. His arms moved nimbly.

An effective pinch of the tobacco was jammed into each of the thing's little eyes. The rest went into its nostrils.

A swipe of a huge paw laid open Doc's coat and shirt. But the metallic skin was hardly touched. Doc's speed was nearly unbelievable.

Springing away, Doc raced for safety.

The prehistoric beast, blinded by the tobacco, its organs of smell temporarily ineffective for the same reason, could only bound about and release its bloodcurdling growls.

Doc joined his friends up a massive fern.

"Afraid you'll be without tobacco now," he told Monk.

Monk grinned admiringly. "I been thinkin' about quittin' smokin' anyway."

Through a lacelike design of vines and branches, they could see the antics of the monster they had just escaped, thanks to Doc's ingenuity and marvelous physique. The thing was alternately pawing at its smarting eyes and ramming its repulsive muzzle into the moist, soft earth.

"There it goes!" Long Tom emitted a sigh of relief as the beast decided to run. It volleyed away with a great uproar.

"Wonder how Oliver Wording Bittman is making out?" Johnny puzzled. "We haven't heard a bleat from that tree where we left him."

"Probably so scared he's lost his voice," said the sharp-tongued Ham.

Doc came to Bittman's defense. "You've got to admit he has something to be scared of. Personally, it's my duty to take care of the man, craven coward though he may become. He saved my father's life."

"Sure," said the big-hearted Monk. "Bittman's nerve was O. K. until we hit this fantastic crater. In fact, it was a continuous source of wonder to me to see how anxious he was to be with us everytime we made a move. Remember how he went with us when we tackled Kar? That took nerve. Maybe his courage will return when he gets used to this strange place—if it's possible to get used to it."

MONK, it seemed, was right.

Oliver Wording Bittman slid down from his fern tree perch as they approached. His features were pale, but his big jaw was thrust out in a determined fashion. He fiddled with the skinning scalpel which still decorated his watch chain.

"I am ashamed of my cowardly performance during the night," he said, embarrassed. "I guess I am not a brave man. At any rate, my courage completely departed at sight of this ghastly world. But I think I have it back, at least in part."

"No one could be blamed for becoming shaky at sight of such an unbelievable, terrifying place," Doc smiled.

"Yeah—it'd give anybody the jitters!" Monk grinned.

Johnny was using the magnifying lens on the left side of his glasses to inspect unusual plants.

"The more I see of this place, the more astounding it becomes," he declared. "Notice there are few flowering plants or trees of the type which shed their leaves."

"Evolution practically stopped in this crater many ages ago," Doc offered.

Johnny began to wax eloquent. "No doubt this was once part of some land continent, probably the Asiatic. The prehistoric animal life entered and were trapped here in some manner—"

"Trapped—how?" Monk grunted.

It was some little time before this question was answered. They moved forward, seeking more open ground. They found it upon a knoll from which an extensive view could be obtained.

"Golly!" muttered Monk, as he gazed at the frowning heights of the crater rim. "We must be at sea level, or below. This crater looks like it was better'n ten thousand feet deep!"

Doc's golden eyes ranged the crater edge as great a distance as possible. Due to the gloominess of the light which penetrated the clouds above the pit, the opposite wall of the crater was lost to sight. Long plumes of steam arising from what were obviously streams of boiling-hot water, helped hinder vision.

The day was really a hot, wet, ghostly gray twilight.

"I do believe I've seen moonlight brighter than this!" Long Tom said.

But they could get a fair idea of their surroundings. The utter denseness of the jungle was a thing to cause awe.

As they stood on the knoll, another sudden rainstorm came. Steam rolled from the hot mud lake like fluffy cotton. The violent downpour seemed to occur several times each day.

"The tremendous rainfall is caused by the moist hot air lifting to the cold air at the top of the crater, where it condenses and falls back as rain," Doc Savage explained. "The great rainfall also explains the plant growth being so rank it is nearly a solid mass."

He glanced about appraisingly.

"This vegetation is only slightly less dense than that which flourished during what scientists call the coal age."

"You mean it was jungle like this that made coal beds?" Monk grunted.

"Exactly. Let a landslide cover some of this jungle, or let water and mud cover it, and in the course of a few ages, we would have an excellent chance of a coal vein. Partial decomposition without access to air would do the work."

FURTHER appraisal of their amazing domicile led Doc to level a mighty bronze arm.

"There, brothers, is the explanation of these prehistoric life-forms being forced to remain here through the ages!"

Johnny, the geologist, quickly comprehended what Doc meant.

"At one time a path gave access to the crater," he declared. "Some natural upheaval, probably an earthquake shock, destroyed the means of getting in and out. And the dinosaurs were forced to stay.

"Through the aeons of time that they have remained here, the outer sides of this cone weathered down. The land sank. Oceans rushed in. And this crater became Thunder Island, supposedly an active volcanic cone projecting from a seldom-visited section of the southern seas."

Monk scratched his bullet of a head. "But, Doc, how do you account for these critters not changin' through the ages, like they did in the outer world?"

"Evolution," Doc smiled.

"But evolution is a changing—"

"Not necessarily," Doc corrected. "Evolution is a change in animals and plants and so on, as I comprehend it. But those changes are caused by slowly altering surroundings. For example, if an animal lives in a warm country, its fur will be light, or it may have no fur at all. But if the country turns cold, the animal must grow a heavy coat, or perish. The acquiring of that fur coat is evolution.

"Conditions here in this crater have remained exactly as they were ages ago. The air is warm. There is a great deal of rain. The luxuriant plant growth makes food plentiful. Probably the seasons down here are alike the year around.

"So the prehistoric animals trapped here experienced no necessity for changing themselves to fit altered conditions, because conditions did not alter."

"That sounds reasonable," Monk admitted.

After this, silence fell. It was a somber quiet. They were thinking of Renny. They believed him dead, on the evidence of what they had seen—his hat and the gore surrounding it.

"We'd better be moving," Doc said at last. "First, we will visit the neighborhood of the hot mud lake, on the chance some supplies might have spilled out of our plane. In case you haven't noticed it, we're practically out of ammunition."

The others hastily examined their guns. They found only a few cartridges in each weapon. Monk, naturally the most reckless, had but four cartridges left.

"Throw the lever which changes your guns to single-shot operation," Doc directed. "We've got to count every bullet. Although the weapons are virtually useless against these prehistoric monsters, they will be effective upon Kar."

"Kar!" Ham clipped. "I had nearly forgotten that devil! Have you noted any signs of him, Doc?"

"Not yet. But we are not giving up our pursuit. Not even these big dinosaurs can keep us from Kar."

THEY visited the hot mud lake. So terrific was the heat of the lavalike stuff that they could not approach within yards. Too, they dreaded a sudden eruption, such as had been caused by the plane plunging into the lake.

Such geyser displays apparently came often. Great splatters of mud, now cooled, decorated the steep slope for some distance below the hot lake.

"Imagine one of them droppin' on the back of your neck!" Monk mumbled.

"Better still, imagine what would happen to the crater floor if this broke!" Ham pointed at the lavalike dike retaining wall which confined the horseshoe-shaped body of superheated, jellylike mud well upon the crater side.

"It would be too bad on a pig, if he happened to be down on the crater bottom, huh?" Monk suggested. Then he watched Ham's features assume the inevitable flush of ire.

They found no speck of equipment from the plane. The craft was hopelessly gone.

To show there was no chance of salvaging it, Doc cast a small chunk of wood out on the crusted lake surface.

So hot was the crust that the wood smoldered and quickly burst into flame!

"Golly!" muttered Monk. "Let's get out of here before that thing takes a notion to cut up!"

"We shall skirt the crater," Doc decided. "You notice the larger vegetation grows near the edges. In the center is a series of small streams. These bodies of water run sluggishly, and are hardly more than elongated bog holes."

"How about lighting a fire and getting some breakfast?" suggested the taxidermist, Oliver Wording Bittman.

Bittman had indeed regained much of his nerve. But it was with a patent effort that he was striving to maintain the standard of calmness before peril set by Doc and his men.

"No fire," Doc replied. "It might show Kar our whereabouts, if he is in the crater. Anyway, we have nothing to cook."

"The breakfast part of his idea still sounds good to me," spoke up Long Tom. "What do we eat, Doc?"

"I'll try to find something," Doc smiled.

They betook themselves from the vicinity of the mud lake.

"Quite a climb!" Ham puffed as they descended the steep slope.

Ham, amazingly enough, had retained his sword cane through all the excitement of the parachute leap and the horror of the ensuing night. He was seldom without that secret blade. But, although it was mightily effective upon human opponents, it was virtually useless against the giant dinosaurs. The tempered blade would snap before it could be forced through one of the thick, wood-hard hides.

However, Ham very soon got a chance to use his sword cane.

An animal about the size of a large calf suddenly bounded up before them. It had four spongy looking antlers, two in the usual spot atop the head, the other pair down below the eyes. It had a cloven hoof and looked edible.

With a swift spring that would have been a credit to even Doc's brawny form, Ham ran the strange animal through with his sword cane.

"We eat!" he grinned.

"I HAVE an idea how we can build a fire without the smoke being noticed," Doc offered. He had suddenly discovered he was hungry. "We'll kindle a blaze near one of these streams of boiling water from which steam arises."

"Talk about necessity being the mother of ideas!" Monk grinned.

They kindled a fire, although experiencing difficulty with wet wood. Too, another sudden deluge of rain nearly put out the flames. But at length they had their breakfast cooking.

"What are we eatin'?" inquired Monk.

"A primitive type of deer," decided Johnny, the geologist.

By dipping a corner of his handkerchief into the boiling stream beside which they had built their fire, then permitting the wet cloth to cool and tasting it, Doc ascertained the water was drinkable, although it had a saline quality.

He proceeded to boil a hunk of the primitive deer in the natural caldron.

"I did that once in Yellowstone Park," said Ham.

Doc and his men kept an alert watch for danger. They were not disturbed. The meat was palatable, but had a pronounced grassy taste.

It was a sober meal, what with the thought of Renny's possible fate.

"The insects are interesting," remarked Long Tom. "There seem to be few butterflies, moths, bees, wasps or ants. But there's plenty of dragonflies, bugs, and beetles."

"The insects you see are the less complex types, for the most part," Doc explained. "They aren't quite developed enough to make cocoons or gather honey. They came first in the course of evolution."

Because the great warmth within the crater would not permit them to keep meat fresh even until the next meal time, they discarded the remainder of their primitive deer. They quitted the vicinity.

"We will now go ahead with our circling of the pit," Doc said. "There may be a path by which a climber as agile as a man might depart."

Monk let out a displeased rumble. "Ugh! You mean to say we may be stuck in here, Doc?"

"Did you notice a spot where you could climb out?"

"No-o-o," Monk admitted uneasily.

Traversing some little distance, they reached a particularly tall shrub. Monk climbed this to look around. He had no more than reached the sprawling top when his excited call came down to Doc and the others.

"Smoke! I see a fire!"

Doc ran up to Monk's side with the agility of a squirrel.

Two or three miles distant across the crater bed, smoke curled from the jungle.

"Sure it isn't steam?" Ham inquired skeptically from the ground.

"Not a chance," Doc replied. "It's darker than steam."

"And I just saw a burning ember, apparently a leaf, in the smoke!" Monk added.

He and Doc clambered down to the ground.

One word was upon the lips of everybody.

"Kar! You think it is Kar's fire?"

"Can't tell," Doc admitted. "But we'll find out soon."

THEY went ahead hurriedly. Ham's sword cane now came in doubly handy for slashing through the tangled growth. There were no forest lanes overhead—open stretches of branches through which Doc and Monk might have swung, anthropoidlike. They had to confine themselves to the earth.

Doc's great bronze form came to an abrupt stop. Strange lights danced in his flaky golden eyes.

He was studying something he had found underfoot.

"What is it?" Long Tom inquired.

"Footprints."

"Let me see!" Oliver Wording Bittman hurried over.

Monk made an angry growl. "Kar?"

"No." A joyful brightness had lighted Doc's golden eyes.

"What are you so tickled about?" Monk wanted to know.

"The footprints are Renny's. I'd know those oversize tracks anywhere. Too, one of his shoes had a cut on the sole, and these tracks show just such a cut."

"Then Renny may be alive!"

They met Renny within the next few minutes. The elephantlike, big-fisted engineer had heard them. He came striding out of the tangled growth—the same as ever!

In one hand, Renny dangled the skin of a small, lemon-colored animal. In markings, this pelt resembled that of an undersized hyena.

"Here's the history of my night!" Renny chuckled after greetings were exchanged.

Rapidly, he told of his wild ride on the great colossus with the three horns and the huge bony shield over its neck, of the playful thunder lizard in the lakelet, of his fight with the odorous and batlike flying reptile chick, and of the creature with the double row of upstanding, saw-teeth protuberance down its back.

He told of ducking into the handy trench, and of being buried. Then he came to the point where he shoved his person out into the hot night—and teeth had seized him.

Renny exhibited a small chewed spot on his shoulder. He shook the pelt of the hyenalike animal.

"It was this little thing bit me!" he laughed. "It made enough noise to be a lion. I choked the durn thing. I'm gonna make a pen wiper or somethin' out of its hide to commemorate one of the worst scares I ever got. When it took hold of me, I sure thought the jig was up."

Doc suddenly remembered something. "That smoke! Did it come from a fire you made?"

"What smoke?" Renny asked vacantly. "I haven't made any fire."

Chapter XIX
ATTACK OF THE GNAWERS

"IT'S Kar!" Ham muttered. "Kar made that fire!"

"Unless there are human beings residing in this place," Johnny pointed out.

"My thumb goes down on the idea that people may live in the crater," said Doc. "Thought that the comparatively defenseless human race could exist in here through the ages is a little preposterous. Anyway, we have seen no sign of monkeys or apes, which some evolutionists claim branched off from the same source stock as man."

"There's not much doubt but that they did!" said Ham nastily, looking intently at Monk's hairy, simian figure. "We have the living proof with us."

"A lot a shyster lawyer knows about evolution!" Monk grinned.

They set forth toward the fire again.

"Use caution!" Doc warned. "If it is only one of Kar's men, we want to follow the chap to Kar. Or capture him alive and force him to tell us where Kar is!"

A stream of boiling-hot water barred their path. It was shallow, but too wide to leap across. They were forced to trail along it. But it only grew wider. It seemed to reach an indefinite distance. It was too hot for wading.

Doc solved the problem. Cutting two tough shoots not unlike bamboo, he fashioned a pair of makeshift stilts. The others quickly followed suit. With these, they negotiated the overly hot stream.

Oliver Wording Bittman, who wailed that he had never walked on stilts as a boy, was helped across the boiling water by Doc.

Soon after, the matlike jungle became horny with great upthrusts of rock.

At the very first of these stony juttings, Doc halted. He examined the rock with interest. He tapped at it quietly with his gun barrel. He borrowed Johnny's glasses to use the magnifying lens on the left side.

"Hm-m-m!" he said thoughtfully.

If the bestial creodont which would have destroyed them except for the tobacco Doc threw in its eyes—if that animal was a mixture of many animals, so was this rock a mixture of many ores. Without proper apparatus for assaying, a great deal could not be told.

"What's so interesting about that spotted dornick?" inquired Oliver Wording Bittman, fingering the scalpel on his watch chain.

"Just the wide variety of ores which it apparently contains," Doc replied.

Renny glanced at Doc. "You mean we may be

near the region from which came the rare element or substance which is the basis of the Smoke of Eternity?"

"It's a thought," Doc admitted.

GREATER was their caution now. The strange rocks became more plentiful. Indeed, the jungle gave way to a wilderness of glistening, mottled stone. This shimmering waste stretched directly before them until it ended against the sheer cliff of the crater side.

They penetrated farther. Signs of rare metals were all about. But it was doubtful if any were present in sizeable paying quantities.

"I'd like to spend a month in here, just classifying rock types," declared Johnny, the geologist.

Doc Savage appraised the stony fastness.

"I want to look this over," he said. "I can move faster alone. You chaps wait here. The fire is on the other side. I'll scout that, investigating this rock formation en route, then return."

His friends spread out among the strange rocks, inspecting curious formations. A couple of them sidled back into the jungle, intent on seeing if they couldn't locate some kind of an edible herb. A meat diet would soon get monotonous, especially a meat with as strong a grassy taste as their primitive deer.

Doc continued into the rocks. They became difficult to get through, as though they were broken glass, the glass being as thick as a house.

This region of strange rocks was larger than he had thought. It must extend for at least two miles. It pressed against the cliff base its whole length.

In order to see the better, Doc clambered atop a vitrified mass.

Spang!

A bullet hit beside him. It sprayed wiry bits of lead into his bronze skin.

A quick leap put Doc in shelter. He was already in safety when the satanic laughter of the echoes came hopping across the arid rock wilderness.

The shot had come from the direction of his own friends!

Hardly more than a bronze blur in the steam-made twilight, Doc sped for his men.

He found them in excitement.

"Who fired that shot?" Doc demanded.

"None of us. It came from the jungle—to the right."

"Where's Bittman?"

Oliver Wording Bittman was not about!

Doc sprang away. Herculean sinews carried his bronze form over knife-edged boulders and ridges around which it took the others minutes to go.

He topped a huge stone block.

Directly below him sprawled Bittman. The taxidermist's body, so thin it was a skeleton and a few hard muscles, lay grotesquely atwist.

It was motionless!

A SAILING spring put Doc beside Bittman. His mighty bronze hands started to explore.

Spang!

Another shot!

The bullet would have slain Doc—if he had been one iota less quick on coordinating eye and muscles. For he had seen a rifle barrel stir out of the jungle foliage. He had flattened his giant form.

The rifle slug slicked through the space his body had vacated. It hit a rock and climbed away with a loud squawk.

Doc's own gun rapped. Once! Twice!

A man came tumbling, slowly, stiffly, out of the foliage. He was a short, broad man. He had the look of a human frog. Doc had never seen him before.

The man piled into a dead heap. One bullet had drilled his forehead. The other had stopped his heart.

Several seconds, Doc waited. No more shots came. He used his sensitive ears to their fullest. His bronze nostrils twitched, sampling the warm, moist air that should bring him any alien odors.

He decided no more bushwhackers were about.

Oliver Wording Bittman stirred. A low, whimpering sound trailed from his lips. His head lifted.

Suddenly he seized Doc's leg. He gave a terrific wrench. Doc, taken by surprise, came lightly to a knee. His brawny hands trapped Bittman's arms.

"Oh!" Bittman choked. "Oh!"

He relaxed. Remorse came into his thin face.

"I—I saw a gun pointing at me!" Bittman moaned. "I realized it was Kar. I—I guess I must have—fainted. When I revived, my first thought was to fight for my liberty. I thought you were Kar's man. I'm sorry. My head wasn't clear—"

Doc nodded thoughtfully. "Fainting was the most fortunate thing you could have done in that case. It dropped you out of sight of the bushwhacker."

Striding over, Doc inspected the dead gunman.

Renny, Ham, Johnny, Long Tom and Monk came up.

"Ever see this man before?" Doc indicated the corpse.

None of them had.

"Come on!" Doc directed. "Let's investigate that fire!"

They made all speed possible across the waste of stone. They were not shot at. The wall of jungle again took them in.

The mysterious fire was close. To their nostrils came the tang of its smoke.

"Quiet!" Doc warned.

Fifty yards more were traversed at a snail's pace. But it is difficult for seven men to move through an incredibly dense tangle of plant growth without noise. Especially when one has no particular woodcraft, such as Oliver Wording Bittman.

"Wait here!" commanded Doc.

Then he was gone like a bronze shadow. The jungle tissue seemed to absorb him. There was no sound.

In a moment, Doc's golden eyes were inspecting the clearing wherein smoked the fire.

NO one was there. The fire had about burned out. It had been lighted for cooking purposes, between two immense logs. The logs alone now burned.

Nearby lay mining paraphernalia—picks, shovels, an empty dynamite box and some stray, clipped ends of fuse.

A long minute, Doc appraised the scene. Then he strode boldly into the clearing—his keen senses had shown him no bushwhackers lurked nearby.

He circled the open space, then crisscrossed it several times. He moved swiftly. And when he had finished, his retentive mind had a picture of what had gone on in the little glade.

Kar's men had camped here. They had been mining somewhere in the waste of strange rock.

They had been mining the unknown element or substance which was the basis of the Smoke of Eternity!

What had caused their departure was difficult to say. Either they had secured what they sought, or had been frightened away by the knowledge Doc and his men were near.

Doc called his men. They hurried up.

"At least six men are in the gang—probably five, now that we got one." Doc indicated a half dozen tracks—only his dexterous eye could determine they were marks of as many distinct men. "Of the four men Kar sent out of the United States on the *Sea Star,* we did for one at the coral atoll, as he tried to bomb our plane. To the surviving three, he has added from the crew of the speedy yacht which took his men off the *Sea Star,* or from some other source."

"But where did they go?" muttered Oliver Wording Bittman. The taxidermist, although his fingers were still too shaky to play with the scalpel on his watch chain, had recovered amazingly.

"We'll trail them," Doc declared.

It taxed Doc's woodcraft hardly at all to find the trail. Broad and plain, smaller ferns and shrubs trampled down, it led off around the crater. A half mile, they had simple going.

Then the way came to an abrupt end!

It terminated at one of the many shallow, wide streams of hot water. As earlier in the day, Doc employed stilts to cross this obstacle.

But he could find no trail on the other side!

"They used a raft or a boat of some sort!" he called to his men.

"We'll take one side and you the other until we find where they landed!" Ham offered.

But this soon proved unfeasible. The slough of hot water quickly became a great swamp. Although this water was far from boiling in temperature, it was still too hot to wade. And some of the channels were too deep for their stilts and too wide to jump.

"We'll have to give it up!" Doc said regretfully.

Time had been passing swiftly. It was nearing dark again, and Doc made preparations looking to a safe night.

"We'll take a lesson from the fact that the top of a tree near us was browsed off last night," he decided. "Each man will seek refuge up a separate tree. That way, if one meets with an accident, it won't spell doom for the others."

The outburst of an awful fight between a pair of reptilian monsters less than a mile away lent speed to their search for a satisfactory location. The prehistoric giants were beginning their nocturnal bedlam.

The adventurers found a grove of the palmlike ferns which made an ideal set of perches. Up these, they hurriedly clambered.

Once more, night poured like something solid and intensely black into the crater of weird Thunder Island.

A FEW words were exchanged in the sepia void. Then conversation lagged. They knew the slightest sound was liable to draw the unwelcome attention of some reptilian titan.

Ham had selected a bower near Monk.

"So I can throw a club at Monk if he starts snoring," Ham chuckled.

Within half an hour after darkness fell, the awful bedlam of the dinosaurs had reached its grisly zenith. The cries of the things were indescribable. Often there came the revolting odor of great meat eaters prowling nearby.

Suddenly Doc discovered a glowing cigarette end in a fern top near the thick jungle.

"Watch it!" he called. "The light might show Kar our position!"

"I'm sorry!" called Oliver Wording Bittman's voice. A moment later, the cigarette gyrated downward, to burst in a shower of sparks.

Doc and his men were tired—they had not slept a wink the night previous. Although the satanic noises within the crater were as fearsome as on the night before, they were becoming accustomed to them. Noises that made their ears ring and icicles roll down their spines now worried them no more than passing elevated railway trains bother a dweller in the Bronx.

But Doc had developed a sort of animal trait of sleeping with one eye open. He heard a faint noise. He thought he saw a light some distance away.

Later, he was sure he detected a distinct, dragging noise very close!

The sound stopped. Nothing immediate came of it. Doc dropped off to sleep. Too many monsters were prowling about continually to be bothered with one noise.

A loud shuffling beneath their trees aroused him again. He listened.

There seemed to be scores of great beasts below!

"Hey!" yelled Monk an instant later. "Some darn thing is eatin' on the bottom of my tree!"

To Doc's keen ears came the sound of grinding teeth at work on the base of Monk's fern. Then big incisors began on his own tree!

Capable bronze hands working swiftly, Doc picked off a fragment of his own shirt. He put a flame to it, got it blazing, and dropped it. The burning fragment slithered from side to side as it fell. It left a trail of sparks. But it gave light enough to disclose an alarming scene.

A colony of monster, prehistoric beavers had attacked them!

The creatures were about the size of bears. They had the flat, black, hairless tails of an ordinary beaver. But the teeth they possessed were immensely larger, even in proportion.

A determined fierceness characterized the beasts. Although they made no snarlings or squealings, the very rapidity of their angry breathing showed they were bent on accomplishing something.

And that was the destruction of Doc and his men!

DOC SAVAGE'S gaze moved quickly to one side. He had remembered the dragging noise heard earlier. He sought the spot where it had ended. A powerful suspicion was gripping him.

He was right!

One of the great prehistoric beavers lay dead! The rear legs were tied together—*tied with a rope!*

"Kar is responsible for this!" he clipped at the others.

"How could—"

"He has visited this crater before. He knows how the weird animals here react. He knew it was a trait with these big beavers to avenge the death of one of their number. So he had his men kill one and drag it here. The animals followed the trail. They can scent us up the trees. They think we're the killers."

At this point, the fragment of Doc's shirt burned out.

To his ears came a *gru-u-ump, gru-u-mp* chorus. Lusty teeth working upon their tree retreats! And from the sound, they wouldn't take long to bring down the giant ferns! They seemed to bite in like axes.

"Thank Heaven!" came Oliver Wording Bittman's sudden gasp. "My tree is close enough to other growth that I can crawl to safety! Is there anything I can do to help you men? Perhaps I can decoy them away?"

"Not a chance!" Monk snorted. "There must be a hundred of them! And they're chewing so fast they couldn't hear anything! Say! My tree is already beginning to sway!"

Doc Savage drew his gun.

He fired it downward. A single report! It sounded terrific.

An astounding thing promptly happened!

The entire colony of prehistoric beavers quit gnawing. They stampeded! Away through the jungle they went at top speed! Not an animal remained behind!

"Bless me!" Monk chuckled. "What kinda magic you got in that smoke-pole, Doc?"

Doc Savage was actually as surprised as the others. Then the explanation came to him. How simple!

"What is the method the beaver uses to warn its fellows of danger?" he asked.

"It hauls off and gives the water a crack with its tail," Monk replied.

"That explains it," declared Doc. "These giant prehistoric beavers use the same danger warning, evidently. They mistook the sound of the shot for an alarm given by one of their number."

Monk burst into loud laughter.

Chapter XX
THE DEATH SCENE

THE remainder of the night was uneventful—if noisy.

With daylight, and the simultaneous retiring of the more ferocious of the colossal reptiles, Doc and his men slid down their tree ferns to see what damage the overgrown beavers had done.

Doc's shot had not been fired any too soon. Monk's tree was supported by a piece no thicker than his wrist. And some of the others were as near falling.

One noteworthy incident enlivened their investigations.

"It's gone!" Oliver Wording Bittman's shriek crashed out.

The skeleton-thin taxidermist was clutching madly at his watch chain.

"My skinning scalpel!" he wailed. "It has disappeared! I had it when I retired, I am certain!"

Doc helped Bittman look for the scalpel under the tree. They didn't find it. Bittman seemed distraught.

"It can be replaced for a few dollars," Doc suggested.

"No! No!" Bittman muttered. "It was a keepsake. A souvenir! I would not have taken five hundred dollars for it!"

Unable to locate Bittman's vanished trinket, the adventurers set out in search of breakfast. They cannily kept close to the giant tree ferns which offered the best safety available to man here in the ghastly lost domain of time.

Doc Savage it was who bagged their breakfast. A large ground sloth flushed up in their path. A bronze flash, Doc's mighty form overhauled it. A rap of his mighty fist stunned the creature. It resembled a cross between a tail-less opossum and a small bear, and looked inviting enough.

"It feeds on herbs and such fruit as there is," Doc decided. "It shouldn't be bad eating!"

It wasn't. But before eating, while the sloth was cooking over a fire near a steaming brook, Doc took his exercises. He never neglected these. The previous morning he had taken them in the tree, although he had not slept a wink during the night.

The kit containing the vials of differing scents and the mechanism which made the high and low frequency sound waves had reposed in his pocket throughout. It was, other than their arms, practically the only piece of their equipment they had saved.

After breakfast, Doc made an announcement.

"I'm leaving you fellows. Stick together while I'm gone. I mean that! Don't one of you get out of sight of all the others! The danger always afoot in this place is incalculable!"

"Where you going, Doc?" Ham queried.

But Doc only made a thin bronze smile. A swift motion—and he was gone! The earth might have swallowed him.

Doc's friends would have been awestricken had they seen the pace with which he traveled now. His going was like the wind. For there was no need to accommodate his steps to the limited speed of his less acrobatic companions. He seemed but to touch the rankest wall of jungle—and he was through. Often he took to the top of the growth, leaping from bush to creeper to bush, maintaining balance like an expert tightrope walker.

Near the slain prehistoric beaver which had been dragged to their nocturnal refuge by Kar's men, Doc picked up a trail. Kar's men had numbered two!

Doc's speed increased. He swept along the trail like a bronze cloud pushed by a swift, if a bit sporadic, breeze. A mile dropped behind him, then another.

His golden eyes missed little of the amazing prehistoric life about him.

One incident intrigued him particularly.

He glimpsed a very black, sleek animal. It had white stripes and spots traveling the length of its body. In size, it approximated an African lion. But it was vastly different in build, being chunky and sleepy looking.

The unusual animal had a black, bushy tail nearly four times the length of its body! This tail waved above the matted tropical growth like a banner—a flag of warning.

And flag of warning it was! Doc realized the creature must be ancestor to the common and obnoxious American polecat!

As he watched the animal, one of the stupendous killers, a tyrannosaurus, came bounding along, its stringlike front legs occasionally batted sizeable trees out of its path. The reptilian monster stopped often, balancing on its enormous three-toed feet, and turning slowly around after the manner of a dog standing on his rear legs. The carnivorous giant must have failed to satisfy its appetite during the night, and was still hunting.

Doc, concealed behind a clump of ferns, kept perfectly motionless. In doing this, he was obeying the first rule of the wild—the same rule that causes a chicken to freeze into immobility when it is sighted away from shelter by a hawk. Common safety commanded that he let the hideous reptilian giant quit the vicinity before he continued on the trail of Kar's men. And motionless objects escape notice best.

Doc was surprised to see the great prehistoric killer, as large as many a house, flee from the black-and-white edition of a skunk's ancestor. It was a lesson in the effectiveness of the latter's gas-attack defense. It was not unlikely that the little animal was the only thing on earth the odious reptile behemoth feared.

The trail of Kar's men worked toward the center of the crater. Several times it was evident they had sought to hide their tracks by wading in the edge of such water pools as were not too hot. But Doc held the scent.

DOC halted to cut a long, bamboolike shoot, not unlike the ordinary cane fishing pole. He stripped off the leaves. He worked on the larger end for some minutes. After that, he tested the heft of the javelin he had fashioned.

For the next few minutes, his alert gaze not only kept track of the trail he was following, but roved in search of something to test his spear on.

He found game in the shape of a small but vile-looking creature which had a back covered with hairs that were stiff and pointed like thorns. No doubt this was the predecessor of the common porcupine.

Doc cast his javelin accurately. He inflicted a minor wound on the beast's flank. It ran off briskly—and suddenly fell dead.

As the animal tumbled lifeless—the trilling sound abruptly came to Doc's lips. Low and mellow, inspiring, but now awesome, it was such a sound that probably had never before been heard in this lost crater—this land of terror. The sound seemed to creep away and lose itself in the weird, luxuriant jungle, and silence came.

It was as though some profound fact had become certainty in Doc's mind.

The bronze master hurried on, following the tracks of his quarry. They had not been able to do an effective job of hiding them, due to the intense darkness of the night and the fear of the prehistoric reptilian giants which must have been gripping their hearts.

Although the larger reptiles had attracted most of the attention, there was by no means a dearth of smaller creatures. Doc saw many armor-backed beasts resembling armadillos. Some of these were no larger than rats. Others reached sizeable proportions.

Very interesting were prehistoric horse types no larger than sheep. Indeed, one who had not studied ancient evolution types might have mistaken them for short-eared rabbits. A close examination would have shown many differences, though. For one thing, the horselike head was quite pronounced.

Many species of chipmunk-like creatures scurried about. These ranged from the size of a mouse to animals larger than dogs. As the ground sloped upward toward a hill, these hole-dwellers became more plentiful.

Suddenly a foul, slate-colored cloud whipped over the jungle. The stirring of great wings like filthy canvas on a skeleton frame made the fronds of the gigantic ferns clatter together as in a gale.

Doc flattened. The slimy wings beat above him. It was as though a great invisible hand were shaking a loose bundle of vile cloth. The rancid reek of carrion was wafted by the squirming wings.

But Doc had been too quick. The immense flying reptile was carried past by its own momentum. Its tooth-armored beak grabbed space with a rattling like boards clattered together.

Not even whipping erect, Doc's bronze form flew like an arrow for the nearest safety—a clump of thorny growth some acres in extent. He had an idea the membranous wings of the pterodactyls were tender. They would not venture into the thorns.

He reached safety! The aerial reptile crashed in after him. The thorns spiked it. With a hideous roaring and gargling outcry, it sprang back.

Doc drew his pistol. He could at least disable this monster with a couple of shots, then be on his way.

But another pterodactyl abruptly came! Then another! The cries of the first had attracted them. And they kept coming.

The great batlike shapes became so thick overhead as to literally blot out what light there was. And the wind their wings made bent and twisted the fern fronds and threatened to rend them from their anchorage. The putrid stench was near overpowering.

DOC was in a dilemma. He didn't have cartridges enough to fight the pterodactyls. To venture out of the thorn patch would be fatal.

Evidently the flying reptiles often chased quarry into the thorns. For, despite the almost nonexistent brains of the things, they knew enough not to venture among the stickers.

Doc relentlessly settled down to wait until the pterodactyls gave up and went away. He believed they would soon depart—if he kept motionless.

But a horrible new development came!

One of the colossal hopping reptiles came bounding up! It was drawn by the cloud of aerial monsters. Perhaps it had secured quarry which the pterodactyls had chased into the thorns on other occasions.

The thorny thicket bothered the terrible tyrannosaurus killer not at all! Its tough hide was impervious! It walked into the thorn patch and began to look for Doc. Hopping a couple of hundred feet, it would stop to turn around slowly.

Its hideous, stringlike front legs—legs that were none the less thick as a barrel—flipped in a ghastly fashion. Probably this was caused by the nervous gnawings of appetite. But it looked to the Doc like the thing was clapping hands over the prospect of a human meal!

Doc moved only when the hideous head with its tremendous, frothing rows of teeth was turned from him. Then he took care not to make noise.

He had an unpleasant feeling the reptile titan was going to find him—unless he did something quickly!

To complicate things, he unexpectedly confronted one of the black, marked, bushy-tailed predecessors of the modern polecat. The noisome thing gave every sign of going into action.

Doc's gun rapped twice. So well-placed were the shots that the bushy-tailed animal dropped instantly.

The reptilian monster had heard the shots. It hopped through the thorns, searching. Its vicious eyes seemed about to pop from its revolting head in its bloodlust.

Suddenly it bounded straight for the spot where Doc had shot the striped animal.

But Doc's accomplished wits were equal to the occasion. He had drawn his knife. With quick strokes, he skinned the beast he had shot.

He draped the distinctive black-and-white hide over him like a coat!

Doc now walked boldly out of the thorn thicket!

The hopping monster, mistaking him for the malodorous animal, in the hide of which he was masquerading, backed off.

Even the flying reptiles, the batlike pterodactyls, made the same mistake. They flopped away from him as though he were a plague.

Doc hurried to freedom!

HE pursued the trail of Kar's men with more caution, aware it was vaguely possible the villains might have located him by the shots and the cloud of reptile bats.

The steps of the fleeing pair suddenly took to an open glade. The length of their paces showed they were making a wild sprint.

The reason was soon apparent.

Doc came upon a scene of carnal slaughter. The spongy ground was rent, upheaved. Footprints were deep as Doc's hips! The tracks of a tyrannosaurus, a terrible killer titan of a reptile such as the one from which he had just escaped!

The prehistoric monster had devoured Kar's two men! Doc, gazing about, saw unmistakable proof of that fact. A shoe, a portion of a human foot still in it, and bits of two different suits of clothing, gave the evidence.

The pair had met a fitting end, considering the evil nature of the journey which had put them abroad in the ghastly night within the crater.

Doc turned back. He ran. The two unfortunate villains, in dragging the giant prehistoric beaver to the grove of ferns where Doc and his men had bivouacked, had undoubtedly left another trail. Doc intended to follow that.

He had pursued the outward trail with great speed, but his return was immeasurably swifter. He carried the black-and-white pelt, rolled tight so it would not smell so badly, under one mighty bronze arm.

A shock awaited him at the spot where he had left his friends. They were gone!

Many tracks were about. They told Doc's jungle-wise eyes a story—told it as perfectly as a book could have.

Kar had seized his friends!

Chapter XXI
HUMAN MONSTERS

WITH the swiftness of a trade wind, Doc took up the new trail. It was broad, plain. Entirely too plain!

Doc knew Kar would expect him to follow. Probably the man would set a trap. He would hope that Doc's excitement over the capture of his friends would dull his keen senses.

But the shocking knowledge served only to sharpen Doc's perceptive powers. He kept wide of the trail, his keen eyes locating it by the most vague of signs. A stalking leopard could not have gone more silently than the bronze giant.

A tiny patch of thorns appeared. Discovering the trail of Kar's men and their captives—Doc's friends—led directly through the burry growth, Doc approached furtively to investigate.

"They're not overlooking any bets!" he said grimly.

For a considerable distance into the thicket, the needle-tipped thorns were daubed with a brownish substance. Undoubtedly a deadly poison!

It was the first of Kar's traps!

Doc went on, not lessening his caution.

Kar's men had taken their prisoners along the crater side, traversing a region Doc had not yet explored. They held a course as straight as possible. It seemed they had a definite objective.

Doc's golden eyes picked up the tracks of Renny, Monk, and Ham in one spot. The trail of Long Tom and Johnny appeared soon after. None of them seemed to be wounded. At least, their footprints did not show the uneven depth and irregular spacing characteristic of a badly injured man.

Oliver Wording Bittman was lagging behind the whole group. However, his tracks also seemed normal.

But Doc knew he would have to make speed. His friends were being kept alive for only one reason, he believed. Kar was using them as a bait to decoy Doc into a trap.

Rather, into a series of traps! For Doc's adamant gaze located a creeper across his path. The vine stretched just a bit too tautly. He investigated.

The creeper was attached to the trip of a machine gun! Had Doc as much as touched it, a stream of lead would have riddled him.

He detached the machine gun and took it along, to use on Kar if necessary.

Sometime later, he found another of the poisoned thorn reception committees arranged for him. There was a deadfall which probably wouldn't have broken his back, considering the speed with which Doc could move. A more dangerous snare came next.

Doc noted a peculiar, dragging movement Monk's big feet made at intervals.

"Good boy, Monk!" Doc smiled.

Monk was making those marks with his feet just before each trap. He was warning Doc!

The mighty bronze man now made better time.

The ground here was higher than any upon which Doc had stood within the crater—excepting only the rim of the mud lake up on the crater side. And this spot was so far from the point where he had surveyed the crater bottom that the ever-present fog of moist, hot air had prevented him seeing much of the detail.

The jungle growth abruptly became scattering. Small glades appeared. Then larger meadows! A rank, crude sort of grass floored these. The ground felt less spongy.

A mass of rock jutted up before him. It lay close to the sheer, nearly two-mile-high cliff of the crater wall. No doubt it had fallen from the wall centuries ago.

To Doc, the rock looked big as a sizeable cut off Gibraltar. Others were behind it, too. They were nearly as large. All had toppled from the hulking cliff.

The trail weaved among these. Doc kept fully a hundred yards to one side, wary of bushwhackers. He came to a vast dornick which had a deeply corrugated surface. This would offer shelter to a climber. Doc mounted to reconnoiter.

He saw Kar's plane!

THE craft was an amphibian—could land on ground or water. It had two motors, both very large. Its cabin would accommodate eight or nine passengers. The long upper wing and the bobbed lower wing and rudder and elevators were joined in a spidery box kite of a framework.

With black fuselage and yellow wings, it looked like a bloated dragonfly crouched in a natural hangar formed by the leaning together of two great stone blocks.

Huge timber had been employed to build a massive fence to keep out lesser carnivora. The cavern between the two blocks of rock was too small at the entrance to admit the king-giant of the killer reptiles, the tyrannosaurus.

The construction work had been done sometime ago! Months past, at least!

"Kar built the hangar on his other trip!" Doc concluded.

Clambering down from his lofty perch, Doc approached the plane. He was not molested. Kar probably had no more than three men surviving. At least, only three had captured Doc's friends. As for that capture—how had a mere three thugs managed to get the upper hand on Doc's men?

Doc had his suspicions. They were far from pleasant!

Doc investigated the craft. He found a few boxed supplies in the cabin. These proved to be canned goods and dried fruit. Although Doc was hungry, having had nothing but meat since entering the crater, he did not touch the grub. He knew in just what subtle forms poison can be administered.

Doc quitted the strange hangar. Tall grass outside the massive timber gates absorbed his bronze figure.

Kar's headquarters should be somewhere near. Doc was hunting it. His men would be prisoners there, since they had not been in the hangar.

In the distance, faint spots in the moonlight-like day within the steam-covered crater, the fearsome bats of reptiles still circled. Probably they had not quitted the thorn patch where they had chased Doc. They were more tenacious of purpose than he had thought.

Somewhere, a prehistoric beast emitted a series of hideous cries. The echoes were taken up by another reptile. For a moment, a bedlam, remindful of the awful night sounds reigned. Then comparative quiet fell.

It was a ghastly spot—this lost land of terror which reposed within the cone of Thunder Island.

DOC came suddenly upon his imprisoned friends. They were being held within another natural cave resulting from the massive blocks of stone piling together. Doc heard voices first.

"You guys just make one move—you're finished!" A strange tone. It must be one of Kar's men.

With no noise at all, Doc's bronzed, giant figure floated nearer. His golden eyes watched the cave mouth—and all the surrounding terrain.

"I'll rush him!" Monk's big, amiable voice offered. "He can't get us all!"

Evidently only one man watched the prisoners within the cavern!

"No need of that, yet," rumbled Renny. Thunder gobbling out of a barrel would have had a close resemblance to Renny's vast voice.

"Let him be a hero!" clipped Ham. The quick-thinking lawyer seldom got in a spot so tight that he neglected to razz Monk.

"Can't you see what they're doing?" Long Tom demanded. "They're holding us as a bait to get Doc!"

"Bait or no bait," Johnny, the geologist, put in, "Doc will take care of himself. And if we went and got ourselves shot, we'd still be bait. I'm in favor of stringing along for a while to see what happens."

"That's a wise guy!" snarled the coarse voice of Kar's gunman. "You birds behave, an' we'll do the white thing by you, see! We'll let you keep on livin'! We'll leave you behind in the crater when we take off in our plane!"

He laughed uproariously at this. He knew life in the crater would be one long living hell! A more perilous domicile would be hard to imagine.

"I gotta notion to rush 'im!" Monk rumbled.

"You have no such idea—you're just working that noisy mouth!" Ham sneered. "I wonder what they're doing to Oliver Wording Bittman?"

"Hard to tell," said Renny. "They took him away shortly after we reached here. I can't imagine why."

Monk made an angry *hur-r-rum* of a sound. "What's still puzzlin' me is how they got us! We had Ham, Long Tom and Johnny on guard. If they'd have sneaked up on Ham, I could understand how they got near enough to cover us before we could put up a fight. But the way it was—"

"Pipe down!" rasped their guard, tired of the talk.

Monk continued, "—but the way it was we—"

"Pipe down, you funny-lookin' baboon!" the

guard snarled. "I'm gettin' so I don't like to watch that ugly phiz of yours when you jabber!"

At this, Ham laughed.

"And the muffler goes on you, too!" gritted the guard. "You cocky shyster mouthpiece!"

Silence fell within the cave.

Doc waited a while. His keen brain worked. His five friends were here in the cave. But Oliver Wording Bittman was somewhere else.

Doc decided to find Bittman. Monk, Ham, Renny, Long Tom, and Johnny were in no immediate danger.

Away from the cavern entrance, Doc crept. The tall grass, coarse as the leaves of cattails growing on a pond bank, concealed him.

He encountered a tiny mound. Starting to go around it, he stopped.

It was a grave! The tombstone was a stone slab. A name and brief inscription had been painted upon it. Doc read:

Here Lies
GABE YUDER
Trampled to death by a Tyrannosaurus

Doc examined the grave. It was months old!

For quite an interval, the mighty bronze man did not move, but remained as quiescent as a statue of the solid metal he resembled.

MEN approaching drew Doc Savage's attention from the grass-grown burial mound. Although his mind had been elsewhere, his full faculties had never deserted the business at hand. He had not relaxed his alertness to danger.

"He probably ain't had time to get here yet," said a coarse voice.

"You don't know that bronze guy!" growled the other. "I tell you, he may already be hangin' around here. He may be waitin' to jump onto us like a cat onto a mouse."

"Listen!" sneered the first speaker. "He never made it past them traps we left! Especially the poisoned thorns! That was good! And the machine gun we left with a vine hooked to the trigger! That wasn't bad, either."

"But supposin'—"

"Supposin' nothin'! If he gets here, we're gonna have our eyes open!"

"He may be too smart to even try to trail us. He may decide to let his men take care of themselves. What then?"

"So much the better! We'll go off an' leave him here! He'll be where he'll never bother Kar again."

"But he might find where we mined the ingredients for our fresh supply of the Smoke of Eternity. They say the bronze guy is quite a chemist. Even a second-rate chemist like you was able to make up a fresh batch of the Smoke of Eternity after Kar told you how!"

"Who's a second-rater?" snarled the other man. "I don't like that crack! Next to Kar, I'm the fair-haired boy in this scatter! Damn you, I won't have—"

"Aw—don't get on fire! I know you're a great guy in certain lines, but only a fair chemist. Supposin' the bronze guy figured out how the Smoke of Eternity was made? With enough of the stuff, he could open a tunnel right through the side of this crater. He might get out—"

"What if he did? Kar would have a new gang together. There'd be no slips like there was this last time. Doc Savage wouldn't have a chance against Kar."

"Maybe," the skeptical one mumbled. "But I'd rest easier if I had the bronze guy in front of a machine gun for about a minute. I just wish I had that chance!"

He got it almost before the words were off his lips. Doc stood up!

But did the Kar gunman shoot? He didn't!

He gave a squawk of surprise and terror and fell on his face in the grass.

DOC SAVAGE never shot a man except in actual defense of his own life, or that of someone else. Hence, he waited for the loud-mouthed one to lift the submachine gun he was carrying. But the man whipped down.

Coarse grass shook as the fellow crawled away. He was taking to his heels!

The second gunman was sterner stuff. He tilted his rapid firer. *Bur-r-r-rip!* It was spewing lead long before it came level. The slugs chopped grass to bits halfway to Doc.

The big bronze man's pistol spoke once. The report was like that given off by the popper of a hard-snapped bull whip.

The gunman melted down as though all the stiffening had been drawn from his body. On his forehead, exactly between his eyes, was a blue spot that suddenly trickled red. The man fell on top of his weapon and it continued to rip off shots until the drum magazine had emptied.

Doc Savage flashed for the cave where his friends were held. He must not let the guard kill them in his excitement.

"What is it?" the guard in the cave was bellowing. "What's goin' on out there? What—"

Doc reached a spot a yard from the cave mouth. He stopped there. Off his lips came a changed voice—a voice exactly like that of the Kar gunman who had just died.

"The bronze guy!" Doc's altered voice called. "We got 'im! Come out an' watch 'im croak!"

"Sure!" barked the fellow in the cavern. "Here I come—"

He crashed headlong into a set of mighty bronze hands. He saw them closing over his face. They looked bigger, more terrible than the whole crater of Thunder Island. The golden eyes behind them were even worse. They radiated death.

The man sought to use his gun. He got a few wild bullets out of it.

Then his neck unjointed! He died quickly. His actual going was painless, whatever the terror of the moments before might have been. For Doc's sinewy hands had brought a merciful end.

Renny, Ham, Monk, Johnny, and Long Tom—all five howling their pleasure—piled out of the cavern prison in a hurry.

"Did you get Kar?" Ham clipped.

"No." Doc put a sharp question. "Have you seen Kar yet?"

"Not yet. They took poor Bittman off to Kar. Or that's what they said. I don't know—"

Doc's uplifted arm stopped Ham's flow of words.

Then, as they all heard what Doc's sensitive ears had been first to detect, horror seized them.

Kar's plane was starting. The engines were already tossing salvos of sound against the gigantic cliff wall of the crater.

Doc Savage left the spot as from a catapult. No word did he speak. None was needed. His men knew that, should the plane get off, their lot would be very hard indeed. It might take them years to escape the innards of Thunder Island.

Renny, Ham, Monk, Long Tom, Johnny—all five trailed in his wake. But from the way they were left behind, they might have been at a standstill in the rear of the bronze master of speed.

Seemingly gifted with unseen wings, such fabulous leaps did he take over boulders, Doc bore down on the makeshift hangar between the two masses of stone that were larger than skyscrapers. He caught sight of the plane.

It was in motion.

Already, the tail was lifting. Another two hundred yards for speed, and the craft would be off. Doc could see the features of the man in the control cockpit.

Kar was handling the plane!

DOC veered left. He put on speed—although he had been traveling faster than it seemed a human could.

He was trying to intercept the plane! Kar saw his purpose. He kicked rudder. The ship veered a little. But it couldn't turn enough to evade Doc. The runway was rather narrow. Great rocks spotted the sides. The plane could easily crash among these.

For a moment, though, it did seem the ship would escape the mighty bronze man. But a great leap sent his Herculean figure sailing upward.

Doc seized a strut which braced the empennage—the rudder and elevators. The plane must have been going forty miles an hour. The wrench would have torn loose the grip of lesser fingers. But the bronze giant held on.

Kar now began to shoot with an automatic pistol. He was excited. He had to aim from a very difficult position. He missed with all his slugs—then had to devote his attention to getting the plane off the crater floor, before it reached the runway end.

The craft lurched. With a moan, it took the air!

Chapter XXII
A LOST LAND DESTROYED

THE plane climbed over the great boulders and the high fern trees. It circled once. Then Kar lifted his pistol to shoot at Doc Savage once more. The plane could fly itself for a time.

Doc had been making good use of the respite. He had mounted to the main tail struts, which extended to the upper wing. He was swinging with a simian ease along these.

Kar's first bullet missed. His second also—for Doc had twisted in a miraculous fashion and gotten atop the wing.

A hollow *clack* came from Kar's automatic. He jacked the slide back. The weapon was empty. Wildly, he started reloading the clip.

The roof hatch whipped open. A mighty bronze form dropped inside. It towered toward Kar.

In a frenzy, the master villain sought to get just one bullet into his empty gun. But the weapon was flicked from his shaking fingers. It was flung through the plane windows.

Kar's voice lifted a screech, "Please—I did not know—"

"Talk will do you no good!" Doc Savage's remarkable voice, although not loud, was perfectly audible amid the engine roar. "Talk will never save you! Nothing can save you!"

Kar looked at the plane windows, longingly.

He had donned a parachute before taking off.

Next, the master villain stared at a large leather suitcase which stood in the rear of the cabin. But he dared not make a move to jump out of the plane or reach the suitcase. He feared those bronze hands that were more terrible than steel.

"I was deceived for a time," Doc Savage's vast voice said grimly. "Your method of deception was clever. It was bold. It worked because you hit me in one of my soft spots. Perhaps I should say in one of my blind spots."

Kar began, "You got me all wrong about—"

"Silence! Your lies will serve you nothing! I have too much proof. I suspected who you were last night, when I saw you signaling from the top of a tree fern with a lighted cigarette.

"You were ordering your men to decoy the big prehistoric beavers to the attack. You had carefully chosen a tree from which you could reach safety."

Doc's face was set as metal; his golden eyes ablaze with cold, flaky gleamings.

"I became suspicious before that," the bronze man continued. "When I was shot at! When you pretended to faint! Actually, you hoped I would come to your motionless body and your man would shoot me."

"I didn't—"

"You did! After the prehistoric beavers had been frightened away last night, I climbed your tree and removed the skinning scalpel you carried on your watch chain. That scalpel was poisoned. I put it on a spear tip and tested it on the ancestor of a common porcupine. The animal was killed by a scratch. You hoped to use that weapon on me, but could not muster the courage, and failed at the last minute."

Kar was now trembling from head to foot. He quailed from each word as from a knife stab.

The plane, no hand at the controls, was flying itself—proof it was excellently made. Straight across the crater, it boomed.

"You had many chances to slay me," Doc continued. "But you did not have the nerve to do it with your own hand. Like all criminals, however clever, you are a coward. You are like a rat. You remained with me, cannily checkmating my moves when you could, and seeking always to have your men kill me. But you dared not do the deed yourself.

"Your craven nature was shown when we landed in the crater. You became a sniveling coward."

KAR was a sniveling coward again now—probably to a greater degree than ever before.

"Your lies were ingenious!" Doc's relentless voice went on. "It was not Jerome Coffern alone who came to Thunder Island with Gabe Yuder. You came also. You and Gabe Yuder found this crater. Jerome Coffern never knew of its existence."

"You got me wrong!" whined the craven before Doc. "Kar is Gabe Yuder—"

"Gabe Yuder is dead! He found the unknown element or substance from which the Smoke of Eternity is made. He probably perfected the Smoke of Eternity. You saw it could be turned to criminal purposes. So you killed Gabe Yuder, and took his chemical formula. I found his grave!"

"You can't prove—"

"Granted. I am merely guessing what happened on your first visit to Thunder Island. It does not matter how near I come to the truth. But I cannot be missing the facts far.

"Jerome Coffern saw something suspicious about your actions. He must have remarked on it. So you tried to kill him. The first time, you shot at him and missed. He suspected you of the deed. He wrote a statement, which you searched for in his apartment and found. I discovered a few lines of that statement upon a fresh typewriter ribbon in Jerome Coffern's apartment. But the important part was illegible—the part which named you!

"The part which said you, Oliver Wording Bittman, were Kar!"

Kar—or Bittman—quailed as though this were the greatest blow of all.

"Yes, you are Kar, Bittman!" Doc continued. "You are a skilled actor, one of the best I ever encountered. And you had aroused my blind confidence in you by exhibiting that letter from my father showing you had saved his life.

"You listened in on an extension phone when I called Monk from your New York apartment, and promptly sent your men after Monk. You also sent one of your gang, a flyer, to kill me as I walked. I recall I told you I was going to walk after I left your place.

"You ordered your men to get the specimens from Thunder Island out of my safe. You ordered the elevator death trap which nearly got Monk, Ham, Johnny, Long Tom, and Renny—and you didn't make a move to enter the cage that had been doctored. You tipped your men to get off the *Sea Star,* and probably hired the yacht which removed them, by telegraphing from New York.

"You even disappeared into the jungle on that coral atoll long enough to tell your man hidden there to bomb our plane. I could name other incidents when you checkmated us. You deceived us. But you did it by taking advantage of the most despicable means to get yourself into my confidence. You knew my affection for my father. So you showed me the letter which said you had saved his life.

"You knew my father—you knew the affection that existed between us. You were certain your trick would blind me to any faults you might have."

Bittman whined, "It was no trick! I saved his life—"

Doc Savage's voice acquired a strange, terrible note, a note of strain.

"Did you? Or was that letter faked in some manner?"

"It was a genuine letter!" gulped Kar—or Bittman. "I saved his life! Honest, I did! I'm not such a bad guy! You read that letter! Your father wouldn't be fooled in a man. I'm not—"

"You can't talk yourself out of it!" Doc said savagely. "I do not think my father did make a mistake. Perhaps you were the man he thought you were—*then!* You have changed since. Perhaps some mental disease, or prolonged brooding, warped your outlook on life.

"There are many possible explanations for a hitherto honest man becoming a criminal. But we will not discuss that. You ordered my friend, Jerome Coffern, murdered. For that, there can be but one penalty!"

The plane was slowly careening off on a wing tip, threatening to crash. Doc's powerful hand, floating out, stroked the controls and brought it level. A wall of the crater was ahead—perhaps five minutes flying away.

Directly in front of the plane, an eruption was occurring in the strange horseshoe-shaped lake of boiling mud which extended nearly around the crater, but high above the jungle-clothed floor.

Kar—or Bittman—suddenly made a frantic leap. He was seeking to reach the leather suitcase back in the plane cabin.

He brought up against Doc's bronze arm as against a stone wall. He struck at Doc repeatedly. He missed each time, for the bronze form seemed to vanish under his fists, so quickly did it move.

Increased terror seized the man. His eyes rolled desperately.

"You'll never kill me!" he snarled.

Strange lights glowed in Doc Savage's golden eyes.

"You are right," he agreed. "I could never kill with my bare hands a man who saved my father's life. But do not think you shall escape with your crimes because of that! You will receive your punishment!"

Kar rolled his eyes again. He didn't know what fate Doc planned for him. But it could be nothing pleasant.

Suddenly the master villain dived headlong through the plane window!

TWO hundred feet below the ship, the man cracked his parachute. It bloomed wide, a clean white bulb in the sinister gray of the crater atmosphere.

Doc Savage gave the oncoming wall of the crater a glance. It was only two minutes away now. Back into the cabin, he flung. He got the leather suitcase at which Oliver Wording Bittman had glanced so longingly.

He did not open the suitcase. The contents might have interested him not at all, judging by his actions.

The speeding plane whipped over in a vertical bank under his mighty hand. It had been almost against the crater wall. The ship seemed to slam against the cliff, then leap away.

Doc's golden eyes ranged downward. They were a cold gold now, determined. They judged accurately.

Doc dropped the suitcase overside.

The piece of luggage revolved slowly as it fell. It hit just below the lava dike which confined the great lake of boiling-hot mud. It burst.

It had contained Kar's supply of the Smoke of Eternity! The crater wall below the lava dike began a swift dissolving. Vile, repulsive gray smoke climbed upward in growing volume. It was such a cloud as had arisen at the destruction of the sinister pirate ship, *Jolly Roger,* in the Hudson River.

The smoke pall hid what was happening beneath. The play of electrical sparks made a weird glow within the squirming mass.

Suddenly, from beneath the cloud crawled a brown, smoking torrent. The lava dike confining the lake of superheated mud had been destroyed. The molten liquid was running into the crater!

Banking, engine moaning, the plane kept clear of the foul gray cloud from the Smoke of Eternity. Doc's golden eyes searched. They found what they sought.

Kar! The river of boiling mud overtook him swiftly. The man tried to run. He held his own for a time. Then one of the giant hopping horrors of the crater, the greatest killing machine nature ever made, confronted him. The tyrannosaurus started for Kar with great, bloodthirsty bounds.

Kar chose the easier of two deaths—he let the hideous reptilian giant snap his life out with a single bite.

But an instant later, the wall of hot mud rushed upon the prehistoric monster. The stupid thing took a gigantic leap—deeper into the cooking torrent. It went down. It rolled over slowly, kicking in a feeble way with its huge, three-toed feet.

Thus perished Kar—or Oliver Wording Bittman, the famous taxidermist—and the colossus of reptiles which had devoured him.

DOC held the plane wide open back across the crater. He landed on the narrow runway among the great lumps of stone which had, centuries ago, caved from the cliff.

Renny, Ham, Monk, Johnny, Long Tom—all five piled into the plane on the double-quick.

Doc took off again.

"Look!" Johnny muttered.

The ruptured lake seemed to contain an inexhaustible supply of boiling mud. It still poured forth. It was flooding the floor of the ghastly crater! The monsters existing there were being enveloped.

And the surviving Kar gunman would perish with them! Nothing could save him.

Steam poured upward. It was thickening in the mouth of the crater over their heads—forming a smudge which less and less sunlight penetrated. The growing darkness, the remorseless progress of the mud flood, the antics of the grisly reptilian giants, gave the tableau the aspect of another Judgment Day.

"Talk about your sights!" Monk muttered.

Then they fell silent. They were thinking of that archfiend, Oliver Wording Bittman, who had deceived them. The fellow was responsible for their recent capture. He had signaled his men where to attack.

From the very first, he had misled them. From the moment when he came to them with a scratch on his chest which he must have made himself and a clever story of being shot at!

They were amazed at the cunningness of Bittman's acting. The man had been a master to deceive them as he had.

Even Doc had not seen through Bittman's fiendish double-dealing until they had reached this crater. But that was understandable. The affection between Doc and his father was extremely great. And Bittman, as a man who had saved the life of Doc's father, had received Doc's gratitude. It had been hard for Doc to look to such a man as an evil villain.

"What about the Smoke of Eternity?" questioned Monk suddenly.

For answer, Doc leveled a bronze beam of an arm. They followed his gesture with their eyes.

The region of strange rocks, where Kar must have mined the unknown element or substance to make the Smoke of Eternity, had already been buried by the hot mud flow. It would never be mined now!

Monk looked curiously at Doc Savage.

"Do you know what that stuff—the Smoke of Eternity—was?" he inquired.

Doc did not answer immediately. But at length: "I have the theory which grew out of my analysis of the metal which was impervious to the dissolving substance. That theory, I am sure, is near the truth. And that is why I deliberately released the flood of mud."

"Huh?" Monk was puzzled.

"The Smoke of Eternity can never be made without the rare substance which Kar mined here. And the supply of the stuff is now buried hopelessly. As for what the substance was, no one shall ever know. I intend to keep my theories to myself."

Monk nodded. "Guess I see the reason for that."

"The world can get along without the Smoke of Eternity!" Doc's voice seemed to fill all the plane.

The ship rammed its howling propellers into steam. Up and up, it climbed. The heat nearly took off their skin. But only for a while; it became cooler at last.

So suddenly that it was like a gush of flame into their faces, they were in brilliant sunlight. Their eyes, becoming adapted to the glare, picked up the coral atoll some fifty miles distant.

"No need of even landing there!" Doc decided.

He banked the plane for New Zealand. Ample fuel for the flight sloshed in the gas tanks, thanks to Kar's foresight.

"From New Zealand to San Francisco by steamer will just about give us time to get the prehistoric reptiles out of our hair!" grinned the irrepressible Monk. "And maybe somethin' else will turn up soon."

SOMETHING else turn up? It would! And Monk did not dream how soon. Even now a devil's cauldron cooked for them on the other side of the earth.

Danger and difficulty such as they had never encountered, awaited them. Upon excitement and adventure, they had just fed. They were elated. The future looked rosy. But they could not foresee the terrible thing that was to befall them.

For this remarkable man of bronze and his five unusual friends were soon to be plunged into a maelstrom of peril and adventure—right in the very center of their native United States!

THE END

AUTOBIOGRAPHY by Lester Dent

Lester Dent—six foot two, weight 210, age 32, born in Missouri. Was brought to Oklahoma, to a farm near Broken Arrow,. when four months old, which practically makes me an Oklahoman.

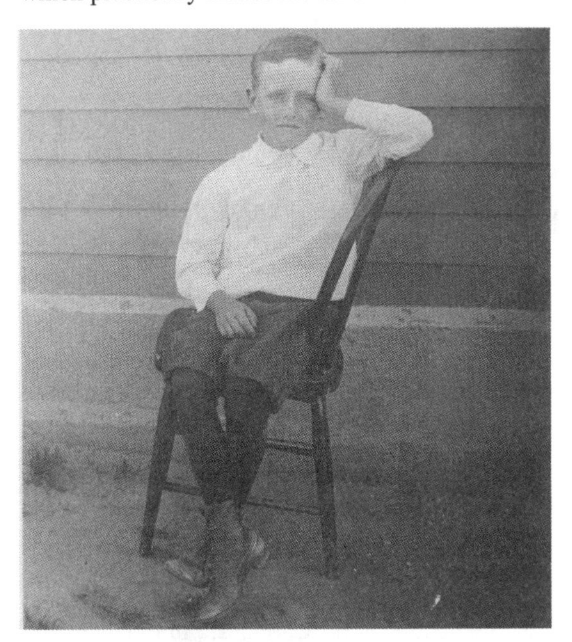

My dad, with the usual Dent luck, sold his Oklahoma farm a year before oil was struck on it, and went to Wyoming. As a small boy, I was taken across Wyoming in a covered wagon.

I lived on a cow ranch in Wyoming, been a prospector, farmer, teacher, and a telegraph operator, winding up by doing my last telegraphing on the Tulsa *World* in 1930.

I flunked English grammer four years running in high school.

I studied law in Tulsa University law school, nights, with an outstanding lack of success.

While working a night telegraph job—the "early" from midnight until eight in the morning in Tulsa—I got started writing. The impulse to write arose from a combination of two things—greed and shock.

The shock came when I reported, by accident, an hour early for work one afternoon in the offices of the Tulsa *World.* There I found another telegraph operator, who was also not supposed to be on duty, bent over a typewriter. The other operator wore an intent expression. I inquired why. The other operator explained that he was writing a fiction story. The resulting dialogue went something like this:

"A what? You're writing a what?"

"A fiction story," the other operator said patiently.

"Haw, haw!" I said. "Imagine a telegraph operator trying to write!"

"Look," the other operator said. He then turned over, for my inspection, a check lying on the desk. It was for three hundred and some odd dollars, and payment for a story the operator had sold.

The result was that I started writing. I turned out thirteen stories, some of them booklengths, and all came back with a perfect record of consistency.

The fourteenth story sold to *Top-Notch Magazine,* a pulp, for $250.00.

A few months later, a large New York publishing house, after reading the first story I sent them, telegraphed me to the effect that, "If you make less than a hundred dollars a week on your present job, advise you to quit; come to New York and be taken under our wing, with a five-hundred-dollar-a-month drawing account." After telegraphing friends in New York to inquire around about the publisher's sanity, I went to New York. That was in 1931.

I have written hundreds of stories since. I have been rated as one of the world's leading writers of the type of fiction which I specialize in—adventure and detective yarns for the pulp magazines.

about a character called "Doc Savage." The magazine, using the same character each month in a story, was so successful that within two years there were almost twenty imitators in the field.

I still write Doc Savage—a 60,000 word story each month. A 60,000 word yarn is a full book-length story. The Doc Savage stories are also put out in low-priced books, and the magazine is translated monthly into several foreign languages and published abroad in Spanish, French, German and Scandanavian tongues. For writing Doc Savage,

Lester Dent (left) and coworkers at the Tulsa *World*

I use the pen name "Kenneth Robeson."

I have also sold to most of the pulp magazines extent, among them such magazines as *Argosy, Black Mask, Crime Busters,* etc.

I write rapidly, having averaged 200,000 words of published fiction a month over a period of two years at one time, and rarely dropping below a hundred thousand words a month.

During the past four years, I have not had a rejected story in the pulp field, due to the fact that most of the stuff is written to contract or on order.

I write mechanically, to a formula, a story blueprint. A writer's yearbook—*Writer's Digest Yearbook* for 1936—published my mechanical plot formula for a 6,000-word short detective story. Over two hundred writers wrote in that they had sold their first story by writing it to the formula.

A considerable amount of my stuff is dictated.

While writing, I have prospected for gold in old Mexico, Death Valley, Colorado, Arizona and elsewhere.

I have done exploration work in South America and the Caribbean.

I am a member of the Explorers Club in New York City.

I spent almost two years on my own schooner, treasure hunting in the Caribbean, finished up with that about a year ago. I did not find any treasure.

At the present time, I am probably on the Atlantic liner *Queen Mary,* with my wife and secretary, bound for Europe.

Lester Dent, March 5, 1938

His schooner *Albatross* at anchor, Dent uses a portable metal detector to hunt for Caribbean pirate treasure.